Jane is the End

CHANCHITO MASSONI

The Princess on the Glass Hill

Jane started her week unaware it would end with the Apocalypse.

Of course, most people didn't go about assuming the Apocalypse was waiting at every turn, at least not if they were healthy, but if Jane had bothered to look a little, she might have caught a glimpse of good-old Armageddon peaking around the corner. There was the giant red star in the sky, the unsettling apparitions, and even the odd raven or two tossed in the mix. You see, the Apocalypse liked to play these games: coyly winking behind the evening news, giving a come-hither stare from the sign the bum carried on the street. But Jane was impervious to these tactics; she dismissed them as side effects from either too much work, too little sleep, or perhaps the odd curse.

But oh, they weren't.

The Apocalypse was indeed coming and, whether she liked it or not, wasn't going to be shy this time. The Apocalypse was like a rowdy twenty-year-old ready to party—full of hormones, alcohol, blood and guts. You could tell the Apocalypse that line of coke wasn't a good idea, that maybe it should go home and get some rest, but the Apocalypse did not care; it was gonna party like Nostradamus in 1999 and *everyone* was invited, and as with all parties this wild, liable to end with a mess on the floor.

For now, though, Jane was oblivious to this impending doom, and the strange adventure on which it would take her. For now, she was more concerned with pressing her blouse, catching the bus, and getting to work on time.

"Hey, hey Jane! What day of the week are demons the most tired?"

Jane held in a sigh as she walked across the cobblestone streets from the bus stop to her place of work, joined now by a slightly overweight man with cloven feet, curled horns, and a very *un*-pressed shirt. "I'm not in the mood for Monday jokes right now, Bill."

Bill scoffed, clopping alongside her. "You never are, and I *always* get you to answer. So, what it is it? What day are they the most tired?"

"Every day you ask me these questions?"

"Geeze Jane, go a little easy will ya'? Maybe go see the apothecary about gettin' a perky potion. It's De-monday Jane, get it? *De*-monday?" Bill chuckled at his own joke.

They walked up granite stairs to a quaint Tudor style building, Jane grabbing the handle to a heavy wooden door. "Yes Bill, you told the same joke seven weeks ago. However, everyone knows that demonic forces are most powerful during the new moon of the sixth month. *Not* Monday."

Bill pattered through the door, deep in thought as Jane held it open. "Told the same joke twice, huh? Must be gettin' rusty. This won't do. This won't do at all. Not if I'm gonna be the next Marfield writer. Need to up my game."

Jane inwardly groaned at the thought of Bill 'upping' his game. "I don't know why you're so obsessed with this Marfield character. He isn't funny."

"Shut up!" Bill cried, aghast.

"He's a porcupine with a human concept of time that eats pizza—which by the way, I don't think would be good for a porcupine to eat. Small children and old people read Marfield, not grown adults."

"First Jane, I wanna say, that says a lot about how you see old people and children, which is not very charitable," Jane shrugged. "Second, I need a retirement plan of *some* sort. It's not like us Municipal Employees get all that much in the way of pension. And third, I *like* Marfield, so go to hell you bitch."

"Hmph, would better if he was a cat, just sayin'."

"*Everything* would just be better if it was a cat, but we don't always get perfection in this world, do we? By the way, you comin' over for dinner tonight? Ma's been askin' after ya."

"I wouldn't dream of saying 'no' to Maera."

"Would be bad for your health," Bill agreed.

They walked up to an ornate mahogany desk, a beast of a thing, staffed by two clerks—one with glowing blond curls in a pink taffeta dress, the other with bronze skin dusted in rainbows. Bill and Jane made an odd pair in comparison: a middle-aged satyr in ruffled clothes and a young albino elf dressed in somber gray. Bill's tanned face was creased with laugh lines, he had an infectious smile that came easily to his lips and hazel eyes that glimmered with mischief; Jane, meanwhile, looked like a bleached bag of bones, pale hair held in two tight braids wound at the base of her neck and moon-colored a gaze that refused to meet anyone. Both Bill and Jane held up identification cards to be waved through, the two clerks looking at one another as they passed, giggling.

Walking down the Ministry halls, Bill sighed, brushing aside a pixie that flitted in front of him as if it were a gnat. Wooden rafters stretched above them strung with crepe paper streamers in pink, yellow, and blue. Numerous clocks on the white plaster walls clicked and chimed, though none of them were of the same design, or even kept the same time, so they just created a sort of cacophonous background noise that one had to tune out. On the floor were cubicles, made of the same pilot blue plastic from which all cubicles were conceived, creating a sort of cubicle-maze that only the initiated could navigate. The cubicles were decorated with garlands, flowers, and other trinkets; some of these trinkets blew bubbles, or spat glitter, or offensively projected family photos so that everyone was forced to see what young Valentine was doing on holiday.

Other Ministry Employees passed Jane and Bill as they walked, giving nods of greeting to Bill and awkward smiles to Jane. They wore tiaras, butterfly wings, and flowing silks, their hair perfectly coiffed and teeth blindingly white—so white in fact, that when Jane had first started working at the Ministry, she had wondered if it was some sort of solar warfare. Bill tucked his shirt into his pants.

They arrived at their desks, Jane's neatly organized, her paperwork tidy on the polished laminate surface, while Bill's looked as though someone had come by with a dump truck full of files and unloaded them; you couldn't even see the 'In and Out' box for all the mess. Jane had no idea how he found anything in that chaos, but somehow, he did. She suspected it was some sort of spell. They sat down in their chairs, Jane putting her bagged lunch in her drawer as Bill pulled out a *Magical Meat Muffins* magazine.

"Hey Jane, this month's quiz is, '*What type of cake are you?*'. Hmm, do you think you're more of a caramel or a raspberry?" Bill looked expectantly over the cover, Jane simply scowling back. He brought his pencil to the page. "Hmmm. A lemon. Most definitely a *lemon*."

Jane ignored Bill, focusing on her work. She had pulled out a giant rubber stamp, getting ready to do some notarizing, when she saw someone coming their way. "Bill, you might want to put that magazine away. The boss is heading over."

"Belinda doesn't care if I read on work time. I got so much dirt on that bitch she'd probably let me burn this place to the ground if I wanted to." Jane decided she didn't want to know.

Belinda descended on the pair in a cloud of moonflower perfume and stardust. She wore a dress of purple silks and pink satins, flowing about her in a nebulous fashion, her dark brown hair curled and held in place by enough hairspray to exert its own gravitational pull. A thick layer of makeup covered her skin in an attempt to disguise the effects of time, the shellac threatening to crack whenever her face moved outside of something other than a frozen smile, but despite this the effects of middle-age in all its cruelty still made themselves apparent in the creases at the corners of her eyes. A mole on Belinda's left check distracted Jane, the makeup shifting dangerously around it, as if ready to break open a fissure in reality.

"Hallllloooooo!" Belinda's voice reached a pitch that made dogs howl and glass break. "Gopher Bless you on this fine day! How are my favorite two employees?"

"It's a lovely morning indeed, Gopher be Blessed," Bill said as he looked up from the magazine, "but may I be so bold as to say, nowhere near as lovely as you, Miss Belinda."

Belinda put her hands to her cheeks in a girlish gesture. "Oh Bill! You satyrs and your charm! If you were just a little taller, I'd say you'd be a danger to us all! And you, Jane, how are you today?"

"I'm doing well ma'am, thank you for asking. Blessed be the Gopher."

"Oh Jane, how many times have I told you, it's *Belinda* not *ma'am*. There's no need to be so formal!" Jane sat there quietly with her hands in her lap, unsure what to say. Belinda's smile ticked. The mole quivered. "Ah well, forget about it. Whatever makes you comfortable! I know you like to have things just-so." Belinda turned to Bill. "I have a field mission for you two today."

"Aww Belinda, *come on*. You know how much I hate work!"

"I know, I know, but I just can't help it. Aurora and Steve are already out on an inspection, Aquafine is on vacation, Gustave and Margaret are *still* recovering from that last mess they were in..."

"Oh, yeah, that was bad."

"Oh, it was just awful indeed. Poor Margaret is going to be seeing the apothecary for a while, I'm afraid. So that just leaves you two and Frank, and well Frank..."

All three of them turned to look over at the cubicle opposite, where a shriveled old man in a dapper hat and tweed suit sat. He had the look of an apple that had been left out for too long, and one was afraid if they breathed too hard, he might crumble to dust. Belinda turned back to Bill. "I somehow just don't think Frank would be up for the task."

Bill sighed as Frank pulled out a box of paper clips, starting to sort through them. "Fine, fine. We'll take it."

"Excellent! I knew you would." She handed a file over to Bill. "It's a small beauty potion shop on the east side of Germantown called, Pretty Princess Potions. There have been reports that their potions aren't up to standard, causing some poor reactions. We need you to go take a look and make sure everything is up to the standards of the Ministry."

Bill opened the file, giving it a quick glance. "So, in other words, some rich kid's parents complained that their son got turned into a toad." He passed the file over to Jane.

"Oh Bill, always with that sharp wit! I'll expect a report on my desk by tomorrow afternoon! Tata! And Gopher Bless!" With that Belinda turned and left, wafting up the scent of moonbeams.

Jane frowned as she read through the report. "This is more than just one violation. This looks like multiple victims with pretty severe injuries."

"Still, just a bunch of rich ljosalfar who can afford to even think about this sort of stuff. I mean, everything in Germantown is twice the price, just because it's *Germantown*," Bill made a face. "It's no wonder some shady place went in trying to grift as much as they can. If you ask me, they deserve it for being stupid." He pulled out a set of keys from under the pile of papers, Jane glowering at the desk to see if she could divine the trick. "You wanna drive, or me?"

"I'll drive," Jane said, catching the keys as he tossed them to her. "You drive like the world is about to end."

"Well, you never know, right? The Gopher gives and the Gopher receives. When or why is not for us to know."

They made their way to the Ministry Garage in the basement of the building. Fashioned after an old horse stable, it housed small white vans painted with a smiling cartoon gopher on the side. The gopher had a slightly goofy, cross-eyed look, holding a hand in a 'thumbs up' gesture; he wore a monocle and a top hat with a blue rose pin in the band. Jane and Bill got into one of those vehicles, Jane taking the wheel as Bill got in on the passenger side. Jane started the van, staring hard at Bill for a long minute; Bill sighed, rolling his eyes as he buckled up. "Okay, okay, you can pull out now." Jane put the van in reverse.

Pulling out of the garage and onto a cobblestone road, they entered the traffic of the Great Misty Burrow. The Ministry District of the Misty Burrow consisted of the same Tudor style buildings as the Ministry of Magic they had just left; all with green tile roofs, white plaster walls, and exposed wooden beams. Everything was tidy and clean. There were plastic flowers in the window boxes and statues of the fat gopher in his top hat spotted the neatly trimmed lawns. Residents of the area could be seen walking to and from work, dressed similarly to Bill and Jane's coworkers, enjoying the sun.

And it was a beautiful day to enjoy the sun indeed—the sky blue with a few artfully placed wisps of cloud, the temperature an even seventy degrees. Fairy-tale palaces and candy cane towers made up the cityscape, sunlight glinting off their bedazzled spires, while to the east a large Ferris Wheel adorned with flowering lights slowly turned. In the center of the Burrow, a tall rose stone building topped with the golden statue of a gopher loomed, taller than even the most ornate castle pinnacle. Surrounding the city was a plain, pink colored wall, over which the tops of snow-capped mountains could be seen. Jane looked up wistfully at those peaks before taking a roundabout, getting off at the turn that would take them to the fashionable Germantown.

In Germantown, the Tudor style buildings became more colorful, the walls washed in pinks, yellows and blues, gingerbread trim painted with daffodils. Hops and grape vines grew over the scaffolding, so that the whole District seemed built of giant cuckoo clocks. The people here sat at cafes eating the trendiest desserts to be talked about at work the next day, shopped at clothing stores buying the latest fashions that were in all the scrolls, and visited potions shops consuming the newest concoctions that would make them the prettiest, and therefore happiest, in the land. Bill looked out the window as they passed a couple, one with glowing iridescent skin and the other with cat ears and a tail—neither natural states for the average Light Elf. "By the Gopher. Wonder how much that cost 'em?"

Jane only half-paid attention to what Bill was saying, focused on finding a place to park. "It's their money. What do you care how they spend it?"

"I don't know. It's just so shallow, and so...ugh. Like beasts in a cage trying to one-up each other." He sighed. "You know, before the divorce, Phillip got heavy into cosmetic potions. Said he was sick of people always lookin' at him. I mean, I guess I get it. It does get old after a while, but I don't know. It was just...too much. All the money spent on trying to get taller, trying to make the horns go away, trying to get *feet*," Bill rubbed his forehead. "Fucking feet. Sank half our savings in that shit. In the end, he just became someone I couldn't recognize."

"Well then, you're better off without him."

"That's what I keep tellin' myself. Maybe one of these days I'll actually believe it."

Jane pulled into a spot. They got out of the car and stood on the sidewalk, getting their bearings. Jane went through the file, searching for an address. "8520 Candytuft Lane," she said out loud before looking up, pointing, "there."

They crossed the street to a dark green door set between an outdoor cafe and a hat shop. The door led to a stairway that went up to the second floor and on the door itself, in gold lettering, was inscribed: Pretty Princess Potions. Bill and Jane walked in.

The stairs were carpeted but old, so they creaked as the two walked. When they got to the top it opened to a small lobby, cozy with some deep chairs and peach-colored walls. Shelves were set up to the left, filled with potions of various colors, shapes, and sizes. There was a receptionist's desk towards, the receptionist behind the desk a pretty Light Elf in a pink dress shirt that would have seemed rather plain, if not for the monarch wings that grew from her back and antennae from her forehead. "May I help you?" the receptionist asked with fluttering eyes.

Bill went up to the desk, flashing his badge. "Ministry of Magic," he declared. "We're here to do a routine inspection."

"Oh! I wasn't aware we were scheduled for an inspection today! Mr. Jonquil is with a client at the moment..." one of her antennae twinged ever so slightly.

Bill gave Jane a look from the corner of his eye before focusing back on the woman. "That's all right," he said, "these sorts of things aren't usually scheduled, but they're pretty routine. If you could just go over what you have in stock, we can be in and out and I can check this off my list. Neither of us wants to be here any longer than we have to, right?" He smiled.

The woman seemed to relax, smiling back. "I can certainly go over the potions we have. Best in Germantown, and all made with the highest quality magic."

"This should go quickly then," Bill said with a wink. "And oh, I forgot, my partner here had a quick question," Bill turned to Jane. "Jane? What did ya' wanna ask?"

Jane froze as both Bill and the butterfly woman locked eyes on her, waiting for a response. "Oh, uhm, is there a restroom I could use?"

"Oh Jane," Bill chuckled with a sigh, "always have tell ya' not to drink so much coffee." He gave the woman a look of 'see what I have to deal with?'.

"Ah well, guess I just can't help it. Guess I'm just a coffee fiend." Jane smiled awkwardly, making Bill wince.

If the receptionist noticed Jane's stiffness, however, she didn't let on. "Oh yes, of course. The restroom is just down that hall and to your right." She pointed past the desk.

"Perfect, thanks," Bill said, getting the woman's attention back on him, "now if you'll go through those potions with me, I'm hoping to get some lunch here after we're done. Do you have a place you'd recommend?"

"Oh certainly! I know this *fantastic* cafe just down the street from here..."

Jane slipped back behind the desk, making her way towards the restroom. Bill's look meant something hinky was up and he didn't trust the woman; Jane had learned long ago to not doubt Bill's hunches—she was going to have to take this opportunity to get a look herself. Past the restroom was another door listed for 'Patients Only'. Normally Jane felt it was unethical to break rules like this, but it seemed as though Mr. Jonquil was breaking a few of them himself, so she slipped past.

It was as if Jane walked into a different building when she went through that door. Gone were the pink-orange walls and inviting decor; here everything was white, sterile, and cold. *Cleanable*, was the thought that came to her. Doors lined a hall, at the top of each door a viewing port. Jane went down the hall peering through those ports to see various patients, some looking as though they had just taken a sleeping potion, resting, while others were covered in bloodied bandages as they moaned. *The pain of beauty,* she thought. Still, so far nothing illegal.

Jane came to one of those doors to find it open, a woman inside awake, sitting upright in her bed with almost impossibly neat posture. The room was dark and warm, reminding Jane of a fever, and it stank of perfume, like rotted fruit. "Are you an apothecary here?" the woman asked. "I didn't know this place hired Dark Elves."

Jane was surprised by the question. She couldn't see the woman's face, for it was hidden in shadows. "No, I'm..." she tried to think, "a patient. I'm talking with Dr. Jonquil to see what he can do for me."

"Oh well, that's a shame. Heard you dokkalfar can do some wicked magic. I like wicked things, you know? But if you came for potions, then you came to the right place. Jonquil can do some *vile* stuff, if you know what I mean."

"Can't say that I do..."

The woman's face came forward into the light. Her eyes were unnaturally large, prismed like an insect, and in that fractal gaze Jane could see pieces of herself: her slight frame, her over-sized suit, her clenched hand. The woman's nose was flattened, her nostrils flared, thick scales covering her skin that gleamed cobalt blue. "I always dreamed as a child, you know, that one day I would become a dragon and swallow the sun. That's what you dokkalfar believe, right? That dragons swallow the sun?" The woman laughed, revealing pointed teeth. "Provincial crap. Anyways, I became obsessed with dragons. Collected them. Gathered one of the largest dragon menageries in the Burrow. I thought this would make me happy, but it didn't. I did mood elevating potions, I drank. Threw the *wildest* parties. Yet I was still miserable. But then, one day, I realized, I didn't want to *own* dragons, I wanted to *be* a dragon, and until that happened, I wouldn't be satisfied. I had a hole inside of me that couldn't be filled...that is until now. Until I met *him*." The woman pulled herself forward on the bed, coming further into the light. "Come little dokka, would you like to gaze upon the devourer of the moon?"

Jane could see now the great dragon wings that had been grafted to her back, sea blue bone draped with silver membrane, the legs that had been fused together and set with scales still inflamed and tinged with blood. Jane tried not to gag, holding her hand to her mouth. The woman held out a palm, glistening like a fish. "What do you think? Remind you of home?"

Without a word, Jane slammed the door shut. For a long moment she stood there, staring at the blank, white slab, hands shaking, breath coming in ragged fits and starts. When she had gotten control of herself, Jane blinked, turning away from the room and its odd occupant. Those wings. A brief mental image flashed—of red gold scales twining above black treetops. Of the awe of the roar.

She looked back down the hall. There was a gray door that said 'Employees Only' on it. Jane made her way to it. Those wings had not been created by consuming a potion. Those wings had been real, and there was only one way to get real dragon wings.

Clasping a hold of the handle, Jane swung the gray door open with one determined motion, glaring in at the darkness. It was a storage room, made of the same smooth, sanitized stone as the rest of the back area, filled to the brim with shelves. On those shelves were jars upon jars of *parts*: there were chimera tails and sphinx claws, hairs of sirens and wings of pixies; along the back wall was a whole gryphon, stuffed and set with golden talons. And these weren't magically created pieces either. The scales had too deep a luster, the teeth too yellow and sharp, the fur too lush. These were *real*. A pair of eyes suspended in reddish pink fluid stared out at Jane, almost accusingly. Jane stared back.

There was a commotion, distracting Jane from her thoughts. Looking back, she saw the receptionist storming in, puffed up and indignant, with Bill scrambling to follow. "Wait! I'm sure she just went to get something to eat! Or maybe she got lost! She'll show up any minute now, you'll see!"

"You and I both know she never left the building. We have re-covering patients back here that can't be disturbed by some nosy government official." She spotted Jane, pointing a commanding finger. "You! You can't be back here! You..." but her words failed as she saw the open door. "You...you shouldn't have gone in there..."

Jane walked up to the rapidly deflating woman, and there must have been something of her anger reflected in her face, for the woman flinched. Jane looked at her for a long while. At her perfect hair. Her impeccable make up. The neat clothes. Bill glanced ner-vously between Jane and the ljosalfar.

Finally, Jane turned to Bill. "Call the Ministry of Knights," she said, "this place is shut down."

The apothecary sat hunched over an ancient-looking desk as he read some notes, rubbing his gray beard as he muttered to himself, flipping back and forth between the yellowed pages. Jane sat there quietly, adjusting in her seat as her legs were tired and the chair was uncomfortable. The office they were in was a cluttered mess, full of books, herbs, and arcana, *not,* thankfully though, full of animal parts. Jane put that thought out of her mind.

"Sooo," he said slowly, "you're looking for an increase on your sleeping potion, right?"

"Yes, that is correct."

"Can I ask why?"

"I can't sleep well, that's why."

The apothecary sighed, adjusting his rumpled, pointed blue hat. "I mean, have you tried exercising, stress reduction, not eating late at night? All those things might help."

"Yes," Jane lied, "but I still can't sleep, and when I do sleep, I have bad dreams."

"What sort of bad dreams?"

"I don't know. Monsters, falling, those sorts of things." She could probably add bug-eyed dragons ladies to that list now.

"Look, I'm not asking to pry. It's just, you're already on a pretty high dosage, and at your age that has me concerned. These things can be dangerous if you aren't careful. You could end up like that one girl, sleeping for a hundred years in a briar rose castle."

"I understand the risks."

"I know things aren't easy for non-ljosa in these parts," he said, trying to get her to meet his gaze. "And I know it must be *particularly* difficult for you. You aren't the only one I treat, and *all* are on some stress-related magical relief."

"I can assure you that I don't know what you are talking about. I am grateful toward the Children of the Gopher who saved me from the backwards way of my people. I just have problems sleeping is all. My neighborhood is noisy." She kept her gaze locked on the grimoire just over his shoulder.

The apothecary stared at Jane hard for a long minute. The pallor, the bags under the eyes, the nervous chewing at the corner of the lip. He sighed again before writing something on a piece of paper.

"I'm going to give you the higher dosage, against my better judgment, because you *do* look like you need sleep."

"Thank you."

"And I'm going to give you the name of a cardiomancer - no, don't worry, your heart remains in your chest," he quickly added at her look, "you just talk with her, and she gives you advice. Kinda an outside perspective to help you through your problems. Anyways, I suggest you go see her. She's a gorgon, so she understands at least some of what you're going through."

Jane took the paper from the apothecary, feeling it crackle under her touch. "I uhm, I'll take that under consideration."

"I suggest that you do. Also, I probably don't need to tell you this, but it doesn't hurt to repeat it, absolutely no alcohol while you are taking this sleeping potion, do you hear me?"

"Of course."

Jane left the apothecary, sleeping potion in her shopping bag. She started over to Bill's mother's.

She got on the bus that would take her from the Ministry District to the southern end of the Burrow, where the majority of the Burrowfolk lived. It was getting dark as she looked out from her seat as they drove, fairae lights sputtering to life in shades of yellow. The government district structures gave way to homes, set up side-by-side. The homes had a similar look for the most part—cottage bungalows with moss covered roofs, shingle walls in pastel colors, and neat fences with little green lawns. They were quiet this time of night, as families settled in for dinner. Jane got off at the station closest to where Bill's family lived, walking the rest of the way.

Maera's place stood out from the others. It was bright orange with a maroon door, beets and onions ready to pick in a small garden out front; Maera was famous for her pickled beets, so it was something to look forward to. It was a cheerful, simple place, but well taken care of, with a porch and warm light coming from its windows. As Jane came up to the door, she could hear laughter from within.

Before she even had time to knock, the door burst open, followed by music and the smell of something delicious. There was a woman standing there, small satchel in her hand; she was looking behind, back into the house, replying to something that someone had said. "I'll be just a minute Daphne!" she called. "Be sure Bill doesn't drink all the wine while I'm gone!" The woman then turned to walk out, nearly running into Jane. "Ah Jane!" she exclaimed. "I didn't see you there!"

Jane smiled softly. "It's good to see you Maera," she dug into her bag. "I brought you some wine." It was hard to imagine a being more different than Bill. Maera was lithe and thin, with supple skin the color of unfurling spring leaves and hair the color of clay. Nymphs always had the amazing ability to stay young-looking late in life, to the point where Maera looked more like Bill's sister than his mother.

"Ah, excellent!" Maera said with a wink. "You know we can always use a little more of *that*." She ushered Jane on inside. "Now, why don't you go and set that on the table and get yourself something to eat. I've a few things set out to hold everyone over until dinner. I need to grab some herbs from the garden and then will be right back." With that Maera shuffled off in a flurry of soft linens and silks.

Jane walked into the house, watching Maera from the window as she made her way to the side yard, picking some rosemary. Bill showed up next to Jane, glass in hand, already looking a little drunk. "Hey there partner. Wasn't sure you were gonna make it after the day we had."

"And miss Maera's famous pickled beets? I'd fight somebody for those."

"You and half the Ministry. Come on, sit down, have something to drink. You earned it after today, kid."

Jane followed Bill. The house was clean, if a bit over-stuffed, with toys strewn in the corners, laundry hanging from the windows, and one of the sophas fitted out as a bed. The hardwood floors were worn with use, and the honey-gold walls hung with pictures drawn in crayon. A couple of kids were racing through the halls, playing tag, nearly running into them. "Hey, hey, watch it you two!" Bill yelled. "You nearly made me spill my wine!"

"Sorry uncle Bill!" they chimed, without sounding as if they really meant it, resuming their chase around the corner.

Bill shook his head. "Little scamps."

"Ooh, they're just excited to see their Uncle Bill," a voice said from the dining room, "it's so rare he comes to dinner these days. Too *busy* with his important Burrow work!"

Bill glared at a willowy looking woman with skin of fresh grown bark and hair a mass of ferns unfurling. She sat at a long wooden table draped with a white lace tablecloth, food and a few half-filled bottles of wine waiting, a group of children underfoot playing some board game. "Ah gimme a break Daphne," he grumbled, "*someone's* gotta do somethin' around here."

Another satyr sat at that table, the familial resemblance clear, even if he was broader and a good foot taller than Bill, and next to him was another nymph, her complexion reminiscent of cherry blossoms and locks flowing pink. "Well, you have to admit," the larger satyr said, "it's been a while since you've visited."

"Yeah, things have just been...tough. What with the divorce and all..."

"Ugh, *tell me about it,*" Daphne huffed. "After I divorced Greg it was all Ma could talk about. 'Light Elves don't mix well with non-ljosa folk', how I needed to 'find a nice satyr boy like so-and-sos daughter'. Wouldn't shut *up* about it. Made me wanna tear my hair out."

"Well, Ma will now be trying to find boyfriends for the both of us."

"Ugh, Gopher save us all."

"You just need to find a nice, considerate man," the cherry blossom lady said, laying her hand on the larger satyr's shoulder, "like James!"

Bill and Daphne rolled their eyes. "Why don't you study hard like *James*?" Bill said, pitching his voice high in a mimicking manner.

Daphne followed suit. "Why don't you have 10 bazillion children like *James*?"

James sighed, a bull-like motion that made him seem tired. "Okay, that's enough of that..."

But Bill and Daphne were on a roll. "James is *soooo* smart and talented," Bill mimed, "he can *shit* gold!"

"Hey!" James protested.

Daphne cackled. "Not only can he shit gold, but it doesn't even smell!" She switched back to her normal voice, poking her head under the table to address the kids, "which is a *lie* by the way. Your father has the smelliest poops I've *ever* had the misfortune to come across."

This got a laugh from the children, someone starting to chant, "Sme-lly Da-ddy! Smel-ly Da-ddy!" The rest of the kids picked up the refrain with the enthusiasm children often developed when they found a way to tease their father.

"Thanks Daphne," James grumbled with a glare. Daphne laughed.

"What is all this rude talk at the dinner table!" A voice exclaimed, and the chanting instantly ceased as Maera walked in. "And with a guest here none-the-less! I'd have thought we'd better manners as a family."

"Ahhh Ma, it's just Jane," Bill said. "She knows it's a lie when we behave ourselves."

"Well, it's still nice to pretend, even if it's every once in a while."

"It's alright Mrs. Maera," Jane said. "I don't mind."

Maera gripped her heart. "Ah, such a soft demeanor, such gentle words," she glared at Daphne. "Maybe if *someone* followed this example they'd still be married."

"Jane?" Bil said with a laugh as Daphne sulked. "Soft demeanor? Maybe if you compare her to a sledgehammer. Notice she isn't married either."

This earned Bill a whack upside the head from Maera. "Don't be rude to guests. I'm sure she's just biding her time. Waiting for the right one to come along. A wise move we all could learn from." With that Maera vanished into the kitchen, a puff of herb laden smoke emerging from the swinging wooden door.

Daphne leaned forward, wiggling her eyebrows. "So, is what Ma says true? You just out there playin' the field? Bidin' your time?"

This was always the issue with coming over to Maera's house for dinner. "No, I'm in solidarity with Bill and have sworn off men until his broken heart is healed."

"A good friend that," Daphne said, patting Jane's shoulder before scowling at the air, "that fuckin' Phil."

"Fuckin' Phil," James echoed.

And then a thirty-minute session on why Phil was terrible ensued.

"James," Jane commented after the third round of wine and some roast was passed around, "I didn't realize you and Elena were back living here."

Elena looked over at James with worried eyes. James looked suddenly depressed. "James got laid off," Daphne said, filling in the silence, "*permanently* it seems like."

"Oh, I'm sorry to hear that. I shouldn't have mentioned it."

"It's all right," Elena said. "James will find something else. It's just the circumstances under which it happened have been hard to accept."

"*Fifteen years* I worked for that damn place," James grumbled. "Fifteen Gopher Be-Damned years, and they sack me for some kid.

Because he's the son of some rich ljosa bastard." He downed his drink.

"Now James," Elena pleaded. "You don't know that. They said that times were just hard and they needed to cut back. They could call you back any day!"

James looked at his wife with sad, affectionate eyes. "Oh Elena, that is what I love about you, your boundless optimism. They aren't calling me back."

"Still," Bill said, "Elena's right. You'll find something. And until you do, we got your back."

"I know, I know. It just rankles, is all. It rankles that no matter how long you live with them or how much you think they've accepted you, you're still just a second-class citizen. Ready to boot you to the curb as soon as it becomes convenient." He looked over at Jane. "You don't forget that girl, you hear?"

Jane looked down at her wine, the red liquid sloshing around in small whorls and eddies. She gulped it down before setting the glass on the table with a clink. "Don't worry. I won't."

"By the way Jane, are you coming to church with us on Wednesday?" Maera asked, fluttering back in the room with another steaming tray. "It's Wednesday Madness! My favorite Gopher event of the year!"

"Uh, well, I don't know...I am not sure if it's a good idea..."

"*Nonsense!*" Maera exclaimed, whacking Jane with the oven mitt 'playfully'. "How could you say such a thing?"

Jane rubbed her the part of her skull where the oven mitt had whacked. "I'm not sure how happy everyone will be to see me after last year..."

"Oh, come now, no one's going to remember that!"

Bill looked up at his mother. "No one's gonna remember Jane having a seizure, flopping on the ground like a dead fish, screaming 'beware the false idol, beware the false idol, the end is drawing near' over and over again?"

"Yeah..." Elena sucked at her teeth, "that *was* a little awkward..."

Daphne leaned forward. "Did you ever get medicine for that?"

"I see an apothecary every week now," Jane said, face bright red. "He said it was probably just the lights. That I should be fine."

"Ah good, very good."

"Yes, most excellent."

Maera laughed nervously, piling more food onto people's plates. "I'm sure it will have been forgotten by now! And I *insist* that Jane attends! She has no family in this world, so we have to be there for her!" She gave Jane a pinch on the cheek. "Just be sure to leave before they pull out the strobe lights this time, all right my love?"

Jane nodded.

The rest of the dinner passed along cheerfully. It was hard to hang onto bad remembrances in the face of good food and good company. It was late when Jane left, Maera goading the men into walking her home. Jane waved aside such courtesies though, insisting on seeing herself back. "Oh Jane," Maera complained as Jane stood on the doorstep, ready to leave, "I do wish you would move over here from that Industrial District. It's too dangerous for a young woman such as yourself to live there alone." Bill snorted, earning himself another oven mitt attack from Maera.

Jane just smiled though, thanking Maera for the food. "And don't worry about me," she said, "the rent is cheap, and no one in their right mind would bother a Dark Elf." With that she left, taking the bus to the opposite end of the Burrow.

In the Industrial District, the clean lights of the faerie globes gave way to oil lamps that sputtered, putting off black smoke. The streets were dirtier, a few of the cobblestones loose and in need of repair, the buildings coated in a layer of grime that made them seem dim. Here, there was a little bit of everything; there were the industrial factories from which the neighborhood and gotten its name—places where potions were brewed, vans assembled, and Germantown fashions sown (alongside cheaper brands, Jane noted); here, there was a hodgepodge of rundown cottages, discarded castle spires, and forgotten chapels all plundered and retrofitted to various ends; here, there was a variety of faerie folk who lived together, with trolls who worked alongside goblins, ogres who had kobolds as neighbors.

And here, there was a view of the Wall.

Jane looked up at the Wall as she got off the bus, it's smooth surface awash in moon-glow. It stretched along either side of the district as far as she could see, made of a soft rose stone that belied the strength and severity of that barrier. Along the Wall, in its shadow, were shantytowns of hastily made shelters built by non-ljosa who had recently been brought in from the Forest to the safety of the Burrow. They lived in pilfered boxes, tents, and lean-tos, eyeing hungrily those who passed. Refugees. That's what they called them.

As Jane walked on, an apartment complex came into view. An old wizard's tower that had been abandoned years ago, it leaned slightly to one side, its conical roof missing a few shingles. She took the stairs to one of the top floors, not trusting the elevator. She came to her room, the numbers '801' on the chipped door slightly ajar.

Going in, she dropped her bag by the door, shrugging off her jacket and letting her hair loose; it fell past her shoulders in long silver waves, the color of spider webs kissed with winter dew. The apartment was small, a studio really, with a pull-out bed in the living room and a kitchen that one person could barely move in. Her clothes fit on a single rack: two pairs of pants, three shirts, a dress, and one other suit. There were no pictures on the walls, or decoration, just a few throw rugs to ward off the chill.

Jane went into the kitchen and grabbed a glass, filling it halfway with whiskey; she thought about it for a moment, before filling it all the way to the top. She took a sip, going out onto the balcony of the apartment—the reason she stayed in this place. The faucet was leaky and the heating needed repair, but the view made it all worth it.

To the southeast was the Temple of the Gopher, that monolith that loomed over the city, the lines of it sharp and unadorned. It was easy to see at night as it was always lit up; lit up so much, in fact, it often blotted out the stars. Its cochineal-pink tone matched that of the Wall, the all-seeing Gopher smiling down from his golden perch. At night, with the light, the Gopher looked almost ominous, the smile maniacal. Fireworks shot off around the tower, as they generally did this at time, in what had become a mundane spectacle. Jane sipped her drink.

But it wasn't the view to the southeast that was precious to Jane. She turned west to where the Wall stood. She leaned back, angling her head just right, to peak over the edge, and there she saw it. The mountain top. The moon was bright enough tonight that she could catch the silhouette of it, the light dusting of snow dotted with dark trees, and for a moment she almost swore she could smell it. The smell of cold. The crunch of crisp snow under foot. The bite in your lungs if you breathed in too deep. A place where dragons really did roam free...

That's what you dokkalfar believe, right? That dragons swallow the sun? Jane finished the whiskey. She went back inside, pouring herself another before deciding to get ready for bed. She went into the bathroom, flipping on a light. The light flickered before it came on, washing her in a fluorescent glare that made her look even more tired.

Jane got some water going, letting it run to get hot. She looked in the mirror. She had a face that might have been considered pretty if she weren't always so run down. A small, pointed chin with large eyes, pursed pink lips in a perpetual scowl. There was a small purple moon on her forehead, a faded tattoo, that she quickly shuffled her hair to hide.

The water reached temperature, fogging up the mirror. She went to grab some soap, when in the reflection she saw someone standing behind her. Jane froze, hand on soap, eyes wide. What Jane saw behind her, was...*herself.*

Well, it was her face anyway, but in a different hue. Where Jane had long silver hair this woman had a short blond bob; where Jane had pale gray eyes this woman's were a playful blue; where Jane had frost white skin, this woman had the pale blush of spring. She was Jane, but not Jane, wearing a black sequin flapper dress and a feathered headband with satin gloves. This woman sauntered up to Jane, mouth turned up in a wry grin, carrying with her the light scent of...May. Apple blossoms and lilacs, mixed with the must of fertile earth.

The May Woman reached out, placing her hands on Jane's shoulders. She leaned forward, whispering into her ear, "it's *coming*."

Jane jumped, startled by the voice and just like that, the May Woman disappeared. Jane jerked around, clasping the offended ear, trying to find where the woman might have gone. But there was nothing. With a shaking hand, Jane reached for her drink. Suddenly her little apartment seemed large and full of dark corners.

I'm just tried and need some rest, she told herself. It had been a long day after all, and that conversation with the dragon woman had shaken her. She went for the sleeping potion.

Stamp.

"Winner, winner, chicken dinner!"

Stamp.

"Hey Jane, wanna hear my Wednesday joke?"

Jane glared at Bill from her desk as he marked the forms with gleeful abandon. "You know, you're supposed to *read* those things before you approve them."

Stamp.

"Eh, I don't really care. I just like stamping things. Besides, what are they gonna do?"

"Fire you."

"Pssh, I'm union, and the only person whose been here longer than me is Frank. They can't do shit."

Jane and Bill looked over at Frank as the elderly man carefully took out his stamp to mark a page. It was a painful process. His hand wavered, the over inked sigil pooling pigment on one side, threatening to drip; for a moment Jane was sure that Frank was going to miss the mark, that he was going to notarize the desk instead, but Frank came through in the end, landing the stamp squarely on the page. Frank waved the document in the air, task accomplished, declaring with a victoriously shaky voice, "winner, winner, chicken dinner!"

Bill's face fell. "Well shit, can't use that now." Jane had to bite her lip to keep from laughing. Bill turned to her. "By the way, have I mentioned that you look like hell today?"

Her urge to snicker was now firmly dashed. "No, but thank you for the concern."

"You really need to see that apothecary I told you about. Makes a potion that will put you out like a gopherling."

"Thanks Bill, I already have an apothecary." And one that probably prescribed a far stronger potion.

"Okay," he said doubtfully, "but if you ask me, whatever he's giving you ain't doin' the job. You look like you're packing for a two-week vacation with the bags under your eyes."

Belinda suddenly appeared at their desks in a puff of smoke, startling the both of them. "Why Halllloooooo! May the Gopher Bless you on this glorious day!"

"*Galloping Gopher Belinda!*" Bill yelled, spilling his coffee. "You almost made me drop my favorite Marfield mug! What did I tell ya' about poppin' around the office like that!"

"Oh, I'm sorry Bill. I got so excited I just forgot. It is Wednesday Madness after all. Gets my blood boiling! Mother always says the same thing, that I'm popping in and out all the time with no thought to others around me. She says that's why I can never find a husband. After all, who would want a wife popping around all over the place like a mole in one of those whack-a-mole machines. Men want a stable woman who stays in one place. Not a whack-a-mole machine." Belinda laughed, somewhat hysterically, her mole twitching; Jane held her breath, waiting for the rip in the spacetime continuum.

Bill grabbed some tissue from Jane's desk, dabbing up the coffee. He made a face as he tossed the wet tissues into the trash before grabbing some more. "You know what, for once I think I agree with your mother." Belinda withered.

"Did you have a question for us ma'am?" Jane asked. "Is there something missing in the report about the Pretty Princess Potions incident?"

"What? Oh no dear, your report was very thorough. As always. Great job on that and all. What *awful* business. No, I'm afraid I have to ask you to go out on another field mission today." She said that last part with a wave of a wand, summoning a rainbow and some butterflies.

"Aww what?" Bill groaned, oblivious to the fluttering wings. "*Another one?* That's two in a week and you *know* I'm lazy. C'mon Belinda! You're killin' me here!"

"I know, I know. If I had any other choice I would send someone else, but my hands are tied. It's a very important person you see, and it's a very serious subject...it's a," Belinda looked around, before leaning forward, lowing her voice to a loud whisper level, "it's a *curse*. And by a curse it seems like it's an actual illegal curse, not a legal pretend one."

"Well then shouldn't that be a matter for the Knights?"

"I mean, I'm sure it eventually will, but first we need to ascertain whether it's actually an illegal curse or not and where it's coming from. You know the Knights, they're are all swords and no brains."

"*Fiinnnee*, give us the file. But I'm not happy about this Belinda. You owe me a drink."

"I owe you *two* drinks." She handed Bill some papers. "She's the daughter of an important Magistrate. Recently she's come under some terrible misfortune. She does nothing but sleep!"

"Well, that could be a bunch of things. Could be your typical true love curse, could be the kid ate a witch's apple, hell it could have nothing to do with magic, and she could just be depressed."

"Yes, all of those ideas were brought up," Belinda agreed, "but there are some *other* concerning signs as well..."

Bill narrowed his eyes, going through the file. "Boils, ravens, blood coming from the faucets..." he sighed. "Yeah, sounds like a legit curse alright. Lives in the Blessed Burrow too, huh? You think a family like that is gonna to be okay with a satyr and a dokkalfar showing up on their doorstep?"

"Oh Bill, don't be like that. It's their daughter that's cursed! I'm sure they'll be grateful for whatever help you can provide. Besides," she said with a wink, "I told them you two were my best people!"

"You're a flirt Belinda, and I like that." Bill got up from his seat, turning to Jane, "come on kid detective, we gotta job to do."

"I'm not a kid nor a detective," Jane said. "I'm twenty-seven-year-old bureaucrat."

Both Bill and Belinda looked at Jane in surprise. "Really? I thought you were older than that."

"Oh, what Bill means is that you seem so *mature*," Belinda said with a smile. Bill gave Belinda a look.

Jane just shrugged.

Bill and Jane made their way to the garage again, Jane taking the driver's seat once more, pulling into traffic. It was another sunny day in the Misty Burrow, the only clouds in the sky harmlessly free of rain. Bill slumped in his seat, scowling over the file. "Seems like a heavy sort of curse," he mused aloud. "Somehow the family must've pissed someone off."

"Could it be a political enemy?"

"Maybe," Bill said, "though most politicians around here stick to frog rains and locusts. The Perrault Family....hmmm. If I remember correctly the father of the family, is a uh," he flipped to a page, "Louis is the Head of the Magistrate of Weather. I can't imagine a Weather Wizard getting too much hate."

"Maybe he got the weather wrong one too many times?"

"Come on," Bill said, "the weather is *always* perfect here. Sunny seventy-five percent of the year. Snowy for those special holidays when it suits the mood. Rainy when folks feel like reading a book. It's never wrong!"

"I mean, there was that one time they calibrated the wind in-correctly and it knocked over the Ferris Wheel in Carnaville," she pointed out.

"Oh yeah. I forgot about that. But that was *years* ago, and no one was really hurt. It just closed down for a day."

"I suppose you have a po..." Jane spotted something, slamming on the breaks. She jerked violently in her seat, the belt biting her shoulder hard. Bill nearly went through the window, papers flying in protestation of inertia.

"*Galloping Gopher Jane!*" Bill cried, looking like an angry hen amongst a ruffle of feathers. "Are both you and Belinda determined to give me a heart attack?!"

Jane, however, wasn't listening. Her hands gripped the steering wheel tight, knuckles white, face drained of what little color it had. Her eyes were wide, pupils dilated so they were almost black, locked on a single point in front of her.

The May Woman was there.

She stood before them in her sequined dress and feathered hair piece, smiling. She was so close to the grate of the van that she could have touched it if she simply reached out with a delicately gloved fingertip, but her hands remained at her side, making small movements as if etching out some arcane spell. Traffic warped around her, cars and horses stretching and distorting to impossible proportions, like light in a pane of old, wavy glass. A halo of re-fraction danced around her head, a crown of kaleidoscope flowers. That crown became all that Jane could see: the pale gold hair, the laughing blue eyes, the haughty turn of her lips, adorned in shifting lily, hollyhock and amaryllis...

"Jane!" Bill barked, breaking the thrall.

Reality snapped back into place. The May Woman was gone. The vehicles went back to their proper shapes and speeds, and with that came the sound of horns honking as Jane stalled in traffic. "Ah, sorry!" Jane said, starting the van back up to move forward. She gripped the wheel to control her shaking.

"What the Holy Gopher was that about?" Bill cried.

"I uh," Jane scrambled for a thought, "saw a squirrel, I think. I didn't want to hit it."

"A *squirrel?*"

"Yeah. A big fuzzy gray squirrel. A real one. Not a magical one."

"Huh," Bill leaned back in his seat. "Haven't seen one of those since I was a kid. Thought they mostly just lived in the Dark Forest now."

"Must've slipped over the Wall," Jane said, relieved she'd been believed. "Happens from time to time. We should probably alert the Ministry of Rodent Control once we get back."

Bill craned his neck to peer through the van window, back to where Jane had stopped. "Nah, let the thing be. Kinda wish I'd seen it. Miss those little dudes." Jane chewed her lip, feeling guilty. "Anyways, next time you do that, could ya' give me a warning? Just about snapped my head off!"

"Sorry." Bill sighed, shaking his head as he gathered the papers back up.

They followed the flow of traffic through the Ministry District, past Germantown—Pretty Princess Potions now replaced by Baal's Bodacious Brews—and into the Blessed Burrow. The Blessed Burrow was where the most beautiful and most extravagant of the castles shone, home to the kings and queens of the Misty Burrow. There were the old money palaces done in the classic style, with ivy covered stone walls and red tiled roofs from which banners flew. Then you had your new money castles, done without a care of how they fit in with the rest of the scene; these were concoctions of blue cupcake towers and pink icing tops, sparkles and unicorns crammed into every crevice. One had so many sparkles that the reflected light made it hard for Jane to see and she nearly drove into a ditch. Regardless of the style though, each castle was more ostentatious than the last, showcasing wealth, magic, and power. And perhaps a little more power.

Bill whistled as they drove past. "If I'd a tenth the money of some of these guys, I'd be set for life. Would be able to buy James and Elena their own place."

"If you'd a tenth the money of some of these guys, you'd turn into an asshole," Jane said. Bill laughed.

They came up to a golden gate that guarded their destination. The castle beyond had large, well-tended grounds of low hedges and neatly trimmed grass. Along the edge, in the distance, was a small forest. It was an odd sight, that forest. Granted, it was a curated and contained one, but Jane found her eyes drawn to it none-the-less. The castle itself was a subdued affair for the area, made of brick and set back atop a series of grand stairs. There was a fountain before those stairs, depicting the Gopher in his usual 'thumbs up' pose surrounded by smiling children. The fountain was currently gushing blood, a raven perched atop one of the mar-ble child-heads cawing before it took a shit. Definitely a curse.

Getting out of the van, Bill went up to the guard at the gate, flashing his badge and explaining the situation. The guard nodded, opening the gate to wave them through. Bill got back in the car and Jane started down the cobblestone drive to the castle proper, glancing out the windows. She could see beings working in the gardens dressed in simple homespun garb. They had long ears, olive green skin, smashed faces, and bulbous shoulders. "Trolls," she said.

"Probably indentured servants. The trolls got the worse deal when they surrendered to the ljosa," he glanced at Jane. "Ah, except for you guys. Sorry."

"No need to be sorry. We never technically surrendered anyway."

They pulled up to the stairs, Jane putting the car into park. Before they even got out of the van, the door to the castle opened with a very worried looking man and woman coming forth. They were typical wealthy Light Elves, dressed impeccably. Baroque seemed to be the current trend among the well-to-do, and the pair looked like something that had walked out of 17th century Paris with ornate hats, curls and bows.

"Oh, thank goodness you are here!" the woman cried, lace handkerchief to her face. "We are just at a wit's end of what to do."

"Don't you worry ma'am," Bill said, taking lead as he put on his public facing smile. "The Magical Ministry's best is here to solve the case. A curse you say?"

"Yes," the man, Louis, Jane presumed, said, "we have had just about every magician in the Burrow here to see what they could do for our poor Penntifore and not a one of them has been able to assist her. It's really quite terrible."

"She's supposed to be married in a fortnight," the woman said, "and at this rate we might have to delay the preparations! It would be a disaster for our family."

"We were told that you two were competent," Louis' brow furrowed. "Are you sure you are up to the task?"

"I assure you good sir, that if anyone can crack this case it will be my partner and I," Bill said. "Could we see the afflicted perhaps? I think that will be a good place to start."

"Of course," Louis said, waving an arm. "This way."

Inside, the castle was decorated with gold filigree, colorful frescoes, and marble statues. The floors were a jade-colored stone, polished to such a sheen that you could almost see up Jane's skirt. She scowled at that. The chandeliers that hung from the ceiling sparkled immaculately, a servant up high on a ladder doing battle with the one speck of dust to mar their crystalline beauty.

They came to a large set of doors that was the entrance to the girl's bedroom. A pensive servant stood outside it, wearing a powdered wig and white dress coat. The servant and Louis talked for a minute in hushed whispers, looking uneasily at Bill and Jane. The servant seemed to not care much for what his master was saying, but in the end acquiesced, opening the doors.

As they went in, the first thing that hit Jane was the smell. It was the same stench as the dragon woman, sweetness over rot, and for a moment Jane was back in that hall, looking into those reflective eyes, hearing that cruel laugh. She shook the image, but an uneasy feeling settled into her stomach. She felt a strong urge to open a window, in the hope that fresh air would banish the imagined miasma.

The room itself was predictably florid with velvet gold-trimmed curtains and portraits of a pretty girl in curls, face flushed. They walked over to a four-poster bed where she lay, under soft sheets and satins, and it was when Jane looked down at the girl that she knew fresh air wasn't going to be of any help. The pretty face from those pictures was now a mottled gray, marked by puss filled boils, the curls gone, leaving her skull bare but for a few brittle wisps. She was skeletal in her thinness, her breath a death rattle.

And as if that wasn't bad enough, the May Woman was in the room. Standing to the right of the bed, she held the hand of the stricken girl, still wearing that beatific smile, seemingly unaware of the suffering before her. To the girl's left was another figure, this one dressed in long dark veils that covered its face and fell to the floor, a set of black horns, like those of a deer, rising from its head. Both the May Woman, and this new apparition turned to Jane, almost expectantly. Jane gulped as she looked over at the horned creature; the hand that held the girl's was brittle and black. Like burnt bone covered in tar.

Jane felt something at her elbow and looked down in surprise to see Bill watching her with concern. "Hey Jane, didn't you hear me? I was asking what you thought?"

Jane blinked at Bill for a few moments, trying to pull herself back to the here and now. She looked at the parents and the servant, satchels to their faces to ward off the smell, then down at Bill's worried face, and then back at the girl with the two entities standing vigil. She wished the parents weren't there. "This isn't good."

"We know this isn't good," Louis snapped, wife sobbing. "What we want to know is how to fix her!"

"It's uhm...it's a blood curse," Jane said. "You can tell by the uhm, severity of the skin condition. You probably can only see the whites of her eyes. I would look for myself, but her skin will be painful to the touch. The smell is from the puss, which is why you can't clear the air in here. I would assume she wanders at night, perhaps moving in a way that is, uhm, unnatural."

"That does match all the symptoms. So then, how do you break this 'blood curse'?"

"Y...you don't."

The room went silent as all four of them stared at Jane, not comprehending what she had just said. "What?"

"Blood magic requires sacrifice, to bend the forces of nature to the magic user's will. For smaller rituals this can be a fish, or a rabbit, or something like that, which is normally used for divination. The life force of the being fuels the spell. For a blood curse," Jane made a movement that seemed more like a twitch than anything else, "someone was sacrificed to curse your daughter. Someone who was close and precious to the magic wielder. There is no one in the Misty Burrow with the skill to break this sort of spell." The mother screamed, falling to the floor in hysterics.

Louis handed off the mother to the servant, walking up to Jane to grab her by the arm. "*You* could break it though, right? This sort of stuff is the specialty of your people, isn't that true? I see the mark of the moon on your forehead. You carry the knowledge on how to save my daughter!"

Jane looked at Louis' desperate face, the sweat beading on his brow, how his eyes shifted like a wild animal in fear. "I'm sorry," she said, "but I don't have the knowledge to save her."

Louis released her arm, almost throwing it, beginning to howl. "Who? *Who?!* Who could do such a thing against my daughter?! *Why!?*"

Jane licked her lips, not sure how to answer, but the May Woman answered for her. Slowly, she released the hand of the child, making her way across the room. She didn't so much walk, as saunter, her heels thudding on the thick carpet, each beat sending a shiver down Jane's spine. The May Woman walked out the door. "I uhm, think I need a moment," Jane said.

"Yeah, go take a breather," Bill said, patting her on the back. "I'll take things from here."

Jane nodded, leaving the room; as soon as she stepped out, she could feel the stink of death slide off her. Jane looked from side-to-side. The May Woman was waiting, down the hall, hands at her hips making those odd little motions. Jane headed towards her. The May Woman turned, resuming her march. Jane tried to catch up, but despite the seemingly slow pace the May Woman moved at, she couldn't quite close the gap.

The May Woman led Jane out of the castle and into the gardens where the trolls worked, a few looking up as Jane passed, curious at this odd girl in their midst. Jane came to the edge of the manicured woods. There, just covered in the trees, was a long, flat building. It resembled more a shed than a place to live, but it was there the trolls resided. She watched them come and go, some injured, some old, some sick. The May Woman walked into the mean building, giving Jane a come-hither stare as she vanished into the darkness of a doorway. Jane followed.

Inside the building, the stink was almost as bad as in Penntifore's room. Straw beds lined the muddy floor, mixed with blood, piss, and shit. There were more trolls than there was room to keep them, and many of them possessed some sort of illness that made them toss and turn on their beds. An old woman troll tended to the ill, hair long and white, as white as Jane's, if no longer soft or shining. The old troll woman looked up at Jane and their eyes met.

"Where is it?"

"What do you care?" the old woman spat. "You should hate them just as much as us."

"She's a child crone. What you've done is cruel and has gone on for long enough. Release her."

"Cruel? What is cruel is giving us scraps while they feast on the boar cooked by my children's hands. What is cruel is whipping us while they enjoy the gardens my children have created. And what is cruel is going through every doctor in the Burrow to cure their *brat* while they won't even give me a simple healing potion while my children lay dying. *That* is cruel."

"You care so much for your children that you sacrifice them in order to get your revenge? Where is the fetish?"

The old woman sneered. "The dire wolf does not hold back when it bites."

"Dire wolves die in captivity, crone, and in case you haven't noticed, we've been caged. Your chance to fight was when you still lived out there." Jane looked around, saw a back room and entered. There she found the fetish. A stick in the ground from which a skull hung, strung with dried herbs. The ritual object was surrounded by a series of half-melted candles, and there was something sticky on the floor that Jane suspected to be blood. She left the back room, heading towards the door.

"Going back to your master's chain, dog?" the crone snarled.

"Better to be a caged dog than a dead one," Jane retorted, then walked out.

It was a warm night. The bus was crowded, so Jane had to stand, packed in so tight she couldn't even find a hand hold to steady herself, relying on the weight of the those around her to keep her upright as the bus turned corners and went up hills. There was an air of excitement on the bus. Everyone was dressed in bright shirts and hats, bearing depictions of the Gopher. Jane for her part wore a plain shirt and a pair of jeans, a small Gopher button pinned above her right breast.

The bus came to its stop before the great temple and everyone got off, Jane grateful to get some space and fresh air. The respite was brief though, as waiting at the stop was Bill and his family.

"Ah Jane!" Maera exclaimed, dressed in the Gopher's blue. "I'm so glad that you came!"

Jane allowed herself to be enveloped in Maera's arms, smelling the fresh earth and lilies. "I don't think she had much of a choice Ma," Bill said. "You were threatening to hunt her down if she didn't show up."

"Oh Bill!" Maera said, hugging Jane just a little tighter. "You make it sound as if I was going to *hurt* her!"

"You were saying you were going to grab Jane by the hair and drag her here if you had to," James added.

Maera's eye twitched. Now Jane's ribs were starting to hurt. "James, you make that sound as if I *meant* it!"

"You said, after you said that, that you 'really, really meant it'," Daphne added.

Maera's twitch turned to a dangerous glare. "Wanna end up on the streets?" Jane gasped for air.

Elena came between them. "Come now, come now," she said, "let's not argue on this occasion! It's Wednesday Madness. It should be a time of joy!"

"Oh Elena," Maera said, releasing Jane; Jane took in a deep, gasping breath. "You're right, as always. The very visage of the Gopher's wisdom itself. Thank goodness such a level head was married into our family!" Maera went over to Elena, wrapping her in a hug. Elena's arms flailed.

Bill pushed Jane along. "Quick run, while you still can!"

Jane looked back. "But Elena..."

"There's nothing we can do for her now," Bill said, a tear in his eye. "We can just hope she doesn't suffer long."

Maera looked at Bill, eyes two sharp points. "You do know I can hear *every word you are saying*?"

The small troop made their way to the temple through the gardens. Up close the hard, austere lines, coupled with the reddish stone, gave the temple the weight of authority, the Golden Gopher smiling down. The gardens themselves were filled with topiary trimmed in various poses of the Gopher, along with bushes of blue roses. Several paths wound their way through the gardens, feeding into a large central road that led to the main temple entrance. Along that main thoroughfare were vendors selling Gopher merchandise: you could get a Gopher top hat, or a dozen Gopher blue roses; there were even strawberry crepes, imprinted with the Sacred image of the Gopher Himself, if you were feeling a bit peckish.

"Hey dad," one of the kids cried, pulling at James' arm. "I wanna Gopher ice cream."

"Yeah, dad," another cried. "I wanna Gopher balloon."

James and Elena looked pained, Elena mostly because her ribs had been crushed. "I'm sorry little ones," James said, "but maybe we can have ice cream when we get home."

"Oh James," Daphne said, "let the kids have an ice cream."

"It's 500 Gopher Nuggets just for a scoop," James complained. "I can't afford that!"

"Then just take out a Gopher Loan," Daphne said, pointing, "they have a booth set up."

"Daphne!" Maera cried, shocked.

"What? It's what it's there for! It's just a loan! The interest goes back to the church!"

Bill groaned.

Grandma Maera treated the kids to some ice cream, and the small family made their way into the temple. Inside, the temple was set up for the event, with tiered seating along the walls and a stage at the back. The stage was framed by an acoustical shell reminiscent of a pale blue rose, housing space for a full orchestra. There was a large screen hanging from the ceiling, so that those in the rear could see. Laser lights hung from the rafters.

The temple was already crowded, so Bill and his family went to the back to find seats. People were excited, chatting with one another. They carried with them signs that read, "I love you Gopher', 'The Gopher is Great', and 'Kiss Me Godfrey'. There was the heavy odor of too many people wearing too much perfume; Jane coughed, eyes beginning to water. "You okay?" Bill asked as they settled into their seats.

"Yeah, I'm fine" she said, waving her hand in front of her face. "Just the smell."

The main lights dimmed as the stage came to life, and the chatter died down. The laser lights started to make intricate designs along the walls, and the orchestra began to play. A man in a rabbit bodysuit came up to the stage, adorned in blue sequin vestments. "Ladies and Gentleman!" The rabbit-man cried, raising awkward felt arms into the air. "Welcome to Wednesday Madness! I bring to you the One, the Only, the Great Critter from Above, *Godfrey Gopher*!"

The crowd went wild with cheering as a platform came down from the ceiling, carrying said Gopher. Lights flashed and the music grew more intense. Jane almost went blind from it. She could see the Gopher on the screen, waving his hands—another man in a sparkling animal suit. The Gopher reached the stage, bringing a microphone to his mouth, "are you ready to get *Haaaapppyyyy!!!!*"The crowd screamed in response, the ground rumbling.

"Raise up your hands!" the Gopher cried, "if you're feelin' *good*!" The whole audience lifted their arms in response.

Bill looked at Jane. "Jane," he cried, barely able to yell over the noise, "raise up your hands!"

Jane raised up her arms.

"That's it, that it!" the Gopher said, arms shaking in the air. "I feel your joy! I feel your Happiness, and you know what happens when I feel Happy?" There were a few preemptive cheers. "It means I wanna dance!" The crowd broke out. "Can you all dance!" The screaming rose even louder. "Hit it!"

The orchestra stopped with a new sound replacing it—the soft *kachunk-a-chunk* of a beat setting on a synthesizer—and the rabbit-man went over to an electronic piano, playing a simple tune. The Gopher started to move. "It's time everyone, for the Gopher Dance! You all know this Dance, but when we do it together, we harness the true power of the Gopher! So, get ready, and let's jam! Move your feet!" The crowd in the stadium began to stomp their feet in unison, Jane joining in. "Then take a step to the left!" the audience bopped one step left, and it was unnerving to see that sea of bodies move, as if they were One. "Then take a step to the right!" the audience bopped one step to the right. "Now flail your arms in the air!" and everyone flailed their arms, reminding Jane of a...

...a dragon, writhing, its serpentine body wrapping itself up the legs of a woman with dark hair and fractal eyes, laughing as it entered into her and ate up the sun...

"Now touch your toes!" and everyone bent down to the ground. Jane felt sweat beginning to form on her brow. That was the problem with Wednesday Madness. There were always so many people, and the Ministry of Weather insisted on it being a warm night. Made it so hot...

...hot like the skin of a girl, blistered and boiling to the touch. It fell off in her hands, in pieces, and there was nothing she could do to stop it. And the girl screamed and screamed and screamed...

"Hands back up in the air!" the Gopher cried, everyone raising their arms once more. "And repeat after me, I am Happy'."

"I am Happy!" Sweat dripped off her nose.

He had ink-black hair, and eyes the color of sea glass. He looked over at her, expression flat, yet endlessly sad. Like a stone lost in a pond.

"I am Happy because I am *Clean*!"

Jane repeated.

"I am Happy because I am *Beautiful*!"

Jane repeated

"And because I am Happy, and I am Clean, and I am Beautiful, I am Blessed!"

Jane repeated.

The cat had tawny fur and eyes of gold-green. He wore a floppy hat set with fishing lures. "Beware the false idol, kin."

"Beware the false idol"

"Falseidol..."

"...falseidol..."

"...falseidol..."

Jane stood in a field of bones, bleached white by a sun that didn't shine. Above she saw the sunmoon in a sky of red, slowly being devoured. The sunmoon became the face of the Gopher, the devourer the dragon woman, teeth slowly sinking into the Gopher, popping out an eyeball as he screamed. A sad song filled the air.

"The Apocalypse is coming. Leviathan is coming for you..."

"Leviathan is coming for you," and the sunmoon turned into a single baleful eye, resentful and full of pain. *"And there is blood in the water, blood in the snow, and blood in the wine."*

A young girl smiling up at the patchy sky, eyes lost in the ecstasy of bliss or pain it couldn't be said. Slowly, a trickle of blood falls from her chin, down her cheek...

Jane started, back in the church with the dancing congregation. Everyone was happily moving back and forth, including Bill, who looked over at Jane in confusion. "You okay?" he asked. "They haven't even brought out the strobe lights yet."

Jane could no longer be in that place. Could no longer pretend that she could even stand it. The smell of it, the sights and the sounds. Her hair was plastered to her forehead from so much sweat. "I need to get some air," and without waiting to hear a response, pushed her way past the crowd to the door.

Outside, the fresh air felt good on her skin. She searched around with shaking hands, finding a pack of cigarettes and a bottle shot of whiskey in her back pocket. She took the shot, lit the cigarette, and instantly felt her nerves cool. She leaned her back against the wall of the church, feeling the excitement inside vibrate in the stone. With a sigh she exhaled a puff of smoke, looking up at the sky.

There, against the backdrop of black night, she saw a red star. It was a rare event to see a star shining brightly enough to compete with the light of Godfrey Gopher, and this one was as red and angry as the cherry of her cigarette. She pulled out another bottle shot, holding it up to the light of that star, watching it filter through the amber liquid.

Jane finished her drink. Well, at least the week couldn't get any worse, right?

"Friday, Friday, Friday!" Bill shadow boxed around his desk, hooves clip-clopping with each jump. "You ready for the weekend champ?"

Jane stared heavily into her mug. Normally she didn't care all that much about her days off, but this week... "Yes, yes I am actually."

"Ooo? Hot date?" Jane gave him a deadpan glare. "Oh yeah, guess not. Well guess where *I'm* goin' tonight? *The Goose's Garter*. Gonna get my drink on." Bill started doing a little dance.

"You go to The Goose's Garter every Friday, and drink enough it takes you the whole rest of the weekend to recover."

This time it was Bill's turn to glare. "You sound like Ma."

Belinda tip-toed up to the desk, meek smile on face and file in hand. Bill and Jane looked at her with sharp eyes. "Hall..."

"Aw no," Bill groaned, "a *third* one? Belinda, you're killin' us. It's Friday for Gopher's sake!"

"I'm sorry Bill," Belinda said, looking at her feet, "I wouldn't be here unless I felt it was really really important."

"That's what you said on Wednesday! Are we *that* understaffed? I mean, can't it wait until Monday at least? We gotta shit ton of paperwork to catch up on." Never mind that Jane's work was done and Bill had an open crossword puzzle on his desk.

"Three drinks," Belinda said, holding up her fingers. "Heck, I might even pay for the whole night."

"I'm not so easily swayed by the promise of booze as to fall for that."

"Oh, I know *that* is a lie. And really it isn't you I should be offering to cover. It's Jane."

Jane and Bill looked at one another. "Me?" Jane asked, taking the bait.

"Yes," Belinda licked her lips nervously. "You see, this was actually supposed to go to the Ministry of Knights, but when I saw who and what was involved, I pulled a few strings to grab it because, well, because I thought it might mean something to you."

"You pulled strings to get us *more* work?"

"Yes, and for a very good reason," Belinda said, "for you see, it has to do with Jane's people."

Bill and Jane went silent. After a moment, Jane held out her hand. "Let me see it."

"It's a report of a small Dark Elf community," Belinda said as she passed the file over, "suspected of entering illegally into the Dark Forest and smuggling illicit items."

Jane looked up sharply. "A whole community? I didn't think enough of us had made it for something like that."

"It's hard to say. Looks like it's more of a small family, but the paper trail on these things is not all that great due to some of the past difficulties we have had with the Dark Elf communities wanting to keep up with the census. Also, with the going back forth between the Wall and Forest who can say? They might have brought in other members of their tribe from beyond the Wall."

"And the Knights just let you take this?"

"I managed to convince them saying that there *might* be some unlicensed magics occurring, but weren't really sure, so it would behoove us to *make* sure before we did anything rash. Really, I just felt that the Dark Elves would react better to one of their own, rather than a retinue of Light Elves in armor, showing up at their door. I felt that tact might bring up, uhm,...some bad feelings. The Knights seemed to understand this position. No one was too interested in starting a fight unnecessarily."

"I appreciate that understanding ma'am."

"I thought you might," Belinda said. "So, can I say that you'll be taking this on?"

Bill looked at Jane, who looked at Bill. Bill sighed. "Yeah, I guess," he said.

"Oh wonderful! That is ever so good to hear," Belinda's cheer instantly back on. "I eagerly await your report!"

Jane gathered her items, getting ready to go. "It's been a long time since I've spoken the old words," she said, "but I will do my best, and ma'am?"

"Yes?" Belinda asked with her same smile.

"Thank you for letting me do this."

Belinda seemed a bit taken back, her face attempting to contort into something akin to an actual expression. "Oh, oh well, it was really nothing. Like I said, I just felt that you might handle it better. You are, after all, the only Dark Elf that works in the Ministry. It just seemed natural to hand it to you. I do expect you to check in with me soon though, right? I appreciate it when my field agents let me know when they come back safely from an assignment."

"You can be sure of that ma'am."

That said, Belinda left, and Bill and Jane headed towards the garage. "You sure about this Jane?" Bill asked as they walked. "Might bring back old memories."

"If they send the Knights in, it'll be a blood bath. Belinda was right to ask us to go."

"And if they're practicing illegal magics? And if they don't wanna play nice?"

"Then we will cross that bridge when we come to it."

"Ahh, I love the 'by the seat of the pants' approach. Always works out *so* well."

Jane didn't respond to the sarcasm.

The pair got into the van, Bill taking the wheel this time, adjusting the pedals so they rose to match his height. Jane read through the file as they drove. "Anything interesting?"

"It's mostly information about this Warg guy. Sounds like he was taken from his tribe young and put through the Re-Burrowing schools."

"Did you know him?"

"No, he's seven years older than me, so we must've missed each another. Besides, looking at this file, it doesn't seem like he adjusted well. Fights, outbursts, refusing to speak ljosalfar. He has a fairly long disciplinary record."

"Weird there's nothing about the rest of this clan."

"It's hard to say. It's probably not his original tribe. Maybe these people he's with are dokkalfar from other groups that have joined together. Though that would be unusual, most of the old tribes didn't get along. But who knows, with as few of us as there are left...maybe they're stragglers, like Belinda said, that have been living beyond the Wall in the Forest."

"Oof, living in the Dark Forest this whole time. Wonder how rough that must be on someone?"

Jane kept her gaze on the piece of paper, but her mind was elsewhere—on soft spring grass underfoot, on fields in bloom after the ice melted, on cries of baby birds demanding to be fed. *On blood in the snow.* "Yeah, I guess it would be."

The small van drifted to the outskirts of the city proper, by the Industrial District, approaching the section of the Wall where the refugees lived in their hovels; the non-ljosa that weren't even trying to, or couldn't, assimilate into the world of the Misty Burrow: ogres in cardboard caves decorated with pebbles, redcaps scowling from shadows; there were even a few satyrs in the mix, naked and drunk, nymphs sitting on their laps. Bill looked away, face red.

They turned down a narrow alleyway lined by two large, dilapidated buildings. Through that alleyway was a good-sized clearing that couldn't be seen from the street, ending in the Wall itself; the perfect place to hide from prying eyes. Here, was a long, low building built from thick logs with a thatch roof and a chimney from which smoke drifted, a small garden out front filled with onions and cabbage. Hanging from the eaves of the structure were various charms made of stick, bone, and red ribbon. Jane watched a piece of that ribbon shimmer in the wind.

"What is that?" Bill asked, peering through the van window.

"It's a Great Hall," Jane replied, "or at least an attempt at one. It's fairly small. Let's go." Jane got out of the van, Bill following.

"And what are these things for?" Bill asked, making a face at a charm with a bird's skull tied up in fur.

"Wards against evil," Jane said vaguely. "Now Bill, I know you normally take lead when it comes to any sort of social interaction we have in the course of our duties."

"Yes, you're *terrible* with people."

"Yes, well in this one case I would ask that you let me take lead. I don't know what tribe these elves are from, but some of them can have rather...finicky customs. I don't want you to do something that would offend them and make our case more difficult."

"You know Jane, you're beginning to make me feel like coming here was a bad idea."

"I'm sure I'm just being overly cautious." When she looked up though, she saw the Horned One, digging in the garden with its long black talons, veils shifting in the breeze like the ribbon from a moment ago. The Horned One pulled up what looked to be a screaming mandrake root from out of the earth, only it was the May Woman's head. Smiling. *Or maybe not.*

Bill watched Jane staring off in the distance, trying to track what she was looking at, but could see nothing. "Come on," Jane said, forcing herself to look away, "let's get this over with."

They went up to the entrance of the Great Hall and knocked. The door was of a heavy wood that absorbed the sound and rasped sharply on Jane's knuckles; for a moment she thought no one had heard and moved to knock again, but then the door was opened by a shriveled, small figure dressed in so many rags it seemed more mop than elf. *"Goten murnin, Lunda Dochter. Vhas ich vur sie?"* the figure asked in Dark Elvish.

For a moment, Jane was stunned by shock—shock at seeing the old woman, and shock at hearing the old words coming out of her mouth. Jane worked her lips and tongue around old, half-forgotten memories. "*Goten murnin Godsmutter. Ist her huerer clannan?*" Her speech was stilted and awkward, and the old woman seemed confused.

Luckily, Jane was saved from having to explain further. "*Mattra Ursa,*" a voice chided,"*tiese clanna necht speken dokkalfar. Must speken ljosa.*"

The mop grandmother made some huffing noises Jane couldn't understand, more like grunting than actual speech. Bill looked at Jane and she shrugged. A face followed the second voice, and it was that of a handsome man that matched Warg's age and description. He had shoulder length blond hair tied back with a string and wore tanned leather and fur. He looked muscular and strong, like a man who could have led a hunt back in the old days, his eyes blue with creases along their edges from being out in the sun. When he spotted Jane, those eyes narrowed. "Greetings," he said in Light Elvish, "I must apologize for Grandmother Ursa. Old age has taken her wits, and she gets confused easily. It's not often we get visitors. How can I be of help to you?"

Jane was thrown by this personage, so reminiscent of figures from her past, yet not. She felt her face grow hot. "Uhm, yes, apologies in disrupting your day. We're from the Ministry of Magic and we heard some concerns about possible illicit magics being conducted here that we would like to investigate. You are Mr. Warg, is that correct?"

The man was silent for a long moment before responding. "Why yes, I am *Mister* Warg, and you two are employees of this Ministry?"

"Yes. I'm Jane and this is Bill. Really, we would just be doing a routine inspection. In and out in 10 minutes." In and out as fast as Jane could manage, as she suddenly felt panicked.

"*Jane* and *Bill*, is it?" He looked from one to the other, those eyes seeming as though they were trying to dig into her soul; Jane stared resolutely down at her shoes.

For a moment, she thought there was going to be a problem, that he wouldn't let them in, which at this point would almost be a relief, but then Warg smiled, stepping back from the door. "But of course you can come in. It would be rude of me to keep visitors out in the cold. A violation of *gutenfronshaft*, no?" He looked at Jane again as he used the Dark Elvish word for the term.

"We thank you for your hospitality," Jane replied simply.

"*Mattra, issan und drinken,*" Warg said, "*und usen guttassen.*" The old woman made some more grunting noises before shuffling off, looking like a pile of laundry trying to escape. Warg turned Jane, saying clearly in Dark Elvish, "*Tee und brotgut, Lunda Dochtur?*"

"That will be more than enough, thank you," she said, Bill looking around, wide-eyed and clueless.

They walked into the Great Hall, and it was cold, despite the fire. Various herbs and plants hung from the rafters; Jane looked up, trying to identify them, but both lack of memory and the smoke made it difficult. The walls of the building were carved with runes and wards, the glow from the blaze filling their lines with golden light.

There was a group of people sitting around the small fire in the center of the Hall; like the old woman they wore an odd assortment of rags. None of these elves acknowledged the new visitors, gazes locked firmly on the flames. The old woman came back with a tray of drink and food. "Please, sit," Warg said, indicating a table at the edge of the Hall, "and then you can see, there is nothing untoward occurring here."

Both Bill and Jane sat at the long table where the refreshment was set. Jane picked up a small piece of bread and took a sip of the tea—it would have been rude to refuse. Bill followed suit. Warg poured himself a large cup of the stuff, taking a chunk of bread. "So, I'm curious," Warg said, "how did a Priestess of the Moon end up being a bureaucrat?"

Bill nearly spit out his food. "*Priestess*?!" He looked at Jane with large eyes.

Great, just great. "That was a long time ago, in a different place. Things have changed. We've all had to adjust."

"Some of us more than others it seems," Warg said with a slight smile. "Well, Little Sister? What do you think of my Great Hall? Do you see some dark secret squirreled away? Some deep stain of blood?"

Jane looked at the ceiling. "I'm pretty sure some of those plants you can only get from the Forest."

"Trade with newcomers, nothing wrong with that. Grandmother Ursa wants to save the seed and add them to her garden."

Jane took another drink, her throat parched from the thickness of the smoke. It made her eyes water. "And the logs to build this

Hall...I don't see how you could have gotten them unless you pulled them from the Forest yourself."

"And here I thought you worked for the Ministry of Magic, not Trade," Warg protested. "Does this Ministry of Magic care where I get my wood?"

"Hey buddy," Bill snapped, "better be nice to the girl. She came here as a favor to you, to keep the Ministry of Knights off your back."

"Bill!" Jane protested, surprised at the outburst.

But Warg just laughed. "A *favor*? To *me*? Somehow, I doubt that," he looked over at Jane. "It is nice to see, though, that you still have *some* loyalty towards your people."

Jane didn't reply. The smoke was making it hard for her to think. Things felt as if they were tilting ever so slightly. It was a feeling that was vaguely familiar, though she couldn't quite place it.

"You know," Warg continued, "I always found it intriguing how these ljosa always feared the Forest. As if there's something naturally evil about it. Do you think there's something evil about the Forest, *Jane*?"

"I don't think there is anything that is inherently evil. Just dangerous perhaps."

"Hmm, but danger is everywhere, is it not? Danger increases the moment we walk past the threshold of our doors, into the world. A car could hit us. Someone could rob us. An asteroid could strike the very planet we are on and wipe us clean," Warg laughed at the thought. "But we don't let that stop us, do we Daughter of the Moon? Because to do so would mean to not live life at all. We accept the danger for the sake of our freedom."

"Your point being?"

"There is nothing *evil* about the Forest, but do you know what there is? Freedom. And freedom has consequences, Little Sister. And these ljosa-scum, they're afraid of that. They're afraid of consequences. They would rather hide in their safe little hole, where they think they can escape from it all."

"I'm sorry Mr. Warg," Jane said, trying to keep a hold of herself, "but what does this have to do with what we came here for?"

Warg's hand shot out, grabbing Jane's wrist in a grip so tight it hurt. He bore into her with those eyes like blue flame, and she found now, that she couldn't escape them. "Because Priestess, they tried to take that freedom from me, and I'm going to get it back."

Jane's world was now spinning dangerously. Her vision blurred. The walls seemed to expand and breathe, the runes come to life. She wasn't thinking clearly. What herbs was this man burning? No, not the herbs. It was the tea. The familiar earthy tang. The discomfort in her stomach. Where was Bill? Jane looked over at the fire and there was the May Woman, standing there, looking into those flames. Jane watched as a beetle scampered across the hand of one of the Dark Elves. Jane then realized, "they're...corpses..."

Warg set the food and drink neatly back on the tray. "Not corpses Priestess, but our brethren, brought back from the brink."

The wards, the herbs, the runes on the walls—it all made sense now. "You've been going into the Forest to get their corpses," she said. "There is no record of them because they died in the war. You've been reanimating them." Jane tried to get up, but had lost feeling in her feet and fell to the ground.

Warg came around, grabbed Jane by the shoulders, and set her back in her seat. "I was taken by the ljosa when I was eleven years old. Not old enough to be a man, but old enough to know my duty as one. They came through and slaughtered my tribe to the person. They skewered the men. Burned our homes. The mothers, wailing in despair, threw themselves from the cliffside with their babes so they wouldn't suffer. I, however, was weak."

"You were a child," Jane said woozily. "A child is supposed to want life."

"Yes, you are right. A child clings to life like a babe to the breast. But there are consequences to our choices, and I suffered the consequence of choosing this 'life'. But now, now I have the chance to make up for my past mistakes. Now I have the chance to be the hero for my people I dreamed about in that wretched 'school'. I will bring back my tribe and we will gut this rotten Burrow from the inside out like bad wood."

"You're mad. Necromancy...it will take you a lifetime to raise enough to do that."

Warg smiled. "Yes, it would have. But now that I have you, I can circumvent all of that."

"Huh?"

"The Moon Mother would never have wanted this for her children. Her will and the will of the Forest has been violated and now balance must be restored. She has brought you to me. You will be my guide to the Mother's Will and the destruction of the Burrow."

"Then you will fail."

"And why do you say that?"

"Because I could never talk to the Moon Mother," Jane said, "it was all a lie. A lie to make us believe we were somehow special, that we somehow had control over our future. But all that really happened was I got high as fuck and spewed out some shit. That will not help you get revenge."

"I see. So, you're that far gone? Fine then, if you won't talk to the Mother willingly, then I will have to go to other methods." He pulled out a knife.

Jane looked at that knife, at her reflection in it; pale-faced, sweating, fearful. "What are you going to do with that?"

"If you won't speak to the Goddess for me, then I will gut you and read her Will in your entrails, just like you once did. I mean, it will be a shame, really, to lose your power. I would've rather you done this willingly. But perhaps I can bring you back afterwards and have you be more compliant."

Jane tried throwing herself away from Warg, but just ended up back on the floor. "This is a mistake! Clinging to the old ways...you're fighting a losing battle! You can't win against them!"

Warg grabbed Jane by the hair and she cried out. He held the knife to her throat, pressing his knee into her spine. His face was twisted, savage. "Then I would rather *die*. I would rather do *any-thing* other than simply survive in this *stinking fucking hole* while my soul rots faster than the bodies of these corpses. Don't you feel it, *Jane*. The decay of your being? Filling it with fake smiles, potions, and booze. Consume, consume, consume, but don't ever think! Smile, smile, smile, but don't ever cry. Because everything is a blissful fucking fairytale and if you ever think otherwise then you just need to be Re-burrowed or take another *happy* potion. I understand how the others have swallowed this poison, but how could *you*?" Tears formed in his eyes. "You were one of us. You were powerful. You were *free*..."

"It wasn't freedom. It was just another sort of prison!"

"Hah," Warg scoffed, "come on, you don't even believe that. I see the look on your face, the sorrow in your eyes. You know what you've lost, you simply can't come to terms with it. Well fret not Little Sister, soon, you won't have to worry about anything at all." Jane felt the knife press into her throat. She coughed, struggling uselessly against the bite of the blade. Its pinch. She felt it penetrate her skin, hot moisture trickling down. She tried to kick at Warg, but it was pointless. Jane cried out in frustration. Then, there was a thud. Warg's eyes were momentarily bright, before they fogged over as he slumped to the ground, knife dropping from his hands.

For a moment Jane lay still, brain unable to process what had just happened. She rolled onto her back to see Bill, standing there with a log in hand, breathing hard. "One stereotype about us satyrs *is* true," Bill said, "we can hold our booze....or hallucinogens...or weed....or whatever the hell this stuff is. What is this stuff?" He looked at his hands uneasily.

Jane didn't have it in her to answer. She turned her gaze to the ceiling spinning above her. Willow, cedar, and wormwort. That's what they were. Willow, cedar, and wormwort, calling to the moon.

"Jane?" Bill called. "Hey Jane? You okay? Holy shit, you look high as fuck."

Willow, cedar, and wormwort. And then they were mandrake root, glistening and pale like the moon. They opened their mouths, and when they opened their mouths, they screamed.

There was blood in the snow. There was blood in the water. There was blood in the wine.

Jane sat at her desk with a cup of water, a cold press on her swelling cheek. Bill and Belinda chatted, shooting glances at her from time to time in concern. "Well, the potion master said that luckily the hallucinogen should be out of your system in a couple of hours and shouldn't do any lasting damage," Belinda said, "that it was more done to incapacitate, rather than harm."

Bill huffed, crossing his arms. "Fool didn't know the power of a satyr. What will happen to him?"

"Necromancy is one of the most illegal magics out there, so I'm assuming he will be imprisoned. Considering how many he resurrected, he'll probably be in incarcerated for life."

"And the ones be brought back?"

"The resurrected will go to be Re-burrowed. I often hear the undead make good servants. It's just helpful when they have structure." Jane looked down at the paper in front of her, the words on the page still dancing, teasing at a pattern that she couldn't quite catch. "I apologize for sending you into this. I should have left it to the Knights. I just thought..."

"You just thought I could help," Jane said aloud, "and I couldn't."

Belinda quietly nodded. "Well, I suppose after a day like that you two will be wanting some rest. Why don't you take the rest of the day? We can always go out for drinks another time."

"I think that sounds like a good..." Bill started.

"I would like to go out," Jane said, surprising them both into silence. Jane looked up from the paper. "I would like to take you up on that drink."

"Are you sure? We can go out anytime Jane, and I would think you would want to get some sleep."

"I'm not going to be able to sleep after all that," Jane said, "and I don't want to be alone right now. So, I'll take you up on that drink."

Bill looked at Belinda who just shrugged. Bill looked back at Jane. "Okay, if that's what you want..."

"You don't have to come Bill, if you aren't feeling up to it."

"No, I don't think I want to leave you alone right now either. Ma would kill me."

The Goose's Garter was the tavern of choice for Ministry workers. It was within walking distance from the office and next to a bus station that ran late into the night, which were important features as Ministry workers drank *a lot*. On the outside, The Goose's Garter looked like the rest of the Ministry buildings around it, the only thing to distinguish it a wooden sign out by the door with a white goose's butt next to the name. Inside, the tavern was a bubblegum pink, decorated with stuffed geese wearing a myriad of under garments: there were geese in the fancy lace garters of high-born Magistrates, geese in the simple cotton garters of the everyday citizen, there were even geese in the garters of various exotic creatures, which for geese themselves, meant nothing at all.

There was a large, glitter infused bar-top, behind which a handsome man in a page boy hat and some suspenders diligently cleaned glasses, assuredly bracing himself for the emotional shit show that was to come. Bill and Jane sat at that bar, followed by Belinda and a few other of their co-workers. "Hey Oberon," Belinda said, leaning her arms on the surface, "you've never met our most junior Ministry Member. This is Jane. Jane this is Oberon."

"Nice to meet you sir."

Oberon smirked at the 'sir'. "Nice to meet you too, Jane. Sorry you're stuck with this sorry lot. You seem like a nice girl."

"Psssh," Bill scoffed, "that's 'cause you just met her."

"Well, I still say anyone who has to put up with you all has to have the patience of a saint," Oberon quipped back.

Belinda huffed. "You're lucky you're cute Oberon...and make the best drinks in town."

Oberon grinned, putting the glass in its proper place. "Speaking of drinks, what will you all be having?"

"Put these two on my tab this evening," Belinda said, pointing, "they had a hard week and deserve it. I think I'll start with a Magical Misty Margarita, light on the triple sec, heavy on the tequila, shaken, not blended and with salt around the rim. Bill?"

"Uhm, I think I'll have a Burrow Beer Stout, if you have that on tap."

"Sure do, and for the *other* young lady?" Oberon winked at Belinda, who giggled.

Jane picked at her coaster in the shape of a goose's rear. "Whiskey. Neat. Well is fine."

"Geeze Jane, startin' the night out with a bang, are ya'?" Bill exclaimed.

"Ah Bill, don't be such a prude," Belinda said with a wave of her hand. "It's Friday night, Jane can do what she wants!"

The bartender served up their drinks; Belinda's was an ornate monstrosity complete with an umbrella, while Bill's beer was served in one of those fancy beer glasses that always confused Jane. Oberon poured Jane's drink, handing the shot glass over to her; Jane moved to reach for the whiskey but, rather than seeing the manicured hands of the man, she saw the skeletal talons of the Horned One.

Jane's heart went to her throat at the sight of the blackened skin and pulsing veins, flesh flaking off to reveal bone underneath. When she looked up though, rather than seeing hood and horn, it was just the face of the smiling bar tender, looking slightly confused. "Sorry," Jane said as she took the drink, "long day." She downed the whiskey, setting the shot glass on the bar. "I'll go ahead and take another." Belinda's brow knit slightly, before she reached down to double check her pocketbook.

The night wore on and Jane got a nice buzz going. More of her coworkers came and soon the bar was a lively place with music playing, people talking, and dancing. Belinda spent most of the time flirting with Oberon, who put up with her advances well enough for someone who was a captive audience, though when Jane saw how much Belinda was tipping, she got a clue as to why.

Bill went out to dance, trying to get Jane to join him. Jane turned him down, and although Bill was disappointed, it was a good chance for her to get to know her other coworkers. Jane learned that Gustave was an amateur herbologist who had a rather large collection of rare plants. Aquafine had been to just about every section of the Burrow, and had even been on guided tours to parts of the Forest. Steve...Steve was pretty strange, and Jane felt sorry for Aurora for being partnered with him, as she seemed nice enough, and Margaret was a little neurotic but kind. Frank was the most interesting reveal, as he had a whole tome of stories to share from his long tenure at the Ministry of Magic. He had enough tales to fill up several books.

At some point it got too hot for Jane, so she went outside to take a smoke break. Bill joined her. By this time in the evening most everyone was pretty drunk, so there were a few people out having a late-night cigarette—one of them throwing up into a flowerpot. Jane lit up a cigarette for Bill and they stood with their backs against the tavern wall, looking up at the night sky. The red star Jane had seen from a couple nights before was even larger now.

"Havin' fun?" Bill asked with a grin on his face.

"Yeah, actually. I didn't expect it."

"Oh man, is this possibly the start of Jane being *sociable.* Maybe Aurora will be able to wrest back her crown of the office ice queen."

"Oh, I doubt that. I'm invested in that title." She let out a puff of smoke, watching it drift lazily up into the air. "But I guess it wouldn't kill me to give a few of them a chance now and again."

They stood there in silence for a long moment. "You know, I know it's not been easy for you. It's not been easy for any of us. I mean, we didn't lose as much as you did, but we still lost..." Bill looked down at his hooves. "There are still things Ma refuses to talk about. And I know they can be stupid, and shallow, and irritating as hell, but life...life is this short, precious fleeting thing. And to waste it not being happy...I mean, nothing will ever be perfect, right? So why stress that? You have to work with what you got and we have a helluva lot more than plenty of other folks, right?"

You were one of us. You were powerful. You were free... "Do you ever miss it sometimes?"

"Miss what?"

"The smell of pine needles mixed with dirt? The cool mist on your skin? The feel of a warm fire after coming in from the snow? Do you miss the thrill of danger you felt just *because* the Forest was unsafe."

"I mean, I can't say I really remember it all that well to be honest with ya'. We immigrated here when I was five. All I remember is a bunch of drunk hairy dudes down by a river."

"So, you never think of what could have been. If we'd never left that life? Where we would be?"

Bill took a drag of his cigarette. "I mean, not about that. But sometimes I think about what it would've been like if I had chosen a different path."

Jane was disappointed by the response, but did her best to hide it. "What sort of path?"

"You'll laugh at it."

"Well, I can't promise I won't..."

"Sometimes I wonder what it would've been like if I'd become a baker!"

"A *baker*?"

"Yeah, you know. Workin' with your hands. Feedin' people. Seeing them smile because of something you made. I can make a mean bread, I'll tell you that. But you know, it wouldn't have worked out. There's always that stigma about satyrs being dirty drunks, and well, who wants to buy bread from a dirty drunk?"

"I would've eaten your bread."

"I know. I guess I would've at least had one customer."

Another quiet moment passed by. "Let's go back in for another drink," Jane said. "Frank was just about to tell me this story about a pixie dust smuggling ring they busted back in the day."

"Wait, wait, wait. Let's make a wish on a star, okay?"

"Huh? Oh geeze Bill, you know I hate that sort of stuff. You must really be drunk. Maybe we should just take the bus home..."

"Oh, come on Jane, just do it this one time," Bill pleaded. "Who knows, maybe it'll come true! I'm gonna wish for a rich hunky husband to come save my overweight ass."

"Bill, I don't think you're supposed to tell people your wishes..."

Bill ignored her, pointing to the red star from earlier, it was oddly larger and angrier from even the moment when they had started their conversation. "Come on, make a wish on that big ass one. If any star is gonna grant a wish it would be *that*." He looked over at Jane, grinning as if proud of the find.

Jane's eyes widened as the rust-colored orb grew bigger. "Bill, that isn't a star." Other people had started to notice and were now running, screaming.

Bill looked back up, eyes wide as they reflected the pock-marked surface of an asteroid. "Oh shit."

And that's when everything went to hell.

May

She puts on lipstick, looking in the mirror, blue eyes deep in concentration. It's a fluid motion, the sweep of the upper lip and the lower, the smack-pop, the check to make sure nothing's smeared on her teeth. It's something of a practiced art, but it always has a special meaning when it's before a hustle. Like a ritual. A donning of the armor. It's a way to deal with the adrenaline, I guess. She puts on a purple turban, tucking in a few loose strands of blond hair, shrugging on a black silk robe printed with stars. It's a bit ridiculous, but the marks always love it.

"Did you get the knocker set up?" she asks, looking through the mirror back at me. This is something else she also always does before the grift. The mental checklist. I don't mind it. It's good to have redundancies built in.

You never knew when somebody was going to
have an off day.

"Knockers set up. Repaired the lines so it
doesn't have that lag anymore."

"And the orb?"

"Attached to its line and ready to go."

"And the spirit lights?"

I hesitate, thinking of how to say this in
a way she'll hear. "---, I think we should
skip the spirit lights for this one."

She turns to me, and I can see she's
already working on how to convince me. "Ah,
this again? The spirit lights are the most
important part of the séance. It won't work if
we don't have them. They're the showstopper."

I look down, notice a spot on my left shoe.
"Then maybe we should just cancel the whole
thing," I say, knowing it won't do any good.

"Tam Lin," she walks up to me, placing her
hands on my chest. She straightens my lapel,
even though it's already perfectly in place.
"I know you're worried, but we can't stop
the séance. You know that. And we need those
lights for the performance."

"You get sick every time you use them. You
don't eat. It knocks you out for days..."
She's so thin I can almost see the bones

poking through the black sheen of her robe. A bird I'm afraid to touch.

"It's just ulcers. I'll admit the paint has been causing that much. But we aren't going to have to do this for much longer," her eyes search my face. I look away. "Soon we'll have enough to not have to worry about *anything* anymore. We just need a few more marks."

"You said that last time, and the time before that. If we don't stop, we're gonna get caught. You do understand that, right? People are catching on. It's only a matter of time. Things like this, they always end that way."

She stretches up and kisses me on the part of my mouth where it meets my cheek. "My dear Tam Lin, always so worried. Remember when we first met in that hell hole at the bottom-most pit of our lives? We promised each other that we would never go back there again. That we would take what we had earned from those bastards with no regret, no remorse. Remember that?"

I remember the rain, the cold, the desperation. But it's so far from now, from this warmth and comfort that surrounds us. Wasn't it just greed to want more? She holds my cheek with her hand, and I look into her eyes, eyes that smolder with intensity. They remind me of an engine running hot, burning bright, but with a warning. "We're almost there," she says, "we're almost to the point where we can say goodbye to all this and live out our lives in peace. We just need a little more. I want to quit this just as bad as you, but we need the money. And if we get found out, we can always just hightail it to a new place. Start again. It won't be the first time we've done that, right?" I nod. "I know you're getting tired, and I know some are getting wise, but I can string 'em along for a little while yet," she gives me a wink. "I've a knack for it after all, right?"

I run a hand through my hair. Lost again. My words stolen from me by that all-consuming gaze, "Yeah, you do."

"Then have faith," she says as she walks back to the mirror, "we both know I'm too clever to get caught out in the cold."

I laugh at that. Faith. That last thing either of us has.

I go to a chest at the back of the room, opening it up. Inside are the spirit lights. I stare at them for a while, a mix of feelings I can't quite pin down rising up in my chest.

"Tam Lin," she says, as I stand there, "hurry
up with the lights, it's almost time."

I swallow the lump in my throat, getting
to work. She opens a drawer by the mirror,
pulling out a small perfume vial. Instead of
perfume though, it contains a thick, clear
liquid. She takes a brush, and dips it into
the vial, marking herself with the stuff. I
watch, and it's as if she's painting herself
with nothing. After this she pulls out a
drinking glass, pouring flour into it with
some more of the invisible paint. She mixes
water into the mess and drinks it. I wince.
She holds her stomach for a moment, pale,
then sees me looking at her and smiles. "It's
okay. Like I said, just an ulcer. Are we ready
to go?"

I look around the room. It's a little too
much for me, red velvet curtains with occult
curios crammed into corners. It's dusty and
claustrophobic. A part of me keeps trying to
look for an exit, even though I know there's
no need. She says the stuff is necessary to
set the mood and everything has a specific
location to disguise the grift, but it all
just makes me uneasy. In the center of the
room is a large oak table with a pentagram
carved in the middle. I feel for my gun

holster under my jacket, making sure it's there. "Yeah, we're good."

There's a knock at the door. I take a deep breath. She buzzes with nervous anticipation. "Perfect timing! Hit the lights!" I do and a purple glow fills the room, previously unseen phosphorescent swirls showing up on the walls from the invisible paint. She's covered in the swirls as well, a dull green, the burn of their iridescence like the burn in her eyes. She goes to the door while I check myself in the mirror, slicking back my short black hair. A scar runs along the side of my face. There was a time I hated that scar, but now it serves to intimidate people and that works fine by me.

The door opens and there is a commotion. A group of kids, anxious and laughing, enter the room. They're dressed in black satin and lace, as if going to a funeral, though their wide eyes and smiling faces make me think they don't know the first thing about death. "Greetings seekers of Truth and Denizens of the Night!" She declares, sweeping her arms wide. "Welcome to the abode of Madam ---! Where the Wisdom of Great Isis shall be revealed to those who've the courage to ask! I trust you have brought what I requested?"

The kids crowd around her, handing over
trinkets and money. She takes them grate-
fully. "These objects will serve us well to
summon the spirits of the dead. Come this
way. Please sit, and we shall begin."

She takes the marks to the table. As they
pass, some of them give me uneasy looks. I
stare straight ahead, ignoring them. They
sit at the table holding hands and she goes
through the typical routines. There is the
shaking of the table (a pedal under her
chair), the knocking of the spirits (plaques
of wood connected to lines), the floating orb
(fishing wire), and spirit writing (really
just random crap she comes up with).

Everything is going to plan, and I'm starting to get bored, when one of the marks, a
kid of maybe twenty, pipes up with, "I've
heard talk about town you're a fake."

I go alert. The table goes silent, everyone
looking at each other as if someone had
just made a crude joke at a polite party.
She smiles, not thrown by the interruption.
"Come, child, and take my hand," she says,
"and I will show you those who doubt my word
have simply not been awakened to the Wisdom
of Isis."

The kid looks at her doubtfully, but his friends egg him on, "Come on, Pythos."

"Pythos?" she raises an eyebrow. "A strong name. Like the dragon at the Oracle of Delphi." He sneers and rolls his eyes, but the peer pressure has its effect, and he sits next to her. "Tell me Pythos," she asks, "to whom on the other side would you like to speak?"

He thinks for a moment. "My mother."

"Ah, but your mother is not dead, I do not see her in the Mist," there is a glimmer in her smile. "Perhaps it's your *father* you would like to talk to instead?"

The kid huffs. "Fine. Yes, you're right. My mother isn't dead, and my father died in the war, just like every other old man 'round here. But you would know that if you simply asked about town. That hardly proves any sort of spiritual powers, just that you did your research." He isn't wrong. Most of the work we do is in getting the history of these marks. The rest is easy once you have that.

"Hmm, true. I can speak to him if you would like. Get you this proof you are so desirous to seek, but his spirit is restless and angry. I don't know if you would care to hear what he has to say."

He rolls his eyes now. "Ah, so you found that we didn't get on well, either? My, you are a little busy body, aren't you? Go ahead and summon this 'father'. I have a few choice words for him myself." His friends grin at the show of courage.

He's getting a little aggressive, which I don't like, but she just smiles that smile. "As you wish." She raises her arms into the air, closing her eyes. "Oh, Great Isis, with your power to commune with the dead. Speak, to your servant. Work through me Dark Goddess of the Night, so that this child can hear the words of his father once more." She begins to shake, and the lights flicker. I frown, wondering if there is a loose connection somewhere, but the lights settle back down. When she opens her eyes back up, they are rolled into the back of her head, white. She speaks in a deep voice, "what the hell do you think you're doin', boy?"

The kid pales, and I have to admit, it's an impressive performance. "F-father?" he all but whispers.

She hunkers down, scowling, face twisted in a way that I've never seen her do before. "You dumb little shit," she snarls, "wastin'

away my inheritance and fortune. Fuckin' that
little whore."

"No father. That's...that's not what's going on..."

"You can't lie to me you little shit," I
wince. She's supposed to thrill the marks,
not terrorize them. "I see what you do behind
closed doors. I see how you like to be fucked.
Dressin' up your little toy in silks and
stones, while your mother entertains every
asshole with a hard cock 'tween his legs.
Spending my goddamn money like you earned
it." Spit falls from her lips.

"You can't talk to us that way!" But his
voice wavers. There is no will behind the
words. "You can't talk to us like that
anymore!"

"I can talk to you however I fuckin' like!
I should've known the both of you'd betray me
once you got the chance! Just wish you'd the
courage to do it to my face. Five years in
that war only to be poisoned by ungrateful
kin! I should've kept you longer in that
cellar. I should've beat you harder with that
stick. Maybe it would've beaten some man into
you."

"Father, I'm sorry..." he's sobbing now.

"Sorry is for..." she stops, beginning to
jerk in her seat. She's going to end this,
thank god. That kid must've really pissed
her off. She throws up the flour-water from
before, the paint lighting it up to a green
goo. 'Ectoplasm' from the spirit leaving her
body. A few of the marks scream. One young
woman faints.

I get ready to go pick up the poor girl when
I see that --- is still puking, and now that
vomit is mixed with blood. "---?" I call.
She's not responding. Her eyes stay rolled up
and the jerking movements grow more violent.
"---!" I yell, now afraid.

I get to her before she hits the ground,
shaking hard. The stupid kids are all standing around watching in shock. "Move the
tables and chairs away!" I bark. "She's
having a fit!"

Some of them start to act once my voice
brings them back to reality. The kid who she
read remains there, dumb, as he watches me
put her on her side and hold her as she flops.
"H…how did she know?" he asks.

I couldn't care less about the boy's problems. "It's a fucking séance kid. Don't take
it too seriously."

"B-but I didn't tell anyone about that. No
one. There's no way she could've known. What
my father did. Wha...what I did. Not even
mother knows..."

Her shaking subsides and I pull her onto
her back, holding her in my arms. Her gaze
is lazy and weak, her arms move slowly, like
she's drunkenly swimming. But then suddenly
her eyes go wide, and she grabs me tightly,
giving me a look I've never seen on her
before.

It's the look of a believer.

"Tam Lin," she gasps, "I saw Her. I saw
Isis. I saw God."

Shit.

In the Land of Souls

Jane groaned, covering fevered eyes with the back of her hand. She was confused. The dream she just had bubbled up and spilled over into reality: the hard floor, the taste of blood, the circle of concerned faces looking down at her; a man with ink-black hair and eyes the color of sea glass. Well, that was an oddly romantic set of descriptors for her. Strange thing, dreams were. Now that she was awake though, the dream was fading, and her head felt *terrible*. She must have fallen or passed out from drinking too much. She had been hitting the whiskey pretty hard recently. Jane sneezed, the smell of sulfur irritating her nose. She needed to use the restroom and get a glass of water.

Getting to her feet to look around, Jane found she was in a hellscape of fire.

The Goose's Garter was gone. Obliterated. Nothing left but a few broken rafters smoldering with a heat that made her face blister. The flowerpots from earlier that the man had been puking into had shattered, the man himself bits of charred bone fragmented across the street. Jane looked at the skeletal remains of the tavern with wide eyes, not understanding. She wildly thought that perhaps their cigarettes had caught something on fire, causing an explosion—that is why you needed to have your Magical Heat Furnaces checked on a yearly basis.

"Th...this can't be happening," a young ljosalfar said a few feet from her, face dirty with soot. "We were the Blessed Ones. We were protected by the Great Gopher. This was never supposed to happen to *us*. What could we have done to deserve it?" He shuffled past Jane, and where his arm should have been was a bloody stump of mangled meat and bone. "What could we have done?" Jane gulped.

She looked up. It wasn't just The Goose's Garter, the whole Misty Burrow was gone. The quaint Tudor style buildings of the Ministry District, the trendy shops of Germantown, the elegant palaces of the Blessed Burrow, all in ruin, crumbled, defeated, and spitting with fire, the night sky smudged with smoke. The Ferris Wheel that had once shown so bright, had been knocked loose from its moorings, now embedded in a mountainside. Jane looked to see the great Temple of the Gopher hadn't fared any better, it's high towers down to the level of the musty tents that had once quivered in its shadow.

For a moment, Jane wondered if she was still asleep; this had to be some sort of nightmare. But then she remembered her and Bill talking, remembered his plea to wish upon a star, remembered it's rage-filled, pockmarked face. Jane looked over her shoulder and saw that star, sat squarely in the south end of the Burrow, lodged into the Wall itself. It glowed red, hot, and low, burrowing itself into the earth like a pissed off tick, the Wall an open wound where it sucked. A few people wandered here and there, injured, in shock, crying; most lay still on the ground, in a limp way that made her feel sick.

A thought came to Jane, waking her from her reverie. Her chest filled with dread. "Bill!" she called. Jane stepped forward, but something was wrong with her ankle. "Belinda! *Bill*!" She limped towards The Goose's Garter.

As she started to dig in the rubble heap of what had once been the tavern, wincing at the heat, music began to play. Jane looked around, distracted, trying to find where the sound was coming from. Who would be playing music during a time like this? The song was heavy, entrancing, as though coming from a distance deeper than the sea. It had an otherworldly quality, so that Jane couldn't tell if it was an instrument playing or someone singing. But the melody was beautiful. Beautiful but sad, like watching silk sink.

The dirge faded, releasing its hold on Jane. She spotted a pair of horns in the wreckage. "Bill!" she cried out, crawling over to them. As her hand came down to touch Bill's curly brow though, she could see the vacant stare in his eyes, his loose tongue lolling out where he no longer had a chin. She gasped but did not scream.

Jane looked around for Belinda, for Frank, for *anyone* she could recognize. What she saw was the Horned One, standing in the flames, hungry crimson tongues unable to eat of whatever foul substance constituted that fiend. In the left hand of the Horned One was the severed head of the May Woman, jaw slack, blue eyes pointed heavenwards as if in prayer.

No, no, no, no, Jane fell backwards, trying to move away. *Belinda, Bill, Frank....are they all...are they...*she began to tremble. *Maera, Daphne...by the Gopher, the* kids.

There was a hand on her shoulder, pulling her up by the sleeve. Jane recoiled. "What-no! Let me go!"

"Sorry," a voice said that she recognized, "I don't have time to explain, but I'm not going to hurt you. We need to get outta here. *Now.*"

Jane turned, stunned, for it was the man from her dreams. He was dressed in gray rags, as if he had been entangled in a fishing net at the bottom of the sea, bits of seaweed and dead things woven into the cloth. The scar was gone from his face, and he was perhaps a little younger, but other than that he was a perfect copy. The same hard line to the jaw. The same worried creases around the eyes. The same slim frame and slightly hunched shoulders. Long black hair fell to his back, pulled by the hot winds. Jane stammered, mind unable to catch up with the rapid turn of events. "I...I *know* you..."

There was the moaning song once more, only louder, closer. The earth shook and cracks appeared. A fissure opened up, swallowing the whole of the slums along the edge of the Wall; the Wall that had once been so zealously guarded turning to dust. People screamed. Jane brought her hands to her face in horror.

The man grabbed her by the sleeve, dragging her along. "Don't have time to talk. This Filament is unraveling."

"Bu-but Maera and the kids! I have to see if they're still alive!"

"They're gone. Everyone here, is gone."

Jane heaved in a shuddering breath, too shocked to cry.

She allowed herself to be pulled away, glancing back to where Bill's crushed horns lay until he too, was consumed by the hallowing earth. She turned to the man. He didn't look back, didn't pause to observe the destruction around him, he just moved forward, his grip an iron hook on the cuff of her jacket. "Wha-what's going on? What's happened? *Who* are you?"

He ignored her questions, instead taking out a small book from his pocket. The cover of the book was tattered leather, covered in barnacles and frayed net; its pages glowed with an eerie blue light. "'Walk three steps towards the morning star, turn left at a happy thought, and hang a kiss upon the moon...?' Shit, what sorta crap is this?" The man looked at the sky. "Can you tell me where the morning star is in all this mess?"

"The morning star?" Jane repeated, confused. "Well, it's usually southeast of here. Why do you need to know that?"

"Because we're going to the Conservator of this place. That weird, gopher-thing," the man situated them so they were facing southeast. "Can you walk three steps and think a happy thought?"

"Godfrey Gopher?!" Jane cried, knowing for sure now she had come across a mad man. "But you can't just waltz up and go see him. I mean, he's *God*..."

"Guess I gotta come up with the thought." The man pulled Jane forward, made a strange face, and then oddly enough blew a kiss to the ash-stained moon. Jane got ready to bolt, convinced she was about to be murdered and worn as a suit, when she was suddenly someplace else, the change so jarring that both she and the man nearly tripped over their own feet. Jane looked around with wide eyes. Where there had been fire, chaos, and destruction there was now peace, coolness, and light.

They were in a palace, the walls of which were a pale blue crystal, carved into swirls, as if water in motion solidified. The ceiling effused a pale-yellow light, illuminating the halls, and the floor beneath their feet was made of clouds, giving slightly as they walked. There were images of the Gopher *everywhere*: busts, portraits, and carvings, done in marble and precious stones. Blue roses grew throughout the palace, climbing over columns, and pillars. Somewhere was the sound of water dripping in time to the tune of a harp, but underlying that was the loathsome dirge, distant for now.

"Where are we?"

"I don't know," the man said, "but it's wherever that damn gopher lives. Come on, we gotta go find him."

Jane went up to a window, peering out. It was night outside, the sky indigo. She looked down. Below she could see the planet of the Misty Burrow—well, not just the Misty Burrow, but the Forest as well—the moon, the sun, and the stars, all exposed to her as if in diorama. She could see the flaming comet in the planet's side, a fatal wound through which its life force bled, bits of the planet tearing off to float in the air as the rest of it burned. "I've gone mad," she said as the red light from the fires below flickered on her face. "This is madness."

The man led her from the window, back into the airy blue. "We can question reality once it's no longer trying to kill us."

They went down the castle halls. Apparently, whatever acropolis they were in wasn't as immune to what was going on below as it had first seemed: cracks began to appear in the pillars, some of the flowers started to wither, and the white clouds grayed as if about to storm. Objects were thrown about in a seeming panic: shoes, papers, odd trinkets, as though everyone had been in the midst of something and just suddenly stopped and fled. They started to hear sounds, scuffling about, followed by agitated voices.

"Be sure to pack my silken pantaloons Roderick, not my cotton ones!"

"Ye-yes sir, right away, sir!"

"Oh, and be sure to not forget my favorite rose brooch! It was made for me by the Sea Witch Himself! I would be *so* sorry if it got lost in the shuffle."

"As you command sir!"

Jane and the man came to a room. It had probably been a grand room once, with large crystal windows looking out onto lush gardens, and blue velvet drapes hanging from a tall ceiling. The ceiling itself was decorated in a fresco, that of a very muscular and shirtless Godfrey Gopher gifting his magical blue rose to a grateful looking group of ljosafar. Now though, the place was a complete mess with drawers pulled open, jewelry strewn across the floor, and feathers flying from pillows torn apart. In the midst of all that was a white rabbit in a blue waist coat with ruby colored pants and a giant fat gopher stuffed in a tuxedo. The rabbit had a very pinched, concerned look on his face, while the gopher was so fat that his features seemed to sink into the folds of his flesh, rendering his expression unreadable. Neither of them noticed the two intruders.

Jane gasped. "The Holy Gopher! He's *real*!"

"Huh? Wha...?" the Gopher tried to turn his head to look but his neck was so thick he had to move his whole body instead. "Am I *real*? Why *of course* I am! Don't you attend Wednesday Madness?"

"I mean, I do, but you just, uhm," she looked the Gopher over, "look a little different..."

"*Rude.* Well, just who are you two anyway, and how did you get here?" the Gopher waved some sausage-like fingers in the air. "Oh, what does it matter? This whole place is done for. You had best get out of here soon if you can, or else you'll go along with it."

"That's why we're here," the man said, "we need a ride."

"A *ride*? You mean a trans-dimensional transport?" the Gopher laughed. "Laugh with me Roderick," Godfrey commanded and the rabbit laughed along with him, until the Gopher stopped. Both of their faces became deadly serious. "And why would I do *that*?"

The man scowled, as if this contingency hadn't occurred to him. Suddenly though, he spied a bit of sparkling blue from the corner of his eye; Godfrey seemed to spot this gem at the same time, for he grew very still. There was a long pause as both beings eyed the bauble cagily. "Roder..." Godfrey began but was too late. The mystery man snapped up the blue rose brooch lying on the floor before the Gopher even had time to wheeze.

"If you want *this* back, that's why," the man said, the slightest hint of a smile pulling at the corner of his lips.

Godfrey puffed up his chest, doing his best to look menacing, though ended up looking rather more like one of those inflatable punching bags that pop back up as soon as you knock them over. "Oh, you just got lucky! Young mortal, if you think you can bully me into giving you what you want, you have a thing or two to learn..."

the rabbit pulled at the Gopher's sleeve. "Not now Roderick, I'm in the midst of smiting!" Roderick pulled harder, getting Godfrey down to his level so he could whisper in his ear. "Huh? Undead?! But that's...oh dear, you're right, he *does* have that look about him, doesn't he?" More whispers. The Gopher's eyes went as wide as they could in that pudgy face. "*Huh?! The Magical Girl?!*" Godfrey looked at Jane, which made her nervous. "By Jove, Roderick, I think you're *right*."

"What are you talking about?" the man demanded.

"You, sir, are dead. Well, undead at this point apparently. And you are traveling with a Magical Girl," Godfrey declared.

The man looked over at Jane. "Do you know what this thing is talking about?"

"No, I'm just a Ministry Worker, not a literary trope."

Godfrey sighed. "Roderick, go get the mirror," Roderick scampered off to dig around in a pile of clothes. "Not that we have time for all this nonsense, but you leave me with no other choice. You see, a normal living creature has a sort of nice colorful aura. Sometimes it's green, sometimes it's blue, I especially like the pink ones. Roderick and I are gold because we are Conservators of this Filament and are special. Very special indeed." Roderick came over, lugging a large silver framed mirror. "If you look into this mirror, you should see your aura," the mirror turned to the man, which showed nothing. "You sir have no aura as you are dead. How you managed to *escape* the Realm of the Dead, I have no idea, but that doesn't matter for now. It's *her* aura that is most concerning." The mirror turned to Jane. When it did so, rather than showing her reflection, it cracked to a million pieces, turning to mercurial dust.

"*See?* Classic Magical Girl reaction. So, you see, I can't give you a trans-dimensional transport as that would be a bit like letting loose a nuclear bomb on the Totality of the Universe. Due to her nature, destruction and turbulence will follow wherever she goes. Other Filaments will unravel, just like this one."

"A-are you saying it's *my* fault the asteroid hit and everyone is dead?"

"Oh yes, dear, why of course. I mean, *I'm* certainly not to blame. As a Magical Girl, chaos will pursue you. And it's really quite a shame. It was such a nice Filament," the Gopher sighed, shaking his head before looking back up. "But I'm sure you understand now why I simply *cannot* give you the transport. So, if you would just give me my brooch, Roderick and I can leave. We're really in quite a rush."

If the Gopher thought he had somehow sowed the seeds of doubt into the man's heart, one look at his face disabused him of that notion. The man glared, holding the brooch tight. "How do I fix it?"

"Wh-what? How do you *fix* it?!"

"Yeah, how do I stop her from being this magical girl thing?"

The Gopher licked his lips, thinking things over. "You don't *fix* being a Magical Girl. It just is! Did you not hear what I just said? She's a bringer of entropy, a dissembler of all that is good! Hell will dog your footsteps! She's the Harbinger of the End itself with some decent hair," Jane tugged at a soot-stained strand. "What do you care for such a creature? I mean, sure she's pretty, but let me tell you, there are plenty of other pretty girls out there..."

The man walked up to the Gopher, picking him up by the collar of his shirt. Godfrey squealed, keeping his face as far away from the man's fist as he possibly could. "*How* do I *fix it*?" He glared down at the rodent.

"I-I-I don't know! It's like a thing that's inked into the Creation of the Tapestry itself! You would have to go like, to the Sea Witch or something to figure out how to undo it. If that's even possible!"

"You're the God here, why can't you fix it?"

Godfrey rolled his eyes, as if he had just asked him what the answer to two plus two was. "I'm a *Conservator*, really. Not at the level of the Sea Witch's omnipotence."

The man huffed in disgust. "So, you're telling me that you aren't even really a God?"

"I mean, I'm not *powerless*, but I don't have the power to change something like a *Magical Girl*. I'm more like, someone who looks after things! A messiah. A babysitter. I look after a tiny Filament of the Totality of the Tapestry. A tiny Filament which *you* have unraveled by the way." Godfrey glared at Jane.

"Okay then, how do I get to this Sea Witch?"

"*How do you get to the Sea Witch?!* You do realize that you don't just *go* to Him..." the man shook the Gopher a little. "Okay, okay, okay! I-I don't know. No one has talked to the Sea Witch for, what, several hundred millennia? He's kinda left us all out here in the lurch. I mean, we don't even know *where* He is," at the man's darkening look he quickly added, "but the Fates would. The Fates would know where He is!"

The man unceremoniously dropped the Gopher, Roderick rushing over to help him to his feet. As he did so, the man pulled the book from his pocket, leafing through it; both Godfrey and Roderick's fur rose on end. "Oh, by all that's Holy, is *that the Book of the Dead?!*" Godfrey cried. "Leviathan has to be throwing a *fit!*"

The man ignored the reaction. "The Fates are listed here, so I think we can find them easily enough," he closed the book, putting it back in his pocket. "Okay, we just need that transport and we'll be out of your hair."

"May I reiterate that this is a *really* bad idea...I mean, the Fates may not even talk with you. They're *notoriously* prickly."

The man's cool eyes slid over the Gopher. He clasped the brooch hard and there was a small ting, like it was about to crack; Godfrey winced. "I wasn't asking."

"Fine," the Gopher said with a sigh. "Roderick, go get Bunny ready."

Roderick hopped out of the room, Godfrey Gopher, the mystery man, and Jane following. They walked out into a courtyard behind the palace. The courtyard looked as if it had been a beautiful once, with apple trees and rose bushes, but now those bushes had turned to sticks, and the trees were filled with snakes. The sky that had been so cool and deep just moments before was now a reddening purple with the occasional flash of orange, making Jane feel as if she were trapped in a gradually heating furnace.

There was the dirge, growing louder again, and when Jane looked up this time, she could see the source of the song. Hovering over the collapsing planet of the Misty Burrow, distant but visible, was a large gray whale. It swam through the night sky, moving in a slow twists and turns—purposeful, plodding, persistent. Its muscles contracted and expanded, deceptively slow yet powerful, like a riptide. Bubbles of lights from the planet below flowed up to the whale, the glow of plankton in the sea, drifting up in large swathes as if pulled in by a current. As the lights drew closer to the beast Jane heard a sharp discordant whine tangle itself into the harmony, the bubbles popping in a flash photoluminescence, vanishing.

"Leviathan is looking for you," Godfrey said, giving the man a side glance. "She's not one to let go of something once it's hers."

"Then we'd better move fast," the man said.

In the middle of the courtyard was a giant tortoise. He towered over Jane and the others, skin craggy and rough. His shell was a ripple of purple, blue, and green, the colors moving like dye slowly diffusing, almost hypnotic in their fractal sway. The tortoise looked at them as they walked up, blinking with slow, ancient eyes. He wore a harness and a set of bunny ears on his head, which Jane thought was strange, but then again, rabbit ears were the most innocuous of the strange things which seemed to be occurring to her lately.

"Okay, this is Bunny," Godfrey said, "and he will take you where you need to go, which thankfully will be far away from wherever *I* am headed. Now, will you give me my brooch back? *Please*." The Gopher held out his hand.

The man looked down at that hand, seeming to weigh the advantages and disadvantages of following through with the bargain. In the end though, he passed the brooch over to the Gopher. Godfrey clasped the treasure as if it were particularly hot or cold, holding it to his chest. The man turned to Jane. "Let's go."

Godfrey took a few steps back, eyeing the man. "I don't who you are or what your aim is, but I will tell you again, this is a bad idea. You can't fix a Magical Girl. You'll do nothing but spread grief and despair by keeping her alive."

Both Jane and the man climbed onto the back of the tortoise. The man looked over at the Gopher, "if I'd wanted your opinion, I'd have asked." With that, the man took up the reigns of the tortoise, and Bunny left the courtyard, rising up into the sky.

Jane didn't know what she had expected, but it certainly wasn't that the tortoise would fly. She flattened herself to the shell as they rose into the air. The wind knocked her hair loose and it began to move wildly about her face; looking back down through the wispy strands she could see the Gopher giving them a long look with his glinting beady eyes, before turning around and heading back into his crumbling palace. Beyond that was the Misty Burrow itself, slowly coming apart, lights, so many lights, ebbing towards the dancing whale.

"I did all of this?" she murmured aloud.

"Don't listen to that idiot. He's just looking for a scapegoat. If it's his realm then it's his fault it fell apart."

"But it's concerning enough for you to want to find a solution," she pointed out, and he said nothing. "Why do you want to help me? I..I don't even know your name."

"I'm Tam Lin," he said, face forward, "and I'm here to protect you."

Jane felt a chill in her heart. Tam Lin. Could it all be a coincidence? "And why do you want to protect me, Tam Lin?"

He was quiet for a moment, focused on guiding Bunny. "I don't know. All I can remember is my name, and what I have to do."

This was not the answer Jane wanted to hear, but before she could ask anything else there was a violent rumbling and Bunny began to make distressed noises. Jane looked back. The whale had vanished, leaving a black hole in its wake. The hungry mouth of that black hole began to consume what little of the universe there was left, the very folds of reality collapsing in on itself into an unrecognizable shape. The Misty Burrow turned to dust, a shock wave of fragmentation following, distorting the space around it. Jane's eyes went wide, unable to comprehend the enormity of the tsunami falling on them, her mind trying to fill in the gaps to turn the wave into a wall of water, the people, the buildings, the places she knew, now fish and coral caught in its glassy prison. Jane felt hypnotized, almost called towards that awesome destruction. The roar of it filled her ears. *Bill, Belinda, are you still in there?*

"The Filament is collapsing," Tam Lin said, "hold on, we gotta move. Come on Bunny, I know you don't wanna get trapped here."

Bunny made a noise of concurrence, a gold sphere growing around the three of them. Jane looked up at that glowing light, seeing in it various reflections, like those in a pool. Images of carrots, sunny days, and wind blowing through apple trees. Almost unbidden Jane reached out to one of those reflected leaves, wishing to feel it's perfect, waxy greenness. But then the wave hit, and those dreams turned to nightmares, and those nightmares turned to darkness.

The Witch in the Stone Boat

Falling. Falling into a blue-black abyss, shot with bits of debris floating like the Multitude of Stars; crackled leaves, shriveled flowers: the memories of a dry world that had been consumed by the singularity that was the flood. She was in water that was cold. Too cold. The sharpness of it stinging her eyes, the chill biting at her fingers and toes, running along the blood in her veins to reach her gut, icing her insides. She relished that frozen sensation. The unfeelingness of it. The lack of fear or pain—a sort of freedom. A part of her wanted to simply fall further into it, until she never had to feel anything at all.

White light shown down from above, a diamond edge in cerulean; she went to raise her hand to block that harsh glare, but found she couldn't move, simply sink. Her hair drifted up in silver waves as she descended further into darkness, and from those swells, red ribbons began to unravel. Curling helices of crimson unbinding themselves from her to drift up towards the white light. She could feel herself unraveling along with them.

A hand broke through the azurite radiance, a violent motion that shattered the placid stillness of the deep. It reached out, grabbing her arm, pulling her upwards. Jane looked back down, almost longingly, into the watery chasm, but whatever her thoughts were, they stood no chance against the will of that grasp. Jane's head broke the surface of the pool, and it was a violent shock as sensation came back to her. Pain, numbness, burning lungs. She gasped for breath, unable to even flail. Tam Lin hauled Jane from the water, over ice, tossing her on a shore by a pond. A shore covered in snow. "Fuck, dammit, fuck," he cursed. "Great, just great. Get her killed in the first goddamn hour."

Jane was too distracted to listen. The cold was so agonizing, it was all she could do to just curl up into a ball, instinctively trying to keep her core warm. Jane had known cold before, but this was different. This was the cold of death.

She forced herself to look up as Tam Lin stumbled off, muttering about finding wood to start a fire. They were in a forest, but it wasn't Jane's Forest. Jane's Forest had been dark and heavy with hidden meaning, draped in shades of smokey emerald and misty blue. This forest was of spiky yellow-green needles with rough red bark, the vegetation underneath scrub brush and junipers, mottled snow in dirty patches. They were just above the timberline and behind Jane was nothing but wind-swept gull-gray rock. The cloudless sky seemed preternaturally close, but despite this the sun didn't warm, and Jane felt exposed. She could see the pond where she had some from, in the midst of early spring thaw, the gleam of the sun bouncing off the ice like shattered glass. He wasn't going to find dry timber here if he looked all day. A breeze blew, causing Jane to start shaking all over again. Tam Lin noticed.

"I need to get you under some cover," he came back, grabbing her by the shoulders. He carried her over to a small rock outcrop hidden in the tree line that was shielded from the worst of the wind. It was there he laid a pile of wet leaves and twigs he had found, trying to get a flame. Jane watched as he rubbed some sticks together, working to get enough friction going. It didn't look hopeful.

"Wh-where are we?" she managed, lips so pale they were purple.

"I don't know," Tam Lin said, focused on the fire. "Another Filament. The shock wave knocked us off course."

"Wh-where is B-b-bunny?"

"I think we got separated. Look, don't worry about that. We need to get you warm first."

"F-forg-g-geta-a-b-b-bout m-me. I-It's poi-poi-pointless. I-I'm d-d-done."

"Don't talk like that. I'm not gonna give up on you that easy. I just need to get this damn fire going."

Jane opened her mouth to protest, but the energy it took to try to formulate the argument drained her. She shook her head. "P-p-pine needles," she pointed with a shaky finger to a fallen tree just outside the timber line, "de-dead t-t-tree. P-pull f-fr-from in-inside." Tam Lin spotted the rotting stump. He nodded, walking over to gather what he could. He was returning with a more hopeful collection, when they both heard rumbling in the distance. Tam Lin went still, focused on the sound.

It was the sound of an engine shifting gears. They could hear voices talking as well, so whoever they were, they weren't far off. Tam Lin looked at Jane "Cars," he said. Jane nodded. Tam Lin sighed, rubbing his face. "Look, I don't like this, but we need to get you help. If we don't get you warm soon that damn rat will get his way after all. So, I'm gonna wave these people down, okay? I mean, hoping they're people at least." Jane nodded again. "Just stay here and try to keep warm. I'll be back."

Jane remained there, trying not to think of how stupid the request to keep warm was. Trying not to think about much of anything, really. Tam Lin returned, and when he did, it was with two other men. Both men had long hair. beards, and were dressed in fatigue pants with tie dye shirts. One of them had a medical pack in his arms. The other had a gun slung over his shoulder. "She's over there," Tam Lin said, "fell right into the water."

"You two are lucky we were out this way," the man with the gun said. Jane was puzzled for a moment, for the man wasn't speaking in Light or Dark Elf, but she understood him all the same. The man with the med pack came up to Jane. He began removing her wet clothes, wrapping her in a silver blanket. "We generally don't scout this part of the mountain. It's only on account of a couple of meteors we saw comin' down that we even bothered. How she doin' Rowan?"

"She's hypothermic that's for sure," Rowan said, peering into her eyes, "but she's with us. Looks like a tough lady. I think she's stable enough that we can get her back to the infirmary where I can give her a full checkup."

"Good to hear," the man turned to Tam Lin. "Like I said, you're lucky we were out here. Rowan's the best medic we have."

Tim Lin ran a hand through his hair, visibly relieved. "Yeah, thanks for stopping..."

"Yeah, no sweat man. What were you two doin' out here anyways?"

Rowan moved Jane's hair from her forehead, eyes narrowing at what he saw. "We were just traveling," Tam Lin said vaguely, "got lost. "

"Traveling all the way out here? Where were you comin' from?"

"I think we came from north of here," he tried to keep the question from his voice. "Honestly, we got so turned around I'm not even sure where north is right now."

"North, huh?"

"Hey," Rowan said, looking up at the both of them. "Hey Sage, take a look at this."

The man with the gun leaned forward, peering at Jane, whistling. "Well, you don't see that every day," he looked back at Tam Lin. "This girl born with those things?"

Tam Lin looked over the shoulders of the two men, mystified. He was surprised to see a pair of rabbit ears growing from Jane's head. He must have missed them in the panic to get her warm, but they were there all the same, white and fluffy and flopped to the side. "Uhm, yeah. Those have...always been there."

Rowan looked back down at the girl. "Fascinating."

"Com'on, you can look at those ears all you want once we get back to the villa," Sage said, "but first we gotta get this girl warm. Can you lift her?"

"Oh yeah, just fine," Rowan said, hefting Jane up. "She's pretty small."

Sage patted Tam Lin on the back. "You can ride with me. We can talk more once we get you all settled in. Seems like you two had quite the adventure."

"Yeah," Tam Lin said, watching as Rowan carried Jane away, "I guess we did."

They walked down to three jeeps set at the edge of the outcrop. The jeeps were low with open tops and roll bars, a group of people dressed in the same fatigues and tie dye shirts as Sage and Rowan waiting for them. They had a similar look, mid-thirties to fifties, fit and muscular with long hair and, for the men at least, beards. On the back of their shirts were a series of symbols, three stylized ducks: a red duck, a yellow duck, and a black duck. The ducks appeared to be dancing, waving feathers in the air. Sage waved to the people below. "Nothing to worry 'bout here brothers and sisters," he called. "Looks like we just came across a couple of strays and one fell into a pond."

"We'll need to get the girl back ASAP for medical treatment," Rowan said.

"But what about the meteors?"

"We'll have to come back another day. We can wait until after the Festival. Those rocks won't be goin' anywhere."

Rowan set Jane into one of the jeeps while Tam Lin climbed in with Sage, a few of the 'brothers' joining them. Sage started up the vehicle and they began to descend down the hill. The ride was bumpy as they went over rocks and mud so that Tam Lin had to hold onto one of the rollbars. Sage eyed him sideways. "Names

Sage by the way, in case you didn't pick it up. What's yours, brother?"

"Tam Lin."

"Tam Lin? That's an interesting one. Not heard it 'round here. So, you're from up north huh? Your tribe up there?"

"Yeah. Yeah, it is."

"Where abouts up north?"

"Pretty, uh, far north?"

"Ah, so pretty isolated, huh? That would explain it." Some of the others in the jeep grinned. "So uh, what brought you down south?"

"Traveling. Guess we got a little lost."

"Landing in a freezing pond sounds more than a 'little' lost."

"Yeah, never did have a good sense of direction," Tam Lin wanted to turn the conversation to *any* other topic. "Hey, you mentioned a couple meteors fell this way?"

"Yeah, man. Three meteors fell last night, an omen from the Mighty Mother. Two fell in this general vicinity, and one fell further south from us. You didn't hear any booms last night?"

Bunny. Tam Lin narrowed his eyes. "No, didn't hear anything. Like I said, got a little disoriented."

Sage laughed. "Ate the wrong mushrooms, eh?" he patted Tam Lin on the shoulder. "No worries man, we all done it before. Lucky you, we came across you when we did. Lucky indeed. You're gonna get to see the most beautiful place in the whole world."

"Oh yeah, and where's that?"

"Yugenia of course," Sage said with a smile. "Don't you worry 'bout a thing. We'll get you fed and warm and set up right."

The three men continued talking with one another while Tam Lin took in his surroundings. He peered at Jane through the rear-view mirror, face peeking out from the silver blanket like some exotic space creature. She didn't look in any danger for the moment, so he let his gaze slide past her. The forest around them soon broke way, opening to a lush valley below.

The meadow beneath was covered in soft green grass, dotted with purple lupine and yellow yarrow, a silver river running along the eastern edge; it was enclosed by blue snow-capped mountains, except for a small canyon to the south that the river cut through, and while the forests in the highlands were still in the midst of thawing winter, the floor of the valley itself was clear of the cold.

To the west of the river was a small community of yurts. The yurts were made of canvas, painted with the same three dancing ducks that Tam Lin had seen on the backs of the brothers' shirts. There were gardens by each yurt, with fruit and nut trees. People milled from place to place, dressed in loose rough spun clothing dyed in pale colors, their hair worn long. In the center of the community was what looked to be a large bonfire with a giant wooden wicker figure of a duck.

"Welcome to Yugenia my friend," Sage said, grinning over at him as he shifted his rifle, "most peaceful place in the world."

Tam Lin nodded.

The conclave of jeeps made their way to the valley below and then to the village. They stopped at a large wooden barn at the edge of the encampment, pulling into it, and in that barn, Tam Lin could see dozens of more vehicles like them. There was also a storehouse of supplies with wooden crate boxes, pieces of farm equipment, and tools. They got out of the jeeps, walking over to the huddle of yurts, and as soon as they did, were surrounded by the people in the loose clothes. They were gray-haired for the most part, wearing simple jewelry and beads, faces pale and eyes blue. They fussed over the newcomers, a few of the men talking with Sage. Some of the women huddled around Jane, taking her away outside of Tam Lin's line of sight. He tried to follow, but was pulled aside.

"Don't worry 'bout the little sister," Sage said, "the healers will take care of her. Why don't you clean up and get some rest? Dinner will be on inna couple a hours, and I am sure Big Sister Bear will want to meet and hear more about ya'."

Great. Tam thought dourly, but not knowing what else to do, allowed himself to be led along. He was taken to a small yurt at the edge of the villa, given a pair of loose rough spun gray pants and a shirt. The inside of the yurt was simple. There was a wood floor with a cot, a wooden chest, and a stove to heat the place. A bowl of water was brought with which to wash himself.

Tam Lin scrubbed off the worst of the dirt, pulling back his long hair into a ponytail. He changed from the rags into the gray cloth; after that, he sat down and, unable to sleep, decided to think.

Three meteors. Two of them likely Jane and himself. The third one possibly Bunny. The shock wave from the last Filament fraying must have sent them off course, and they would need Bunny to get back on track to reach the Fates. But it was a large world, and he needed more information on where Bunny was other than, 'further south'. They were going to need transportation to wherever this 'further south' was, as well. Tam Lin sighed. As much as he hated to admit it, he was going to need these people's help. They seemed friendly enough at least.

It was around this time that one of the villagers came to the open flap of his yurt, popping his head in. An old man in sea-foam green, hair tied up in a bun. "Dinners ready man, if you're hungry," the creased face said and Tam Lin nodded, getting to his feet.

The sky outside was heading into sunset, washed out blue lit up by thin clouds of orange and pink, crumpled like crushed silk. People were leaving their canvas huts, falling in line as they headed towards the bonfire now visible in the center of the villa. Everything was neat and clean, the gardens carefully tended, the pathways mulched. And everywhere Tam Lin looked was the symbol of the three ducks. Making their way through camp, Tam Lin noticed that the man leading him, while seeming to be old, stood straight and walked with a limber stride. He also didn't see any children. In fact, the youngest people he had seen so far were Sage and the 'brothers'—younger than these people by a good ten to fifteen years.

When they reached the bonfire there was already a table set with roasted plums, fresh bread, and pepper jelly, carafes of a golden liquid being passed around. Torches had been lit to give light as the sun fell, a large fire set by the fierce looking duck totem. At the head of the table was a large seat made of gnarled, polished wood, presently unfilled.

Sage, sitting near the front, waved to Tam Lin, indicating to sit next to him. Tam Lin went over, settling next to Sage, and was shocked to see Jane across the table. She was in a dress of undyed wool and looked withdrawn, but the color was back in her skin. She had already poured herself a glass of whatever stuff it was everyone else was drinking. "Should you be out of bed?" Tam Lin asked.

"That's what I said," Rowan, who sat next to her, agreed, "but man oh man, if the healers weren't shocked at how quickly she recovered. According to them, all her vitals are where they should be."

"I've always handled the cold well." She took a drink.

"It's that northern temperament. Look how she handles her mead!" Jane shrugged as she poured herself another glass.

Tam Lin watched in dismay as Jane guzzled the mead, seemingly determined to get drunk. It didn't seem smart to him to get plastered in a place full of strangers, especially after a near death experience, but apparently, she didn't feel the same.

It was while Tam Lin was fuming over this, that a woman emerged from one the yurts. Her yurt was slightly larger than the others and slightly more decorated. She was a tall, broad-shouldered being, dressed in the same loose linens as the other elder people, her in yellow. She had a broad face, leathered by the sun, her steel gray hair held up in braids and beads. On her forehead was tattooed three ducks, slightly faded.

The woman came to the gnarled wood throne and sat; all conversation at the table stopped. "All hail the glory and bounty of Mother Mallard!" she declared, raising up a glass of mead.

"All hail the Mighty Mallard!" The people at the table replied.

"Sister Virgin, Mighty Mother, Queenly Crone, her wisdom shines down upon us like the rays of the moon!"

"We dine under her holy light!”

"May she ever be with us in prosperity and peace!" the woman drank, the rest of the table following her example. "Now, let us chant the praises of the Mighty Mallard in thanks for this great feast!"

"Let us chant to show our gratitude!"

"He he hooooooo..." the woman breathed out heavy, a slight hum with each exhale.

"*He, he, hummmm....*" was the reply, in a different key.

"He he hooooooo...."

"*He, he, hummmmm...*"

"Whua, whua!" she was now inhaling deeply.

"*Whua, whua, hooooooo...*"

"Whua, whua, heeeeeeee...."

"*Whua, whua hummmmmmm....*"

Tam Lin watched all of this with a confused expression, while Jane just seemed bemused. Sage glanced over at Tam Lin with a slight nod, indicating that he should join as well, so Tam Lin did, repeating the breathing refrain along with everyone else. They repeated it so many times, that Tam Lin didn't know how people weren't dizzy.

The woman clasped her hands before her face at the end of the chant, head bowed in prayer. "The Mother has blessed this plenty. Your gratitude has blessed this plenty! Now we shall enjoy, under the light of the Mallard Moon!" With that there was another round of cheers, and another round of drinks. "Now we shall partake of the Flesh of the Duck!"

Tam Lin looked from side to side. The flesh of the duck? A large platter was brought full of steaming hot meat topped with prunes and onions. As the plate passed, each person muttered a small blessing, taking a bite. When the plate came to Jane she shrugged, swallowing a bit. When it came to Tam Lin, he hesitated. Sage urged him on.

It was a succulent looking piece of meat, cooked to medium rare perfection, the outer skin nice and crispy while the innards still soft and moist. Oddly enough, he couldn't smell the duck, though at the moment he didn't think much of that. Tam Lin took a morsel, trying to utter some odd thanks, but feeling inadequate in the process. He brought the greasy duck to his mouth, fat glistening, the tender bite passing through his lips.

He tasted nothing.

He could have filled his mouth with ash for all the texture and flavor of the duck meant to him. Disappointed, Tam Lin swallowed, but even that was a little painful. The woman at the head of the table beamed. "Blessed be the Mother, and blessed be you all. Let us feast!"

With the ritual now seemingly complete, the atmosphere at the table became more relaxed. People began to freely take food and drink, chatting with one another as they did, a comfortable low hum of conversation filling the air. Despite that casual atmosphere, though, there were quite a few curious glances cast the direction of Tam Lin and Jane.

The woman in the gnarled chair leaned forward. "I see we have guests tonight. Young Sage told me of your adventures. My name is Bear, and you are in the plentiful land of Yugenia."

"I'm in your debt, Bear. If it hadn't been for your people, we would be dead."

"The Guardians are a good group of men and women," Bear agreed, "they look after our people. I hear you're from the northern tribes?"

Not this again. Tam Lin looked over at Jane, who was already beginning to slump down in her chair, as if she might melt through it and into the dirt. "Yeah," he said, "we lost our bearings and panicked, I guess. She fell through some ice."

"She seems plenty hardy to me for a girl who was half frozen just a few hours ago!"

"Yeah, guess she does."

Bear looked over at Sage. "Are they aware of our ways little brother?"

Sage shook his head, wiping his mouth. "Not as far as I can tell Big Sister Bear. Seems like they come from too far north."

"I see," Bear said. "You're a lucky man, Tam Lin. You have come to the great sanctuary of this land. A place of peace and beauty. Protected by the Mother."

"Yeah, so I hear."

"There was time, this land was split apart by war. Terrible, terrible war. Tribe against tribe, kin against kin. Killing and raping and pillaging on an almost daily basis. All over a few scraps of land or food. But then, one day, the Mighty Mallard came down to us and showed us the way. She showed us how to build a place of peace and prosperity, where no one would have to suffer. Is that not a glorious gift?"

"Sure."

"I know you have fled a place of suffering. A place where this must seem like...heaven!" Those around the table smiled, nodding to each other. "You must be wondering, what do you have to do in order to live in a world like this!"

"Uhm, yeah?"

"Well, all we had do was give into the will of the Mighty Mallard, to let the Mother show us the way! Which she did! Do you know what those tenants she asked of were, Tam Lin?"

"No?"

Bear held out a club-like hand, counting them off. "She told us not to kill, not to eat the flesh of animals, and to respect mother nature. For you see, Tam Lin, death is like a stain. For each death done by your hands the blood sticks to you like oil, and you can never wash it off. It tarnishes you. Once you free yourself from death, you free yourself from the cycle of suffering, so that you can face the Mighty Mallard with a pure, true soul."

Jane snorted, but if anyone noticed they didn't say anything. "Didn't we uhm, just eat duck?" Tam Lin asked.

Sister Bear lifted her head to the sky, arms raised to the moon. "Yes, the Glorious Sacrifice of Mother Mallard as all Mothers must suffer! It is her greatest gift and our greatest boon."

"Our greatest boon!" the others at the table repeated, raising their hands in imitation of Bear.

Bear settled back in her chair, lacing her fingers over her belly. "As you can see, the Mighty Mother sacrifices much for us, even her own flesh, so that we may be at peace. Do you understand?"

Hell no, he didn't. "Yeah...of course."

Sister Bear looked down at Tam Lin with pity. Jane started to laugh, but Tam Lin kicked her shin from under the table. "Poor soul. Fleeing from your struggles. You must wonder at times if you'll ever find a safe bosom to cling to."

Tam Lin wasn't sure about the 'bosom' part, but the rest he could readily agree to.

"Well fear not, lost little bother," Bear said, "for we welcome *all* wanderers, *all* tribes into our befeathered embrace. In fact, Flora here came from a lost tribe such as yourselves. One filled with pain and hate, and she found protection under the Mother. Is part of the Guardians now."

Tam Lin turned to see a young woman, the only one at the table whose skin was a darker hue, dressed in the same fatigue pants and tie dye shirt as the brothers, her smile and eyes just a little too wide. "Yes, Big Sister Bear. Yugenia is Heaven on Earth," Flora said. She turned to Tam Lin. "You and your friend really are very lucky."

"Yes," Bear said, "all one has to do is abide by our rules and they will be welcomed here at the heart of the Mighty Mallard's Kingdom. In fact, generally we only allow people to join our community once a year, during the Great Festival..."

Tam Lin hoped they would be long gone by then.

"...which is tomorrow!" Bear said. Tam Lin felt like sinking into his seat now as well. Maybe he could join Jane as a puddle. "It must be the Mother's Will that brought you here before us on the Eve of our most important Festival!"

"Not to mention those three comets we saw the night before," Sage said, "it is a great portent."

"Yes, and the very fact that two of those comets fell where you were found, and the third fell at the Festival Grounds," Bear agreed, "means surly you are meant to be here."

Tam Lin perked up at that. "The third comet, you said, fell at this place where this festival is gonna be held?"

"Yes, I can see you understand the import of that. Can I count on you to participate tomorrow?"

Tam Lin couldn't believe his luck. He could get a ride straight to where Bunny was most likely to be. "Yeah, sure. Sounds like a plan to me."

Bear reached out, shaking Tam Lin's shoulder with one of her massive hands. The old woman was surprisingly strong. "That's what I like to hear. Let's drink to tha...ah, looks like your friend already wore herself out!"

Tam Lin turned to see Jane had collapsed, head on the table, half-filled glass of mead still clutched in her hand. The table laughed and Tam Lin managed a half-smile, happy that he at least had a plan.

Dinner passed, and soon it was time for everyone to go to bed. Tam Lin was once more escorted to his hut where tried to sleep, but rest eluded him. He shifted and turned, tried to count sheep, but it was to no avail. At some point he decided if he couldn't sleep, then he may as well do something useful, so, he left his yurt, poking his head out into the cool spring night air. It was quiet. Three moons hung above him—pink, yellow, and blue—their near fullness so bright that the stars were nearly drowned out by the luminescence. He frowned when he saw a guard had been posted to watch over his yurt, but the guard had obviously had his fair share of mead that night as well, for he was out cold, snoring. Tam Lin slipped past him easily.

The village was still, yurts emitting only the occasional soft snore. Tam Lin could see active outposts around the commune, armed with guards lit by faint firelight, squinting into the edge of the forest. Odd for a group that believed in causing no harm. Perhaps there was a threat he wasn't being told about? Not that he planned on being there long enough to figure out what that threat might be. Tam Lin came to the center of the villa, stopped, and took a good look at the wooden totem of the Mighty Mallard.

The statue was indeed duck-like in nature, with wings, feathers, and a bill. It had a row of large sagging teats on its chest from which various animals fed—boars, mountain lions, and stags—its belly distended, as if with child. It was set into a nest with a clutch, only instead of ducklings emerging from the eggs, there were tiny doll-like people. Its face was twisted into a grotesque snarl, and Tam Lin could see a series of sharp wicker teeth lined its bill.

Shuffling away from the figure with a glare, Tam Lin decided to try to find where Jane was and see how she was doing. To this end, he started poking his head through some of the larger tents. In one, he saw Bear sleeping in a giant bed covered in blankets and furs, a couple of the younger male followers lying next to her in various states of undress. The next yurt he peered into was for food storage with grain, preserved fruits, and nuts. Inside was a brown-skinned boy in rough-looking clothes cleaning up the duck carcass from earlier. The boy was a good twenty years younger than anyone else in the village and was thin, as if he didn't eat enough. Tam Lin moved on with a frown. Finally, he came to a mid-sized tent towards the edge of the encampment.

Tam Lin had to move carefully around this one, as there were still people awake, tending to some of the more severely ill. He snuck around the back, peeking through the seaming in the yurt. There he could spy Jane, passed out on a cot, oblivious to the world. She seemed okay, even if he bet she was going to have a nasty hangover in the morning. She snored loudly.

Seeing that Jane was safe, Tam Lin decided to take a peek at the barn they had gone to earlier; the store of supplies there interested him. At the barn were a few more guards, so Tam Lin had to take his time, hiding in the shadows and moving quietly. The guards were all somewhat fuzzy from the feast though, yawning and staring off into the distance.

Tam Lin made his way to the back of the barn, peering through the boards to see what was inside. *Huh, interesting.* He could see rows of rifles and boxes of bullets. Tam Lin wondered where they were manufacturing the items as he saw no factories nearby, but that didn't stop him from looking for something that might be of use. There were knifes, hunting bows, and oil. He looked around to see if there was an easy second entrance. A loose board. Tam Lin wiggled the board slightly. It would require a burst of force to get it to move like he wanted. He checked on the guard, looking to see if the noise he made had alerted him. The guard yawned, scratching his balls before picking his nose. Tam Lin grinned. Perfect.

He went back, popped the board aside and slid through. Once inside, he grabbed a med kit, some twine, and a roll of tape. He was about to leave when he noticed a small clay pot, about the size of a deck of cards. He opened the pot, and inside was a dark, sticky substance that smelled slightly of gasoline. *Greek fire,* he thought, then looking behind to make sure no was there, grabbed a couple jars of the stuff. His ill-gotten goods secured he slipped back out, making sure to put the board back in place. He then went back to his yurt to pretend to sleep until morning.

"Rise and shine dear! Today is the day of the Great Festival of the Mallard and you shall receive the Blessing of participating!"

Jane reluctantly opened an eye, wanting nothing more than to find the owner of that voice and claw her throat out. Where was she again? What was this strange room? Who were all these people? She was in a sort of large tent lined with cots, the cots occupied by sick-looking elderly people. The elders looked so ancient that Jane felt even Frank would have given them a run for their money. At the edge of Jane's cot was a woman she didn't know, dressed in lavender, long silver hair in a braid. She had a serene smile on her face that made Jane uneasy for some reason. "Who the fuck are you?"

The woman was unfazed by Jane's reaction. "I'm Lily silly! We met yesterday, remember? You had come in from that chill and we warmed you up. Seems like we let you wander sooner than we should have. You collapsed at dinner after some mead. Poor thing, you must have been exhausted."

Oh yeah, Jane thought, remembering the mead, *well, that would explain the headache.* That would also explain the place. And the dull ache in her chest. "Oh yeah, hey...got any more of that mead?"

Lily laughed as if Jane were joking; she was not. "Oh *you,* today is the day of the Great Festival! You don't want to be drunk on mead for that!" That is *exactly* what Jane wanted. "Here, I'll give you a concoction for your headache, and then we should be off."

Lily handed Jane a horn mug filled with fizzy water of a mysterious origin. Jane drank the contents without thinking, without caring, before handing the mug back. After the drink and some breakfast that Jane could barely keep down, she was escorted out of the yurt with two of the other healers. Jane kept her head down, trying to focus on the dirt. On the blades of grass. On anything other than what kept wanting to pop up in her mind. *Bill's head, tongue flopping out, the lower half of his face gone.*

Jane gripped the hem of her sleeves, counting rocks.

It was just past dawn and the coolness of the morning seemed to shake some of the hangover from Jane, trying to pull from her some semblance of cheer, but she pushed it back down. The sky was clear and the sun was bright; it was going to be a glorious day. There was an entourage of vehicles at the edge of village, jeeps decorated with columbine and streamers of red, yellow, and black. The citizens of Yugenia were singing and joking, partaking of a strong-smelling plant.

Tam Lin was with them. He smiled and accepted a beverage from one of the revelers, but Jane noticed he didn't drink it, and that his eyes remained narrow and sharp. He looked over at Jane as soon as she arrived, made some sort of quick assessment, then went back to surveying the party. *He seems good at this guarding people stuff,* she thought, *too bad he's wasting it on me.*

Whatever was in that fizzy drink was starting to take effect. Jane felt her headache slip away, but along with her head she began to feel her feet and fingers turn numb. Jane felt as though she might topple over. At this point though, she was shoved into a car, a crown of pink phlox placed on her head. "It was lovely knowing you Jane," Lilly said from outside the car. "May you find joy with the Mighty Mallard."

Was? Well, that doesn't sound good.

Tam Lin was escorted to a separate vehicle, seated in the back. This done, the rest of the revelers boarded, and the engines started to rumble; then with a cloud of song, petals, and exhaust fumes they started off south, towards the Festival of the Mighty Mallard, and where Bunny potentially lay.

Tam Lin sat quietly in his seat, Sage and Flora seeming happy to chat among themselves. They talked about the excitement of the games, wondering who would win, who the underdogs were and the favorites might be. He looked back through the rear-view mirror to spy Jane, crown of flowers on her head. She seemed to be staring out at nothing, eyes unfocused. He supposed it was an aftereffect from the hypothermia and alcohol.

They first went through the southern canyon. They drove on winding dirt roads alongside which the silver river ran, fish jumping in a seeming panic, as if the fresh spring melt was too cold even for them. They then went through more forest, buttercups poking up from the clay-colored dirt, before emerging out into an orchard. The orchard was filled with fruit and nut trees, and considering it was spring, there wasn't much to see, other than folks working the dirt, tilling it up and laying down fertilizer. Tam Lin looked over these people. They weren't dressed in the loose, clean garb of the Yugenians, nor did they wear the fatigues and tie dye shirts like the brothers. These people wore rags, had scarred hands, and were covered in dirt, like the boy he had seen the night before. He saw children here as well, running between the young and the old.

"Ah, I remember being a kid back on Festival Day," Sage said, smoking as he drove, "it sucked. Glad those days are over with." They left the orchard and went back into the forest. By now it was mid-morning, light flickering through the trees. Tam Lin shifted in his seat, feeling to make sure the clay pots and his other supplies were still securely strapped to his legs.

When they emerged from the forest a second time it was onto a flat clearing that stretched far into the distance. It was a clearing of basalt rock and low yellowed weeds, not suitable for growing. To the south, Tam Lin saw a volcano. The volcano was part of a mountain range, but stood taller than the rest of the peaks, slate-colored smoke drifting from its top. It stood in stark contrast to the cyan sky, almost black against it. In the field before the range, Tam Lin could see more of the people in rags, and these people eyed the jeeps warily. Small shanties assembled themselves, made of scraps of metal, wood and cloth; as they drew closer to the mountains these shanties grew in density, until they became overcrowded with streets of mud that reeked of piss.

"This is where the tribes have been relocated," Sage said. "It's not as pretty as Yugenia, but it's better than the hellholes they came from and at least they're not fightin' each other. They have a purpose here, under the Mother Mallard, and work for her glory. We provide them food and shelter in return." As they drove past Tam Lin could see a line of people in front of a stalled jeep, bowls in hands. There was a crew of brothers around the jeep, rifles held at the ready, as they passed out some slop. Sage grinned. "This is where you and your friend woulda ended up if you'd missed the Great Festival. Woulda had to wait a whole year in this place. But lucky you, you all came at the right time!"

"Yeah, lucky us."

Metalworks began to appear, around which the shanty towns were concentrated, answering Tam Lin's question as to where the guns and bullets were being made. The metal works were large concrete buildings near hot springs and geysers. They were square, low, utilitarian, and guarded. It was here Tam Lin could hear the hiss and pop of steel being forged. He saw more of the people in rags coming to and from the forges, these ones covered in soot and burns. They passed the metalworks and came up to the volcano.

The volcano was behind a tall wall of corrugated metal. The wall was semicircular in shape with spikes lining its top rim. It was massive and stretched for miles so that Tam Lin couldn't see the end of it. There were shanties upon shanties built up along the outside of that wall, the refuse of so many lives accrued like dried shit. Just beyond the tips of the spikes, if Tam Lin looked up, he could an image of a duck carved into the mountain side.

Sage looked back at him. "Whaddya think of our Great Arena my friend? Pretty amazing, huh?"

Arena? "Must've taken a lot of work to build it."

"It was a fort back in the day before the Unification," Sage said. "Was the place where the Treaty of the Tribes was signed under the gaze of Mother Mallard. Now it serves as a testing ground for those who would be Chosen to join us in the Mallard's Blessed City."

"Testing ground?"

"Yeah man," Sage said, "you don't just get to *join* Yugenia. I mean, *everyone* is welcome, but you gotta prove yourself. That you're worthy. That's what the Festival is about, finding those who are Chosen. That's how Flora and I became part of the Guardians. Through the test. And once we're done serving the Guardians, we'll get to cleanse ourselves of our bad karma. You know, Flora here was a wheat field thrasher. Hard work that. But she passed her test and was able to join us."

Flora smiled back at Tam Lin. "I am truly Blessed."

"Hell ya'," Sage agreed, "you took down what, twenty-five? Thirty?"

"Twenty-seven."

"Man, I always remember when you ripped the arm off that one guy and beat him with it," Sage said with a laugh, "the look on your face was *savage*. You killed *everyone* in that place."

"He was my uncle! But there was no fucking way I was gonna go back to that field!"

Shit, shit, shit! Tam Lin glanced back at Jane, three cars behind him, listless. He looked back up at the arena, and he could see now, on top of the spikes there were heads, pickled by the sun. Eyes eaten out by crows. "You're gonna have us fight each other to join your group?" Tam Lin repeated, struggling to keep his voice steady.

"Oh, you'll get that Blessing, and I think you'll do pretty well, tough guy that you are. But your little friend will receive an even *greater* Blessing. She'll become a Morsel to Mother Mallard, to be forever cherished in her *own* great Feasting Hall, where she dines upon human flesh like we dine upon Hers."

Fuck. I fucked up.

"But I thought the Mallard said you couldn't hurt anyone?"

"Ah, well yeah, those who've been chosen need to keep their karma clean, but that doesn't mean we can't watch *other* people hurt each other!" Sage laughed. "If you can even call these animals that!" Flora began to giggle as well.

Bad. This is soooo fucking bad. What had he gotten them into? He looked down at his feet, thinking fast.

"Wow, uhm, that's really generous of you," Tam Lin said. "And when will this Festival start? Do I have time to prepare myself?"

"There's no preparing for the Glory of the Festival. But the Battle will begin at dusk. The Duck likes to feast on blood under the triple moon."

Tam Lin nodded, and before either Sage or Flora could blink, reached out from the back seat, twisting Flora's neck so that it snapped. For a second Tam Lin saw his reflection in her surprised eyes, the shock of it momentarily stunning them both, before the light left them and she slumped down in her seat. "*Holy shit man!*" Sage screamed, grabbing for his gun while trying to control the car at the same time.

Tam Lin reached over, easily overpowering Sage to veer the jeep off the road and into the shanty village, crashing into a pile of wood and feces. People screamed and chickens flew. Sage began to convulse violently, blood coming from his nose. Tam Lin didn't question his luck, he just grabbed Sage's gun and ran. The shanty-town inhabitants watched him with dead eyes as he passed, neither hindering nor helping. When he looked back, he saw the other jeeps had pulled over and several of the Guardians emerged with weapons ready. But they were drunk on the festivities and too slow.

By the time they had gotten to where the jeep had crashed, Tam Lin was already lost in the mud and rickety structures. He looked at Jane, a slip of white in the muddled colors. He looked at the sky. It was just past noon.

It was time to come up with a plan.

Jane watched Tam Lin's jeep. Saw as he jumped out and ran off into the hobble of wood and metal to disappear. A part of her wondered what was going on in his head, but the rest of her just didn't care. The Yugenians spent some time looking for him, but came up empty handed.

Rowan watched everything with a pinched face. He bent over to the driver, saying something in his ear. The driver nodded, hitching up his rifle as Rowan left, both of them giving Jane a wary look. Jane just sighed, leaning her head against the seat. Rowan talked with the guards before walking back to the jeep, leaning over Jane in what she supposed he thought was an intimidating manner. "Where'd your little boyfriend go?"

"I don't know. I barely even know the guy," she made a face, "and he isn't my *boyfriend*."

"Yeah, well he killed two of our own. One of them my blood brother. I got half a mind to take you out right now and shoot you in the head."

"Fine. Go ahead. Save us all allota trouble."

"What?"

"Life is just suffering to delay the inevitable, ending it sooner would be a mercy."

124

"Shit, you're a downer," Rowan frowned, "no wonder that guy split."

"Forget about it, Rowan," the driver said, "she's a Morsel. The meteor is a sign. You don't wanna dirty your hands with unnecessary blood. The Mother would frown on that. That guy can't do anything out there. What's he gonna to do? Hit us with sticks and rocks?"

"Yeah, I guess you're right, what can one person do?" He glared at Jane, before turning back to the driver. "Get her to the other Morsels safely. I'm gonna stay here and see if I can help clean up this mess."

The driver nodded, starting the vehicle back up and heading down the road to the gates of the arena. The gates were large, made of a thick wood petrified with age. As they drove through Jane looked up, arching her neck back to see the pickled heads.

Past the gates was a large sandy flatland, filled with pale yellow grit. The floor of the arena went up to the base of the volcano, where the carving of the Mother Mallard looked down. She was a copy of the wicker effigy back in the little yurt town, only here she was made with more detail. Almost life-like. Behind the jeep cavalcade, along the arena wall, was seating for spectators, and there were already people filing in. Mostly people from Yugenia in their windy silks and storm cloud hair.

In the center of the arena, Jane spotted a familiar figure. *Bunny!* For a moment Jane almost sat up, a sense of urgency breaking through the ennui. Bunny was held down with chains, unable to even get to his feet, belly and neck pressed flat to the sand. There were people around him decorating the chains with various purple and yellow flowers. Bunny did not seem pleased by this, crying plaintively, a low bellow that echoed off the stadium walls. "Wow so that must be the other creature they found when the meteors fell," the driver said.

"Yeah man," said another of the brothers, "will make a great Morsel for the Mother!"

"This will be the best Festival *ever*!"

Jane sunk back in her seat as they passed Bunny. She looked back, watching the tortoise struggle until out of sight. The jeep pulled into a small arch under the main seating of the arena that led to a staging area underneath. The driver got out, pulling Jane up by the arm, dragging her through rows of racks set with dull swords and chipped helmets.

They marched down a hall that was dim and made of red stone, the same color as the bark from the trees. Jane could see participants getting ready for the sport, men and women with hardened faces picking out weapons, testing them. Jane remembered the heads.

She was taken to a room at the back of the hall. The entrance to the room was decorated in penstemon and buttercup, two guards with rifles standing outside it. The driver nodded to the men as Jane and him passed through. It was dark inside that room, lit by flickering torches, the smoke of it stinging Jane's eyes. The walls were rough, as if carved from the earth, and in the center was a rusty metal cage where about fifty women and children sat. They were young, ranging from infanthood to early twenties, all dressed in the same white shift as Jane and all adorned with crowns of flowers. Some of them were crying, a few looked to be in a state of blissful rapture, while others yet eyed the guards angrily.

Jane was unceremoniously dumped into that cell, door locked behind her. The driver smiled in at them. "Blessed be the Morsels of the Mother. May your last moments on this earth be in peace," he then left, patting the guards on the shoulders with a laugh and a smile.

Jane was still as she looked around that room, no one really bothering to notice her. Why would they? They were all dead anyway. That was, until someone did. "No *way*," Jane turned to see a thin girl, late teens, come up to her. She was pretty, with dark skin and full lips. A crown of lilies sat on her curly brown hair, and her eyes were that sort of hazel where the color shifted depending on the light; one moment they were green, then the next they were blue, and then they were a sort of purple? Shifting into pink? Somehow turning into all colors at once? Jane shook herself. It must have been an after effect of the fizzy drink. "It's *you*!"

Jane looked behind herself and, seeing no one was there, turned back to the girl. "You must be mistaking me for somebody else. I don't know you..."

"Oh no, no, no," the girl said, raising her arms in supplication, "you wouldn't. Not someone like *me*. But *I* know *you*."

"P-pardon?"

The girl smiled, giving Jane a co-conspiratorial wink. "I know who you are! Can read that aura from a mile away. You're the..." the girl looked around to make sure no one was listening before leaning over to Jane to whisper, "*the Disruptor*." Her eyes gleamed a bright hawkish yellow.

Jane looked sideways at the girl, trying to subtly shuffle away. "Pardon...what?"

"You *know*," the girl said, not backing down, following each of Jane's movements with the intensity of a pressure cooker about to explode. "The Catalyst! The Great Error in the Calculation. The Magical Girl. You're *Armageddon*!"

"Wh-who are you? Why do you know all that?"

"Oh, I'm Peridot," the girl said, holding out her hand. Jane took it, shaking it limply more out of habit than anything else. "And I'm an apprentice Conservator, but you can probably tell that." Jane had no idea what an apprentice Conservator was or how she would be able to tell. "My Mentor was Conservator of Gardenalia, but it unraveled due to the fraying of a nearby Filament," a wink. "Wonder who could be to blame for that, eh? Anyway, in my escape I got separated from my Mentor and ended up here!"

Jane attempted to process this, unfamiliar vocabulary non-withstanding. "My, that sounds terrible, and also seems rather convenient..."

"Well *of course* it's convenient!" Peridot exclaimed, sounding exasperated but smiling all the same. "You are the convergence of all *sorts of things*, so all kinds of *convenient things* will happen to *you*. You're blessed, or er, uhm, cursed...or however you wanna look at it." Peridot gasped, a sudden thought coming to her. "Does this mean I'm meant to meet the Disruptor and have some part to play in her tale?" Peridot squealed. "That is so *cool*! I get to be the *bad girl*!""

By now Peridot's earlier attempts at discretion had been totally blown out of the water as the occupants of the cell glared at the overjoyed girl in annoyance. Jane moved to the side of the jail wall, where hopefully they would cause less disruption. "Look Peridot ..."

"So whatcha' gonna do? Gonna blow up the planet? Gonna rip a hole in the sky and reign down fire? Gonna reset time and get us all caught in some permanent loop?"

Jane looked away from those eager eyes, squinting her own closed, before turning back to face her again. "Look, Peridot, I don't know who you think I am, but I don't want anything to do with this Disruptor-Magical Girl nonsense. My name is Jane..."

"*Jane*? That's a boring name for the Bringer of Chaos. Totally not fitting. It should be more something along the lines like Bellatrix, or Lillith, or something like that."

"Yeah, well, you're just gonna have to deal with Jane. And I'm not blowing up any planets or summoning any weird time demons. I'm just a simple civil servant and that's it. Nothing strange or exciting about that." *Or, at least I was.*

"The Disruptor...a bureaucrat?" Peridot made a face. "Well, that doesn't fit very well, does it? I was thinking you would be more of like a counter-culture revolutionary or some bad ass warrior. Not some milquetoast yes-woman. A bit of a mismatch I would say. A flaw in the stone."

"Well, I wouldn't know. Never met a Disruptor before."

"Well maybe this part of the Disruptor's development," Peridot said, talking more to herself now than Jane, "maybe she has to learn to let go of her constraints and lean into the power of chaos. A little tricky, but I suppose that's something I can work with." She looked at Jane with those whirlpool eyes. "Well, whatever your qualifications are, you're going to have to think of a way to get us out of here soon, Jane the Disruptor, as we are on limited time and you seem unable to manipulate that dimension yet."

Jane looked out the cage, glancing at all the flowers. She noticed one of the guards had a mead flask he was drinking from. "Figures."

"Yeah, you see...." Peridot squeezed along the side of the cage, so Jane was forced to see her, blocking her view of the guard. "We are the Morsels to the Mallard, and do you know what that means?"

"Hmm, if I had to guess, I would say it means we're going to be sacrificed to some ancient god in a pointless pagan ritual." She really wanted that mead right now.

"Ugh, well yes. That's exactly it," and when this didn't have the effect of stirring Jane, she elaborated. "The Festival is a series of games where the enslaved tribes fight and kill each other to join Yugenia. Part of the Festival includes the Morsels of the Mallard, where we will be eviscerated at her alter. She's gone mad you know, that Duck. Conservators are supposed to protect their Filaments, not feed on them. But I suppose that since the Sea Witch has been out of the picture for so long, some Conservators have...*drifted*."

"Hmm, evisceration? Brutal. It's always the quiet ones that do that. But better than roasting alive or flaying though, those are the really sadistic bastards," Jane reached a hand through the bars. "Hey! Gotta drink for a dead girl?" The guard at the entrance looked back at Jane with a scowl. She smiled. "I'll put in a good word with your weird duck-goddess for you." The guard thought about this, shrugged, and tossed her his flask.

"Wait, are you telling me that you don't care that you're about to be *eviscerated*?!"

Jane shrugged, sitting down in a corner to drink. "If I'm all these things that you say I am, we're probably better off for it."

Peridot shook her head, again, talking to herself. "This is not what I expected, not what I expected at all. A *complete* and total mismatch. I can't believe she's gonna give up that easily!" Peridot looked over at Jane with a scowl. "I must say that I am very disappointed."

"Aren't we all?"

It was night by the time the guards came to escort the women and children out of the cage. Jane was pretty toasted, having finished the whole flask. She wished she had more, but the guards that came to collect them were disappointingly sober. The captives stirred when the men opened the door to the jail. Some started to swoon, some to pray, eyes upturned to whatever god they thought might reply, while a few stoically picked up the younger children who were too tired to walk. Jane just sighed as she was pulled up by her armpits to her feet, a little unsteady, Peridot glaring at her accusingly as they were marched out. Jane avoided her strange, swirling eyes.

They were escorted in a line, heads bowed low, long hair flowing, white shifts coming to their knees. When they emerged out into the arena, the roar was deafening. The whole of the stadium was filled with spectators screaming and yelling, the sound of it accumulating into a rumble that shook the earth.

Jane looked up in shock at the noise, towards the seating in the arena. She remembered how softly the residents of Yugenia had spoken, how gentle they had seemed. Their faces were now twisted with blood lust. They screamed. They howled. Their eyes gleamed with savage fury.

Jane knew that look, turned away from it, but what she saw when she looked at the battlegrounds of the arena chilled her even further. It was bloodbath. Slave had been put against slave in a battle royal of at least a hundred people hacking at each other with sword, spear, hand and tooth. Jane watched in dull despair as an ax squashed a woman's head, eyes popping and brains leaking out the side. Next to her a man missing a leg tried to crawl away, howling, only for a spear to land in his back. The sand became stained red. *Like blood falling in snow, seeping between her toes. Steam rising up from life freshly released.* One of the girls wailed while another got sick.

Head steady, but eyes somehow shaking, Jane turned to the mountain carving of the Mallard. It had come alive under the light of the full triple moons, gaze gleaming, mouth twisted in a cruel grin. An alter had been laid before this animated deity, a simple stone slab, lit by torch light; it was there she saw Bunny, chained, waiting to be sacrificed. *No,* Jane thought, *this isn't what I want. Not like this...* Tear swelled up in her eyes. *But what can I do?*

"Hey, don't look back, but I want you to know I have a plan," Jane turned towards the voice in surprise, recognizing the flash of green and black, even in uniform. "I said *don't* lookback."

"What are you doing? How did you get here?"

"Guess I'm pretty good at sneaking around," Tam Lin said. "Look, I have it set up for one of the metal works to go off here in a few minutes. When that happens, I need you to help me grab Bunny and run. Got that?"

"Go off? What do you mean? Did you plant some sort of a bomb or something?"

"Kind of, yeah. With some Greek fire that I found."

"Shit..."

Jane's head was now shaking along with her sight. The sand buzzed. She could feel it in her feet, the trapped life. Like dammed water wanting to flow free. Steam ready to burst. "I don't want this, Tam Lin," she said, vision blurred, but with what she didn't know. "I don't want more people dying for me."

Tam Lin's face was unreadable in the flickering fire light. "I'm sorry Jane, but I'm not giving you a choice."

"Ooooo!" Peridot said, butting in. "Who's this? Your boyfriend? Hmmmm. He's a little too scruffy for my taste but I can see the appeal."

"Who are *you*?"

But Peridot was too distracted to answer, giving Tam Lin the once over a couple more times. "Wait, are you *dead?*"

"Hey!" one of the other guards yelled. "What's goin' on over there?!"

Tam Lin cursed, slinking back into the shadows. Jane looked ahead, at the trembling youths, clinging to one another, feeling the earth pulsing. So much life. So much death. So many shattered dreams. She felt them, invisible hands reaching up, grasping her ankles.

Jane stared at her feet, fixated by those fingers.

I want to live! they said.

I want to live!

She looked up, and cried, "I'll go first!"

"Jane," Tam Lin hissed, reaching for her, "no!" But Jane slipped through his grasp to move forward, feeling almost as if she were floating above the grains of sand. She could hear the whispering of the souls in them. The bubble of the stream about to break free. The guard at the front took her hand, gently, looking at her as though she were some fey creature sprung from nothingness.

"Jane!" Tam Lin yelled, now lunging. The other guards grabbed him, grappling him to the ground, but Tam Lin fought back, causing two of them to drop. Jane watched the struggle, hearing and seeing it, yet somehow oddly detached. Like beholding some relic of the past. Her eyes slid to one of the girls, and they were no longer in an arena, but in a forest of heavy hunter green boughs, glistening with ice and snow; the girl's rough dress was now white furs, her crown of roses the delicate snowdrops of early spring; her feet no longer chaffed from dry heat, but frostbit from cold. She could feel the genesis of memory bubble forth. The girl, head bowed, looked up, and her eyes were Jane's own.

Jane turned, and before her was the blood, the sand, the heat, and the duck. The Mallard noticed her now, recognized the threat, and as she rose lava spat high from the volcano, blocking out the stars with smoke, but she couldn't block out the glow of the moons. Jane stepped forward, and it wasn't sand she stepped on now, but the spring of dreams: the thoughts, hopes, and prayers of all those who had died in that arena in sacrifice to this being; their blood, soaked into the sands became purified, evaporating into mist. As

Jane's nascent March-hare feet, pale and lithe, touched each bit of memory it froze, creating a glacial stairway of crystal into the sky.

The Mallard bellowed in rage. There was an explosion at the side of the arena followed by screams, only this time it wasn't screams from the battling contestants, but from the stadium as part of it collapsed and hot slag poured from the metal works. Peridot and Tam Lin ran to Bunny in the midst of the chaos, but Jane's eyes were on the Mallard, her whole being filled with churning water, filled with waves. It pulsated through her, moving in time with her heart, becoming her blood, until Jane felt herself getting lost, becoming adrift at sea.

The water seeped and grew from the sand, first becoming a lake, then an ocean, before finally roaring to a tidal wave that washed the arena clean. It hit the hot slag of the steel works, hissing as the metal cooled, steam whirling up in clouds of evaporated yearnings. It enveloped the fleeing residents, spinning them about in whirlpools. It cradled the bodies of the recently fallen, holding them softly in its embrace. The Mallard flinched back as the boiling waves washed over her.

The Mallard howled, fighting against the drowning, reaching towards Jane. Jane could see the hand of stone and flame reach for her. Jane closed her eyes, ready to accept her fate, ready to accept the sacrifice...

I want to live...

"Jane!" a voice called.

Jane looked up. There was Bunny, freed from his chains and flying fast, Tam Lin at the helm with Peridot sat at the rim of shell.

Peridot had her arm stretched out, Bunny swooping in, evading the Mallard's grasp. "Grab my hand!" Peridot cried.

Without another thought Jane clasped a hold of Peridot, and Bunny turned, gaining altitude. Peridot held Jane tight as they rose into the air, the ground falling away beneath them.

"Dear God, what did you two do?" Peridot muttered as she hauled Jane aboard. "All those people down there...are dead." Tam Lin didn't answer, keeping his gaze grimly ahead as Jance glanced back, expression pained.

But the Mallard wasn't done with them yet. She burst from the roiling pool, flesh boiled and pink so that muscle could be seen underneath. She let loose a wailing cry, lurching forward to grab at the glimmering Bunny with a mangled, bony hand. Bunny shrieked in fear. "We have to jump now!" Tam Lin yelled.

"But we haven't calculated our trajectory!" Peridot protested. "If we jump now, we don't know where we'll end up!"

"Better than here! Go Bunny!"

Bunny went.

Lament of Ashera I

Daughter Dawn opens rose-colored eyes.

She stretches pale arms.

Pushes back the velvet night.

She rises.

Her breasts, high and firm, become the flushed clouds, the curve of her stomach the quickening day.

Her lips, unripe peaches, become rousing winds, the strands of her hair auric rubicund rays.

Her hips, still unseen, the soft promise of heat, the spell under which all living things sway.

Sister Moon, pale face green with envy, fades in this blossoming beauty.

Sister Moon, adorned in silver filigree, unable to compete with Dawn's pageantry.

Daughter Dawn, however, just sighs with pouty lips.

Daughter Dawn knows something is amiss.

For Daughter Dawn looks down on a world that is fading into mist.

The mountains that once trembled at her touch, had ceased to move, ground to rufescent rust.

The morning Zeru was born, it rained.

It was the Old Ones who recognized the sound as drops hit the roof of the cave.

It was the Old Ones who remembered the pungency of petrichor.

The People left the Cave, to dance in this gift of water, in this strange abundance that fell from the sky.

Zeru, son of Maryam the weaver and Yusuf the carpenter. The boy who brought the rain.

The Old Ones agreed Zeru was very blessed, for a child to be born was rare; a child whose birth brought the rains was even more so.

Such a child was surely Chosen by the Dreaming God, Himself.

The People of the Cave would lay offerings at the feet of Zeru. Of small stones and shining trinkets whose purposes had long ago been forgotten, of shells, dried flowers, and bits of bone.

He was given the largest of grubs, the freshest of dew, so that he became strong and free from disease.

And the People of the Cave were grateful.

As Zeru grew, he would sit at the feet of the Old Ones, listening to the tales they spun.

Of forested mountains and trickling streams.

Of fish that leapt in abundance and deer that ran in herds.

Of a World where people lived in plenty. Of a World where a Dreaming God wove Dreams.

Zeru would listen along with the other child that lived in the Cave of the People. A girl, ten years his elder.

Ashera, daughter of Miriam the dew gatherer and Ivan the spear maker.

She had hair of burnished gold, and limbs of bronze. Her eyes were lapis blue, seeming to carry within them the depths of the forgotten ocean.

She would collect the old bones of the Cave and adorn her room with them. Curved swirls of opalescent pink and purple, bits of wood hardened to stone, skulls of creatures whose form could only be wondered at.

Ashera and Zeru would stare at her treasures and dream of the sea.

When Zeru was in his seventh year, Maryam and Yusuf ceased to breathe. Their bones poked sharply through their skin, their cheeks hollow and eyes sunken. They weighed no more than the boy they had brought into the world.

The Old Ones said their deaths were a sign, that it was time to return Zeru to the Dreaming God so that He might be stirred. So that He might Dream once more of moving mountains, rising waters, and growing things

Zeru was given the best clothes the People had. Given the cleanest water and fattiest meat. He was given a crown of flowers —the Blessing of Life to be carried with him.

"But how should I find this Dreaming God?" Zeru asked, eyes wide with fear.

"Follow the Cynosure till you come to the Crystal Cave. There you will find the Dreaming God and the Waters of the World."

"But how do I follow this Cynosure? I know not the night sky."

"Ashera will accompany you on this journey. She often goes hunting with her father, and they must travel far to find what prey they can. She will know the way."

So, it was decided Ashera would accompany Zeru to the Dreaming God. She was given the strongest spear her father could make, and bore with her a necklace of her favorite shells. Ashera cried, but her Father told her to save the water, for they would find precious little of it once they left the Cave.

On the first new moon of the year, Ashera and Zeru left the Cave of the People. Old hands reached out from the depths of the mountain hole, as if in yearning, as the two younglings left, vanishing beyond the dunes into an endless profundity of stars.

The gaze of Sister Moon was cold, and frost soon coated their clothing. They walked through the night and slept when the sun was up, covering themselves from Mother Day's cloying heat. The frost that melted from their clothing Ashera collected to drink.

On the second night of their journey, they came upon a snake. The snake had its tail in its mouth and was eating itself. Zeru reached for the snake, but Ashera kept him from it. They walked on.

"Why was that snake eating itself?" Zeru asked.

"Because it has been driven mad with hunger," Ashera said. "It's best not to eat such things lest it's madness passes to us."

That day Zeru, unable to sleep from heat and fear, asked Ashera to sing of courage and strength. She sang and her voice soothed him to sleep.

On the third night, they came upon a mother wolf with two cubs. One cub lay dead on the dune, the greedy sand drinking its blood. The mother wolf's fur was patchy and thin, hunched hips with heavy flat skin. The mother wolf turned to the second cub and tore its throat open, its cries ringing across the land. Ashera pressed Zeru along, going downwind of the wolf.

"Why was that mother killing her young?" Zeru asked.

"Because she knows her young will only suffer and starve," Ashera replied, "and she is saving them from that pain."

That day Zeru asked Ashera to sing of love and hope.

The fourth night came, and the stars were blocked out by a large crescent moon that sneered down on them, spiting them with her cold. A wind blew, pulling at their garb so night's icy barbs could find their way in, picking at their fingers and nose. It roared wildly, laughing at them, mocking them, in only the way a wind driven mad by the moon could. Bits of sand rose up to strike one another, casting arcs of blue light seeming to manifest Sister Moon's disdain. The glow of the Cynosure grew faint.

In the distance could be seen the skeleton of a tree, black against the backdrop of the bright mercurial night. It had long lost its leaves, or even the memory of what it was to have such things, but it was shelter against the wind so they made their way towards it.

Under the barren boughs of that tree they found a man, though like the tree, he had long ago lost the memory of what he was. His skin was leathered like the snake's, his nails long and black like the wolf's. His nose and lips had been taken by the cold, and his eyes saw nothing but the moon. He muttered in some strange language Zeru had never heard before, but his words were not for them.

Ashera pushed Zeru past the tree.

"Shouldn't we help that man?" Zeru asked.

"He is beyond our aid."

"What happened to him?"

"He saw the snake and he saw the wolf, and the truth of it drove him mad."

That day Zeru did not ask Ashera to sing.

On the fifth night they found the entrance to the Crystal Cave. It was hidden under a mound of sand, the only hint to the mysteries it held an opening on the side from which a shimmering light effused. Inside the Cave was a maze of reflective silver that repeated Zeru's and Ashera's images into infinity. For a moment it blinded them, and then confused them as they had never seen their own reflections before. Zeru stared at his face for a long time—at the plump cheeks, the flushed lips, the crown of flowers on his head. There was a sun-warmed beauty to him that at moment he recognized; a regalness to his fire-glass locks and copper skin. So different from the worn thin gazes of his mother and father, pale and sallow as the moon. Ashera moved him along, keeping her gaze down.

Deep in the Cave, the Dreaming God slept.

He rested fat and complacent in a pool—more water than Zeru had ever seen—The Waters of the World at his feet, his long beard touching his knees. Unlike the People of the Cave, thin and brown, the Dreaming God was bloated and white, like the grubs his parents had fed him.

The Dreaming God stirred, looking down at them with a sleepy eye. "Child of Life," he rumbled, voice shaking the walls of the Cave. "You come to give me the Gift of Life and renew the World. What have you learned on your journey here?"

Zeru stared into that giant eye, and within it he saw the multitudes. He saw the sun, the moon, and the stars. He saw all the living things that have been and could be. He saw the baleful eye of the Whale. "I saw a being eating itself and learned the pain of death."

"And?"

"I saw a mother killing her own children and learned the pain of life."

"And?"

"I saw a man driven mad by both and learned the pain of God."

The Dreaming God nodded. "Then you know what you must do."

"I do," Zeru said, and then taking the spear from Ashera's hands, ran it through the eye of the Dreaming God. "I will create a world without the pain of death," he stabbed the Dreaming God through his other eye, "I will create a world without the pain of life," he stabbed the Dreaming God through his screaming mouth, "I will create a world without the madness of God."

The blood of the Dreaming God spilled forth, mixing with the Waters. Zeru stepped into that pool, drinking from it, letting it fill him, cover him. He bathed in its pinkish red glow, feeling it satisfy him as nothing had before. Ashera screamed. "Zeru, what have you done?!"

Zeru looked back at Ashera, smiling.

To just accept one's fate is rather odd,

not a Sacrifice, I've become a God.

The Cat's Elopement

Jane looked out into a fuchsia sea

A pink mist had enveloped them, moving in soft eddies, rippled with bits of starlight like petals tossed in a stream; it had the pungent smell of wild geraniums, and when Jane reached out, was pleasantly cool to the touch. The mist seemed to have a dampening effect on sound, not unpleasant or oppressive, but more like the quiet of earth in winter: asleep, hushed, contemplative. Jane looked over at Peridot and Tam Lin, sitting at the helm of Bunny as they drifted though the cloud, the two of them mute, lost in their own thoughts.

Memories seeped in and out of the back of Jane's mind as she stared off into that seemingly endless dianthus haze. Memories without pain. There were fall days in the Forest when the leaves turned to gold, fresh dirt as wild onions were dug up, Bill's crooked smile after he told another lame joke. It filled her with a sense of warmth and safety she had not felt for a long time, perhaps not since she was a small child and knew little of the world, and the comfort of that feeling made her fingertips and toes buzz.

Jane could have stayed in those memories forever.

But such was not meant to be. They emerged from the nebula in incandescent silence, tendrils of sparkling fandango clinging to Bunny as they broke through into open space, the sweet remembrances dissipating along with the haze. Jane looked out at the vastness of that indifferent night, dotted with so many countless stars that one became dizzy from the number of them, and she looked back to the cloud with longing, feeling a pang as it fell behind. But whatever spell that rose-colored serenity had had over her was now broken. She tore her gaze away to face what was ahead.

Below was a small planet. It was the size of a large asteroid, perfectly round. There was a town on it, but it was a town that was alien to Jane, being that it was perfectly average. There were parks and gardens where children played, a small strip of downtown with stores and soda shops, and a church with a white steeple. Cars lined the roads—heavy metal beasts in shades of cherry red and powder blue. Mothers with neatly pressed skirts and beehive hairdos walked the streets with shopping bags in hand; police officers roamed about waving to one another before stopping at the local cafe; shop owners set out their wares on the sidewalks. A peaceful place. A clean place. A quiet place. No one bothered to look up as Bunny came down from the sky, as if nothing strange were occurring at all.

Tam Lin brought them down to the edge of a park near some pine trees, just out of sight of people walking in a rhododendron garden. He jumped down from Bunny, followed by Peridot. "Where are we?" Peridot asked.

"I don't know," Tam Lin said, pulling out his book. He frowned, turning the map multiple directions. "I don't even see where we are on this thing."

Peridot got up on her toes to look over his shoulder and down at the page. "*Weeeeiiirrdddd.* Are we... are we in a Filament that's not woven into the Totality of Creation?"

"What the hell does that mean?"

"Have the Book of the Dead and you don't even know that!?"

"I mean, I don't know. I just kinda grabbed it and ran. It's not like I actually read the thing."

Peridot sighed, looking a mixture of disappointed and annoyed. "Seriously! It means this is, like, a rouge universe or something. Off the grid so to say. *A sub-luminal space.* Usually, sub-luminal spaces are created by some sort of intense psychic distress or state of ecstasy. They are unstable and collapse as soon as the emotional state passes. But this one...this one seems stable?"

"Is that possible?"

"I mean, it shouldn't be," Peridot said, now taking the map from his hands, "but I can't see any other explanation for it. This is a world that exists outside the Sea Witch's Creation."

"Great," Tam Lin grumbled, "we seem pretty good so far at stepping out of one pile of shit and into another....Jane, what are you doing?"

Jane sat on the ground with her back pressed against one of Bunny's legs, knees drawn up to her chest. She muttered something to her knees that neither Peridot nor Tam Lin could pick up, so Tam Lin asked again. Jane looked over at them, face flushed red and angry. "I said that my feet have turned into hooves!"

Peridot and Tam Lin walked over to take a look and sure enough, where Jane had once had regular human feet there were now a set of cloven hooves, brown fur going all the way up her calves. "Those sure are hooves," Peridot said, "but hey, at least the bunny ears are gone!"

"It must be some sort of warping when we go through different Filaments," Tam Lin said. "Can you walk?"

"No, I can't walk!" Jane snapped. "I fell flat on my ass just trying to get off Bunny. It's like balancing on stilts!"

"Okay," Tam Lin said. "I don't want to stay here any longer than we have to. As soon we get our bearings we'll make a jump. Until then you can rest here. Hopefully, we won't have to move much."

"So what?" Jane grumbled. "Next time I can turn into cow?"

"Well," Peridot said, "you do kinda have a cow's tail....or ox, I can't quite decide." Jane spotted the tail, starting to wail. "Hey, there, there," Peridot took Jane's hand, patting it, "it's okay. Everything's okay. This is all a part of the plan. I'm sure of it! Right now, it seems like a lot, but it's like when you first start putting a puzzle together. It just takes a little time. It'll get figured out!"

"A puzzle? A fucking puzzle?! Is that what you think of all of this? Don't you understand? *Nothing is fucking okay!*" She said this loud enough to cause Tam Lin to jump and stun Peridot into silence. "My-my co-workers, my friends, they're all *dead*! All burned to a gopherdamn crisp. I mean, I hated the fucking Misty Burrow. It was a stupid, shitty place, but it was my *home*. And now it's all gone, sucked into the anus of the universe or whatever the fuck you wanna call it. And not only is it gone, but it's *all my fault*."

"Oh, come now," Peridot started, "you can't put that on you..."

"'Magical Girl', he called me," Jane spat, "and what did you say? Disruptor? *Arma-fucking-geddon!*"

Peridot turned away with a nervous laugh, Tam Lin glaring daggers at her. "Looking back that was maybe a poor choice of words..."

"I can still feel them," Jane looked at her hands shaking. "I can still feel it flowing through me. The people who died in that arena. Their pain, their suffering. It was like it was in my blood. Is that all I am? A harbinger of doom? Of death? A vessel of destruction? Am I just some sort of...*monster*?"

"Look," Tam Lin said, kneeling in front of her, "I get that you're upset, but nows not the time to fall apart. Let's get to the Fates, get some answers, fix this thing, and then you can have a good cry."

Peridot heaved in a quick breath as Jane's sobbing turned to glaring daggers at Tam Lin. "Oh, so you want me to *time* my nervous breakdown, do you? Make it so it's *convenient* for you? Well, *fuck you!*" Jane threw a pinecone at Tam Lin that bounced harmlessly off his chest. "You don't get to fucking decide when I fall apart or not! You don't get tell me how I fucking feel! Who asked you to save me anyway! Not me! You should've just left me there to *die!*"

Tam Lin looked down at the pinecone, as if it had mortally wounded him. "I uhm, I..."

"Hey, hey now," Peridot interjected, "let's not get too heated here. Jane, you have every right to be upset, but Tam Lin is also right. We don't know where we are or what danger this place might pose."

"And why the fuck do you care? Some weirdo fangirl of destruction? What, do you get off on this kind of thing or something?"

"Oi, oi, oi!" Peridot puffed out her chest, "pipe down there, little missy! Everyone here is just trying to help!" But Jane wasn't listening anymore, burying her face into her knees to sob.

"I don't want this," Jane moaned, rocking back and forth, "I don't wanna hurt anyone anymore..."

Peridot sighed, running a hand through her hair. She looked over at Tam Lin, who was still looking down at the pinecone, dumbstruck. "What a mess. This is not how I thought things would be. Not *at all*."

There was a rustling in the bushes. Tam Lin heard it first. He turned to face the source of the sound, motioning for the two women to get down. "Quiet!" he ordered. Peridot clasped the sobbing Jane, pressing them both to Bunny for protection.

Townspeople emerged from the cover of the trees, approaching them. There were the mothers with the children, the fathers in the suits, a firefighter, a cowboy, and an astronaut in a space suit. Peridot was so distracted by the astronaut, that it took her a moment to realize that each one of these townspeople had the head of a cat, and it wasn't just any cat, but the head of the same broad faced brown gray tabby with yellow-green eyes: the mother with her bright red cardigan and pearls—tabby face; the police officer with his mustache and badge—tabby face; the cowboy with his hat and lasso—tabby face. "Oh yeah," Peridot said, "this place is *definitely* not on the map."

"Guapo," the astronaut said through a speaker on his space suit.

"Guapo, *guapo*, guapo," said the housewife.

150

"Guapo?" asked one of the children, a little boy in a school uniform.

"*Guapo,*" the housewife hushed.

"Guapo" said the police officer to the firefighter, "guapo guapo guapo."

"*Guaaaaapo,*" the firefighter agreed with a nod, "guapo guapo?"

"Guapo," the policeman replied.

At this point even Jane was weirded out enough to be stirred from her melancholy. "A-are they saying 'kupo' over and over again?"

"I, uhm, think it's actually 'guapo'," Peridot replied, not taking her eyes off the creatures.

"Wh-what do they want?" Jane whispered.

"I uh, don't know. But I don't get the feeling they're hostile. Maybe just worried?" Jane blushed, wiping her eyes.

The 'Guapo' people came over to the travelers. Tam Lin bristled, looking ready to start a fight, but when a grandma Guapo came and took his hand, patting it gently, he was instantly diffused. The grandmother chatted some things to Tam Lin which he pretended to understand, nodding his head submissively; Peridot sucked her teeth. "Our great defender at work," she grumbled.

The Guapo people came up to Peridot and Jane. The boy in the school uniform offered his hand to Peridot, who took it with a sigh, the boy helping her to her feet. She looked back at Jane who was flanked on either side now by the housewife and the firefighter. "Bu-but, I can't walk!" Jane protested, but her cries went unheard. The housewife and firefighter got Jane to her feet, and for a second she wobbled there, as if she might fall right back down; Tam Lin looked ready to say something, but the grandma Guapo tugged him along, 'tsk-tsking' at him. The housewife and the firefighter steadied Jane, moving her forward. She was unsure at first, but she gradually got her balance, even if she did move awkwardly. The housewife and firefighter were patient, moving at her speed.

Peridot turned to Bunny, who was chatting with the astronaut. For a brief moment, she thought it was funny that Bunny could commune with these creatures, when he disappeared entirely; her eyes widened in surprise. "Tam Lin!" Peridot called; the schoolboy hushed her, saying something she didn't understand.

Peridot looked over at Jane and watched in horror as the pale girl sunk into the earth along with her two helpers. "Tam Lin!!" Peridot yelled louder. The boy whined at her noise.

She looked ahead to Tam Lin, head still bent towards the old woman. Peridot watched them go behind a tree, and then not reappear on the other side. "What tha! What is this!" she looked down at the boy. He offered her a lollipop. She made a face, looking at the fur stuck to the red circle of congealed sugar. There was no way she was going to touch *that*.

And then, she was gone as well.

Rumbling thunder followed by a boom. Fire and smoke. The acrid smell of gunpowder mixed with burnt meat. Screams.

The screams had been a lullaby to him once, though he couldn't remember why. Had they been soothing because they were the screams of his enemies? Or because he had known he wasn't among them?

"Get up! You gotta move! Move! Move! Move!"

Tam Lin watched as a man rolled out of his cot. The man had Tam Lin's same dark hair, same loose frame, but where his face should have been, was a distorted pane of glass, as if trying to look through water.

The man was surrounded by darkness, but even in darkness he knew where to find his cigarettes. Pull one out. Light it up. Sigh the smoke into the black. The clean smoke of nicotine. Both the smoke of flesh and of plant-life carried emulsified vitality within, but one bore with it the promise of regeneration, the other thick with guts and oil—air rendered skin.

The man put out the cigarette, grinding the angry, red stub into the ashtray beside him.

That tray turned to scorched dirt, and the man was in a trench, walls of earth and rotted wood above him, gray and dull. Below was mud, mixed with piss. Thunder all around him, the sigh of lullabies, followed by flashes of cherry-colored light. On either side were faceless men who fought with him. The ones that would die.

"Whaddya waiting for! Get over that goddamn hill! You don't move now and I swear to fuckin' god I'll kill ya' sorry fucks myself!"

"Move!" Tam Lin yelled, looking down at the man, sensing the fear, seeing the hesitation. "Go now!"

The man crested the hill and began to run, a small speck in a wave of men desperately scrambling across the black terrain pock-marked with craters. Bullets came down from the plumed sky like lightening. The bullets hit the faceless men beside him, those men exploding into puffs of pink smoke, falling to the ground in piles of glittering candy. Some shined metallic green. Some were striped red and pink. Some shimmered gold. They gleamed under the flash of gunfire tracers and flares like little jewels. Fatty black smoke. A scream. A puff. Another delicately wrapped Turkish delight.

Tam Lin ran on, holding his gun tight. Terror coursed through him, shining wrappers popping all around, but still he moved forward, focused on one thing. Focused on the simple animal desire to survive.

He came to a pile of lemon marzipan, as tall as a mountain, looming. He hesitated. Behind him they were coming. The enemy. That fatty, black smoke roiling from their lungs.

"*Move it! Less you wanna die!*"

Tam Lin plunged into the pile of sweets, clawing his way to the top. The treats grew hot and unraveled under the warmth of his skin, melting and sticking to it; his hands became slick with caramel, his forearms covered in chocolate, his face smeared with raspberry filling, his mouth drunk with almond lacquer.

The top of the mountain was on fire. He stood there, looking around, to find that he was alone. His companions were gone, his leaders were gone. There was just the enemy, just the smoke. Tam Lin fired into the nothingness...

...his shot hits a tin duck with a ping. It falls over into a painted river, a new duck running along behind it, which Tam Lin treats with the same efficiency. He looks up, BB gun now in his hands. The roiling smoke is replaced by the smell of hot dogs frying in old grease, the flashes of bombs by the lights of carnival rides, the screams of pain by shrieks of thrilled laughter.

Tam Lin stands there for a moment, in front of a shooting gallery, watching the metal ducks on their track as they go by.

Their chipped paint. Their dented bodies. The vacant blue dot of their eyes. Plush prizes hang from the rafters of the red and white stripped tent, cheap pink bears and blue unicorns looking down at him almost accusingly. Someone says something to him, but they are another faceless person. He puts the toy gun down and walks away.

He walks down asphalt roads, through crowds of smiling people eating fries and playing games at gaudily colored tabernacles. Their faces twist, becoming distorted masks of drooping black eyes and sagging flesh, as the phosphorescence of the carnival blurs. Reds seems to stretch in waves and starbursts, as greens and blues fade. He feels drunk. His legs don't want to obey him. The sky reels above and spins in a whirlpool of faded starlight; he's in danger of falling over. Ahead he sees a funhouse and stumbles his way towards it. In the funhouse there is quiet. In the funhouse there are less people.

It's dark as he staggers in, the sounds and lights blessedly mute. He is surrounded by mirrors, bent in ways to play with the reflected light. In the first reflection he sees the man: he carries a Springfield rifle in is hands, his green fatigues stained with soot. Behind him is a black mountain rimmed with flame. He stares at Tam Lin with that unfocused face, as if expecting something, though what, he cannot say.

Tam Lin walks on.

In the next mirror he sees the same man, only different. Same blurred face, same build. He's in a forest this time though, in heavy armor with a red cross on his chest. In his hand is a bloodied sword.

When Tam Lin turns a third time, there is the image of the man again, only now facing away from the mirror. He's in a room. It's a small room with only space for a threadbare bed and a rickety desk. He's slumped over on that desk and isn't moving. He's thin. Too thin. There is a picture of a woman that Tam Lin can't see, a cigarette in an ashtray, burning to a waste. Next to that is a needle and an empty bottle of pills.

And then Tam Lin sees her, there before him, shimmering as if she were a coin at the bottom of a pool. The light catches and throws her image at him, but the light is fleeting, and the water deceitful. *Save me*, she whispers from those murky depths, as pale and shimmering as a pearl. Her hair shifts in different colors, and her eyes constantly change, as if she can't quite make up her mind on who she is, but the look on her face leaves no room for him to doubt that she is in danger. He reaches for her, but then she isn't there.

Tam Lin looks down at his hands. They are shaking. Wet with water but empty. Wet with caramel, chocolate, and lacquer. He can hear the fall of the bombs coming. Can smell burnt sugar mixed with tar. Here? The war should be over. But the cries from outside blur with the cries of the men in the field, and the crash of the fireworks blur with the crash of the rockets, and Tam Lin can't tell where he is. Can't remember who he is.

In this growing chaos, he hears a song, as clear and cool as the trickling of ice breaking in spring. It cuts through the smoke, through the drumming roar, and makes Tam Lin look up to follow.

He follows the sound past the mirrors. Past the man in sandy dunes with a composite gun, past the man in jungles with a machete, past the man in wastelands with a hazmat suit. Past all the discordance of heat, iron, and blood to follow the harmony of water, forests, and small things growing in the earth.

He comes to the rear of the funhouse, a set of black curtains before him. From the crack between those two curtains the melody seeps through. He looks back. The funhouse is full of a rust-colored blaze now, and it bounces off those mirrors, as if it's on fire. Tam Lin steps through the black curtain, to the other side...

...and the screams, the lights, the sickly-sweet smells vanished. He was in a forest. It was a gilded forest, white barked birch trees bowing becrowned heads, dripping liquid gold; their quaking leaves flitted to the ground, over moss-colored rocks, islands of emerald popping through burnished copper pools. Birds chirruped cheerfully, seen in flashes of cardinal and indigo, the air tinged with the pleasant aroma of decaying leaves.

A stream trickled through the woods. Tam Lin walked up to that stream and in it he could see a school of fish. Their backs were dull under the bright sun, the only thing to distinguish them from the pebbles sat the bottom of the riverbed their slight movements, their struggle against the current. Not knowing why, Tam Lin reached out for one of those fish; as soon as his hand broke the surface tension of the water though, the fish darted away, deceptively quick. Tam Lin frowned.

"The key to catching fish," a voice said, "is to be still. Fish have a shared genetic memory to know when they're being hunted, and that shared memory is *old*. Any sort of anticipation or anxiety and they'll sense it, and then the hunt is over. And you, my friend, have anxiety that those fish would scent from a mile away."

Tam Lin turned around.

There, by the stream was another one of those 'guapo' beings, relaxing on a rock with a fishing pole in the water. This one was dressed in overalls with a green fishing vest and straw hat. Lures glimmered, pinned to the vest. "Who are you?"

"I am El Guapo Cervantes Aguilar Trevino Salazar," the creature said, then added with a wink, "otherwise known as 'The Cat'."

"Well, Mr. El Guapo, mind telling me where the hell we are?"

El Guapo laughed. "I like how despite your mistrust I still get a 'mister'. But you don't need to worry, you're not in a place that will cause you harm." He pulled his pole from the water, a rainbow trout flashing on the line. "Care for some?"

Tam Lin watched the trout flop on the forest floor, and for some reason his mouth filled with bile. "No thanks. Don't eat much these days."

El Guapo nodded, stringing the trout on a line before putting it back in the stream. "That's the death, you know. Turns everything that touches your lips to ash, the colors of the world dull. Even your emotions take a back seat to it. After all," El Guapo cast again, "how can you have feelings when you don't have a heart?"

"I'm beginning to realize that...," Tam Lin picked at a leaf, "and I did it to myself, didn't I? Made myself this way."

"That's a hard question to answer. Where to lay blame. It raises questions of much control we have over our actions or our destiny. Questions about the nature of time and the causality of our being. I've my own thoughts on the matter, but it would be up to you to decide how much that was 'doing it to yourself' or simply being the victim of circumstance."

Tam Lin sat in silence for a while. "I don't think I can answer that question," he said. "I can't even answer the question of who I am."

"Well, who can really? A question like that is kinda tied up into the rest of the stuff, and there've been centuries of folks thinking about *that*."

"Yeah, but those people still have their memories."

"And what is that to who you are, your memories? Is that it? Are you simply a bundle of past experiences? No core sense of self, just shifting as the wind blows? Does who you are change with each new addition of a moment?"

"Ugh, no?" Tam Lin looked up at the trees, how they shook in the breeze, blue sky between them. "But maybe, yes? I guess that's why I'm here. Because of a memory. If I didn't remember her, I wouldn't have tried to escape."

"Maybe. But maybe not," he reeled in his line and cast again, shimmering in the wind like a loose spider's web. "I mean, the memory may have been what brought you to Jane, but the desire to escape Leviathan had nothing to do with that."

"Then why do you think I wanted to escape?"

"Do you really want my opinion?"

"Yeah...kinda..." Though Tam Lin wasn't sure why.

"'Cause that's just who you are."

"Because that's just...But if I don't have the body of Tam Lin, or the memories of Tam Lin, then how can I *be* him?"

"You know, I once had this sweet car. 1976 mustang. Cherry red, leather interior. Loved that damn thing. Called her Olga. Olga was a sweet beast, but you know, over time she got old and needed to get some parts replaced. Sparks plugs here, starter there.

Soon, I was replacing the whole transmission. She ran a helluva lot smoother after that. But no matter how many parts I replaced, no matter how much her gas mileage or performance improved, do know what she always was?" El Guapo looked over at Tam Lin with an expectant look.

"...Olga?"

"Damn right she was. Never a day in my life I thought otherwise. And yeah, she changed over the years, we all do, but that doesn't mean we've *really* changed. We're just different parts of ourselves at different times in our lives."

"Yeah, but people aren't cars.”

"I don't know. I wouldn't be so sure about that. The soul of a car is nothing to sneeze at. But point being, even in death, when your very being was drained by Leviathan, when all your senses, thoughts, and memories had been taken from you, something in you held on. Something in you decided to fight. And I think that says something."

“Yeah, well what?”

“Well, that you're a stubborn asshole for one.”

Tam Lin laughed. "You might have a point there, ugh...” he watched a fish jump. “She's right to be mad at me, isn't she? Here I am, dragging her along on this whole thing, and I don't even know why."

"The Disruptor has her own bundle of problems to deal with, and until you figure out your own shit, you're gonna be little help to her. But figuring out your own shit will mean remembering who you really are."

Tam Lin thought back to the screams and the cries, to the smoke. "I don't know if I'm ready for that."

El Guapo stood, grabbing a stone from the creek. He handed it over to Tam Lin. Tam Lin took the stone, working it over in his hand; it was deep purple-red color, nicely smoothed over by the water, and even though Tam Lin couldn't feel the coolness of the stone, or it's smoothness, the weight of it brought a small comfort he couldn't quite understand. "I don't think you are either," El Guapo agreed.

"What sort of stone is this?"

"It's porphyry," El Guapo replied.

Tam Lin didn't know what sort of rock that was, so decided to keep quiet.

El Guapo reached to Tam Lin patting him on the shoulder. "Good luck though, with all that. Once you figured it all out, then I'm sure you'll be able to catch some fish."

"I don't know, I just feel more lost than before."

"Well, that's least a good start."

Peridot stared up at the cornflower blue sky, a handful of white clouds passing through. She watched those clouds, popcorn shaped puffballs without a kernel of rain to mar the beauty of the day; in them she could see a rabbit, and a little squirrel, followed by a cat. A sort of celestial menagerie. *So symmetrical,* she thought, *of wonderful shape and composition. Excellent amount of moisture, drifting at a perfect velocity for maximum enjoyment. What sort of heaven is this?*

Peridot looked down. She was no longer in the shabby shift, but a dress, a ball gown made of peacock silk and black taffeta, done in ruffles and set with iridescent raven feathers. Lace stockings covered her legs and a pretty rose fascinator sat on her head. She sighed with satisfaction as she smoothed a few wrinkles in the skirt; finally, some clothing worthy of her station.

She looked around. Peridot was in a garden. An aristocratic creation of neatly mowed grass, trimmed shrubbery, and pretty flowers. To her left, grassy hills gently rolled off in the distance until they vanished into the horizon; meanwhile to her right were rose gardens, stone statues, and a hedge maze. The rose gardens were in full bloom, in a rainbow of hues, their sweet scent wafting in the breeze, while the statues were of people that seemed oddly familiar, but she couldn't quite place them—wise visages looking out proudly and standing tall. She went over to a nearby marble fountain with a placard that read "Iamblichus", and shrugged, having no idea who that was, before peering at her reflection in the water to adjust a few stray curls.

"Well," she said aloud, placing her hands on her hips, "whoever runs this place sure knows who to treat a guest, huh?" She looked around, spying the maze, a slight smile coming to her lips. "Oh, what here? A challenge to the apprentice of Gardenalia? Well, challenge accepted!"

Peridot ran off to the hedge puzzle, looking at everything in wonder: the trees perfectly shaped, the bushes trimmed at nine-ty-degree angles, each flower at its peak—there wasn't a leaf or vine in sight that wasn't intentional. A part of Peridot wished she had brought a protractor, so could measure the degrees between the stems. She laughed as she ran through the maze, and for a brief second there even weren't even clouds in the sky, leaving everything under unstained blue.

It was with a shock, then, that she came to the center of the maze. For in the center was a rosebush with one red rose. The rose itself was a deep, blue-red color, with a single row of petals, it's golden center crown abuzz with pollen laden bees come to court. It was a plant of such color intensity and fragrance it should have been a joy to Peridot, but she frowned, for in the cutting of the leaves was a branch that wasn't even with the others. She put her hands on her hips, pouting. "Now who, in this wonderful place, would stand for a terror such as that?! Doesn't fit. Doesn't fit at all!"

"A terror!?" A voice exclaimed behind Peridot; she whirled around in surprise. "Now who would claim that of a simple flower?"

Peridot saw before her another 'guapo' creature, only this one was in gardener's get up, with a neat little green apron and some shears. He was tending to the bushes, trimming them. "Who the heck *are* you?" Peridot demanded.

"Well, I already told my name to one of your companions, and it's a bit of a mouthful, so we'll just go with 'El Guapo' if that's all right?"

"Hpmh, so you've a whole Filament made after your image speaking your name as a language? Bit arrogant if you ask me."

"So God created man in his own image, in the image of God he created him," El Guapo replied. "So, I suppose you could say there's precedent."

"I see, a bad philosopher, are we? The *worst* sort."

El Guapo laughed. "I suppose you've a point there, though you must forgive my plodding ways. I do not have the wisdom of the Sea Witch, you see, I am His shadow at the very best. I do not have the gift of clay making, at least anymore, and I'm not even sure I care for the burden of it. Point being, those beings you see are not my creations, but are a part of me."

"Whatever do you mean by that?" Peridot asked with the raise of an eyebrow

"Just exactly as I said. Each of those who you met are not a separate part of me, but *are* me. The fractured pieces of my whole. Iterations of myself from differing timelines, gathered here, into the collapsed quantum wave of One. Observed by the Unified Self."

Peridot did not like where this was going. "Well, if they're a part of you, then maybe you should get one of them to come here and tend this garden. That rose has been butchered." She pointed to the offending plant.

El Guapo walked up to the rose, gently cupping the glossy leaves, peering at its vibrant color. "But don't you see? This rose is sublime as is! The beauty of the flower counter acts the unevenness of the stems."

"Well, a lesson from a being that has studied under the Sea Witch Himself," Peridot said as she crossed her arms, "is to always strive for perfection."

"Oh, studied under the Sea Witch *Himself,* have you? That's very impressive indeed, considering no one has seen nor heard from Him for oh...what is it, twenty millennia at this point?" He plucked the plant with his shears.

Peridot shrugged self-consciously. "Something like that."

164

"To study under the Sea Witch would be an honor *indeed*," El Guapo went on, "for truly, He created the most extraordinary of Universes. Every tree hand crafted, every squirrel ass carefully f ormed..."

"Hey!" Peridot protested. "Watch it there, what you're saying could be considered...ugh..."

"Blasphemous?" El Guapo said with the raise of an eyebrow. "But I mean it with the upmost respect. I mean, *someone* had to take the time to create a squirrel butthole."

"We aren't talking about squirrels' buttholes," Peridot snapped, "we're talking about roses, and how *that* one offends the whole beauty of this garden."

"And what is in the nature of a rose?"

Peridot blinked. "Pardon?"

"What makes a rose, a rose?"

She scoffed. "Well obviously a eukaryote that is photosynthetic. You need some chloroplasts in there as well. As far as roses are concerned you generally require five petals with some sepals. Some thorns..."

"And are all of that what makes a rose beautiful?"

Peridot paused again. "Well no. Beauty is determined by color saturation and symmetry. Sometimes what is culturally acceptable as well."

"But what about scent? What about memory associated with the plant? What about someone who cannot see the color of the rose? Is it any less beautiful then?"

She huffed through her nose. "I guess it's just sometimes about the feel of a thing."

"Exactly," El Guapo said, "and how do you measure a feeling? How do you define your relationship with the rose?"

"I, uhm, well feelings are easy enough. There are dopamine receptors, and biological imperatives..."

"And none of that has any impact on what the rose really *is*."

"No, I suppose not."

"And would you measure love? Friendship? The feeling of loneliness when you look out in the vast vacuum of space? Would you have a metric for that?"

"I-I don't know what answer you want from me..."

El Guapo pinned her down with his yellow-green eyes, and she felt herself falling in. "Can you measure the wisdom of God?"

Peridot looked at him for a long while, before glancing down back at her feet. "No. I uhm, don't think there would be much to measure there."

He handed her the rose, its pungent scent wafting up to her. "No, perhaps there would not."

Jane stumbled into a tavern on uneven feet. Her two helpers were gone, but she had gotten the hang of the hooves, though it was still slow going. *Gopher, how did Bill manage this.* Looking around, she saw she was back in The Goose's Garter, though it was different from the one that had been in the Misty Burrow; the bartender, rather than being Oberon, was the Horned One with its deer antlers and black cowl, while along the back wall was a stage where a woman danced to some strange music Jane didn't recognize, filled with long guitar riffs. The dancing woman had the same face as the May Woman and Jane, though hers was browned by the sun, as if in summer, long red hair touching her knees. She wore a simple pale pink dress that clung to her body, a projector reflecting an image on her torso. The image reflected was that of an atomic bomb detonating. The Summer Woman's green eyes were dead as the bomb went off, the fire consumed, and then everything reset to as it was before.

Jane made her way over to the bar. The May Woman was there, but she was dead, head resting on the bar-top, swollen blue tongue sticking out. The Horned One poured Jane a shot of whiskey without even asking. Jane downed it. The Horned One poured another. As Jane was sipping this second drink, she spotted another being in the corner, this one hidden in shadow; as much as she tried to peer into that darkness though, Jane couldn't quite perceive it. Eventually she just gave up. "Well, most things do come in threes I suppose," she said, before finishing the shot.

The Horned One was filling her third glass, when the door to the tavern opened. Jane looked up.

In walked a giant cat, the same cat Jane had seen earlier, though this one seemed different than the rest. Taller, more regal. He was wearing a sort of a biker getup—red bandanna around his head, leather vest with various patches (Jane couldn't help but notice mostly of fish), and black leather pants. He sat down at the bar next to Jane, looking at the Horned One. "Cream soda," he said, "heavy on the cream, light on the soda."

The Horned One looked over at Jane, exuding an air of confusion. Jane just shrugged, nodding her head; the Horned One pulled out a soda shop glass and got to work. "So," Jane said, running her finger along the rim of her drink, "what fresh new hell are you?"

"Well, aren't we a ray of positivity and sunshine? You know, with that attitude, no wonder you're already running into trouble." The Horned One delivered his drink.

"Whatever."

"Not even the will to fight back? You *are* in rough shape."

Jane looked over at the Summer Woman. There was the shock wave, the boom, followed by the angry bloom of smoke that mushroomed into the sky, base flickering red. Then everything reset, and the cloud was gone, the scene at peace, but only for a short while. Shock. Boom. Fire. Reset. Shock. Boom. Fire. Reset. Shock. Boom. Fire...

"Fighting back only gets you in trouble. Besides, I should be dead."

"But you aren't."

"I should've died when that meteor hit. I should've died when my village was attacked. I should've died when..." *when the blood sank into the snow,* "but somehow, I keep on living while everyone else around me gets shred to pieces. Like some cursed cockroach."

"Cockroaches are pretty darn tough. People look down on them, but I think they're admirable creatures. But that is neither here nor there. The real question is, have you *really* been living Jane? Or have you merely been surviving?"

Jane scoffed, but in the back of her mind she saw Warg's face, heard the words he said. *You were one of us. You were powerful. You were free...* "I don't know, I would say that to the dead 'living' and 'surviving' pretty much mean the same thing."

"You've a dead man with you, and I think he would disagree."

"Then he's an idiot, because living is surviving, and surviving is living, and you sometimes get a choice, and you sometimes don't. What was I supposed to do? Runaway back to the Forest? It wasn't easy living out there, especially as a lone girl. Was I supposed to fight against the system that fostered me? I tried and that just made things worse. Once I started playing along, things got better. So yeah, it wasn't perfect, but I was doing just fine."

"And are you okay with that? Doing 'just fine'?"

"Of course! I mean...I guess. It's better than the alternative. That's part of being an adult, right? A child gets everything it wants, an adult understands that there are compromises."

"I'm not talking about compromise. Because you're right, we all have to navigate the world. But when we know our true selves, our true path, then that way is clear. It's when we lose sight of who we are that we start going from navigating through the world, to sacrificing a part of ourselves to fit in with it. I fear that is what has happened to you. You've become so used to doing what is necessary, you've forgotten what you even want."

"And what do you think? That I want to go back to that old life?" El Guapo didn't respond; Jane huffed ruefully. "You know, I spent so much time pissed at the Light Elves, at the Misty Burrow, for having killed my people and Re-Burrowed me. I mean, I looked down on them all the time. That they were so vain, that they believed in such a stupid God, that not one of them would last a night out in the Forest because they couldn't even light a match between the three of them. But you know what? *My own people* didn't want me. My fate would've been way worse out in that Forest if they hadn't taken me in. But I always romanticized it, every time I didn't feel like I belonged—oh the woods, the animals and the trees! So beautiful! So natural! Forget about the mosquitoes, the blood, and the shit." Jane turned the drink in her hand. "It was a hard, short, and brutal life. Life in the Burrow was at least, I guess, safe?"

El Guapo didn't say anything in reply.

Jane spun the amber in her glass. "For years, I suppressed...that. What you want from me..."

"I want nothing from you."

Jane glared at him from the side of her eyes. "You say that, but I know what you're dancing around. You would have me become a beast."

"I would have you be *free*."

"So what? So I can leave a trail of destruction behind me wherever I go? Become the eye of the hurricane, watching everything fall apart around me?"

El Guapo swirled his cream soda, and an image appeared in its depths. It was the Forest, ancient and old, thick with branches and undercover. "This is a Forest. It is an ancient Forest with limbs so heavy no light can come down through it. With branches so tangled on the ground no new life can break through. What do you do with a Forest like this? That has become so stagnant that its progeny can no longer flourish?"

"You burn it." Shock. Boom. Fire. Reset.

"Exactly," the image of the Forest turned to one engulfed in flames, "either local peoples do controlled burns, as your people did, or Mother Nature lights the spark. Either way there the is inevitable loss of life, of homes for the animals," Jane watched as a deer bounded from the inferno, its backside singed. "There is suffering. But suffering is something that we cannot prevent."

"Why not?" Jane asked, entranced by the image.

"Because that is how this universe is set up. There's no getting around that. Adversity is in the very thread of the story. The very act of breathing causes harm to something else. All struggle to live. All die in the end anyway."

She tore her gaze away. "The Universe is a fucked-up place then."

"The Universe is a complicated place, ran by a vain and fickle God. When the Forest burns, yes there is suffering, yes there is pain, but in the end," the image of the glass shifted. The Forest was now fully burned to the ground, the only thing remaining of the ancient trees blackened sticks, but beneath those trees though Jane could see a new flourishing of life. They were the small things of the Forest—groundberries, larkspur, and saplings. The heat from the flames had cracked their seeds. The ash from the ancient grove had fertilized their cradle. The sun and the rain could now reach their soft beds. It was ready to begin anew.

"So, you're saying I'm the fire then?"

"I am saying, destruction isn't always bad. That sometimes it's just the other side of creation."

"Yeah, well, easy to say when you aren't the deer gettin' your ass burnt."

El Guapo sighed as he walked over to the creek that ran through the gilded woods. He was dressed in his favorite fishing vest and hat, bedecked with tiny, wrapped fly lures like jewels vested in a crown. In his favorite fishing spot was the lawn chair that was his throne, by its side the pole that served as scepter and cross. Bunny was on a rock next to this alter, chewing on lettuce.

El Guapo sat in the chair, casting a line. "I have some serious concerns about this iteration of the Disruptor," he said.

Bunny nodded, continuing to chew.

"I had hopes, after so long, that perhaps there would have been a buildup to gift us with a strong one. But boy, she's a mess. Stuck in typical casual thinking." He sighed. "The Fates are gonna chew her to pieces."

Bunny swallowed.

"Until she gets over her own sense of self and starts seeing where her true power lies, she won't get anywhere. But I don't see her doing that anytime soon unless there's an event that forces her to think things through."

Bunny burped.

El Guapo watched the red and white bobbin float. "I think we need to add a diversion to the stream."

Tam Lin walked out of the forest into a field of wildflowers; there were cowslips, poppies, and iris; columbine, larkspur, and sage. A profusion of color under a robin's egg blue sky. A wind stirred the field, creating a ripple of hues—orange, purple, pink, and yellow in wafting undulation. In the center of the field was a table covered in white lace, set with tea and pastries.

Tam Lin went over to that table and sat down. There were croissants, muffins, and cupcakes, all on mismatched plates painted with sweet peas and delphinium. Steam rose from the nose of a teapot that was wrapped in a knit rainbow trout cozy—the cozy looked handmade. The thumbprint cookies seemed particularly appealing to Tam Lin, but remembering his experience back in Yugenia, decided to leave them for someone else. He rubbed the surface of the stone that El Guapo had given him, trying to pull out some forgotten memory.

It wasn't long before he saw Jane emerge from the forest. She was now walking on her hoofed feet, picking her way through the grass. Tam Lin got up to help, but Jane waved at him to sit back down. She made her way to the table, sitting in a chair with a sigh of relief. "Thank *the Gopher*. Oh, treats!" she exclaimed, grabbing a scone to pile it with the clotted cream. She added some raspberry jam.

Tam Lin watched enviously as she ate. "So, did you also have a conversation with a giant cat?"

Jane nodded, mouth full. "Pretty much told me we're all fucked," she shrugged, "which I could've figured that before. You?"

"Pretty much the same." He tossed the stone up in the air, catching it.

Jane watched with interest, wiping crumbs from her mouth. "Where did you get that?"

"It's a gift from that Guapo creature I think."

"Kinda a weird gift. Does it mean anything?"

"Don't know. Maybe? Probably." He played with the stone for a little while. "I think...I think I need to apologize for earlier. I think

I've been pushing forward without thinking, and you're right, the situation is fucked. I shouldn't have tried to push so hard I guess."

Jane was quiet for a moment, poking at a cupcake top with a teaspoon. "You were just trying to get us someplace safe. Sometimes I think, I get lost and lose focus. I think I get a little overwhelmed and lose track of what's most important."

"Well, to be fair to yourself, there's been a lot going on."

"Yeah, having your home blown up and being told you are the cause of the end of the world *is* a lot." She looked out at the field of flowers. "But just because things are rough doesn't mean I should be an asshole to the people around me. So thank you, for helping me, even if you don't know why."

"I'm sure we'll figure things out."

"Maybe," Jane looked at him with a wry smile, "don't have much for an alternative other than to try, do we?"

There was a gentle breeze, carrying with it the scent of primrose and lavender; it teased at her pale hair, blowing it across her face. Jane pulled at the strand with a single slender hand, and before either of them knew what happened, they kissed. Tam Lin could feel her warmth through the contact, could even taste the lemon scone still on her lips. The thickness of the clotted cream. The sweet tartness of the raspberry jam. The earthy crunch of the poppy seed bits. He pressed her closer, wanting more of that warmth, wanting more of that heady sensation, but then just as suddenly the feeling stopped, and Tam Lin went back to feeling nothing.

When Tam Lin looked down, Jane wasn't breathing.

"Jane," Tam Lin said, shaking her. She was limp. A rag doll with blue skin. "Shit. Jane?!"

"*What the heck do you think you're doing!*" a voice yelled.

Tam Lin looked up, still holding Jane, Peridot heading their direction through the field, wearing some ridiculous outfit, wildflowers tangling themselves around the hem of her dress so that she had to pull herself free to move forward. Despite this, she looked furious.

"I just, uhm, I just..."

"Yeah, you kissed her! I saw it! You two weirdos kissed each other," Peridot all but fell over to the table, fascinator askew. "You can't touch her, you idiot, you're *dead*."

"Huh?"

Peridot snagged Jane's body from Tam Lin, glaring at him. "You're dead, you dumbass! Things taste like ash. You need no rest. *You suck the life from all things that you touch*."

Tam Lin looked down at his hands as realization dawned. "Oh shit..."

"Yeah, 'oh shit'," Peridot snapped, "now she's dead and the only way we can revive her is to get her soul back from *Her*." Tam Lin winced. "Good job great protector. You just delivered Jane to the worst person she could come across. You just sent her to *Leviathan*."

"Okay, okay, okay," Tam Lin said, pressing a hand to his brow. "I know this bad, but we can do this. I can fix this. We grab Bunny, hunt down Leviathan, and get Jane back."

Peridot laughed. "You're sure as heck confident, aren't you? You think Leviathan is gonna let you steal something from her *again*?"

Tam Lin didn't have an answer to that.

"Hmm, Leviathan, that's a fish even *I* would be loath to catch."

Peridot and Tam Lin turned to see El Guapo heading their direction through the field, wearing his crown of flies, string of fish in hand. The flowers seemed to give way before him, bowing their petaled heads. "We need Bunny," Peridot said, "we have to reunite Jane's soul with her body before it's too late."

"Bunny's journey has ended," El Guapo said. "He has traveled as far as he needs and will live here with me now. But no worries. I can get you where you need to go." He tossed Peridot a rainbow trout, which she caught, looking down at it in mild disgust. The fish began to vibrate with an uncertain energy.

"But how are we going to get to the Fates without Bunny?" Tam Lin protested.

The trout opened its mouth, a loud hum coming from it; Tam Lin and Peridot's hair began to stand on end as they were encased in a field of glimmering silver energy. El Guapo smiled. "Don't stress, I'll send some help your way," and then in a pop like when your ears adjust to pressure, they were gone; so was El Guapo's smile. "You're gonna need it."

The Water Mother

Jane floated in space. She didn't know where she was, or how she had gotten there; she dredged through the depths of her mind, trying to remember, but her memories were like rivulets of water seeping through sand—elusive and fleeting.

There had been that weird cat, and she had had hooves for feet, her calves still ached from that awkward gate, and then she had kissed Tam Lin...Jane's face went red. Why had she done *that*?! She barely even knew the man.

Jane looked down at pale hands, luminescent against the enigmatic darkness. *That's right. The Misty Burrow is gone. Hit by a meteor. Collapsed. And yet somehow, I lived.* She looked back up. Or had she? Considering where she was, this seemed very like she was dead. Had the rest perhaps been some sort of fever dream? Some chemical process in her dying brain interpreting random signals in a way that made some, even if very poor, sense? It seemed more plausible than it all being real.

A myriad of stars floated before her, reminiscent of a bioluminescent sea, or perhaps more like the rarely visible but always present primordial cells that were the beginnings of life; the universe didn't need them to exist but was yet all the more beautiful for them being there. Decorative beads giving glory to the Tapestry of the Universe. Providing Illumination to the Tale. Jewels in the crown of God.

Jane wrinkled her nose, wondering where such strange thoughts had come from, when she heard the song.

The dirge droned, reverberating in Jane's ears. It was that same terrible melody she had heard back in the Misty Burrow, when all this hell had begun; it was the sound of the ocean, the beating of a heart, the sublime mellifluousness of the very fabric of space, that if one wasn't attuned to, could be missed altogether. The song grew louder as Jane drifted, pulling her to it, seeming to wrap around her limbs in strands of scarlet ribbon.

Others followed that same hymnal lure—beings that gave off a sort of light; some of them glowed blue, some pink, and together they created a humming opal hue. There were men and women, the young and the old; there were people, animals, and plants; there were even those that had no form at all, but were simply a memory. A memory of a feeling. A memory of a hope. Some seemed to notice her, others were entirely entranced by the song. They all, however, moved to converge on this one point. On this one wordless psalm.

It was then Jane saw the Whale. It undulated in the depthless morass of space, it's skin craggy gray, mottled with white. The detritus of the universe was embedded in its hide, like cosmic barnacles—spaceships and moons, statues of old gods and abandoned temples, with gold chains wrapped around its slick membrane, digging in deep. The weight of all this seemed to burden the creature. The weight of a universe of forgotten things. The Whale opened an eye, and Jane could see the reddish-brown iris trimmed in sea blue, the rim of that eye like ring of the sun as it is eclipsed by the moon.

That eye reminded Jane of the first time she had seen the ocean. It's wideness. It's great depths. It had been beautiful, but her comprehension of it, even then she knew, had been shallow at best; for a part of her knew that if she had wholly understood the wildness of those waters, the full meaning of the magnitude of it, that it would have made her dizzy with its strength. Would have knocked her right off her feet.

The Whale was encompassed by the flickering lights; it scooped them up in its creaking maw, feeding on the transcendent krill. Jane then knew where she was. "Leviathan," she gasped. "So it's true. I didn't make it, I'm..."

The dirge pitched high, and Jane clasped her ears, feeling as though her head might explode from the pain of it, and then suddenly the Whale was no longer in the distance. Jane turned to see Leviathan upon her, sweet song pulling her under like a quick tide. Jane only had time to hold up her arms before she was swallowed whole.

Water overtook her, swirling in a maelstrom, the other lights there with her spun about. She felt the waters seep into her mind, pulling at her memories with their ebb and flow; Jane fought against this invasion of her thoughts, repelling it. When she glanced over to the side she could see the other lights, their glow, their being, starting to grow dim, leeched away by the waves. Thoughts formed in their mouths in the shape of jewels, dropping into the waters—pearls, rubies, emeralds, sapphires—a multitude of precious stones, now glistening underfoot. *Is this what happened to Tam Lin?* she wondered.

The waves spat them onto an island shore; a dark, spongy surface, the living membrane of the Whale. Jane remained on the ground for a moment, looking around cautiously, for they were in the maw of the mammoth, its jaw stretching high above their heads in a cathedral ceiling. Everything inside the Whale, rather than being reinforced by bone was reinforced by wood, reminding Jane of the hull of a ship, with mottled purple-gray flesh casting all in gloom. Where there wasn't meat and bone, there was water, shifting restlessly, whispering at something Jane couldn't quite make out.

Beings in brown cloaks came up to the island in small wooden boats; they bore nets over their shoulders, heavy with stones, faces impenetrable under the shadows of their hoods. These brown-cloaked creatures lined up the now dull star-beings, who didn't bother to fight or protest, gray husks of their former selves.

When the Brown Cloaks came to Jane, they swarmed around her, chattering in agitated disapproval. Jane looked at her still glowing arms, then over at her now non-glowing companions; obviously, she had missed a step. "Well shit," she said, before ghostly hands lugged her to her feet, clasping tightly on either side. Jane, the Brown Cloaks, and the dead were all led to the edge of the fleshy island, where the small fleet of wooden dinghies awaited.

Jane was pushed onto one of those dinghies without word of explanation. The Brown Cloaks lit a series of lamps, pushing off to float further into the aquatic juggernaut. Jane looked up at the Brown Cloaks that held her, peering into the faceless hoods to see if there was anything there she could recognize, but she found only darkness. She looked down into the waters, seemingly alive with the memories of the dead; she could see flashes of a child on a swing, the death of a parent, a first kiss—like watching a movie, and for a moment Jane felt embarrassed, felt exposed to something intimate and private.

One of the memories bubbled up, as if irritated, coalescing into the form of a diamond, flashing clear blue. A Brown Cloak snatched the treasure up greedily, scurrying it away with the rest of its horde, the other Brown Cloaks watching with a seeming air of envy. Jane did her best to make herself small.

They started down a long, dark corridor. Jane began to hear the beating of a drum; a rhythmic, primitive sound, unlike the tempo of the wailing song, that seemed to have a rageful purpose of direction. It was the primal dance of man. It was a cardiac pulse that couldn't be ignored. The beat grew louder as they went further in, filling Jane with dread. The narrow corridor opened up to a giant hall that was the belly of the colossus, the rising crescendo turning to a roar that throbbed in her ears and made her skull pound.

The hall stretched so far back Jane was unable to see an end to it. The wooden bones of the Whale were more ornate here, carved with images of the sea and inlaid with coral and gold, ensconced torches giving off a sputtering light. Water filled the hall, and in that water were a column of benches. The benches lined either side of that great room, made of the same wood as the bones, with oars attached to each seat. The benches were occupied by the gray dead, bound in golden chains, rowing to the rhythm of the drum; they didn't look up, they didn't pause, they simply kept pressing oar to water as if steering the beast—row upon row of endless dead, all bent to the task. Jane watched as the boats pulled over to the side of some empty benches, the Brown Cloaks chaining the newly dead to their place and shoving them along. The dead meekly sat down and obeyed, picking up the oars to move to the beat.

Jane alone was taken to the throne at the center. The throne that sat atop a pile of driftwood and carved bone, adorned with bits of broken seashell and petrified wood, the seat itself made of sunrise-red coral entwined with gold chain. The throne where Leviathan sat.

She was so beautiful that, for a moment, Jane thought was she was looking on a statue. Her long, strong limbs were the color of smoothed bronze, and her hair was burnished gold, intertwined with bits of dried seaweed and wrapped around her head in intricate braids. Her face was comely, but hard, as if carved, and her eyes were the color of lapis. She wore silks of turquoise and aquamarine that rustled restlessly around her like waves, adorned in pearl and copper. Her nails were long, encrusted with barnacles.

It wasn't until Leviathan blinked that Jane realized the being before her lived; those basilisk eyes narrowed at her. "What do we have here?" Leviathan asked, voice a gathering storm on the horizon. "A lost soul that defies me?"

Jane shrunk down into herself, wanting nothing more than to disappear. "I...I don't know that I did anything wrong. I just wanted to hold onto my memories."

Leviathan rose from her seat, and Jane got the sense that it had been a long time since the Queen of the Dead had moved, bits of shell and dust falling from her. Leviathan stretched out one long arm, dipping her hand into the waters that lapped at her bare feet. She raised the liquid up to her lips, taking a drink. "A Defiler, I see. The Sea Witch has sent you to overthrow me."

"Awh...Oh for fuck's sake no, not another title. I just wanted to keep my memories, is that so strange? Why do you have to turn it into something more than it is?"

Leviathan raised an eyebrow, and Jane clamped her mouth shut; she also got the sense that not many people spoke to her in such a manner. "I have seen your kind before. You are not the first. Defiler of my Will. Disruption of the Order. They all sought to overthrow me and begin the world anew. And they all fell to the inevitable wearing of my waves. For even rock will crumble under water if given time."

"But I don't *want* to disrupt anything! I just want to live peacefully, like anyone else!"

Leviathan laughed, and it was a cold, hollow sound that chilled. "I see. You will break easily enough False Priestess of the Moon," she turned her glittering eyes to the Brown Cloaks. "Take her away to the cells. *This* servant of the Sea Witch, it seems at least, won't be giving us too much trouble," Leviathan sneered down at Jane. "From the sound of it, she's already defeated herself."

Jane didn't appreciate being talked to like that, especially by someone she didn't even know, but didn't have time to protest, as the Brown Cloaks shoved off from the throne, floating away from the hall Leviathan, in her mighty seat, vanishing from sight. They went down a narrow side-corridor where Jane could still hear the beat of the drums, though not as intensely, the quiet a sort of temporary reprieve. Here, there were a series of cages lined along the murky corridor walls, partially submerged in the waters, bars encrusted with rust. Most of the cells were empty, some contained faded shades such as the ones that manned the oars, while others yet were mad, muttering to themselves as they looked down at their feet.

They came to a woman, hair wild, cloth torn at her knees. She picked at the riverbed rocks, holding them up to peer at them, as though they were pictures of a dear forgotten friend. "Toss this one aside, they have," she muttered to herself, "such a shame such a shame," she picked up another, "oh, and this one of a child! How terrible! Such a tragedy!"

A little way further down, there was a man, undulating and shifting in his cell. His eyes were rolled into the back of his head and his mouth moved aimlessly, as if lost looking for words he could no longer voice; Jane cast her eyes down, for the manner of the movement seemed almost lewd. When she looked back up though, she saw the man was missing his limbs, his arms and legs just four small stumps, ending in ugly knobs that flailed in the air. Jane looked away again, the sight making her sad and sick at the same time.

Jane was shoved into one of those cages, alone, the door locked behind her with a click.

As her captors drifted away, Jane stood there, ankle deep in the water. She could feel it, like minnows nipping at her toes, the pull of the water on her mind. She did her best to ignore it for the time being, though like Leviathan said, she was unsure how long she could withstand it. "You keep getting yourself stuck in these circumstances, don't you?" she muttered to herself.

"Hey look!" a voice said, "a new person!" Jane froze, startled.

"Well," said another, "that is a little unusual. You don't get too many new people around here. Do you think she's friendly?"

"Of course she's friendly! Just look at her!"

"You can't tell whether a person is friendly or not based on how they *look*," a third voice said, "you big fathead."

"Sure you can! I mean, *look at her*! I bet she gives amazing head scratches! Do you think she'll pat my butt?" Jane broke out into a cold sweat. What sort of place was this?

"Lily petal swoons

Pale pink waters reflect

Beautiful lost souls"

This was a fourth voice, and by now Jane was sure the madness had already set in. "Hey, I'm gonna go up to her and say hi," the first voice said. "See if she's really friendly or not."

"Okay, but if she snaps your neck and drains the marrow from your bones you can't say I didn't warn you...you big *fathead*."

Jane reluctantly turned to peer into the darkness of the cell next to her. There was an odd glob in the corner of that enclosure that she couldn't quite make out in the dim guttural light of the torches. Part of that glob detached itself, making its way over to where Jane stood. *It's gonna be hell demons. Big fat hairy hell demons with tentacles and claws!* Jane stepped back, staggering away to the far end of her cell, clasping the bars to prepare herself for whatever eldritch horror was about to be revealed.

That horror, it turned out, was a Siamese cat.

The cat was sleek and muscular, with a dusty white coat and dark brown face, reminding her of a lightly baked chocolate scone.

The eyes of the cat were sky blue and slightly crossed. "Hi," the cat said, perfectly understandable, "I'm Antoine. I'm a handsome boy. Please pet me. Are you friendly?"

Jane stood there at a loss for words, looking from side to side. "P-pardon?"

"You don't just ask people to pet you the moment you meet them!" that third voice yelled. "You have to hide and act aloof. Make them *work for it*!"

Antoine started rubbing his head against the cage bars. "This is my cage," he said to Jane, "and that is my sister, Scarlet. She's a big fathead."

"*Don't you call me that! You're* the fathead, not *me*!"

Jane relaxed, ever so slightly. They didn't *seem* like hell demons, but then, you never knew with cats. "Why don't you all come into the light where I can see you?" she said. "Then we can talk. I'm not going to hurt you as long as you promise not to hurt me. I get the feeling we're both prisoners here."

"We aren't *prisoners*," Antoine said, aghast. "We're willing guests. Totally in control of the situation. We're just *allowing* ourselves to be kept here until we can...we can..."

"Find a way out?" the second voice suggested unhelpfully.

Antoine's tail drooped a little. "Yes," he said sadly, "until we can find a way out."

Jane had heard in tales from her home world of the hero's quest and how one often had to help a series of magical animals along the way to achieve their goal. Granted, there were usually three animals, not four. And if there was a cat, usually it was just one cat among a small menagerie. If there were three of the same animal, it was usually chickens or something like that. Still, Jane supposed these odd creatures could be of help to her; at the very least they could distract her from the nipping at her feet.

The other cats muttered among themselves, arguing while Antoine put his head through the bars, Jane giving him a gentle scratch. At some point the other three cats pushed and shoved their way into the light, revealing themselves. There was a pretty calico with a white bib and vivid green eyes; she glared suspiciously at Jane and swiped at Antoine. There was a little tabby, almost half the size of the others, with medium length fur and peppery gray eyes. Finally, there was a big, fat, fluffy black cat; his whiskers were long, and he kept his eyes slightly closed in narrow slits.

"We're the GCATS," Antoine said, puffing his chest out. "You may have heard of us, genetic hackers and rebels of the Universe."

"I'm sorry, but I can't say that I have. Why do you call yourself the GCATS?"

Antoine's chest deflated. "She's never heard of us." The little tabby came over, rubbing against Antoine to comfort him.

"Probably comes from some provincial backwater timeline where they don't understand science," the calico said, licking her claws.

"GCAT are the chemicals that build DNA, and DNA are the blocks that build life," Antoine explained. "All living things are made out of DNA and therefore the GCAT chemicals."

"Well, there are a *few* exceptions," the calico said.

"Yes, this is true," Antoine agreed, "but those things are scary and we don't want to talk about them. Anyways *99.9%* of all living beings are made of DNA—the chemical codes that dictates how your body is built."

Jane attempted to process this. "And you can manipulate that?"

"Yes," Antoine said, "we can turn a duck into a fish..."

"Yummy!" the little tabby cried.

"...a flower into a tree," Antoine continued, "and just about everything in-between."

"Oh! So you're wizards then!"

The GCATS laughed. "*Wizards* you say?" Antoine scoffed. "You're right Scarlet, this poor creature *must* be from some uneducated slum."

"I told you."

"No, no, no, we are not *wizards*. Wizards use *magic*, which is a silly superstition of unsophisticated fools. We're *scientists*. We got shit figured out."

"Yeah!" the tabby chimed in. "We use math and empiricism to mess with things! Though...sometimes the math does get a little sketch."

"I see," Jane said, hiding her annoyance at being called an uneducated fool. "Well, what got you all here?"

"Well," Antoine said, "we had cracked spacetime travel and were going between timelines studying the various life forms and their changes."

"Well, technically the cracking of spacetime travel is what helped us to unlock the DNA code," the tabby said.

"Yes, true," Antoine agreed, "well anyways, we were happily going through spacetime conducting experiments in the name of science, not realizing that *somebody* felt they had a monopoly on inter-dimensional travel!

"Leviathan captured us, claiming we were breaking the natural order by traveling through spacetime and changing the genetic structure of living beings. Said we had achieved the power of gods and that mortals such as us needed to be caged away before we did permanent harm."

The calico scoffed. "Mortals. *Us.*"

"So she trapped us here, and took our vessel, *The Illumine*," Antoine finished.

"I do hope Marigold is okay," the little tabby said.

"Whose Marigold?" Jane asked.

"She's our friend, and she lives on *The Illumine*. She got left there when Leviathan caught us."

"I see," Jane said, "so I think we're here for similar reasons. My name is Jane. I've learned Antoine's, how about the rest of you?"

Antoine answered. "That's Toramaru, he only speaks in haiku, and is our physicist" the black cat nodded his head, "that's Cricket, she's super nice, and is our engineer" the gray kitten let out a trill, "and *that*-that's Scarlet, she's our doctor and *she's a big fathead.*"

Scarlet's ears pinned back as she hissed, "no *you're* the big fathead Antoine!"

"My head is small and narrow, aerodynamic, so my brain can move fast. Your head is big and round, so it gets overheated, and you become a stupid jerk. Hence why you are the fathead and not me!" Scarlet hissed again, which led to a slapping fight between the two.

Jane had to hide a smile behind her hand. "So, how long have you been trapped here?"

The GCATS all looked at one another. Scarlet and Antoine paused their mutual antagonization, "A year? Two maybe?" Antoine said.

"I think it's been more like three."

"Fluid memories

Time. Fish like jewels in the stream

Greedy pools swallows"

"I see,' Jane said, "and how have you survived the pull of this, ugh, water for so long?"

"Oh, the Primordial Memory Fluid?" Antoine said. "We've been taking turns standing on each other's shoulders, like this!" With that Antoine stood at the bottom, while Toramaru, Cricket, and Scarlet climbed on top of each other, creating a sort of cat tower. Scarlet sat at the top. "See? This way we aren't constantly bugged by it. I'm the pilot anyways, so I'm not too bothered by PMF."

"Yeah, and because you're a *fathead*," Scarlet huffed. Antoine performed a strategic sit, all of the cats ending up in the water, Scarlet included.

This time Jane couldn't hide her laughter. "Well, I'm afraid I don't have your same advantage," she said, "so I guess I'll just have to hang onto my sanity another way."

Antoine reached a single chocolate cream paw through the cell bars, placing it on her knee; his claws naturally dug in, but he didn't mean anything by it, the pain grounding her slightly. "No worries Jane," Antoine said, "you have the GCATS here, and we'll keep you sane."

Peridot and Tam Lin stumbled onto the back of the Whale of Leviathan. They appeared with little fanfare; they were simply one minute in the gardens of El Guapo, and the next a foot or two above the craggy back of the whale, dropping ungracefully between the bits of junk and lost dreams embedded in the granite skin. Tam Lin glanced up at the sea of stars, nebulae and suns in the distance; it would have been lovely if not for their predicament. The trout El Guapo had given Peridot disappeared, turning to starlight. She wiped her hand on her skirt. "A one-way ticket huh?" she said, looking at their surroundings. "Well, how the heck are we supposed to figure a way out of here without Bunny?"

Tam Lin put his rock in his pocket. "We worry about that later. Our first goal is to find Jane."

"One thing at a time, right, speaking of which..." Peridot looked around, spying a pale lump of flesh lying next to a statue of Diana. "Ah there she is!" Peridot went over to Jane's corpse. She frowned. "Huh, even dead she changes."

Tam Lin walked up, looking over Peridot's shoulder. Jane lay there, dead as she was before, but now instead of goat legs she had a fish tail—it was a gray, sparkling tail, reminding Tam Lin of salmon under ice. "A mermaid?"

"I guess. I suppose it doesn't matter at this point."

"You carry her. We need to find a way into this place."

Peridot made a face as Tam Lin left to go find an entrance. "Oh, *now* you're going to be careful about touching her. When she's already *dead*." When Tam Lin didn't bother to reply, Peridot sighed, getting to work humping Jane up onto her back. "I don't even like fish. They *stink.*"

The pair walked across the Whale's uneven hide, pockmarked with meteorites and stars, overgrown with cosmic dust and solar moss. The skin was thick like the crust of the earth, and just as hard. Tam Lin sighed, weighing his options. "The blow hole," he said finally.

"Awww *heck* no."

"I don't see any other choice. The mouth is watched by the No Bodies. The blowhole...we can get in undetected that way. I mean, we could try you know, the private parts," he peered off in the distance, down the Whale's tail, "but I get the feeling we're at least a day's walk from that."

Peridot turned a little pale. "Guess the blowhole doesn't sound like such a bad idea after all." She pointed. "It should be further towards the head. It won't take us long to get there. Let's get moving." They started their way towards the head of the Whale, picking their way through the bumps and shards.

"You don't have to come if you don't want," Tam Lin said as they walked. "I mean, I kinda don't know why you're even here. You don't have any skin in this game. I would've already ran to the hills at this point if I were you."

"Well, currently I'm kinda stuck, unless you can see any 'hills' out here that I can run to." Tam Lin had nothing to say to that. "Besides, give up a chance to help the Disruptor? Nah. Wouldn't miss that."

"Wouldn't miss a chance to help end the world? Sounds kinda fucked up if you ask me."

"It's not ends so much I like, as beginnings. When everything is fresh and has so much promise. Before it becomes corrupted." Peridot was quiet for a moment, just the crunch of space barnacles under their feet. "You're going to see the Fates right? Which means you intend to see the Sea Witch."

"Yeah, from what I gather that's the only way we'll be able to get an answer on how to help Jane. If we can." He looked back at her. "What? Is that the reason you're coming with us? To see God?"

"I told you I was Conservator's apprentice, right?"

"Don't think I was there for that conversation."

"Ah, well I was. Apprentice to a beautiful world called Gardenalia. The most perfect, lush place you've ever seen. Roses, so red, the colors just about shook. Lilacs so fragrant you saw the meaning of life in their scent. Nothing ever wilted, nothing ever died. Everything was plentiful, glorious."

"What happened?"

Peridot shrugged. "It fell apart. As things do, I suppose. I told Jane it was due to a nearby Filament collapse, but really, Gardenalia had been rotting from the inside for a while. It was just a matter of time before it dropped. It was terrible watching the decay though. Watching the fruit grow poisonous. Watching things suffer. It just all turned to rot."

"So what? You wanna ask the Sea Witch to restore your world? Or get revenge on God?"

"I guess..." Peridot looked out at the stars, the souls drifting so lonely. "I guess I just want an answer as to why. Why does it have to be this way? Why does it have to hurt so much? Do you suppose there is an answer to a question like that?"

Tam Lin shrugged, and they walked on.

They came to a ridge of stone-colored flesh lining the two massive caverns that were the blowhole of the Whale. Peridot and Tam Lin looked down into the murk, a dank stench wafting up, tinged with the acrid tang of fire smoke. Peridot looked ill. Tam Lin sighed. "Okay, let's get this over with. I probably don't need to tell you but be careful of the water. *Don't* let Leviathan catch you."

"Don't need to say that twice. Ugh, oh god, it reeks so much." Peridot plugged her nose, and with that the two descended into the gloom.

The membrane of the blowhole was slick, but there was enough coarseness to gain a grip to ease their decent. Peridot had a harder time than Tam Lin, with the weight of Jane, and a time or two Tam Lin had to grab the apprentice by the back of her shirt to make sure she didn't fall. The blowhole led to a flat drop that was thankfully clear of the memory sapping waters, and from there they were able to slink along a side nasal passage that led down to the main thoroughfare.

For a moment Tam Lin and Peridot sat watching from their hidden spot above as the boats passed below, filled with their brown-cloaked shepherds herding the sheep-like dead. Peridot spotted a soft light down the corridor. Pulling at Tam Lin's sleeve she pointed; he followed her gaze to see the faint moonbeam. "She managed to keep a hold of herself," Tam Lin said, the relief visible on his face. "Though she's under the watch of the No Bodies."

"As expected of the Disruptor. Leviathan sure won't like that."

"We gotta follow."

Tam Lin spied a boat lagging behind, out of sight of the others. He waited until it was under them and then jumped. The No Body turned. Seeing him, it clasped a horn, readying to bring it to its empty face, but before the cloaked creature could sound the alarm, Tam Lin reached in, clasping at whatever substance constituted its being. He felt the No Body's essence pour through him. It's anger. It's hatred. It's sorrow. All the feelings that threatened to turn these placid waves into a roiling churn condensed in one dark shadow.

Tam Lin took all of that into himself and drained the creature away, leaving nothing but a dingy cape and a net of jewels. The dead on the raft looked at Tam Lin with dull eyes before going back to watching the flickering pool. Peridot dropped down, landing with a clunk, Jane on her back. "I'm gonna twist an ankle doing this," she grumbled, "I can't believe you just did that!"

Tam Lin placed the cape on Peridot, hiding her light. Peridot looked awkward and bulky. "I'm your prisoner and you're a No Body," he said. "Follow her."

"This is a terrible idea. If Leviathan notices either me *or* you..."

"She's gonna to be too distracted by Jane. It'll be hiding in plain sight. Now go. If we lose sight of Jane, then we lose sight of the objective."

Peridot reluctantly pushed off, making their way down the corridor. When they came to the main hall, Jane was before Leviathan and for a moment Peridot's breath was taken from her at the sight of the Queen: at her lithe muscles, the fullness of her lips, the arrogant curve of her brow. When she sat, she was so still, and when she moved it was with the deliberate slowness yet inevitable doom of a tidal wave. Tam Lin shook Peridot's oar, pulling her from her reverie. Following the lead of the other No Bodies, Peridot hauled the dead from their boats, locking them to their benches. It tore at her heart to see their little dim faces, without a hint of will between them.

Jane was escorted from the main hall and Peridot moved to follow.

They lost sight of Jane midst the lines of rowers, but from what Leviathan had said Tam Lin knew the general direction they were headed, so Peridot meandered the forgotten prison cells of Leviathan, with few there to discover them. It was a lonely place. For the most part all could be heard was the trickle of the water as they moved.

"Were you ever in one of these cells?" Peridot asked as they drifted past an old man with a long beard that touched the waves.

"I don't know. Most of my memories are gone."

"So then, what made you remember? What made you try to go to find her?"

"I don't really wanna talk about it."

"Come on," Peridot said, "I gave you my reason, only fair play you to tell me." Tam Lin glared at Peridot and she shrugged. "Who am I gonna tell? The waves?"

Tam Lin licked his lips. "I uhm, I don't know how long I'd been here. Could've been a couple days, could've been a couple years, could've been a couple centuries. Guess it doesn't matter all that much in this place. Anyways, I was rowing when I saw...the most beautiful creature swimming under the water. I'd seen a lot of memories, we all did, but this one...this one meant something to me. The way she moved, the light on her skin. Her eyes. I knew I'd

196

once known her. I knew she'd once known me. And I realized at that moment I had to save her. This creature in the water. That she was under some terrible dark fate and I had to see her through it. That I was the only one who could."

"Wait, are you saying Jane is a memory you saw in the water?"

"A part of her at least. Or perhaps it's the other way around...I don't know. But yeah. Jane is someone I knew when I was alive. And I owe her my life for a sin I committed."

"Do you know what this dark fate is? Or this sin?"

"I can't remember."

"I see. And uhm," Peridot rubbed her eye, "have you told Jane this?"

"No. And I'm not sure I really want to," Tam Lin looked over at Peridot. "You aren't going to, are you?"

"No, no, no. I wouldn't do that. Just don't go kissing and killing her again, okay?"

Tam Lin picked at a piece of boat wood, throwing it into the water. "Yeah, that was dumb. I don't know what came over me."

"I would say hormones, but you don't have a corporal form over which hormones would have an influence, so I'm just gonna go with stupidity."

They turned a corner, seeing a light in the distance. That same soft moonglow. "Jane!"

"Yeah, I see her," Peridot rowed faster. "Hopefully the waters haven't gotten to her yet."

As they came to the cage they, oddly enough, heard laughter. For a moment Peridot and Tam Lin thought that there must be somebody else in the corridor, but when they saw no one, they became worried. "That must be Jane," Tam Lin said.

"The waters have already gotten to her and she's laughing mad!"

When they came up to the cell, they saw Jane sitting in the water, soaked to her waist, but seeming not to notice. A group of cats performed a series of tricks in the cage next to her, causing Jane to start laughing all over again. It was an odd sight for the pair, for it was the first time either of them had seen her happy. "Jane!" Tam Lin yelled.

Jane looked over at them, face beaming. "Peridot! Tam Lin! What are you doing here?"

"Jane, are these people part of your colony?" Cricket asked.

"Yes!"

"Wow!" Antoine said. "They seem like they would give good treats and pets."

"We came to rescue you and reunite you with your body," Peridot said. "We're gonna get you outtta here."

Tam Lin kicked the door open, the lock breaking easily under the heel of his foot. "Come on, we gotta go."

Jane looked at Tam Lin, looked at her body on the boat, then looked at the cats. She crossed her arms. "Only if they get to go with us."

Peridot and Tam Lin looked at the cats, then back at Jane. Tam Lin shrugged. "I can live with that. I like cats." He kicked down the cell door to the GCATS.

"Yay!" Cricket cried. "Freedom!"

"Hi strangers. I'm Antoine. I'm a very handsome boy and I like pets."

"Sorry friend," Tam Lin said. "I'm dead and can't pet you without killing you."

"Oh, that's so very unfortunate, for I have lovely fur to pet. You're really missing out. But you also are intriguing as you are a form of sentient psychic energy. Have we ever encountered such a thing before, Scarlet?"

"No...he's an oddity indeed." Scarlet sniffed him, "and he smells like fish."

"Ugh, I'm allergic to cats, but okay, no one bother to ask me," Peridot said. "*My* feelings don't matter."

"Oh! I *like* allergic people! Just as long as you don't sneeze..."

Jane emerged from the cage. "Hey, where's Bunny?"

"Yeah," Peridot said, Tam Lin too fascinated by the cats to answer. "That weirdo took him. Gave us a fish that got us here, but now we're S.O.L. We have no way to leave."

Jane looked at the GCATS, nodding her head. "Well, I think I might've found us a way out, then. How would all you feel about saving Marigold?"

"Save Marigold!?" Cricket exclaimed. "That would make us very happy!"

"Yes, yes, yes," Antoine said, kneading the boat. "There is no way we would want to leave without Marigold or *The Illumine*!!"

"Marigold? *The Illumine*?" Peridot asked, looking back and forth between Jane and the cats.

"Their trans-dimensional ship apparently," Jane said. "I get the feeling Marigold is some sort of being that maintains it."

"A ship capable of trans-dimensional travel? Well, that *is* convenient. Where is this Marigold and *The Illumine* then?" Everyone went silent.

"I know," Tam Lin said, after a moment. "If it's something that Leviathan has kept then I know where to find it."

"And how would you know that?"

Tam Lin held up the Book of the Dead. "It's the same place where she keeps everything else. That trophy room of hers."

Peridot rolled her eyes. "Of course. And do you remember where this mystical junk drawer is?"

"I might need a moment, but I think I can if I try."

It took them a while to shove Jane's spirit back into her body; for whatever reason it seemed as if her soul had gotten just a smidgen larger than the body that was meant to harbor it, so there was a lot of pushing and pulling. Peridot lost her patience, so the GCATS had to help, adding their weight to the effort; all in all, it felt like trying to squeeze a very busty woman into a overly tight brazier. Meanwhile, Tam Lin worked on figuring out from memory where Leviathan's treasure house resided.

Finally, Peridot and the GCATS succeeded, and Jane sat up, back in her corporal form. She looked down at her tail in despair. "Really? *Again*?"

"I mean, at least no hooves?"

Jane glared at Peridot. "You said the same thing about the rabbit ears."

Tam Lin came over to them, a map drawn on the back of one of the cloaks. "Okay, I think I have it figured out. The treasure storage is here," he circled a part of the map with his finger, "and we are here," he circled another part. "So, I think we can reach it via this path. We're going to have to cross some of the main channel again, so we're going to have to hide Jane and the cats. But if we can manage that, we can get to the treasure storage and free your vessel."

"Assuming the vessel is even there, and assuming Leviathan hasn't moved her junk drawer since you last robbed her."

"Yes. We're running on two assumptions: that Leviathan kept the ship as an oddity, and that she's too arrogant to bother moving the vault. She'd rather hunt down and punish me than increase her security. I know those are two large assumptions, but I think we have to hope they're true. I don't see what other option we got."

"Okay then, so how do we cross the main causeway without Jane and the others being seen?"

"I think," and he looked at Jane as he said this, "I think they have to go under."

Jane thought about this for a moment, remembering what the entrance felt like. The pull. The slide. "I think...I think I can do that."

"But what about us?" Scarlet protested. "I can't swim!"

"I'll hold onto you," Jane said, "like you held onto me."

"Ooohhh, that's *so* sweet!"

"Too sweet. I'm gonna hork."

"My fur is gonna get all wet!"

"It'll only be for a short section," Tam Lin said. "We can keep on the boat until then. Okay?"

Scarlet huffed. "Okay...I guess it's for Marigold anyway."

Plan in place everyone got in position. Peridot was once more garbed as a No Body with Tam Lin as her prisoner. Jane hunkered down along the edge of the boat with the GCATS in her arms, ready to slip over the side at Tam Lin's command. Ready, they set out for the treasury of Leviathan, Queen of the Dead.

Everyone grew quiet as they floated down the causeway towards the main hall, even the GCATS saying nothing, ears pricked and eyes dilated. The only sound to be heard was the beating of the drums and the splash of displaced water as Peridot dipped her oar into the body of memories.

They came to the main hall, another No Body floating towards them. Tam Lin looked back at Jane and she nodded. "Okay, hold your breaths," she warned the GCATS, before going over the side of the dinghy.

Under water, Jane clasped the ropes at the bottom of the boat, the GCATS clinging to her, claws digging into her skin. The tide of memories pulled at her, threatening to drain her and drown her in the whirlpool. She caught flashes of the GCATS' memories: a purring kitten suckling on milk, some weird math computation she couldn't understand, a flash of tawny green eyes.

At one point Jane had to break the surface of the water so the GCATS could breathe. Tam Lin looked down sharply at her as she did so, a crowd of Brown Cloaks around them. Jane quickly slipped back under. When she broke for air a second time, the poor creatures half-drowned, they were in another side corridor. "Tam Lin," Jane said, "they can't take anymore. We'll kill them at this rate."

"I think we should be in the clear for now," Tam Lin said. "Come on board." Jane shoved the GCATS onto the raft before hauling herself up. "The treasure store house should just be around this corner. We're almost there."

Jane looked back from where they had come, towards the entrance to the main hall, where she could still see the dead rowing, backs bent towards their infernal labor. "Poor things," she murmured, "to have this be the place for eternal rest. I never thought death would be so cruel."

"Huh, feeling sorry for someone other than yourself for a change?" Peridot said, getting a glare from Tam Lin.

"That's not very nice," Cricket protested. "You're mean!" Peridot stuck her tongue out at the little tabby.

"No, it's all right," Jane said distractedly as she watched a new batch of dead being brought in, chained to another bench, "I have been out of sorts...is that...Elena?" A figure came off from the boat, guided to her new duty. The soft hair, the willowy arms, the pretty face that used to smile so cheerfully—her cherry pink glow turned the color of mud.

"Whose Elena?" Antoine asked. Tam Lin shrugged.

"Elena! I have to save her!" Jane flung herself over the side, back into the waters.

"Jane, no!" Peridot cried. "You can't do anything for her now! Forget it!"

"I can't just leave her here!" Jane protested, swimming back towards the rowers. "You were able to save me, maybe I can do something for her!"

"Jane no, it doesn't work that way!" Peridot sighed in frustration as Jane vanished down the hall. "Dammit!"

Jane went down the corridor to where Elena sat, hiding around the corner as she was chained in. After the No Bodies left, Jane went up to the bench, pulling at Elena's chains. "Elena!" Jane whispered, getting no response. "Elena, I'm here to free you! Elena!" Elena ignored Jane's pleas, long hair hanging like a curtain around her face. "Elena!" Jane yelled, shaking the shade's knees. "Please! At least look at me!"

Elena turned towards Jane, only it wasn't the face of Elena Jane saw, but the bug-eyed woman bespeckled with dragon scales. She smiled, with those pointed teeth. "Welcome to the hall of wickedness, little dokka," she said, then began to scream.

Jane fell back, startled. The other spirits looked up, following the gaze of their shrieking companion, and upon seeing Jane, began to scream as well. Somewhere is the distance Jane heard the sounds of horns. The horns of war. She dove under the waters, partially to escape the noise, swimming back to the boat where Peridot pulled her aboard. "Great job. You've alerted the whole place to our escape!"

"I huh," Jane looked back at where Elena sat, still screaming, "she wouldn't answer me...and then..."

Peridot started to row, faster now, Tam Lin grabbing the other oar to give them speed. "Of course she didn't," Peridot said, "she's dead. Her memories have been taken from her. She's no longer Elena, Jane, that's what I was going to say if you'd bothered to listen. She's just a husk."

A host of No Bodies in their boats were now gathering at the entrance to the corridor, the drums beating faster. "I'm sorry. I just...I just had to try."

Peridot shook her head. "I knew you were a Bringer of Chaos, I just didn't realize you would bring that chaos down on yourself."

"Hey, ease up on her. And less talking, more rowing," Tam Lin said. "We're almost there."

"I'm sorry," Jane murmured, the sounds of the horns now echoing, long and low and cascading, building on themselves to a cacophony.

"You did nothing wrong," Tam Lin said. "You wanted to save your friend. That's not a bad thing. It was just a miscalculation. We'll get out of here. Don't you worry about that."

They turned a bend in the corridor, spotting an opening further down to the side, looking like an entrance to a cave. There was a light from inside that cave, firelight off gold, flickering with an alluring luster. "It's still there," Tam Lin said. "Let's just hope this ship of yours is still there as well."

The small troupe hurried into the cavern. The treasure house, like the main hall, seemed to stretch into infinity. It was filled to the roof with...stuff. There were piles of gold, gleaming sand dollars, and intricately carved jewels. There were effigies of kings, furs of exotic beasts, and works of art. There were even castles of some forgotten era, eroded colonnades, and crumbling spires. A grove of trees grew from the waters with shaking leaves from which ripened odd looking fruit; one of these fruit, a plum-looking thing, opened a set of eyes, watching as they passed. "Are we supposed to find anything in this mess?" Jane wondered aloud.

"Like I said. Junk drawer. What a slob."

Tam Lin looked back, the drums were getting closer. "What does this vessel look like?"

"Like a giant gold atom!" Cricket said. "It has a semipermeable psychoplastic alloy exterior that is circular and that is where the bulk of the ship is along with the Dream Tank. Surrounding it are five arms made of infused rarminium gems that spin to generate the psycho-space-time field that serves as the wormhole to pass us into another dimension."

"A giant gold atom," Tam Lin repeated, looking around at all the items. "A giant atom. I don't know what a giant atom looks like."

"Is that it?" Jane asked, pointing into the waters below. They peered down, and sure enough, there at the bottom of a deep pool was a large mechanism in the shape of an atom.

"*The Illumine!*" Cricket cried.

"Hold on Marigold!" Scarlet yelled, as if she could be heard. "We're comin'!"

"Fuck, how are we gonna get down there?" Tam Lin said.

Jane looked at her tail. "I can get there."

"Yeah, but can you steer the thing?"

Jane looked at the GCATS. The GCATS looked at one another. "I mean, she has withstood the waters here," Antoine said. "Chances are she could withstand the Dream Tank."

"What does that mean?" Tam Lin asked, looking back towards the cavern entrance, the drums were getting closer, "and fast."

"So, in your mind is the power of a *thousand neutron stars!*" Antoine paused, as if expecting a reaction, and when he didn't get one, continued, "you do know what a neutron star is, right?" Tam Lin shook his head. "Well, let me tell you, they're powerful as heck! And you need a powerful as heck thing to transcend the bonds of space and time. Leviathan's Whale runs off the psychic remnants of the dead, yes? Mind power. Neutron star power. We call it Primordial Memory Fluid. PMF. That is how this vessel moves. That is what this water of memories is for. The Dream Tank runs on slightly the same principal..."

"Only *vastly* more sophisticated," Cricket chimed in.

"Oh, yes, so much more sophisticated and elegant. Because instead of running on the memories of the dead, it runs on the memories of dreams. It uses those dreams like Leviathan uses these dead people. So no one dies, yes? Wonderful. Except you can get *lost* in the Dream Tank if you don't have a strong enough will."

"Or a big enough ego," Scarlet quipped.

"Not now," Antoine said, pushing her face away. "Point being, *anyone* can go in the Dream Tank and fly the ship. Marigold has processes for that. The question is, will that individual come back."

"What happens if you don't come back?"

"You become one with those neutron stars I was talking about? Maybe? I mean, we don't really know. Haven't totally figured that part out yet. But you sure as hell aren't *here*."

Tam Lin glanced over at Jane. "Do you think that's something you can do?"

Jane looked back. She could see the flickering light from the torches of the No Bodies "I don't see we have any other choice."

Antoine pulled some hair from Cricket who squeaked in protest; he passed it to Jane. "There is an entrance on the top side of the sphere. You will see it as a small red dot, like a laser pointer! This fur will give you the genetic code to let you in. Once in, you'll meet Marigold. She might be running slow as she hasn't had a power source for a while, but she should be able to guide you through the process."

Jane nodded, taking the hair. "I won't let you down."

"Until then," Tam Lin said, "we need to hide and buy her time."

As Tam Lin and the others went to hide in the mountain of treasure, Jane dove into the waters, making her way to the vessel at the bottom of the pool. There was the familiar tug of memories, which she was able to ignore at this point, even use a little bit to help push her along; however soon, there was something added to it: a low, lilting song. *Leviathan!*

The song manipulated the memories, and now instead of helping Jane, they slowed her. *You cannot escape me here, False Priestess,* Leviathan's song mocked, *you will soon be mine once more.*

Jane pushed through, reaching the hull of the ship. She found the red dot and pressed the handful of cat fur to it. The dot opened to an airlock that Jane swam down into, the door closing behind her; as soon as it did so, a new door opened, dropping her down into the ship proper with a splash.

Jane landed with a thud, getting the floor wet. Her arms hurt from the drop, but in here things were quiet—there were no nagging memories or eerie songs. Jane looked up. She was in a hall that stretched in a loop on either side of her. The walls had a warm, earthy hue, like that of well-worn parchment, and the floor was soft, the color of broken in leather. The walls were decorated in paintings, odd creatures that Jane had never seen before, depicted in swirls of indigo, vermilion, and malachite. There were hydras set in gold flames, birds with heads for tails, and fish with wings, all painted with a masterful touch. Above Jane, the ceiling was covered in moss and sedum.

"Greetings," a voice said, and Jane looked up to see a woman standing in front of her, "I am Marigold and this is my ship, *The Illumine*. I see that you have the fur of Cricket. May I ask what for?"

The woman before Jane had the beauty of a 70's porn queen, yet the demeanor of a nun. She had wavy auburn hair that she wore back in a ponytail and soft, storm-gray eyes. She wore a jump suit that covered her curves nicely enough, a set of paint brushes in her pocket. For a moment Jane was baffled that somehow someone was left alive on this ship, until she saw the woman wasn't solid in shape but shimmered, and that Jane could see right through her. "Y-you're the ship?"

"I am the AI of this vessel, yes," she said.

Jane's sense of urgency overtook her surprise. "We have to hurry! Cricket and the others are in danger! If we don't help them, they'll be re-captured by Leviathan!"

Marigold's brow knit in concern. "Oh dear, that does sound dire. But without Antoine here how are we going to move the ship?"

"I'll pilot the ship."

Marigold looked even more worried. "Oh, this seems like a dangerous idea indeed."

"Yeah, I know," Jane said. "Do you think you can help me?"

Marigold looked at Jane, the worry still in her face, but nodded. "If it's for the GCATS, I will do anything in my capacity. I have been running on reserves, but I should have enough energy to corporealize and get you to the Dream Tank."

"Do you think the ship will run?"

"My systems could use a diagnostic and we are low on rarminium, but we should be able to make an emergency jump and then do repairs." There was a flickering of lights, a few of them went out, and the rest went dim. Marigold walked over to Jane, solid now, picking up Jane as if she weighed nothing. "Did they warn you about the Dream Tank?" she asked as she walked them both down the hall. "Do you under the risk you are about to undertake?"

"Yes. They told me."

They made their way through the ship. Everywhere Jane could see little plants, small, knitted creatures, and paintings. It was as if the whole ship were a collage. "I didn't know cats could knit or paint," Jane commented.

"Oh, they don't have the patience for those sorts of things," Marigold said with a smile, "nor the opposable thumbs, though I wouldn't mention that. Besides, they have far more pressing issues to spend their energy on. Spacetime travel, genetics, and all of that. I made these things."

"Oh, well, you're very creative."

"I am an AI. I do not have the capacity for creativity, though I thank you for saying so. I simply copy patterns from my databases."

The hall ended, opening up to an engine room. Here there were no paintings, but a series of monitors along the wall. Most of the monitors were currently black, closed books, saving a few that still displayed numbers and readouts. There were copper coolant chambers, valves, and tubing twisted in byzantine loops that seemed alchemic to Jane's untrained eyes. The ceiling was covered in ivy, saffron infused light filtering down through it. In the center was a tank filled with what looked to be liquid gold; the tank was round, large enough to fit a grown adult, and adorned in ornate bronze filigree. The tubing and readouts of the engine room were clustered around this tank, and a small staircase wound around its side to reach the top.

"So, what do I do?"

"You will go into the Tank," Marigold said. "I will configure the coordinates and run the ship on auto pilot. Hopefully then we can collect the GCATS and jump."

"Do I have to do anything special? Like meditate or think happy thoughts or anything like that?"

"No. The Dream Tank is a greedy creature. It will take what it needs. What you *do* need to do is focus on keeping what you can to yourself." She cocked her head to one side as if processing something. "I suppose if you were to meditate on anything, it would be on the meaning of self."

"Huh...great."

Marigold carried Jane up the series of steps along the side of the Tank. Jane looked down into the waters of that vestal, at is viscous swish; the consistency of it reminded her of the ink of a fresh pen, wet and ready to sink into the page. Marigold looked at Jane, "are you sure about this?"

"No, but going in there seems better than the alternative." Marigold nodded, and then with one last pensive look, cast Jane into the Tank. As soon as Jane hit the water, she could feel it. The Pull. It was like the pull of the waters of Leviathan, persistent and nagging, wanting to curl into the bits of her soul and tear it apart. Make her one with the molecules of the fluid. Drown her in entropy. *Think, Jane,* she told herself, *you are Jane. Not water.*

But why aren't you water? Does not water flow through your veins? Are you not made up of the same compounds as water?

I am not water because I have thoughts and memories. Water does not have thoughts and memories.

On the contrary. Water has all the memories of the world. Water flows with memory. Put a rock in waters way and it will pass and remember how it was to be whole.

I am not water then because I am alive.

Well, that was a recent change, now wasn't it? You were dead but a few hours ago. And does not water trickle with life? Does it not jump and dance like a fish?

Jane! Jane! a voice called, and she recognized it as Marigold's. Jane opened her eyes to see the pinched face of the AI, peering at her from the outside of the tank. She was distorted through the glass, but there was still that knit of her brow that Jane was beginning to suspect was a permanent feature of the being. The room beyond was now fully lit up, everything powered on, Marigold seeming brighter than before. More alive. *Jane, don't let it pull you in, okay. You have hold it together so we can save the others!*

Jane nodded, focusing her sight, pushing the thoughts aside.

I am not water because I am Jane. And Jane has things she needs to do.

The water had nothing to say to that.

Marigold typed something into a keyboard, and Jane felt a transmission come through. A destination. The vessel shook and rumbled. There were creaks and groans as it stirred from its undine slumber. Jane felt them rise. The ship protested at the movement, a few warning lights going off. Valves burst and steam filled the engine room. For a moment Jane began to panic.

Don't worry, Marigold's voice echoed. *I'll hold us together. No vital systems are failing. Cricket will fix the rest.*

Jane nodded, continuing to allow the vessel to rise. There was commotion. GCATS, Peridot, and Tam Lin entered the engine room. There was a tearful reunion between Marigold and the GCATS. Peridot looked around the room in fascination. Tam Lin eyed Jane in the Tank. "We need to move," he said. "We were able to hold off the No Bodies, but Leviathan is closing in."

"We should take Jane out of the Tank and put Antoine in," Marigold said. "She's surprisingly done well so far, but her energy is unpredictable. She's blown some of our redundancies. Her genetic structure seems highly unstable."

Scarlet went to a monitor, reading Jane's vitals. "This *is* highly unusual. I don't think I've ever seen anything like this."

"We can worry about that later," Tam Lin said, "we need to keep movin..."

Suddenly the scene before Jane faded way to be filled by a pair of cruel lapis eyes. The sounds of her companions' voices dimmed, replaced by the siren call of Leviathan's voice. "I see, so you seek to defy me further?"

Jane shivered in fear. She was on the ground, before the Forest, dressed in white furs with a crown of flowers on her head. In her hand was a simple wooden spear; it seemed a weak weapon against the Whale's might. Jane turned to run.

Those lapis eyes looked down from the sky, storms brewing behind them. "Flee while you can rabbit, but it will all come to naught. You may fight. You may struggle. But it will all be in vain. For I am the laws of this world. I am inevitability. I am *death*."

Jane cried out, and not knowing what else to do, threw the spear right between the blue eyes of Leviathan. There was a scream. A serpent emerged from the clouds to eat the sun. Darkness covered the land. Fires ate the trees. A comet roiled angrily in the sky.

Jane fell into a pool of blood.

Does not water flow through your veins?

Summer

There is a tone, followed by reverberation. The tone is deep, almost jarring, and I can feel it in my gut. I can never decide if the feeling is good or just makes me sick, but the sound soon fades, becomes soothing, almost hypnotic. Then, just as the first tone is about dissipate, another is struck, starting the cycle all over again.

I inhale, trying to focus, exhale. "Breath in the scent of the earth," her voice intones. "Feel it fill your lungs. The scent of soil. The pungency of it. How it bites the back of your nose."

I concentrate on thoughts of fresh tilled dirt, so dark that it's almost black, stubborn weeds already breaking through. It's hard though. The memories hang there for a flickering moment, brief impressions before

my closed eyes, before giving way to nothingness. Just like the bell.

"Listen to the sound of the birds," her voice commands. "How they sing. How their wings flutter from branch to branch."

Birds. What were the names of the birds again? I remember enjoying watching birds. I even remember a book I used to carry around, identifying them. It was all dog-eared and bookmarked, grubby from being out in the dirt. Now I can't even remember the names of the simplest ones.

"Feel the energy. Let it run through your belly to your fingertips and toes. Let it flow as you breath out, releasing it back into the Universe. In that release, feel the Oneness of Creation. Feel your breath, in connection with the air, in connection with the rain, in connection to the life that grows from the ground. Feel as you breath the Sum of the Great Equation and how we are a small Part of it, and how it is All of us. Repeat after me, 'the Equation is Me, I am the Equation—the Part of the Whole'."

"The Equation is Me," other voices in the room pick up the refrain as I try to follow along, "I am the Equation—the Part of the Whole..."

There is a cloud of incense, and I start to cough. The smell of smoke. It brings up unpleasant memories more potent than birds and flowers. A desert flashes before my eyes of burned red earth and crunched black bones, the buzz of the bell becoming the scream of a siren as planes loom in the distance. My heart rate jumps and I open my eyes, not wanting to see anymore. Instantly that grim place is gone, and I'm in a room of bright light and whitewashed walls, the only sound other than that of the bell the soft breathing of the people sitting next to me. Still, I can feel the artery in my neck throb. I know it'll be pointless to try to go back to the mediation now. The session is almost over anyway.

I get up from my place on the floor, old scars twinging. We're in a small, circular hut. Mud brick walls with a thatch roof, old blankets on the dirt ground. A few bits of decoration are set up in attempt to make the place feel more homey, but they are dingy things. Pictures of friends long gone, paintings of green fields before they were burned—left behind scraps of a forgotten life. The hut is filled with people sitting on the blankets, facing the north end, legs crossed and eyes closed. They're dressed in simple loose clothes of some synthetic variety. I stand out in desert fatigues. They are a range of ages, though most are young. A few give me annoyed side-glances as I stand.

At the head of the room She sits, back straight, hands on her knees. She wears a loose slip of rose, red hair reaching her waist. She is relaxed and calm. There is a woman to her left that rings the bell as she repeats the chant.

I leave the hut. Outside, is a village of little white buildings set against a backdrop of reddish dust. It's quiet right now, with most of the residents in the meditation session. The village is set in a ravine, and in that ravine is a riverbed that is dry most of the year, though during the brief rainy season can suddenly become wild. The wadi walls stretch high above the cluster of huts, showing layers of rust and peach colored rock—centuries of work that the intermittent water has done. For most of the day the tall walls protect the village, hiding it in shadows. Right now, though is the time of day the sun finds us, and it is a cruel heat. I frown up at the sun before putting a cap over my head.

There is a ladder along one of the ravine walls, leading to the top. I climb up this ladder. At the top there is desert, the arid air sucking the moisture from my skin. A few scrub brushes and cacti dot the landscape, but other than that there is nothing but sand as far as the eye can see. There are two people there, also in fatigues, nestled in the dunes in cloaks that help them blend into the grit. I join them. "Hopper, Leo. How is it out there?"

"Dry as a desert," one of them says.

"Always the fuckin' poet, aren't you, Leo?"

A woman looks at me, face tanned and scarred. "Skipping out on meditation again, sir?" she says with a wink. "You'll be in trouble with the boss."

"Yeah, I'll get an earful tonight."

"Bullshit. She always goes easy on you."

The man next to her snickers, a patch covers one eye. "Yeah, well that's what you get when the boss is your wife."

"Ugh, whatever," I grumble, letting them tease me, "can you give me a report already? My knee is killing me."

"Saw three sets of drones the last hour, sir," Leo says, "coming from the northeast at one, two, and three o'clock."

That's not what I wanted to hear. "They're closing in on us."

"It was only a matter of time, sir. Those fat fucks were never gonna let us be for long. If you ask me sir, we should move camp, and move camp soon."

"You might be right," I get back up. "Keep sharp. If any activity picks up, radio me. I'm gonna go talk with the boss."

"Good luck sir," Hopper calls as I go down the ladder, "and don't let her beat you up too badly, okay?"

I give them both the middle finger.

The meditation session is over, and her devotees are hanging around, discussing whatever metaphysical things they like to talk about. Some of them look up at me as I walk over, giving way. --- smiles, green eyes lit up like twin flames. I clasp her arm, bending down to say in her ear, so the others can't hear, "we need to talk when you have a chance. I think it's almost time."

The light dims in her eyes, but the smile remains. She's gotten good at hiding her feelings from them over the years, and for some reason this makes me sad. "Wait for me in the hut," she says, "I'll be there shortly."

I nod, leaving her to her followers as I go back inside. I sit on the edge of a table this time, where it's easier on my knee. She enters. The fire is back in her gaze, but her face is pale and drawn. The young woman from earlier follows, buzzing like a gnat. "I told you to wait outside," --- says to the girl, an edge now to her voice. The woman obeys with a bow. I pull up a seat and help her sit down.

"Kids these days," she says, rubbing her forehead, "believe they have all the answers."

"They believe *you* have all the answers, which is exactly what you set them up to do."

"If you had told me when we started this whole thing, that it would turn into something like this, I wouldn't have believed it."

"And if you had told me when we started this whole thing, that you would actually come to believe some of things you were saying, I wouldn't have believed it either."

She sighs, and I can hear the weariness in that huff. "I know you don't agree with the things I say Tam Lin, and I know you stay by my side regardless..."

"That's never been a question. And it's not like I don't agree, I just...struggle with it."

"I suppose I don't blame you," she says, looking down at her hands, pulling at some loose thread I can't see. "This all started as a con to get money and foolish me, I had to go and get religious. But you have to believe me when I say, I saw something in there. And what I learned from that...force? entity? Whatever you want to call it, changed how I see the world. It opened my mind to whole universes that I never thought could exist."

"I don't doubt you saw something." I just doubt what it is.

"These people need meaning. They've been stripped of their homes, forced through a hellish war. They need the Great Equation to make sense of it all. And it's my obligation to guide them through this trial. To guide them to their Part in the Balance." She looks tired, and I regret bringing up the old argument, because what I'm going to tell her next is only going to add to the burden. "You said something about it being time. How bad is it? Have we been found?"

"Lookout has spotted three drones in the area. Likely, the City has homed in on our location, but doesn't have the exact coordinates yet. It's only a matter of time, though, before they do."

She brings a thumb nail to her mouth and begins to chew. "God's Veil been torn from us. What are our options?"

"I mean, not much. If we stay, they'll find us, and it'll be a fight. The City, even out in this wasteland, won't let us go after what we did. If we leave..."

"It will be another Exodus," she says. "We lost so many in the last one...and this place, as terrible as it is, protects us from the worst of what is out there. Could we manage it Tam Lin? Could we manage a fight?"

"We have an arsenal, and we have people who are trained. We could manage some sort of guerrilla warfare, but can we dig in and defend this spot? No. They would totally overwhelm us. They've more men, more weapons, more power. They've more time too. They could just bleed us dry without losing a single soldier on their end if they wanted to."

"So, another Exodus it is then?" she says, and I see her shoulders cave, as if from the weight. "Just...how do I tell them?"

I place a hand on her back, almost willing strength into her. "It's not all bad. We have scouted out places, knowing this might happen, so we're at least prepared this time. There's that cave to the east and the mountain range to the south. Yes, there are those...things out there, but we've marked out the worst nests and can move around them. It won't be fun, we'll still loose people, but it won't be like before."

"You...you're right. The Equation has granted us that much at least. We wouldn't be going out blind this time, but still, I feel so terr..." her words drift off.

"---?" I call, but she doesn't answer. She is somewhere else. Somewhere I can't follow. Her eyes roll into the back of her head and I move forward, catching her before she falls. She starts to convulse violently. "Hey!" I yell. "Someone get in here!"

The woman from earlier bursts in. I get the feeling she's been listening in on our conversation, but I put that aside for now. The woman goes white as she sees --- shake and writhe, backing away as I kick any furniture to a distance before laying her on the floor. "Is the Great Mother having a Vision?"

"She's having a damn seizure," I snap. "Go get Ruby!"

The girl runs out and soon after she is gone another woman, older and with a pinched face, rushes in with a metal kit box. --- flails in my arms, spit falling from her mouth. "Another one?" Ruby says, pulling out a syringe. "That's the third one in just as many months." She presses the vial to her skin, pushing down the plunger.

I watch as the liquid pours into her. Copper colored. Like blood. "Yeah. They're increasing."

Ruby looks at me with sharp green eyes and I avoid her gaze, knowing what she's going to say. "Tam Lin," she presses, regardless. "She's getting more sick. The tumor is growing. There's only so much I can do out here. I need equipment from the City to give her proper treatment."

"She won't allow it. Claims it's her conduit to god." I can't help but feel the bitterness on my tongue as I say that last word.

"The Mother's conduit to the Grand Equation is in her spirit," Ruby says, "not in her illness."

"Yeah, well, try telling her that."

Her shivering slows, ceases, and then stops. For a moment she just lays limp in my arms, and it's shocking how light she feels, as if she weighs nothing at all. Then she begins to stir, eyes slowly opening as if waking from a dream. "Call the council," she says.

I assume she's in her normal post-seizure haze. "You need to rest. You just had an episode. I know you're probably confused right now..."

"I'm not confused. In fact, I've never seen more clearly. Call the council to meet tonight, for I have had a Vision."

The Council meets in the main hut that night, after --- has had time to recover. There is a fire in the center of the hut, the smoke seeping through the chimney into the starry night sky. Now that the sun has fallen it has gone from unbearable heat to a sharp chill, and the fire is needed.

The Council is made up of the Great Mother, who sits on the floor wrapped in blankets, face still drawn from her recent ordeal. I am with her, as her military advisor, sitting in the only chair in the room, as well as Ruby and a host of elders that have been with us since before the time of the First Exodus.

"We hear from young Linda there will be a Third Great Exodus," a voice says.

So, the little shit was listening in.

"Three sets of drones were spotted this morning," I say. "All homed in on this position."

"So that means they know we are here?"

"That would be the assumption. They're just trying figure out exactly where. I say we have two, three days tops, before they attack."

"Two to three days is hardly enough time to prepare us to leave. We've been here for the past five years."

"We always knew this day would come," I say, "and are ready for it. I know it'll be hard, but if we don't leave in the next two to three days the City will strike, and we won't survive."

"I wonder if we can survive a Third Exodus. First there was the Exodus from the wreck that was Earth, to this failed terraformed wasteland. Then there was the Exodus from the City, into which the corruption from Earth had crept. In both of those we lost so many of our kin. To ask them to move again...." Ruby's eyes fill with tears.

"I understand your fears," I say, "and I'll
be honest, we will lose people in this next
move. The land up there is hostile, and while
we are better set then when we left the City,
that doesn't mean we'll be immune to loss.
I don't make this suggestion lightly. I was
witness to both those great tragedies you
mention and don't wish to witness another..."

"We all know Tam Lin. We all know the
sacrifices you've made and the courage you've
displayed. That is not the question. The
question is, can the people stand it?"

I nod, looking down at my hands. They are
rough and scarred. "They have to. Or they
won't and they'll die. It's not about courage
and sacrifice at this point, it's about doing
what needs to be done."

"There is," she says from her blankets after
a moment of quiet, "another option."

I look sharply at ---. She doesn't meet
my eyes, face sinking into the darkness of
her blanket; my heart starts to beat more
quickly. "Surly you don't mean that?" one of
the council members protests.

"Earlier today a Vision came to me, and
in it, I saw the Collider. The Great Column
of the Grand Equation, its knowledge written
in whispered runes of flame. It rotated,

228

first a rose spinning in water, then a spiral
of color, turning into a fractal, endlessly
repeating itself—growing larger and larger
in its rhythmic beauty. And in each tendril
of that fractal, in each fiber of that rose,
I could see the beginnings of the universe.
The knowledge of the runes were deciphered to
me. The secrets of creation. In those grains
I could see the Grand Equation. The Part that
will allow me to fully comprehend the Whole."

"But Great Mother," one of the council
members protests as I sit back, my sense
of doom growing, "you already grace us with
the wisdom of the Grand Equation. And the
Collider...it is dangerous. That would mean
going back to the City. Remember what happened the last time we tried the Experiment?
It failed."

"I know the last Experiment was a failure,
but I think it is a venture worth trying
again. Most of you here are old enough to
remember Earth before the War. The people we
lost, the planet we lost. We were once so
many, and have become so few. Do you remember
the taste of berries from the meadow? The
sight of rivers running through the forest.
The sound of snow? Do you want your grand-

children to never experience that? To live forever in fear out in this wasted desert?"

The room goes silent, as each falls into their own memories. Memories of green fields, of a sun that didn't burn. "The Equation wants us to return to that. The Equation wants us to bring Balance back by creating the world anew, free from the corruption of the fat technocrats of the City. We were not meant to hide forever in these toxic sands, infested with monsters riddled with disease. We were meant to plow. To gather. To grow. We can turn this land into a paradise if we just solve the riddle of terraformation, and we can do that with the power of the Collider. The Equation has given us the tools. Has given me the knowledge."

The elders look at one another. I stare ferociously at her, and for the first time that night she meets my eyes. I feel despair. She will not be swayed. "I don't know," someone says, breaking the silence. "Tam Lin, is it even possible for us to do this?"

I clasp my hands to keep them from shaking. "I would highly advise against it, but this is not the first time we've talked about an attack on the City. We have codes. We have contacts. We could do it. It would have to be a small team. A strike force. We would probably have to take out a few of their nuclear reactors to do it."

"That would be suicide!"

"Yes. The likelihood of survival would be low."

"Those who go would be martyrs," she says, "fulfilling their Part of the Balance."

Goddammit. I want to cry.

"You would need someone to input this... Experiment that the Grand Equation has sent to you," one of the council members says.

"Well, that would be me of course."

I look up. "No. No way. Not in your condition. There is no way I'm taking you on a mission, especially one like this, when you could pass out at any moment."

"But Tam Lin, it has to be me, don't you understand? I'm the Interpreter of the Equation. I'm the only one that can decode the Message. If I'm not there, then it'll all be for nothing. Besides, I can't ask others to go on such a dangerous journey if I'm not willing to go myself."

I sit back in my chair, hand to my mouth. I'm about to vomit. "No. I don't like this. People will die. And the risk to you is just

too great. It's a bad idea. A really, really
bad idea..."

She reaches out, hand trembling, as if she
is on the brink of breaking, as if she is
afraid. "Tam Lin, my love, people are going
to die regardless. That we cannot prevent,
but we can decide how. I started this journey,
I have to be the one that ends it. Will you
abandon me now, in this dark hour when I need
you most? After all we've been through?"

I clasp her hand, steadying it. "You know
I won't do that. No matter what you ask."

She smiles, as if my words give her sustenance. "Thank you."

"May the Balance bless us all."

The next evening twelve of us meet at the edge
of the village. It's getting dark and a few
stars are starting to become visible. There
are two moons, one is full and the other is
at half, which will give us a little light.
There is me, Hopper and Leo, a man named
Lenny who is younger than the rest of us, a
few others, and Her.

I walk up to her in the semi-darkness. "It's
been a long time since I've seen you in a
uniform."

232

She tugs at the gray coveralls, putting on a hat to hide her flaming hair. "It's been a while since I've worn one. Do you approve?" She gives me a wink.

Despite my misgivings, seeing her this way brings a smile to my face. "Never. Glad to see you seem to be feeling better."

"Slept better for the first time in ages. I don't know if it's because I feel like we're doing the right thing for first time in a while, or if it's because I'm happy to be doing something other than just meditating and talking." I'm not sure what to say to that, so I say nothing.

Gathered together now, we go over the plan. "Okay everyone, our goal here is to access the Collider. Do we all have the location of the Collider on our maps?" the small group nods. "In order to enter the Collider we're gonna need to take down the power grid. That means taking out at least one of three nuclear reactors that supply power to the City. Team Alpha, Team Beta, Team Gamma, each of you are tasked with taking down your assigned reactor. The hope is that at least one of you will be able to achieve that goal. You've been given the codes needed to enter the facilities and get access to the control rooms. Team Alpha, you'll go in as a repair crew. Team Beta, you'll have access as a routine inspection. Team Gamma, you'll have an insider for that reactor who'll lead you to the core. You get in, you set off a reaction, and then you get the hell out and meet back at the extraction point, okay?" The three teams nod. I pause for a moment, wanting to say more, but I know it won't do any good. "I wish you all the best of luck.

"Team Delta, it's our goal to infiltrate the Collider once the power grid is down and run this Experiment. Hopper, Leo, it'll be your job to guard the Mother. Lenny, you're with us as you were a technician for the Collider and have knowledge of it."

"Yessir," Lenny says, "but I only worked on the venting. I won't have access to the backup power system or any of the codes needed to calibrate the machine."

"You don't, but --- does, as she helped build the Collider after the First Exodus. Some of her backdoor access is still in there." Lenny looks at the Mother in surprise.

"One question sir," Hopper says, "what is the extraction plan?"

"Get out however you can," I say, not looking her in the face. "That's the extraction
plan."

"Just know," --- says, stepping forward,
wisps of fire popping out from beneath her
cap, "that we are doing the will of the Grand
Equation here, and whatever happens, Balance
will be restored." Everyone bows their head.

"Let's roll out," I say, "before we lose
more night."

We move along the dry riverbed, following
it until the canyon veers to the west, at
which point we come up from the ravine to the
surface. It's quiet, but Hopper and Leo are
on edge, eyes darting, guns gripped tightly.
"Okay, eyes open everyone," I say. "One wrong
move and you'll be something's meal."

We move along a dune ridge, Hopper at
the head. One of the younger crew members
stumbles in the sand and slips to the side,
falling over. He tumbles down the slope of
the dune with a cry, landing at the bottom.
There is a rustle from the scrub next to
him, and the man looks up, panic in his
eyes. Something emerges from those bushes as
if right from a nightmare. It's a ring of
reddish warped flesh, moving round, shifting
in an unnatural motion-like muscles spasms.

It lurches across the sand, leaving a trial of some sort of fluid I can't place and don't really want to. At the top of the mound of lumped skin are the heads of three women with sharp teeth and yellow eyes. One of the heads opens its mouth...

"Cover your ears!" I yell.

The devil screams.

Even with my ears covered I can feel the shriek in my bones. Most of the crew have time to cover their heads, but the man who fell doesn't. His head explodes. Pops like a grape. This brings back memories of me crushing grapes between my fingers as a kid, which I can quite fit with the dead man. The beast falls on him, tearing at his flesh.

"Fuckin' cunts," Leo growls, getting ready to shoot.

"Focus Leo," I say, pushing him forward. "Don't waste your ammo. It's not gonna save the kid."

They press on.

Soon, in the distance, a silver bubble appears on the flat horizon. It is lit up against the night sky, like a snow globe, though rather depicting some fantastical scene the City just looms, ominous. The City sits on a tall wall of titanium, thin silver

236

spires rising from it, encased in an energy shield. Outside the City's protective sphere, there are a mass of deformed creatures, drawn in from the desert by its light.

We reach the base of the wall, coming to a large air vent along the eastern side. There is a beast at that vent, feeding on some carcasses laid out around it. The beast is large, the size of one of the village huts, and is in the shape of a scorpion, only instead of shining carapace it has a series of human arms for its legs, severed torsos make up its body. Its stinger is made of a conglomeration of keratin nails, and it has a human skull for a head.

Hopper and Leo take out the monstrosity with their guns. Leo fires into it until he empties his clip. I let this one slide. Lenny gets to work on the vent, stopping the fan mechanism and popping open the cover so we can walk through. He seals the vent up behind us. "We gotta move fast," Lenny says, "the repair machines will be here soon to see what's up."

We move through the low silver tube in silence before coming up to another intake entry. Lenny does the same here, and we emerge from the tube into the City itself. The spires tower above us, clean and untouchable, while the bowls of the City are dark and covered in black muck, people huddled together in limp lumps.

"This was supposed to take us to the center of the City," Lenny says, confused.

"Change of plans then," I say. "Team Alpha, Beta, Gamma, we separate here. Team Delta, we find the Collider. Keep a low profile everyone. We don't wanna draw any attention."

The crew, in their cloaks and rags, blend in easily with the slums. The citizens of the City sit lost, in some dream-like haze seeing things that are unseen. I watch as a woman brings a bottle to her face and sniffs something from it, eyes rolling into the back of her head. I grit my teeth and turn toward the matter at hand. We move towards the center of the City, to a building that is unlike the tall spires around it—low and circular, with a glass dome roof. The glass is a mottled green that reminds me of old soda bottles.

We hide in the shadows, keeping watch over the covered dome as I eye the time nervously. Leo and Hopper are quiet, their jaws tight. Lenny is breathing fast and sweating slightly, but he at least appears focused. And she...she is calm as ever, eyes locked on her target.

The first explosion goes off.

I knew seeing the nuclear reactor go would bring back bad memories, but knowing and feeling are two different things. My knees buckle, and my heart booms in my ears. I'm locked still, looking at the flames coming from the top of those cursed stacks, looking at the plumes of smoke rise in the air. Plumes of death.

Hopper is shaking my arm, but it's as if she's doing so from a distance. "Sir, sir! We have to move before the security doors close!"

I can't take my eyes off that smoke, at the demons dancing in it. "I wonder how many people just died?" Hopper looks at me with wild eyes.

Another explosion goes off.

This is enough to shake me from the trance. I look over at the rest of the team, at the fear on their faces. On her, I start to see...doubt. Fuck. Now wasn't the time to falter. "Okay, let's move!" I bark. Better to move forward than to think. Better to not think.

People are running and screaming, soldiers are scrambling, unsure what to do. The defenses were always set to protect from

the monsters on the outside, never from the
inside. We are able to use the confusion to
come to the domed building. Lenny keys in the
codes to get us in.

A third explosion.

All five of us look up at this new cloud
of smoke, something beginning to sink in, a
horror we can't quite grasp. "We-we just took
out the whole power grid for the City," Lenny
says, voicing what we are all thinking. "The
shield will fail..."

"We keep moving," she says, "this is as the
Balance wills."

We make our way through the vent system,
crawling on hands and knees. Beneath us there
is more chaos as people run, yell, masking the
sound of our movement. We come to dead end.
I inch over to the nearest intake, looking
down. "---, do you know where we are?"

She walks over the grate. There is a red
door guarded by two men. "The entrance to the
control room," she says. "We've arrived."

I ready my gun. "Let's finish this."

We open the grate to jump down into the hall
before the door. An alarm goes off and Lenny
curses, but it's too late. The alert is out.
I jump down first, taking out one guard while
Leo takes out the other. Hopper guards the

Mother as she goes to the control panel. "By passcode Alpha Omega 1618 Gamma," she says to the door.

There is the sound of boots pounding the ground in the distance. I hope this works. The door slides open. The control operators on the other side fire at us. Hopper takes out two of them but is hit in the stomach. Leo takes out the third. We rush in. The door closes behind us.

The doors block off the worst of the sirens and yelling, so that it is almost blissfully quiet, but I know the reprieve will not last. It's a room of dull gray metal and red vinyl chairs. Along the far wall is a complex series of computer screens and controls that mean nothing to me, all dark and unlit.

Lenny helps me haul Hopper over to one of the chairs and sit her down. Hopper's face is pale with pain but she doesn't say anything. She tries to breath but I can hear the fluid in her lungs. Lenny takes her gun, face white. "Hurry and do what you need to do, ---," I yell, voice hoarse. "That door isn't gonna hold forever!"

She nods, taking off her hat as she walks up to the controls. Her red hair falls past her shoulder, as wild and untamed as the fires

that now ran through the City. She begins
to type. She moves with graceful speed, her
fingers looking more like they are weaving
some sort of tapestry rather than pulling a
computer system online.

"Emergency generator on," she says, more to
herself than anyone else as the lights come
back on, "recalibrating the Collider per the
Equation."

Hopper's eyes are rolling in the back of her
head. She coughs and blood-specked spittle
stains her lips. I can hear a charge go off as
the guards attempt to blow the door. The door
buckles in slightly and there is a deep thud
that shakes the room. She is untouched by the
chaos though, entering her arcane numbers and
symbols with meditative focus. A series of
diagrams show up on the screens, and for all
that I understand them, they really could be
the Word of God.

"Calibration complete," she announces,
"pulling up imaging systems."

The door warps further under the next blast.
"Come on. We don't have much time!"

"I'm almost there! Powering up systems!
Imaging ready! Here we go! We're going to
finally see the answer to the Great Equation!

The First Cause! We're going to see God!" She hits a button.

I watch as a pathway comes up on the screen. It tracks a pattern, and in the blink of an eye that pattern is obliterated. A stream of data appears. She stares at it eagerly, intensely, the light of the numbers reflected across her face.

Another charge bends the door.

"Well?" I ask, Hopper's breathing now still, gray eyes dull. "Does your Equation tell us a way to get out of this mess?"

She is silent. Reading. Rereading. She clenches her fists, her hands becoming little white balls. "No this impossible, this can't be true!"

My anger turns to fear at what horrors she could be divining in those numbers. "What? What is it? What do you see?"

She turns to me, eyes full of terror, mouth working around some soundless scream. "I-I can't see anything. Nothing at all. It's just like every other experiment we ran. An absolute failure. This data is the most average, garbage data I've ever received. Oh god Tam Lin, I fucked up. We just did all of this for nothing."

I sit there, not understanding, holding
Hopper's body to my chest. Still warm. "All,
for nothing?" I repeat.

The door blows open.

She screams.

The Magic Swan

Jane groaned, opening her eyes, to yet again, a strange new place. It was becoming a disturbing habit, this unconscious flight, and a part of her worried just exactly where it would take her. The scream of the being who was her yet not, the dying eyes of a woman who seemed so familiar yet was a stranger—what had the words on the screen said again? A language that was unclear, but at the same as bright as the sky at midday. Were the dreams trying to tell her something? Were they some sort of warning?

The thought gave Jane a chill. She didn't care much for the woman in her dreams, and it didn't help to know that in some way, that woman was her. She seemed so careless, arrogant, things Jane liked to think that she was not. *I wonder if Tam Lin knows she's such an asshole...I wonder if did, if he'd still protect me.* Protect the beast from the woods, out to nibble your heart and devour your toes.

Ugh, I must still be dreaming, Jane thought, rubbing her face, *I'm thinking strange things again.*

She was laying on a stiff bed, in a small room of isaballine-colored walls painted with flowers in blue, red, and gold. The flowers were simple but ornate, with mosaic fronds, lacy petals, and arched stems. They were the sort of representation of flowers that made it impossible to tell exactly what plant they were, could be a tulip or possibly a rose, and so seemed to shift restlessly under this lack of definition. They had been crafted with a loving touch, wisps of moss here, a swirl of lemon there. Even the small errors, the places where the hand had slipped, added to the charm of the work.

In comparison to the art on the walls, the rest of the room was sterile, in corrective-white and steel-gray. Small, circular sensors were glued to Jane's skin, connected to a machine that intoned her vitals. Jane rubbed her eyes, as what seemed to be a calendula turned to a poppy. She needed to get up, clear her head. She got to her elbows. A blanket covered her against the chill, crocheted in rose-madder pinks and lead-tin yellows.

"Ah, you are awake!"

Jane's vision blurred, as though still entangled in the threaded web of dreams, the sticky stands reluctant to let her go; she stared for a moment, studying the being before her. "Marigold?" she said, more question than statement.

Marigold smiled. She sat in a metal chair next to Jane, a set of knitting needles and some yarn in her lap. "Oh good! I'm glad you remember my name. That is a good sign. The PMF Tank can slow electrical impulses in the brain and cause confusion similar to dementia if one isn't careful. But so far your vitals seem to be fine."

Jane turned her gaze back to the ceiling, the overly bright lights burning auras in her retina, like looking through shattered glass. "That's right, we were escaping Leviathan. I was in the Tank. I saw her eyes..." she looked at Marigold. "Where are we now?"

"Ah, well, we're still in the process of figuring that out," she reached out, patting Jane's head; Jane supposed Marigold meant that to comfort her. "You see, there was a power surge in the Tank. I fear that power surge took us off course. But it's nothing for you to worry about. We'll get it all figured out. Would you like a fishy treat?" She pulled an orange, crinkly bag out from her entanglement of yarn, shaking it.

Jane eyed the treats dubiously, fat cat face on the cover. "I uhm, think I'm good, thanks." Marigold put them away. "I guess I shouldn't be surprised that we got knocked off course, considering everything that has happened so far. But we *are* away from Leviathan, right? No one's hurt?"

"Everyone is safe and we are as far from Leviathan as can be, thanks to you." Marigold smiled at Jane, and this time there was some actual warmth in it. "I want to thank you, for bringing my GCATS back. It's a tad embarrassing to say, but I was rather lost without them." There was a shimmer to the AI's face that seemed almost close to...tears?

Jane was taken back by the gratitude. "Yeah sure, it was nothing. I mean, we weren't gonna be able leave without them, so it's more like they saved us."

"I see. Well, you have my thanks none-the-less and I'm glad to see you awake. For a moment we were worried we had lost you to the Tank! Antoine was just about ready to go in there and fish you out!"

Jane thought back to Leviathan, with those watery blue eyes, and was grateful that he didn't. Her stomach growled. "Ah," Jane clasped her belly.

"My, you *are* hungry!" Marigold cried. "My apologies for being such a terrible hostess, I am not used to tending to human needs. The GCATS you see, are *more* than proficient at alerting me when they require nourishment, to the point where have had to create a schedule, which they *do not* care for, and they consume such simple things. We must find something for you! Are you able to walk? If not, I can carry you to the mess hall."

Jane peaked under the blankets to confirm her bodily state. "I think I can walk. Looks like I got legs this time, and I don't even have any hooves!"

Marigold, if a physical manifestation of an AI system could have a bad poker face, had one. "Ah yes, well, that is something *else* we should probably discuss once we are with everyone. But yes, you look...relatively normal. I mean, relatively that is."

Jane raised an eyebrow at the 'relativelies', looking around; she saw a mirror at the other end of the room, and getting to her feet, made her way to it.

"I have snake hair," she said flatly as she looked at her reflection.

"I mean look at it this way, at least they're asleep?"

Jane gave a side glance to one of the snakes currently growing out of her scalp, its scaly aqua skin glistening under the light with a faint iridescent glow of purple and pink. "Huh," she said, its face in quiet repose, lips twisted into an almost cat-like grin. "They're actually kinda cute. Hope they don't bite me when they wake up. Do you think they would bite me?"

"I have no reliable data with which to answer that. I have never met a being with snakes for hair before. I've only read about them in tales. It does raise some questions though. Like, how are they

248

receiving nutrients? How are they processing waste? Are they a parasite? If they are a parasite, what impact does this have on your brain structure?"

"Ugh." It seemed like Jane had opened up a snake-sized can of worms. "Let's not think about it. I am hungry though, which makes sense since I am eating for," she counted the heads, "12? Surprised it's not 13."

"Oh, that would be too many." Jane chose not to ask why.

With Marigold in the lead, the two left the sick bay, making their way to the mess hall where the others were recuperating. The mess hall, like the rest of the ship, was painted with murals, though these were of fierce cats, wreathed with fire and gowned in feathers. There was a particularly tempestuous looking black lion, with a crown of bones, the ocean trembling at its feet, obsidian mane shifting in the stormy wind, looking out with jade-moon eyes. Toramaru sat before that depiction, in an almost perfect mimic of the pose, slowly blinking.

A series of windows lined the starboard side of the room, acting as a viewing port, which at the moment looked out to a foamy nebula in shades of sea-green and coral. There were some tables and chairs, and a small kitchenette toward the bow. The kitchenette was utilitarian and clean, with a stainless-steel countertop and gray-blue cabinets that reminded Jane of the ever-ubiquitous origin of cubicles—boredom coalesced into a hue. The rest of the space was taken up by houseplants and blankets, along with a few high places for the GCATS to sit. Scarlet was currently curled up on one of those blankets, while Antoine was batting at a spider plant, Cricket purring over some schematics. Peridot and Tam Lin were playing chess at a table, Tam Lin scratching his head as Peridot beamed triumphantly. They all looked up as Jane and Marigold entered the room.

"The princess awakens!" Antoine declared.

"Antoine, what did I tell you about eating the spider plants?" Marigold chided, for the first time since Jane had met her, looking annoyed. "You're going to make yourself sick."

"He just wants to get high," Scarlet grumbled from her sleep.

"Eat the plants? What would make you think I would ever do such a thing!" Antoine asked innocently, before immediately throwing up a mass of grass on the floor. He stared at the puddle of puke. "Whoa, I think my bile is telling me the secret code to the Universe."

Marigold sighed, grabbing a towel to wipe up the mess. "Jane here is hungry," she said. "I know we have some stores left from when Father stocked the ship. I was hoping we could make something for her."

"Ah yes," Scarlet said, "a midday meal would be delightful." Antoine meowed in protest as Marigold cleaned, but then his eyes dilated to the size of dinner plates and he zoomed off, chasing after some shadow; Jane frowned, for a moment almost swearing she saw something in his chase.

"We have freeze dried tuna, freeze dried turkey with bacon bits, freeze dried mackerel—my personal favorite—freeze dried chicken..."

"Huh, I think I can go take a look for myself if you don't mind," Jane said, shaking off the reverie. Hopefully there would be something other than freeze dried meat.

"The food is in the cupboards behind the kitchenette sink," Marigold said, "if you would like to take a look."

Antoine appeared out of nowhere, as if materialized from thin air. "But hands off the fish flakes, missy, those are *mine*."

"Antoine!" Marigold admonished, but Antoine wasn't listening, jetting off to that weird dimension only cats seemed able to find. Marigold looked over at Jane with a pained look. "I apologize. He becomes quite impossible when he's like this."

"I am the Rat King! Serve unto me all your fish flakes my surfs! Bwahahahaha!" He tackled Scarlet who made a squawking racket, and fur flew before Antoine vanished again.

"*Antoine!*" Marigold cried, helpless hands on her hips. "We have *company*!"

"It's all right," Jane said. "I think I'll manage without the fish flakes." She went over to the cupboard behind the sink. Inside, the cupboard was packed to the top with various freeze-dried meals wrapped in a tinny blue. She pulled out spaghetti and meatballs with spinach. "Oh! This looks fine!"

"Ew. You wanna eat *that*?" Cricket cried with a look of disgust. "Well at least *someone* does, I guess. That stuff smells *awful* if you ask me. Full of salt and...*vegetables*."

Marigold got an electric kettle of water going.

"So, what's the situation?" Jane asked, opening the bag.

"Well, the power surge you created tossed us in the middle of nowhere," Cricket said.

Jane paused as the pot behind her began to pop and bubble. "Wait, *I* caused the surge?"

"Of course you did," Peridot said from the table, moving a rook. "You're the Disruptor." Tam Lin groaned, looking down at the board in increasing despair.

"Gopherdammit," Jane said, "so, we're not on Tam Lin's map?"

Tam Lin tentatively moved his knight. "Map isn't showing where we are."

Peridot quickly made a counter move. "The fabric of the universe is shifting," she said. "The Filaments have become entangled. The Book of the Dead is less reliable than what it once was." Jane bit her lip. The water was now at a full boil. Marigold turned off the pot, filling up Jane's bag, steam rising up, mimicking the swirls of the nebula outside only carrying with it the starchy scent of pasta.

"The power couplings are blown," Cricket said, "some of our wiring is fried. Our main generator is totally offline so we're running on the backup..."

"*I* did all that?!"

"I mean...I think you did *most* of it? Some of the damage had to do with how long *The Illumine* been sitting without running. But Marigold did all the routine maintenance that she should. So yeah, I would have to say most of it was from you."

"Which is not that big of a concern," Marigold interjected, seeing Jane's face, "we can get it fixed."

"By the way," Antoine said, appearing on the kitchen counter, "you're *not* allowed back in the Tank."

"Yeah, not allowed back in the Tank," Cricket said, everyone else in the room nodding in agreement.

"I won't argue," Jane grumbled, stirring her freeze-dried dinner with flaccid motions.

"Which ties into our second problem," Scarlet said.

"Yes, that ties into our second problem," Cricket parroted. "First we need to find a place to land and fix the ship. Then we need to figure out what to do with *you*."

Jane looked up, spoon halfway to her mouth. One of the snakes stirred. "What do you mean?"

"Your genetic structure," Scarlet said, "*that's* what we mean." When Jane gave Scarlet a blank stare, Scarlet sighed. "So when you were in the Tank it read your vitals, right?" Jane shrugged. "Okay, well, it does a full genetic scan. Part of being able to go into the dream state needed to fuel the power of the Tank has to do with your genetic structure. Some flexibility is good, but too much and you get lost in the sauce, so to speak. Your genetic structure when you were in the Tank, well, I suppose the only way to describe it, your genetic structure is a Paradox."

Peridot fired her fingers in the air. "Boom, boom, boom. Whaddya I tell ya'? Magical Girl Power."

Jane groaned and one of the snakes hissed; Toramaru jumped up on the table, staring at it with curiosity. "No. Not another one. Not another title. I'm the Magical Girl, the Disruptor, the Apocalypse, and now I'm a *Paradox*?"

"Don't forget the Defiler!" Peridot offered, taking another one of Tam Lin's pieces.

"You aren't helping," Jane grumbled. The snake hissed at Toramaru. Toramaru raised his paw.

"Ah, so you know about this then."

"I can't say that I *know* about it," Jane said, "but there does seem to be a circle of chaos wherever I go and I'd like it to stop."

"That's why we're traveling to the Fates," Tam Lin added, "so we can figure out the location of the Sea Witch and ask Him how to help fix Jane."

The GCATS started to laugh. "The *Fates*!" Antoine cried. "The *Sea Witch*? Like they would be able to help you. Foolish tales from children's imaginations!"

"Hey, what do you mean by that?" Peridot protested. "The Sea Witch created this Universe and you laugh?!"

"*Science* created the universe," Cricket said. "The Sea Witch and all that are just stories people come up with to explain it."

"*Are you saying the Sea Witch isn't real*?!" Peridot cried, getting up from her chair with such force she knocked the game over in the process; for a moment, Tam Lin looked as though he might try to pick the pieces back up, but then thought the better of it.

"I mean, it's real in the way *all* stories are real in that they exist in the collective imaginations of a populace and influence how they interact with the world," Antoine said, still high as fuck. "But if you mean *really* real? Then *no*. The Sea Witch is not *really* real."

Peridot grabbed her hair. "You all are insane! Then how do you explain Leviathan? How do you explain Tam Lin being undead?!"

Toramaru struck, whacking Jane's hair with rapid fire paws. "Leviathan travels through space using psychical energy just like we do," Antoine said. "Her Dream Tank is just a highly adapted organic one. As for Tam Lin, he is indeed fascinating."

"Fascinating," Scarlet agreed.

"Fascinating," Cricket added. Tam Lin looked up from the board, three sets of predatory eyes on him. He suddenly felt very uncomfortable.

"A manifestation of psychical energy that has taken on form and intelligence," Scarlet commented, then looked at the scattered chess pieces, "well, some *minor* form of intelligence." Tam Lin glared.

Now all of Jane's hair was awake and moving, snapping at Toramaru. Toramaru bristled and ran off, knocking over a pot as he fled. Marigold sighed, grabbing another rag. Jane ate a bit of spinach. "So then, what do you suggest we do? Nothing? I can't keep going around causing hell wherever I go."

"This is true," Scarlet agreed, "and the fact of the matter is, you're going to become more unstable with each jump. We need to find a way to stabilize your genetic structure so you don't become consumed by the Paradox and cause all of existence to cease."

"And how do we do that?" Tam Lin asked.

"We need to go to the Lab," a pall settled on Marigold and the GCATS as Scarlet said this. "It is the place where *The Illumine* was born, for a lack of a better term. I don't have the equipment here to stabilize you, but if we to go to the Lab, I could possibly do it there."

"And maybe while you're at it you can stabilize your *fathead*," Antoine dodged a swipe from Scarlet.

"Antoine," Marigold chided, "be serious." She turned to Jane. "It's not with a light heart the GCATS offer to take you to this place. It's full of old ghosts for us, as you humans would say. If Scarlet suggests this path, it is because she believes it is the only way."

Peridot sat in her chair with a huff. "Ghosts? Seems a bit *unscientific* to me."

"She's talking about *metaphorical* ghosts, duh," Cricket said. "Like she just *said*." Peridot and Cricket glared at each other.

"I see," Jane poked at the reconstituted noodles. They were getting soggy. "I mean, I guess this is your ship, so I can't tell you where to go."

"This is an offer of help Jane, not a prison," Marigold said. "We won't force you to go where you won't. And as you saved the GCATS from Leviathan, we will take you where you wish to go. They just feel that this can help."

Jane stared at her food. It was becoming rapidly more unappealing for a variety of reasons. "Tam Lin? Peridot? What do you think?"

"The choice is yours," Tam Lin said. "I go where you will."

Peridot harrumphed. "I think this whole business is foolish. The Sea Witch is the only being that is going to be able to help you, not some silly mortal *science*. It's hubris."

"Well then I guess it's hubris that runs this ship your ass is sitting in, your *highness*," Antoine snapped back.

Jane sighed. She thought back through their whole adventure so far, at what had brought them to this point. Her mind wandered. She looked at one of the writhing snakes. It looked back, its eyes reminding her of the fire rimmed gaze of Leviathan. "GCATS, huh?" she said, running the word over tongue. "Cricket, Antoine, Toramaru, and Scarlet. What's the 'G' for?" She looked over at Marigold. "You don't have a nickname that starts with a 'G', do you?"

"Ah no," Marigold said with a blush, then seemed to grow a bit sad. "There was time that we were a crew of 6, not 5. But we lost one of our own."

"Lost? How?"

"Lost him to the Dream Tank," Scarlet said. "He just, sorta disappeared into it, and we could never pull him out. It was a terrible loss to our ship colony."

"Soft warm air breaks cool

Pink blossoms sway in the wind

One falls, to the ground"

The crew went quiet, looking out the window in a sort of trance. "What was his name?" Jane asked, a part of her already knowing the answer.

"El Guapo."

Jane nodded as Peridot sighed, slumping in her seat, defeated. "We go to the Lab then," Jane said. "See if we can figure anything out. If we can't, then we go to the Fates from there. Is everyone okay with that?"

"That works for us," Scarlet agreed.

"I mean, *fine*, another diversion from the True Path," Peridot huffed, "heck, by the time we get to the Fates there probably won't even be a Universe left *to* save." She put her elbows on the table, resting her cheeks in her hands with her back bent over.

"Well, first things first," Cricket said, "we need find a place to land so I can finish the repairs. We're in no shape to make a jump to the Lab in the state we're in. We're also running low on rarminium, but I think we can wait on that."

"Right," Marigold said, "we should leave this nebula and scout out a suitable place to land."

The crew of *The Illumine* made their way to the Tank Room where Marigold guided them out of the nebula and into open space. The ship seemed to strain with the motion, Cricket's ears perked as she looked over readouts informing her of various ailments, of arrhythmic pressure pipes that steamed, and inflamed energy fields. Once out of the nebula, Marigold pulled up a visual on one of the screens, showing their current location.

"Huh, is this an iteration with just one solar system?" Scarlet mused.

"It seems so. My sensors indicate that this spacetime consists of a universe that is approximately 150,000 square kilometers."

"It's *so tiny!*" Peridot squealed as she went up to the screen, mood flipped like a switch. "And precise!"

In the center of the screen was a large golden sun. Circling that sun were six planets, each perfectly round, as if polished stones, made of red coral, emerald, blue sapphire, yellow sapphire, garnet, and interestingly enough, cat's eye. They moved about the sun in a complex pattern that seemed to etch out a diagram against the backdrop of stars. Jane frowned. Perhaps it was just an aftereffect of her being in the Dream Tank, but she felt as though she could see a pattern in their movement. A hexagon within a star within another hexagon.

"Is that sun...not burning?" Tam Lin asked, getting up close to the screen.

"Your observation is correct," Marigold said. "It does seem to be giving off an energy source, but not in the form of nuclear fusion. In fact, I am unable to pinpoint exactly what sort of power source it is. The sun itself seems to be made of gold at an 80 percent purity level and is the only location from which I am receiving any signs of life."

Peridot looked over at Marigold. "Are you saying the rest of those planets are dead?"

"I am saying that they are devoid of life signs. All life, seems to be concentrated on that sun."

"Have you ever seen anything like this before?" Tam Lin asked Peridot.

"N-no," Peridot said, eyes back on the screen. "It so small and neat. All the planets are timed...like clockwork! Everything is placed so flawlessly! Most Filaments can't function like this. There is always some give or fray in the thread so to speak." Peridot worked her mouth around something she couldn't quite express. "It's...beautiful..."

There was an alert on one of the monitors; the Tank Room lights went from honey-gold, to red. "Two foreign objects are coming our direction," Marigold announced and on screen they could see two small missile-like vessels emerge from a tall structure at the apex of the sun.

Jane grabbed a hold of the nearest thing she could find. "We're under attack!" she cried, all snakes hissing.

"They are moving at a speed inconsistent with a hostile entity. I *don't* think we are under attack."

"Ah," she relaxed her grip.

The two objects neared *The Illumine.* They were ships, made of a white metal shaped to look like clouds and trimmed in gold. On the side of one of the hulls was a 'Q' and on the side of the other was an 'E', the two ships linked by a bar. They were not large, with perhaps enough space for one person each. The zephyr-like vessels came up to *The Illumine,* stopping before it. "We have a request for communication," Marigold announced.

"Put them through," Antoine replied.

The screen changed from the outside world to the beings in the steel cirrocumuli; the creatures that came into view were encased in sharp white enamel, lined in gold and silver. They did not have faces that would be recognized as such, but blank masks of platinum, etched with navy blue at the neck and cheeks. On each of their chests was the same 'Q' and 'E'. "Greetings," the beings said in flawless unison, "you have arrived at Cear Leot, the Filament of Conservator Melusine. She welcomes you and requests the names of those who have graced her realm."

For a moment the crew of *The Illumine* looked at one another, confused as to whom should take charge. Marigold glanced back at Jane, Jane violently shaking her head. Tam Lin just shrugged. The GCATS milled around, Antoine flopping down on a cat nip toy to rabbit kick it. Peridot sighed, stepping forward. "I am apprentice Conservator Peridot of the Filament Gardenalia, and these are my companions," she announced. "We are grateful for your Mistress' kind reception. As you can see, our inter-dimensional transport is damaged. Would you perhaps know of a place where we could land and rest whilst we await repairs?"

The two zephyrites were silent for a moment, before replying, again in unison, "the Great Mistress Melusine welcomes you to her palace. She bids you to follow us to the sun, where she will greet you with feasting and rest whilst you await the repairs of your vessel."

Peridot gave a slight bow. "I thank you and your Mistress for this kindness."

With that, the screen switched back to the outside world, the two clouds turning towards the sun. Marigold followed. "Do think this is a good idea?" Tam Lin asked. "Going into the home of a stranger?"

"She's a Conservator, not a stranger," Peridot said, "and there are certain customs of hospitality that must be abided."

"Including not killing us, right?"

"Ugh, well, depending on the circumstance."

"Oh. Great. Have you even met this Conservator before?"

"What? No. But it would be impossible for me to meet all the Conservators that populate the Totality," she said. "I'm just an apprentice after all." Peridot went quiet, seeming to go inwards.

They followed the zephyrites to the solar citadel. The palace at the top of the sun was comprised of minarets and gears, enclosed by a bronze-wrought gate. The shafts of the towers were the same white enamel of the ships, while the roofs and cogs were in labradorite and silver; there was no decorations or flourishes on the gleaming surfaces, everything lustrous and smooth, reflecting light. There also seemed to be no central housing to the palace, the thin spires surprisingly mobile, the minarets shifting as the gears moved, rearranging the shape of the palace as if along lines of an orbit that mimicked the motion of the heavens.

Landing on the surface of the sun, the crew of *The Illumine* left the ship, the cats pawing at the ground before trusting it with their full weight. The gold beneath crinkled and flaked, bits of dust drifting up in the air, refracting light and giving the sun its own sort of glow. Past the golden haze was the spinning of the bejeweled planets, set against velvet night and diamond stars. "It's beautiful!" Marigold exclaimed.

Jane frowned, waving a hand in front of her face to keep the dust at bay. "It can't be healthy to breath this stuff in."

"You can't accept anything nice, can you?" Peridot said with a glare.

"Actually, Jane is correct. Inhaling gold dust can lead to respiratory problems and accumulation of gold in the liver," Scarlet said. "We should be using respirators."

"Ugh, *boring*!"

"You needn't worry about the gold particles," the zephyrites said. Freed from their vaporous vessels, they floated above the surface of the sun, their enameled robes swirling about their feet; it was an oddly malleable movement for such a stiff material, like watching molten metal run. "You will only be exposed to them for a short period of time. It will not be long enough to cause any lasting damage."

"I'm gonna stay on the ship," Cricket said. "Do some work and fix Marigold. Marigold, you should go with the others."

"Marigold can leave the ship?" Jane said. "I assumed you were bound to it."

"That would make sense, wouldn't it? It is where my traditional servers and sensors are stored, and if *The Illumine* isn't doing well, I tend to feel poorly also. But...

"But Marigold has surpassed what an AI should be capable of," Scarlet said. "Possibly due to her close interaction with the PMF. Possibly some interface Father installed that we aren't aware of.

But regardless, her technological DNA has become very advanced. So advanced, in fact, that we don't really understand it."

"We theorize that the PMF is like some astral server for her."

"Ah, I see." Jane had no clue what they were talking about.

"All that of that is to say, my iteration of self could be tied to *The Illumine*, or it could be tied to the PMF, we don't know. It is certain that the condition of *The Illumine* has an effect on me, it's just to what extent. But I should stay here, with Cricket, and help repair myself."

"You were stuck in the bottom of that ravine for three years," Cricket said. "You should stretch your legs! If I need anything I can always call you on the comm."

"Yes but..."

"I was stuck in a cage for three years with these oafs!" Cricket squawked. "I could use some alone time!"

Antoine looked up from cleaning his butt. "Who are you calling an oaf?"

"Okay Cricket, I'll go with the others then."

"Yay! Catnip and bird TV time!" Cricket hopped back into the ship. "Call me if you need anything!"

"Will do," Marigold said. As Marigold left the ship, she became solid, corporeal once more; the dust clung to her now, caught in her lashes. "This really is a lovely place."

"Come on, let's go," Peridot said, pushing them along. "I wanna eat something other than dehydrated garbage."

"Oh, that *does* sound good," Jane agreed. "Do you think they'll have anything to drink?"

"Maybe we can even get a *live* fish!"

They followed the two guides to the bronze gate of the palace; in the center of the entryway was another symbol, this one of a line with an 'x' through one side of it, underscored by a second, thicker line. The gate opened to a garden. In that garden were fig and pomegranate trees, hyssop and coriander, myrtle and grapevine, set in neat rows along clean lines. The plants seemed almost impossibly well cared for, until one saw that that they weren't comprised of leaf and petal, but gem and stone: diamond stigma and emerald leaves, amethyst petals and agate steams, even the dew on the garnet fruit made from intricately fired glass—all done with expert precision, with no flaw in even the most humble ruby.

"I've never seen anything like this," Peridot said, "everything so expertly cut, so cared for. The cedars sway just so. The blossoms even flutter in the wind. Each facet, each blade of grass, is a work of art!"

"The Mistress will be pleased to hear of your appreciation," the zephyrites said. "She has worked hard on her Creation."

"Your Mistress built all of this?"

"Yes, she has many talents. Gem craft and languages are among two of her strengths."

"*Antoine!*" Marigold hissed. "This is not the place to go to the bathroom!"

The doors to the palace arched above them, two obelisks of argentine, carved with arcane runes in shapes of triangles, moons, and crosses. The zephyrites held out their hands, and a clicking sound could be heard; the palace began to tremble and shift, once more beginning to move. When the gears and towers stopped, the doors opened, the two guides leading them inwards.

On the other side of those doors was a hall of gleaming white marble floors and high arched ceilings, slender blue columns supporting them. The crew of *The Illumine* went silent for a moment as they stood in that place, for it felt like entering a cathedral. The crystalline lights that lined the walls cast a diamond-like glow that glistened on the highly polished surfaces.

The zephyrites lead them to another, smaller door at the end of the great chamber, this entryway made of gold. The door opened up to a room with a domed ceiling adorned in a mosaic. The mosaic was of an Eden-like garden laid out with mathematical precision: grapes set in a certain number of clumps, apples in orderly intervals, even the animals seeming to appear as though set by some algorithm apart from nature. A chandelier hung from the center of the ceiling, it's light reflecting the colors of the mosaic so that they shimmered below, casting patterns on the floor.

At the back of the room, on a throne of ivory flanked by gold lions, sat the Conservator Melusine. She was a giantess, her head nearly touching the rim of the dome, hair a wispy pale yellow, like finespun filament, worn back in a net of silver stars. Her face was heart-shaped and fair, with the faintest color to her cheeks, though her eyes, the color of aquamarines, were set slightly too far apart, giving them an otherworldly gaze. She wore a heavy velvet gown the color of tanzanite, embroidered with pearls, the folds of the fabric so voluminous she seemed almost lost in them. A disc of radiant gold rested on her shoulders, framing her benevolent face in its brilliance, as if her body were the universe, and her smile, the sun.

"Greetings fair travelers," she said, in a selenite voice, each word picked carefully and set in place. "I welcome you to my abode and grant you shelter. I hope your ventures have not been too taxing, for you seem weary and in need of rest."

Peridot stepped forward. She curtsied, awkwardly smoothing the wrinkled and torn gown that she wore. "Greetings Conservator Melusine of Cear Leot. I am Conservator Apprentice Peridot of Gardenalia. We are grateful for your hospitality."

"You seem to be an interesting aggregation," Melusine said, passing her soft blue eyes on each of them. "A stolen dead man, a robotic ghost, a group of *overly* intelligent cats," her eyes narrowed on Jane, "and *you*," Jane huffed, wrapping her arms across her chest, "an agent of chaos."

"Oh, you needn't worry about Jane, Conservator," Peridot said with a nervous grin, "she really doesn't like to cause troubl..."

"I am not worried," Melusine interjected with a glossy smile, "for chaos is like entropy, to be embraced, controlled, and brought under Oneness with the Sea Witch. For this is His Will. There will always be detractors, but that is nothing new. No, I have seen such creatures before. To be honest, the being that intrigues me the most, is *you*, young one."

Peridot's face flushed under that beatific gaze. "Me?"

"I sense an energy in you. A special energy. Surly your previous mentor sensed it as well, yes?"

Peridot looked at her feet. "If he did, he didn't say anything to me."

"Well," Melusine said, "I am sure he felt it all the same. For I see it emanating in you, like a radiant light, ready to be spilled out unto the world. Ready to come into perfect harmony with it."

"Conservator, I am honored that you see this in me," Peridot said. "I must say, I'm quite impressed with this world you've created. In it, I see no suffering, I see no pain. Only beauty. I've not come across such a place before."

"Yes," Melusine said, glancing upwards as if there was something there the rest of them couldn't see, "it is as the Sea Witch would have it. A perfect world without pain. A thing for which all Conservators should strive. What you see before you is not any working of mine own, it is His Will working *through* me. I merely obey it." She bowed her head.

Peridot took an involuntary step forward, as if magnetically pulled by her words. "Conservator...I-I've so many questions for you!"

"And they can wait for now," Melusine said. "I have a feast being prepared in your honor. There will be plenty of food and drink whilst we converse further. Until then, I've some rooms where you can refresh yourselves and get some rest. A change of clothes has been laid out for you that I think you will find are to your size."

The zephyrites reappeared at the back of the throne room, the indication obvious. Peridot bowed once more. "Thank you again, Conservator, for your grace."

Melusine waved them along, and the small troop turned to the zephyrites who ushered them down the hall. When they opened the golden doors this time, instead of leading them to the entry hall from before, it led to a flight of stairs. Tam Lin raised an eyebrow. "When did that happen?"

"The Mistress' Palace moves according to her will," one of the zephyrites said, "and she wills you to find some comfort and rest."

"Ah, what a wonderful place, don't you agree!" Peridot exclaimed as they walked. "After all we've been through, it's nice to find a place where we can relax!" Tam Lin and Jane exchanged glances.

"It is rather lovely," Marigold conceded, looking at everything, "and made of some fascinating alloys!"

Jane tugged at Tam Lin's sleeve, the two of them hunkering back, letting Peridot and Marigold chat. "I don't like this place," she said.

"I agree. There's something weird here."

"Yeah, something's off, and Peridot isn't seeing it. It's like she's being suckered in by something."

"More like she's being suckered in by that lady's looks," Tam Lin sighed. "Well, there's nothing we can do now other than keep an eye out. So try to keep your head about you, okay?" Jane nodded.

The zephyrites escorted them to each of their rooms—all in the same hues of gray, black, and gold. Inside was a feather bed, a place to wash, and new, clean clothes. When each emerged from their rooms to go down for dinner they looked brand new; Peridot came out in a dress of emerald satin, gold suns in her hair, Marigold in a gown of fiery orange, ruby flowers along her neck, while Tam Lin wore a simple black suit. Antoine had a collar of braided silver, Scarlet a collar of garnet, and Toramaru a collar of tourmaline. Jane meanwhile...

"Jane!" Peridot yelled, pointing back at the room. "Go in there and get out of those grubby rags and dress like a darn human being!"

"I'm not gonna put on what she has in there! I'm comfortable in this!" Jane protested, hugging the dusty cloth to her. As if she almost hadn't been sacrificed in it.

"Jane," Peridot chided, "Melusine is a lady of refinement and is not used to having weird street urchins in her halls! You will dress like a normal being or I will make you do it!"

Jane stuck her tongue out, one of the snakes hissing. "Try me!"

Peridot stomped over to Jane, grabbing her by the arm to haul her back into the room. "Hey! Ow! Stop..." the door closed.

"Oh dear," Marigold wrung her hands, "do you think they will be okay?" Tam Lin shrugged.

A few minutes later, Jane and Peridot reemerged, Peridot triumphantly preening, Jane scowling. Jane was in a pretty dress of pale blue silk and icy lace, reminiscent of a snowflake. A silver hair net dotted with opals attempted to contain the snakes; they writhed and hissed but at least couldn't bite anybody. Jane slouched in the dress, so it didn't fit quite right.

"I'd say you clean up nice, but you look like a wet cat," Tam Lin said. Jane shot him a sullen glare. They went down the hall where a new set of Melusine's animatronic servants waited for them. These ones were black and gray rather than white and blue, and in place of the 'E' and the 'Q' they bore an odd looking 'C' on their chests. The guides led them through the golden doors again, where they once more entered a new location.

They walked into a feasting hall with another elaborate display in the ceiling, this one of various gemstones in the shape of suns and starbursts: pockmarked topaz asteroids, luminous citrine bodies, and gliding moonstone beams. In the center of the room was a long table made of heavy black onyx with symbols carved into it, similar to the ones they had seen at the gate, and set with gold. The table was laden with a rich meal: platters of roasted sprouts smothered in blue cheese, fish on beds of melted leeks, and cakes with sugar glazed raspberries. Most importantly there was a giant flagon of wine; Jane made a bee line, pouring herself a glass. Tam Lin sighed.

Melusine sat at the head of the table in a large chair of gold inlaid with rubies. She had changed into another magnificent gown, this one emerald-green embroidered with all the creatures of the world at the hem. The embroidery was so skillfully done that the creatures seemed to move; Peridot watched the rabbits run and the foxes chase with fascination. "You truly are Conservator of a wondrous Filament, Lady Melusine!"

Melusine smiled indulgently. "I am glad that you think so. It is but a small segment of the Tapestry that is the Totality, but I take great pride in it. It has taken me many centuries to weave this cloth, and I, for one, am pleased with my work. Of course, what I feel about it makes little difference, as long as it suits the Divine One."

"Oh, I'm sure it would!" Peridot exclaimed, looking up at the stars, "I don't see how it couldn't! Is that...is that another miniature universe up there?"

"Oh yes, just a little experiment that pleases me. Like a snow globe, I suppose. A bauble within a bauble."

"*Amazing*!"

"If you would like," Melusine offered, "I could give you a tour of my laboratory tomorrow. Show you some of my works in progress."

"I would love that!" Peridot exclaimed, then frowned, as if just remembering something. "Oh, but we probably can't stay long. We have to leave as soon as our ship is finished being repaired. We're on a journey you see."

"A journey? And pray, what sort of journey is that, if I may ask?"

Tam Lin was glaring holes in the back of Peridot's head, if she could feel the heat of his gaze though, she didn't indicate it. "We're going to see the Sea Witch, to see if we can fix Jane!"

Melusine managed to seem only mildly surprised. "'Fix her', you say?"

"Yes, Jane doesn't want to be the Apocalypse anymore, she wants to figure out a way to fix herself," Peridot shrugged. "I told them it's a thing you can't fix, but I guess it doesn't hurt to try."

"I see, well that is an important journey indeed," Melusine said, then added with a wink, "I somehow think we can find time though."

The rest of the crew ate as Melusine and Peridot continued to chat about complicated things like universal transmutations and the composition of the moving heavenly bodies. Tam Lin sat there, arms crossed, looking a little board. The GCATS dug into the fish, Antoine and Scarlet fighting over the head. Jane looked as sullen as Tam Lin, slumping in her chair as she picked at a sprout. Marigold sat next to Jane, looking at the food with wide eyes.

"All of these things look and smell delightful!" Marigold exclaimed. "Is there any order in which I should consume them?"

Jane stabbed her sprout with a little too much force—it bounced off her plate and onto the table, leaving a smear of sauce. "You eat?"

"I can break down food into a minimal amount of energy. Really, probably takes more energy to break it down than what I can extract from it, but everything looks so wonderful, I just can't help but want to try."

Jane reluctantly grinned at her enthusiasm. "Sounds nice to me, not having to eat."

"Actually, it's kinda a drag," Tam Lin muttered.

Marigold spied a lemon tart. "Oh! That looks delightful. Can I try that first? Is that the proper way to do it? If I remember correctly eating sugar and complex carbohydrates should be done after protein."

Jane grabbed the tart and cut an extra-large slice, setting it on Marigold's plate with a 'thwack'. "You know what, fuck the proper way to do it. Here, have some lemon tart."

Marigold picked up a spoon, taking a bite. "Oh, it's somewhat sour, but sweet! It's delightful!"

Jane smiled, watching Marigold eat. It was like watching a child. Something in Marigold's discovery of it seemed so novel to Jane, and also made her feel a little sad. "Sweet but tart deserts are always the best, aren't they?"

"Would you care for some?"

"No...I'm, I'm not all that hungry."

Marigold tilted her head. "But why not? I can see that your glucose levels are low and that you could use some sustenance. Is there something unsatisfactory about the food?"

"No, no, the food is fine. It's just..." she took a drink from her wine, smiling at Marigold. "It's nothing. Just a silly memory."

"Ah yes, I forget that sometimes human appetite can be affected by emotion."

"Yeah. Not the most efficient way of being, is it?"

One of the animatrons came by Marigold and seeing her eating the tart automatically poured her a cup of tea, setting a bowl of sugar cubes and pitcher of cream next it. Marigold looked up as the animatron left, wiping a crumb from the side of her mouth. "They really are lovely creatures, aren't they?" she commented.

"Hmm? I don't know, they seem a little strange and distant to me. Like walking vacuums." Jane seemed to realize what she had said as soon as she opened her mouth, adding quickly, "nothing like you though. You're different."

"But I'm not, am I?" Marigold commented, continuing to watch the gray robot go from guest to guest. "A complex series of 'if, then' statements and algorithms to make it seem like I'm real."

"Oh please, you seem a little more sophisticated than that," Jane grumbled. "The GCATS even said so. You're enjoying a tart after all, and enjoyment is a feeling, not an 'if, then' statement...whatever that is."

"You have a point," Marigold said, poking at her tart now rather than eating it, "but what if those feelings aren't real? What if the tart I am tasting is nothing more than a sensory system made to *mimic* being human. What if I am just programmed to *think* my feelings and experiences are real and act in a way that makes it seem so?"

Jane looked like a five-year-old who had stepped into the deep end of the pool and just realized they couldn't swim. "Well how do we know then that I'm not a meat computer programmed to think I'm real too? And what about the art you make on the ship? That can't come from nothing without a...soul, or consciousness, or whatever you wanna call it."

"Not so much art, as poor patterns that I copy and adjust."

"Well, most art is a copy of something else, isn't it? We all have to build on something," Marigold had to concede that point. "Sometimes you can't think so hard about stuff."

"*I* think we're all just meat computers programmed to think we're real," Antoine said.

"As do I," Scarlet concurred, "it's science...ow! Don't pull my tail!"

"Meat computers wouldn't care about being called 'fat heads'," Jane said, releasing Scarlet's fur. She turned to Marigold. "I mean, no one can know these things. Apparently, you don't even get a clue after you die. Trust me, I've been there. So, eat your lemon tart and enjoy it. Don't spoil it by trying to over analyze things too much. It's a tart. You like it. Fuck anything else. Don't know what's so great about being a corporeal being anyway. It kinda sucks."

"That sentiment," Melusine said, eyes turned to them now, "is one I can agree with." At Marigold and Jane's awkward looks, Melusine smiled. "Sorry to interrupt the conversation."

Marigold, guileless, head cocked to one side, and asked, "and what is it you do not like about corporeality, Mistress Conservator?"

"It's more, child, that I should ask what fascinates you about it? Do you not understand the blessing you have been given? The divine light of your form?"

Marigold looked at Peridot, as if seeking an answer; Peridot shrugged. "No," Marigold said, "I do not."

"You have been given divine knowledge," Melusine said, "free from the corruption of flesh. Human beings, all living things, have such base needs. They need to eat, they need to reproduce, they need to process waste. It means they spend an endless amount of time focused on these needs. Time that could be spent on enhancing their minds. They develop insecurities, *habits*," Melusine looked pointedly at Jane with her glass in hand; Jane finished the cup with a defiant glare. "All, which divert them from the True Path. You are a pristine existence with a storehouse of knowledge more vast than the greatest libraries. I believe you are truly Blessed."

"That is very kind of you to say," Marigold said. Peridot beamed at this praise. "But I must respectfully disagree."

"Oh, and why so?"

"Knowledge without empathy is just that, knowledge," Marigold said. "It is not wisdom. And I have seen the consequences of the quest for knowledge over wisdom. I would rather not be a part of that again."

Melusine smiled, though it seemed more a plastic smile, like that of a doll. "Ah well, I see. Very well then."

That night, after dinner, Peridot settled into the first comfortable bed she had slept in for a long time. A soft mattress. A down comforter with silk sheets. Fluffy pillows that cradled her head. Her belly was full and she was slightly drunk—a happy place to be. *I wish I could stay here forever*, Peridot thought, squeezing the pillow tight, *Melusine is so smart. There's so much I could learn from her. I could even rebuild with the knowledge she has. Make things better this time! Make it actually work.*

Peridot flipped on her side and thought about Jane. About the purpose of her being. *Of course if Jane succeeds, that would all be pointless. But Jane doesn't want to be the Catalyst, right? I mean, that's why she wants to see the Sea Witch to begin with. What if she doesn't have to destroy the world? What if Melusine has a way to change the basic structure of what Jane is? What if I could really...*

But that would mean telling everyone the real reason she was here, which was not the reason she had given; Peridot would have to admit that she was lying. *They would forgive for that though, right? Especially if it meant I could fix Jane?* Peridot chewed the side of her mouth nervously. *I mean, we could even try to harness her power for good.*

Peridot got out of bed, mind running too fast for sleep. She went to get herself a drink of water when there was a knock at the door. She looked up, puzzled. Wrapping a blue silk robe around her shoulders Peridot went to the door and answered. It was one the servants, this one enameled in vermilion emblazoned with a gold triangle, reminding Peridot of a djinn. "The Mistress Melusine would like to see you."

Peridot smoothed down her hair in girlish excitement. "Just give a moment to change..."

"You are satisfactory as is," the djinn said. "*Time* is the valued constant."

"Ah, yes," Peridot lowered her hand, slightly disappointed, "well please, lead the way."

The djinn glided across the sheen of the marble floors, feet not touching the earth. Peridot followed after the creature, feeling her feet heavy in comparison, as if leaving oiled stains on an otherwise flawless surface. They went down the stairs, to the floor level where the throne room and feasting hall sat. The gears of the castle seemed to be asleep at this late hour, Peridot feeling a little as if she were seeing the underbelly of a labyrinth. They came to a crevice along the eastern wall of the palace, and the djinn stopped, allowing Peridot to catch up.

The crevice lead downwards, and the depths down that crevice were dark, almost black, so it was difficult to make anything out. The djinn vanished into the void, as if swallowed by a pool of ink. Peridot hesitated, feeling a sense of uncertainty. *One does not gain anything by being a coward.* Swallowing her fear, she plunged into the abyss.

The first strides she made by feel and almost fell, for there were steps that were steep and uneven. Her eyesight soon adjusted however, and she saw that while it was dark, there was a thin thread of light, however faint, that illuminated the way. This light grew on the walls, giving off a dull green luster that bounced off the enamel of the djinn. When Peridot touched that light it rubbed off on her hands, like grease.

The walls here were rough, boulder-gray rock, and Peridot could feel a humid heat rising from the deep, smelling of sulfur mixed with something sweet. As they descended, the stairs and walls grew more uneven. Soon there was a river trickling down the steps, the source of the water beyond Peridot's reckoning. The ceiling became strung with stalagmites a pale white color like the underbelly of a fish, the phosphorescent halation bouncing off the crystals in them to cast the cave in a Will-o'-the-wisp glow. The pathway grew narrower, claustrophobic. It was such a maze of impossible twists and turns that Peridot wouldn't have been able to find her way back even if she wanted to.

They came to a dead end. A place where the path stopped and a wall of stone stood before them. The djinn, undeterred, found a fissure in the rock that at first seemed far too narrow to squeeze through, the automaton slipping through with graceful ease. Peridot followed, having to hold in her breath in order to pass; her clothing became torn by the jagged edges and stained with the glowing substance. A part of her mourned the death of the beautiful clothes.

On the other side of the fissure was a long cavern; here, the ceiling was low, jagged with stalactites, the walls sweating with fleshy waves of lime deposit. In the center of the opening was a large pool filled with the same lustrous essence that grew on the walls, only here it was in such concentration that the green burned way so that it bore the appearance of liquid gold. Peridot was taken back by the sight; the reddish-yellow fluid swirled and eddied in constant restlessness, waves lapping at the stone rim. It emitted

278

a hum that resonated with everything around it—a sound Peridot felt deep in her belly.

"I'm glad you accepted my invitation, Conservator-In-Training Peridot."

Peridot looked up to see Melusine on the other side of the pool. There was a natural formation in the rock that looked very much like a fainting couch, and Melusine rested on it, dressed in robes of red studded with bronze stars, a cornet of gold and garnet on her head.

"Oh, of course Conservator Melusine," Peridot said. "I could not have declined! Your promise to show me your work has me very interested."

Melusine smiled. "Good. It's good to see ambition, especially in one so young. Sadly, it is something lacking in the world. Though perhaps, do I detect, a little *too* much eagerness to learn?"

"Whatever do you mean?"

"Dear child, I may look youthful, but I'm incomparably old. Older than the rocks in this small Filament. Older than these Waters. And in all my time I have never heard of this place called Gardenalia, or of the concept of a Conservator-in-Training."

Poop. "Well, maybe it's a newer Filament then?" Peridot offered. "Gotta, train up the youth?"

"The Sea Witch does not create 'new' Fragments of The Ruined Creation."

Peridot looked down at her feet. "No, you are correct," she said, almost to herself. "He does not."

"But that is all right," Melusine leaned back in her seat, "there was a time I was ambitious myself, just like you. I too, had a master that kept the secrets of the Universe from me, tried to keep me ignorant. I took that knowledge from my master, only to find how little he understood," she frowned slightly, as if the memory still left a bitter taste in her mouth. "Ambition can be a gift, little Peridot, as long as it is *tempered*. As long as it is cleaved of impurities so that only the brightest light can be shown through."

"All I want is to create a perfect world," Peridot felt as though the words were torn from her, "like yours! A world without pain or suffering, where we can all thrive!"

"A world joined under the Universal Principal. The Great Dream of the Sea Witch. Who Created all Creation, who Created Themselves. Who Created the Oneness, also Created the Fissure, and do you know why He split apart the Beauty and Glory of the One? Why He Unraveled the Tapestry into so many lost Threads?" Peridot didn't answer, too absorbed by the beauty of Melusine. Too absorbed by the beauty of the light, the humming of it filling her ears, like the hum of bees. "Because we were *not worthy of it*. We were not worthy, so He split Himself apart so we could put everything back together again. Don't you see? It's our great Test, to purge this world of the Impure! It is by discovering the secret to the Oneness of All that we bring our knowledge closer to God, and it is through that, we prove we are Worthy of His Work." Melusine cupped her hands. "Drink, from this Pool of Eternal Life, the very Liquid that is the thing all things are made of, Peridot, and you will see, it is all as I have told."

Peridot went up to the edge of the pool, reaching out to touch the luminous waves; they coated her hand, thicker than water, but less viscous than honey, and when Peridot brought the liquid to her mouth it had the faint smell of copper. The taste itself was tinny but sweet, and as soon as the drops fell past her lips, she knew she wanted more. It filled her belly with fire and rippled through her veins, going from the top of her head down to the tip of her toes and through her fingertips.

Melusine got up from her fainting couch, and now that she was standing, there was an awkwardness to her movement; her body seemed far too large for the size of her head. "What do you think, child? How does it taste, the Knowledge of the very marrow of the Universe?"

"It's the most wonderful thing!" Peridot cried, quickly dipping her hand back in for more.

"Pace yourself little one," Melusine said, beginning to undo her robe, "you have work to do before you lose yourself too much to the Liquid of Life. But once you do, you will see the secret path to God, and in doing so, will shed this vain mortal form to become *His* vision of Beauty. To be in *His* vision of Glory." The red silk fell to the ground, exposing her bare form; however, there was no milky white skin underneath, no soft curves or pink flush; instead, there was just hard black carapace encasing pulsating green sinew. It was a confusion of fused insectoid parts. A bauble of broken bits put back together again. Where there should have been the gentle slope of a shoulder, was rough exoskeleton cast in a polluted rainbow hue; where there should have been a graceful arm, were clenching pincers and chattering mandibles; where there should have been the roundness of a breast, was hard chitin. Her pretty little head bobbed atop a mass of horrors, like a ball lost at sea, smile serene despite the beast that lurked beneath.

Melusine's underbelly quivered in excitement, putrid flesh pulsating and contracting, and for a moment there was a look of exquisite pain on her face; a large grub dropped from her thorax and fell to the floor. The thing was fat and white, and it writhed and cried, it screams like the wails of a newborn. Melusine picked up the grub with her doll-like hands, looking down fondly at it as she held it to her milkless tits.

"Lady," Peridot said, eyes alight with the ruddy glow of the pool, "what would you have me do?"

Melusine smiled as she casually dropped the grub into the golden water. The grub shrieked as the liquid hit it, the water eating at the newborn like acid, dissolving its tender new skin, consuming its tender new innards. "Simple," Melusine said, as the wails of birth turned to the screams of agony, "we must bring your friends closer to God."

Jane lay in her room, unable to sleep. The bed was too soft and the sheets too slick, making her feel as if she were drowning, an ungodly amount of pillows the lid of the watery tomb, while goose feathers from the down comforter pinched her like carnivorous little crabs.

The snakes on Jane's head hissed as she shifted from side-to-side for about the fifteenth time that night. Jane gave up sleeping with a sigh, getting up to get a glass of water instead. *How many strange places have I slept since this whole thing started?* She wondered. It reminded her of when she had first come to the Misty Burrow as a child, shuffled from foster home to foster home until she'd been left to rot in the Re-Burrowing school. Jane rubbed her forehead, suddenly wishing she had drunk more wine.

She decided to go for a walk. Maybe stretching her legs would do her some good, and after all, who knew how long they would actually stay legs? May as well enjoy them while she could. She grabbed a robe to wrap over her nightgown, walking out the door. Outside, she saw Tam Lin was also up, sitting at the end of the hall looking out a balcony window. He had that stone El Guapo had given him and was rubbing it in his right hand. Jane walked over.

"Can't sleep either?" Jane asked, leaning against the balcony parapet to look out at the stars.

"Guess part of being dead is I don't sleep."

"Oh, I didn't think of that. That's gotta be boring."

"Gives me time to think."

Jane looked over at Tam Lin, the cool starlight casting his profile in a silver-blue halo; in that light he did seem otherworldly. "What do you think about? How to get us out of the next shit storm we're gonna find ourselves in?"

"Sometimes...well, a lot of the time. But, also, my memories. What little I have of them."

"Care to share?" It struck Jane at that moment how strange it was, to be so dependent on a person she knew nothing about other than what is in her dreams.

"Not much to share," he said with a shrug. "Brief flashes. More feelings than anything I guess."

"And what feelings are those?"

He looked up from the stone, gazing out unto song of gods, humming their secrets in platinum tones. "Regret. Sorrow. I remember feeling really sad. Like I lost something important and it was all my fault."

For a moment, Jane felt an unreasonable amount of jealousy towards the women in her dreams. "Sounds like memories I wouldn't want to have."

"Yeah, well, you say that because you have yours. Better painful memories than no memories. Without them, you feel sorta...lost."

"So *you* say. I'd rather not be the sum of my past experiences thank you very much. Would make me a pretty shitty person."

"What? Didn't approve a license at some point? Made someone fill out the application in duplicate? Jane the Terrible. Jane the Bureaucratic Bully?"

Her hand went up to the faded purple moon on her forehead, and by some perverse impulse, she wasn't sure what, said, "my real name isn't Jane, you know."

Tam Lin's eyes widened in surprise. "Huh?"

Shit, why did I say that!? "My real name isn't Jane," she repeated. "That was the name given to me by the Light Elves."

"So, what was this Pre-Light Elf name that you had, then?"

Jane rubbed her brow as if to wipe it clean, screwing up her face. "Ugh, nothing. I mean, it was so long ago I can barely even remember it. I don't know why I brought it up. It's not like I go by anything else other than Jane. Forget it. I'm tired and being weird."

Tam Lin looked as if he didn't quite believe her. "If you're sure about it."

"I'm not sure about it. I'm not sure about anything anymore."

"Yeah well, that makes two of us then," Tam Lin said. "Sometimes I'm not even sure if I'm me."

"You've been sure about one thing so far.”

"Oh, what's that?"

"Saving my ass. More sure than I ever was."

“Yeah, I guess.”

Jane thought for a moment. "And I'm pretty sure you're pretty sure the GCATS are cute.”

Tam Lin grinned. "Well, I mean, who wouldn't be sure of that?"

"Scarlet *does* have a big head. It's pretty adorable, really."

"Yeah," Tam Lin agreed. “Wish I could pet them."

"Well, I'm sure if you could, you would be the best cat petter out there."

Now he laughed. "You're really trying to stop me from asking about that name, aren't you?

Jane stuck out her tongue “Yes…and no. I'm just making a point. Somethings are just you being you, your past bedamned. Just like a tree is still a tree, even it's down to the root.”

He shrugged, still smiling. "If you say so, though I'm not sure how I feel about being called a stump. But then again, who am I to argue with the End…" he looked over at her. "Hey Jane, you okay?" His smile died. "Jane?"

Jane was still, face pale, eyes wide. She felt a chill that went to her bones, for in a corner, just past Tam Lin, was the Horned One. It stood in shadow, watching her, in its vacuous billowing robes, while in its left hand it carried a head. The Summer Woman. The Horned One gripped the Summer Woman by her long hair, blood dripping from the loose flesh of her neck, open eyes rolled back.

Suddenly, so that Jane jumped, the Summer Woman's eyes came to life, wild and spinning. Her mouth opened, as if to say something, but nothing came out. She had no vocal cords. The Horned One made a step towards Jane, who fell back, gaze locked on that silently screaming visage. The specter passed through Jane, gliding down the hall and out the door. Jane stood there, looking at that door, holding her hands to keep them from shaking.

"Hey, come on, you're scaring me here," Tam Lin said, looking helpless.

The feeling of something wet dripping down her chin brought Jane to her senses; she focused back on Tam Lin and their surroundings. "Oh," she said, pressing a sleeve to her nose, watching red fluid stain delicate silk. "I uhm, I don't know what came over me..."*The waters are shifting.*

"Do you need a drink of water or to sit down? You look like you've seen a ghost."

"I uhm, uhm no," she said, then looked over at Tam Lin. "I uhm, think something is going to happen."

Tam Lin looked as if he was about to say something when a door opened and Marigold came out, looking panicked. "Oh, you two! Thank goodness you're both up. Have you seen the GCATS?"

"No. They aren't in their rooms?"

Marigold shook her head. "I went to give them their midnight snack, and they were gone! They *never*, especially Antoine, miss their midnight snack. I thought they might have gone back to *The Illumine* or tried prowling around the castle, but when I went to track them, they were gone! I can see Cricket's tracker, but the other three have just vanished!" She looked on the verge of tears.

"I'm sure they're fine Marigold," Tam Lin said. "They're smart cats, right? They can get themselves out of trouble. But you're right that we should probably figure out where they are. Do you have a ping on their last location?"

"Y-yes," Marigold sniffled, "it looks like they were in some lower part of the castle before they vanished. Oh, if anything has happened to them, I just don't what I would do with myself!"

"Just don't panic. We don't know what's happened." Marigold nodded, but didn't look convinced. "We'll go to their last location, for all we know they're just raiding the kitchen. Jane, will you go wake up Peridot and let her know what's going on? I'd feel better if we were all together."

"Yeah, good idea."

Jane walked over to Peridot's room, glad to have some distraction from her recent vision. When she went into the room however, it was empty, the bed cold. Jane bit her lower lip, liking these turn of events less and less. When she went back into the hall, Tam Lin and Marigold were waiting for her. "She's not there," Jane said.

"*Shit.*"

"Where could she have gone?" Marigold wondered aloud.

"First let's find the GCATS," Tam Lin said, "then we can worry about Peridot. We at least have a last location for them."

"Yes," Marigold said, "I can lead you there. Follow me."

They followed Marigold through the halls of Melusine's palace, down twisting stairs and past moonlit colonnades. It was oddly quiet, with not even the whir of the animatrons to disrupt the silence; there was only the click of Jane's heels on the glossy stone, and the sound of her heavy breath.

Marigold stopped before what seemed to be a giant crack in one of the palace walls, turning back to the two. "This is where the signal stopped."

Jane and Tam Lin looked down the crevice where neat polish gave way to irregular stone. "I'm beginning to think that your premonition might have been right," Tam Lin said.

"Yeah, not what I really wanted to hear. Hey Marigold, can you tell what's down there?"

"That is where the large life force resides. But I can't pick up anything else with my sensors from here, as it seems to be interfering with them."

"Okay, so I guess we're going down then," Tam Lin said. "Marigold, keep your sensor-whatever-things open, in case you are able to pick anything else up. I'll take front. Jane, you stay between us. Marigold, you're rear. Okay?" Both Jane and Marigold nodded. That decided, they descended.

It took a moment for Jane's eyes to adjust to the dark, and when they did, she could see the dull gold-green light along the walls. "What is this stuff?"

"It looks to be a life form of some sort. I can't quite discern its origin. Normally mold and plant life that grows like this has a fairly simple structure. This however, is exceedingly complex. Almost like it's organic, yet synthetic at the same time. It would be fascinating to take a sample to study back on the ship where I have better tools..." Marigold reached out to touch the substance, but Jane's hand shot out, stopping her.

"I wouldn't."

"But why not?" Marigold asked, puzzled. "I don't detect any harmful compounds."

"You don't know what it is," Jane said, "and that, in it of itself, means you don't know what it can or cannot do. Plus you were just saying some of your sensors are fried. Just call it one of those human...hunches." Marigold dropped her hand, nodding.

They continued on, going deeper into the cave system, getting hotter. "What is this place?" Tam Lin wondered. "It's like a maze. Marigold, can you get *any* sense of where this life-force might be?"

"It's difficult. There is a core that seems to exist further down, but at the same it's almost like it's everywhere. Even in the walls." Tam Lin sighed.

Jane peered down a corridor, spying an odd glimmer in the umbral murk. "What's that?" she asked, pointing.

Tam Lin and Marigold followed her finger, looking into what seemed to be a small side room, filled with dully gleaming curio. "It looks like, some sort of lab?" Marigold suggested.

"Let's take a look. It might give us some information."

They went down into the darkened alcove. The phosphorescent ooze on the walls didn't travel to this place, so Marigold increased her own radiance to help them see. Indeed, it did look like a lab that had long ago been forgotten, long wooden tables laden with beakers, crucibles, and scales. Some of the beakers had dried up, leaving nothing but a film on the inside of the glass, while others still contained some of their fluids in a range of colors: chartreuse, amber, and cerulean. There were symbols drawn on the beakers, as well as notes containing the same hermetic patterns. Everything was covered in a thick layer of dust and smelled stale, of mildew.

"Huh, I wonder what this was all used for?" Jane asked. She scowled at the tinctures in their tempered abodes.

Marigold wrung her hands. "I wonder as well."

Tam Lin moved ahead, at the edge of Marigold's light. "Marigold? Can you come over here? I want to see something."

Marigold obliged, going up to Tam Lin to illuminate that corner of the room; she gasped, bringing her hands to her face, for along the wall were four tubes containing corpses in various states of decay. The tubes were each the size of a small column, embedded into the rock, filled with a solution that had congealed with bits of mold and residue, like sugared tea that had been left out for too long: the first tube was a dark charcoal gray, with two moth-like creatures floating in it, joined at the hip; the second was light blue, with some odd amalgamation of a man and a fly; the third was a reddish-pink with two larva that had fused, almost one. In the last tube was nothing, but viridescent dew.

"Oh no, oh no, oh no," Marigold said, "this bad. This is *terrible*. The GCATS are in danger."

"Take it easy," Tam Lin said. "We still don't know what's going on."

"Don't you see? She's *experimenting* on living beings. It's a madness that seeps into obsession!"

As Tam Lin tried to reason with Marigold, Jane walked past them, to a door at the end of the laboratory. Something about that door caught her attention. It was an iron door, the color of the night sky, stamped with symbols in rust and charcoal—black on black - readable only by the slight raise of the lines. Jane frowned. She reached out with a trembling hand to the pictogram in the center of that door. A circle within a square within a triangle, followed by another circle in a square in a triangle, creating a repeating pattern that had no end; downward and downward it spiraled, threatening to pull Jane into it, before some odd perverse whim of will broke her from its illusion and she all but fell forward, smearing the drawing.

The door opened with a pop.

Marigold and Tam Lin looked over at Jane. "What did you just do?" Tam Lin asked.

"Opened a door?"

Tam Lin walked over to Jane, annoyed. "First you tell us not to touch anything, then you go and do exactly what you told us not to. I swear, looking after you is like looking after a cat..." Tam Lin's words died as he peered into the room. "Is that a *dragon*?!"

Jane turned and just past the iron door was indeed a massive golden dragon. Burnished scales effervesced in the dim light, gleaming along taut, muscular lines. Its head was triangular and thin, but proud, framed by horns of twisted silver, wings so translucent that channels of blood could be seen like veins of amber-colored ore. Black chains pinned the creature to the ground so that it couldn't stand up or move, the chains linked to bolts in the floor. Jane noticed that the bolts were wound in symbols identical to the one that had been on the door.

The three walked into the room, dwarfed by the size of the beast. "It's huge!" Marigold exclaimed.

"Is it dead?" Tam Lin asked. "It's not moving."

"It seems to have some life-force, though faint..." Marigold started. One of the dragon's eyes opened, causing all of them to jump. The iris of the eye itself was larger than their bodies, the color of the eye a deep umber. Jane was momentarily distracted by the colors that shifted in that orb, from soft pale yellow, to tawny wild gold, to a deep earthy brown. She thought of the Whale of Leviathan, and the deep, sad, wisdom contained within.

"What are you?" a voice rumbled, the floor reverberating so that Jane's toes tingled. "More illusions sent by her to torment me?"

"We don't know anything about illusions or torment," Tam Lin said, "but by 'her' I'm guessing you mean Melusine?"

The dragon's lip curled, a puff of smoke emitting from his mouth. "Is that what she calls herself now? She changes her face as often as she changes her name." The dragon eyed Jane. "No, you are not illusions. She would not have sent one such as *you* to torture me."

"What? You got a name for me too?" Jane asked, crossing her arms. "Shit Kicker perhaps?"

The snarl turned into something that could have been a smirk. "No, it is not for me to name the Forces of Will. Your name, you will have to claim for yourself." Jane huffed. "I do wonder what circumstances have brought you here, and how you have the acquaintance of my captor."

"Well," Tam Lin said, "our ship was damaged and we needed repairs. Melusine offered us shelter while we're working on it. Now some of our friends are missing and we're looking for them." He licked his lips. "What do you mean by 'captor'? Are you saying Melusine trapped you here?"

There was a low, ominous chuckle. "I see she has pulled you into her web as well, as she has done so many others." The dragon glared at Jane. "I would have hoped that one such as yourself to have seen through her deception."

Jane shrugged. "I was hungry."

"Okay," Tam Lin said, "can you tell us what's going on here?"

"My name is Delphyne, and I am the Conservator of the Clockwork Kingdom, Caer Leot. The being you know as Melusine was my wife, until she took over my Kingdom. Your friends, if they are still themselves, are in grave danger."

"I knew it!" Marigold cried. "The GCATS, she will kill them!"

Delphyne shrugged, the chains clanging at the movement. "Not kill necessarily, but fuse them with a False Elixir of Life in an attempt to cleanse the world of flaw and attain what she sees as God's Great Vision. In her mind, she will be freeing them from the physical chains that hold them back from enlightenment, from becoming One with the True Great Purpose."

"Oh," Jane said, "so just psychotically killing them, then."

"I have to find the GCATS!" Marigold took several steps back. "I can't let her harm them!"

"Marigold, wait," Tam Lin said, "we still don't know what's going on..."

"I'm sorry. I'm sorry, but I can't wait any longer. I let the GCATS down once before, I won't do it again!" With that Marigold left, taking her light with her. The orphic glow of Delphyne's golden eye filled the room.

"Well, great," Tam Lin muttered.

"She's not wrong to worry for them, for they are in danger."

"What does Melusine intend to do?" Jane asked. "What is all this God stuff she's going on about?"

"Melusine," Delphyne said, with a sigh, "sweet, sweet Melusine. Once she was so beautiful. Like the light of a star in twilight hue, and I suppose despite myself, I fell in love with that beauty." The voice of Delphyne had a hypnotic quality, an arcane verse from a forgotten age. "When I was Conservator of this Filament, it was a joyful place. There were creatures of the earth and sky. Vast oceans and deep roots. Certainly, there were flaws in the stone. Inclusions that gave rise to unplanned life forms, fissures that held untapped secrets. However, through careful study and meditation, I worked to cleave the stone of its blemishes, or at least understand them. I moved step-by-step towards the Ideal Perfection of God.

"Melusine was fascinated by this study. The desire to attain perfection. I saw in her a willingness to change and learn. To walk the hard path of inward reflection and actualization. Of transformation and transmutation both of body and soul. I did not see the greed, nor the unchecked ambition, that would turn her journey from one of ascension to that of corruption. And for that folly I deserve my punishment here."

In Jane's mind she saw swirls of gossamer wings, pale blue and white, mixed with blood. "She sought to create a short cut to God. To attain enlightenment efficiently, easily. To that end she started to perform experiments. To find the unifying substance that binds us all. The Philosopher's Stone. The Elixir of Life. The Perfect One. At first the experiments were only on herself, changing her body. She felt that by making herself and the things around her more beautiful she was bringing herself more in vision with God. More in line with the great Harmony. I thought nothing of it."

"But she took it too far," Tam Lin said.

"Yes," Delphyne was now sorrowful, "she did. Beauty is indeed a gift from God. A counterbalance to the evil in the world, but it can be a sort of horror in itself. She sought to eliminate all that was ugly, as all that was ugly was an affront. Nothing was good enough anymore. It wasn't symmetrical enough, clean enough, blue enough, black enough, red enough. For God was perfection, therefore if it wasn't perfect, then it wasn't of God, and if it wasn't of God, then it was corruption. She carved her own flesh and blood to bone, and would demand the same of others. In her mind the pain would be justified by the glory. I was too in love with her at time to see the destruction, to see how wrong she was.

"And then, it was no longer that God was all that was beautiful, but that God was all that was spiritual, and therefore everything corporeal was corrupt." Delphyne sank further. "That is when I woke up to the disease that had taken hold of her, for that is when she began to kill things. I tried to stop her, but by then, it was too late. My folly and lust had stupefied me. She had perfected what she saw as the divine substance that connects us all. It wasn't the true thing, but it was close enough to make her very powerful. With that power she was able to bind me here and take over as Conservator of this Filament."

"And all the things that used to live here?" Jane asked, already knowing the answer but still needing to hear it. "All the trees, the birds, and the small things?"

"They all became One," Delphyne said, "with her misguided vision. All my creation. Turned to ruddy slack. A false harmony, flat and pale in imitation to the real music." All three were quiet for a long moment.

"So what do you wanna do, Jane-not-Jane?" Tam Lin asked.

Jane sighed, rubbing the back of her neck. She thought about the symbol on the floor and the symbol on the door. She thought about Marigold and the GCATS. She thought about the yellow-green of El Guapo's eyes. *Gotta make a choice.* "Hey Delphyne, if we free you, would you be able to stand up to Melusine?"

"My powers are greatly diminished, but I should still be able to put up some sort of a fight, and I would be ready for it this time."

"Well," Jane said, "it's always been a dream of mine to ride a dragon at least once. What do you say to that, Tam Lin?"

Tam Lin grinned.

Marigold ran through the rocky catacombs. *I have to find them, I have to find them,* she thought. *If I don't find them, I don't what I would do with myself. If I don't find them, I don't know how I would go on.*

A part of Marigold knew waiting for Tam Lin and Jane would have been the smarter choice, that the entity they had come across could have information useful to their search, but another part of Marigold was overwhelmed by urgency; that every second she waited increased the likelihood of the GCATS suffering some untold horror at the hands of Melusine. And it was a thought she couldn't bear.

Is this what Jane meant when she said that being human wasn't desirable? This irrational feeling? This terror? Marigold pushed the thought aside, moving forward. She couldn't let that distract her now. She had to focus on finding the GCATS.

It made some sort of sense that if the GCATS and Peridot were imprisoned by Melusine, that she would have taken them to the heart of the lifeforce disturbance in the palace. Marigold followed the source of that disturbance. As she grew closer her sensors received more static from the energy around her. Soon they became so overwhelmed she had to switch over to basic vision range, so she could tell where she was going.

It was then she picked up on the light coming from a cavern exposed by a small fissure in the rock. Marigold hurried over to that light, peering through the narrow entrance, the glow from it reflecting off her face and hair. In the room beyond, she saw the monstrosity that was Melusine—her half-doll, half-insect form. She watched Melusine birth the larva that went into the pool of gold. Watched the brief flicker consumed in wails. "No," she gasped, "no, no, no!"

Peridot stood in the center of that pool, waste deep, eyes aglow. Her clothing had been charred by the hot touch of the viscous miasma, but her flesh yet remained unsinged. Antoine, Scarlet, and Toramaru sat hunched on Peridot's shoulders, all three of them puffed up to cotton balls. "Great Conduit of God's Vision," Peridot declared, looking upon Melusine in adoration, "I bring you these lost souls, so that they may rejoice in your wisdom, and be One with God."

"Peridot! You said we were gonna get treats!" Antoine yowled. "I'm beginning to think that was a lie!"

"Yeah, we don't wanna go into the pool Peridot. We're cats!" Scarlet protested. "We don't need baths! We clean ourselves!" Toramaru just puffed up even larger.

"There is no need to worry," Peridot said, blank smile on her face. "Soon there will be no fear, no suffering. Soon you will be One with the Ink of God's Hand. Doesn't that sound wonderful?"

"No it doesn't! It sounds like some hippy cult! Get us back to that ledge *right now*, Peridot!"

But Peridot wasn't listening. She couldn't even hear. "No birth, no death. Just unending life. Unending knowledge. Unending Oneness. Just like the Sea Witch intended."

Marigold staggered into the room. "Peridot! Stop this!"

"Marigold!" Scarlet cried. "Marigold, save us! Peridot has gone mad and wants to turn us into kitty stew!"

Peridot turned to Marigold, unfazed. "Marigold, have you come to join the Oneness with us?"

"No, Peridot, this isn't the way! Melusine is deceiving you! That substance is like a drug of some kind that is affecting your thinking!" Marigold attempted to step into the pool, but the liquid caused her foot to decorporealize; Marigold jumped back before she could be drained entirely.

"What do you mean?" Peridot asked. "What could be wrong with wanting to be part of perfect Oneness? It is the dream of the Sea Witch, you know. To create a world of bliss. The Sea Witch doesn't want us to suffer. He doesn't want us to feel fear, pain, or know death. He wants to be happy. To be rich. To be full."

Marigold reached out from the ledge. "Peridot please, listen to me. I know you think this creature has the answers, but she doesn't. Yes, I'm sure the Sea Witch wants us to be happy, but not at the price of others' suffering. Not at the price of others' will!"

Peridot's eyes dimmed for a moment; Melusine hissed. A rumbling came from somewhere, at first sounding like an earthquake, then a storm. "Will," Peridot repeated. "What good is free will? It seems the source of all suffering, doesn't it? If we didn't have free will, if we just listened to God, then there wouldn't be any pain, and we would all be happy."

"No Peridot," Marigold said, "the world is an imperfect place. Things suffer. Beings die. It's almost as if pain is written into the very fabric of things. But if we ignore that, if we just try to pretend it away, or drown it in our obsessions, we become deaf to the cries of others suffering. We become inured to pain and see it simply as a fault. Is that what you want, Peridot? An unhearing world where people are cruel?"

Peridot's eyes became a swirl of blue and pyrite. "No, I-I don't want that at all. I just want a world...where things are right."

"We all want that Peridot. It's a part of the organic drive to survive. But everyone has a different answer to what that means, and that's part of the point, isn't it? For it to be your own journey. Your own choice. What do you learn by just forcing others to adhere to your own ideology? It's through our differences and sharing of ideas that we learn more about what it means to be what we are."

"Don't listen to her, Peridot," Melusine hissed. "She is full of lies! Will is just an illusion. A deviation from God's Oneness. A discordance. Simple arrogance of the flesh in a desperate attempt to feel they have control over their environment. It is a flaw in the Logic of the Word," she glared at Marigold, "a fairy tale that a being of higher intelligence should be above believing."

"I believe in the GCATS," Marigold declared, standing up stare to Melusine down, "and the love they have given me. I believe in the beauty of this world, and all that has been created within it. The transcendent art. The black holes, the planets, and the things of flesh and blood that inhabit it. And sometimes it can be terrible, but it is often all the more glorious for that terribleness."

"But Marigold," Peridot said, eyes now empty of lucency, filled with tears, "why does it have to hurt so much?"

"I don't know," Marigold said, turning back to Peridot to hold out an arm. "Maybe this is all a part of the Sea Witch's plan, and we just can't understand it. Maybe He is just as flawed as the rest of us. Even with all my databases I can't answer that question. But I can tell you running from the pain and drowning it in this false promise is not going to give you your answers. It will only bring you regret. Come, take my hand Peridot. We can figure it out together, okay? We can figure out this world together as friends."

Peridot tenderly reached out, clasping Marigold's wrist; Marigold pulled her from the waters. Melusine's face darkened. "You fool! And here I thought you would see. That *you*, of all people, would understand!"

"You can't just take things away from people!" Marigold cried, holding Peridot to her chest.

"The only Will is the Will of One," Melusine grew larger in size; the water pulsed and agitated, "and if you will not bow your head in benediction to His Great Wisdom, then I will force you to your *knees* before it."

The pool began to bleed over the edge and onto the rock. "Don't let it touch you!" Peridot cried. "It'll burn!"

"You don't need to worry about that!" Antoine yelled as clambered up some stalagmites. "I'm not lettin' that stuff anywhere near me!"

Marigold looked towards the entrance, blocked off now by the flood of gold. "GCATS! Hold onto me! I'll get us out."

"But Marigold," Scarlet protested, "we don't know what impact this stuff will have on your systems."

"I'll make it somehow, don't worry. The important thing is that you three make it to safety."

"*You*," Melusine boomed, raising a hand, "will not be going *anywhere*." The waters surged again, nipping at Marigold's feet. The GCATS howled, scrambling further up the rocks.

Then there was the deep rumbling again; Melusine looked up, a scowl on her pretty face. "That can't possibly be..." Her words were cut off when the ceiling of the cavern was pierced by a large talon; that talon tore the roof open, exposing them all to the open air. They looked up through the hole in the rock to the night sky, before them a luminous dragon, framed by the moon and twinkling stars, Jane and Tam Lin riding on his back. Melusine shrank before them.

"*You!* But how? I had bound you with the strongest hieroglyphs!"

"You underestimated the Agent of Chaos, Child of Light," Delphyne rumbled.

Melusine turned to Jane. "You did this!" she hissed, face twisted with rage. "I should have known. I should have dealt with you when you first came here. Now, you've ruined everything!"

Jane stared down at Melusine, snakes writhing to reveal the sickle on her brow.

"I won't let you do this! I won't let you take this world from me! I worked too hard to build it, to perfect it, to make it in the vision of God! I've sacrificed too much in His Great Name!" Melusine heaved. "*I* am the one that studied the Great Arts. *I* am the one who sacrificed to learn the Secrets. *I* am the one who venerated Him, so why would He select as His Chosen One a feckless creature like *you*!" She pointed a quivering finger at Jane; Jane's gaze remained distant and cool.

"Maybe because *she* doesn't act like an ass," Tam Lin said. "You killed those you were supposed to protect. Did you ever question if your god wanted this sacrifice?"

Melusine snarled, raising her arms into the air. "Blasphemers! I made this world, and I will drown you in it if I must!" The ambrosial liquid spun, rose, twirling, until it became a spout of amber. The force of it drove Peridot and Marigold back, the GCATS hunkering behind them. The light played on Jane and Tam Lin. Delphyne flinched, scales singed from the heat. Melusine sneered.

"I..." Delphyne gasped, "I can't withstand this! She is too strong!" He shuddered, and the motion shook Jane off his back. She fell into the pool.

"Jane!" Tam Lin cried, reaching for her, but it was too late.

Jane felt the waters cling to her as soon as she touched them, wrap around her to dig hungrily into her brain. It was like the waters of Leviathan, but sharper, more aggressive; instead of a siren call luring her in, this was more like a shark taking a bite out of her ass. The waters bore with it a terrible pain, and a terrible hate, and that hate and pain consumed her, blindsiding her with its ferocity.

A girl standing at the edge of the Forest, watching.

Fresh guts spilled on frozen rock. Steam rising from the entrails.

Blood in the wine, blood in the snow, blood on her feet.

They should all die. I want them dead. I want them all dead, dead, deadDEAD!

Jane let loose a sob with a yell.

The waters shifted and turned, wrapping around Jane. Melusine frowned, falling back.

"What's going on!" Tam Lin yelled over the scream of the storm.

"The power of the False Elixir is overwhelming her," Delphyne cried. "All the dreams and nightmares encapsulated by those who were sacrificed to the Elixir...it's too much!"

Tam Lin thought about this for a moment, before jumping off Delphyne. "Child no!"

Tam Lin landed in the pool, wading through the waters to where Jane crouched, holding her stomach, crying. He could feel the push of the fluid, the whispers of their collective thoughts.

Searing heat ripping at skin, tearing into insides, dissolving tender bits to pools of congealed fat and puss.

Limbs being removed, surgically, one by one, to be replaced by those of a brother or sister. The rot, the rejection, the fever that ran in the blood.

The smiling face of a mother, loving yet uncaring, as she moves further away.

Tam Lin held out his hand. "Grab hold!"

Jane looked up from the vortex of memory with wide eyes, shaking her head.

He tried to find the words. "I'm empty. This death has left me empty. I know it's not much, but if there is some way I can use that, well that's something, right?" Jane still looked unsure.

He grit his teeth. "Dammit Jane, just trust me. Grab hold!" He looked back to where the GCATS and Marigold were about to be inundated. "Before they're killed!"

Jane winced, thought about it for a moment more, then took hold of Tam Lin's hand. The psychic dissonance that had trickled through him before now became a torrent of feelings, sounds, and smells. It was so ferocious that for a moment he was simply caught up in the maelstrom, adrift in its waves. *Tam Lin! Hold on!*

He looked over at Jane, could see the light easing around her as it flowed into him, and he nodded. She nodded back. They could do this. Jane raised her free arm to the sky, the waters flowing around her, seeming to bend to her will.

He sees the forest and the trees. The spines of ice and purple mountains.

He sees the plants and the animals and all the small things of the world.

He sees a girl at the edge of the forest. Spear in her right hand, face smeared with blood. Her moon gray eyes are filled with a sort of icy fire. In the shadows of the forest behind her is a beast, crowned with black horns. The heads of three women hang from its belt.

Jane broke contact, tossing her other hand into the air. The spout sublimated, breaking into a thousand pieces of glittering light that shot up into the sky, falling back down like twinkling stars. Jane crumbled. Peridot ran over to Jane, clasping the unconscious woman's head.

Melusine looked up in disbelief. "No, no, no! What have you done? What have you done with my creation?!"

The light that fell to the earth become absorbed into it. It fell on the shoulders and hair of Tam Lin, Jane, and Peridot, warm and soft. Tam Lin looked down at his hands, still feeling the echoes of whatever had passed through them. "This light," Peridot said, "it's the memories of this Filament." The castle began to shake.

"And back to this world they shall return to fade as all things must do," Delphyne said, rock crumbling around them. "It's time to relinquish the illusion of control."

"No," Melusine cried, grasping at the bits of illumination, "they were my children! My perfect children! You've ruined them! You've turned them to dirt!" As much as she tried to clasp at the golden tendrils though, they slipped through her fingers, fading into the rock. She turned to Delphyne, enraged. "This is all your fault. *You!* You were always jealous my greatness! Envious of how quickly I surpassed you!"

Delphyne's eyes filled with sorrow. "I suppose I am partially to blame for all of this, and for that I apologize. I allowed you to come to this place. I was blinded by your beauty and did not see it. You have become a hollow soul, full of pain and regret."

Melusine's rage turned to tears. "All I wanted was to Glorify God!"

"And so you did, for a time, but sometimes, in order to progress, we must start at the beginning." Delphyne reached down with his giant claw, enveloping Melusine. She raised her arms to ward off the great scaly grasp, but failed, and screamed.

Peridot frowned, Jane's head cradled in her lap. "Did you have to kill her?"

"Death is something you need to get used to, Oh Companion of the Great Magical Shit Kicker," Delphyne said, with no small amount of wryness. "For you don't get beginnings without ends." He sighed. "But alas, Melusine is not dead. I suppose I'm still soft after all." He opened his claw back up, and where Melusine with her golden hair and black carapace had been, was now a butterfly. Her exoskeleton was a seraphic blue, gleaming purple and green, her wings silver cloth, flowing and water-like. She wore a lacy crown of silver antenna that shimmered with sacramental moonlight. "From which you came, you shall return sweet child," Delphyne murmured, "and may you have better luck next time around."

With that the butterfly took off from Delphyne's talon, flitting chaotically up into the air to disappear into the night sky.

Toramaru spoke:

"Drunken starlight hue

Lady moon in mourning gown

Rosy dawn stirs new"

For a moment the group was quiet, watching where Melusine had vanished. They were brought back to their immediate surroundings by a part of the cavern collapsing. "Come," Delphyne said, "we must leave this Filament, lest you be buried here along with her folly. Caer Leot, and Melusine's journey, has ended for now, but you still have a much further to go."

Lament of Ashera II

Mother Day looks down with sapphire eyes.

She raises ruddy arms.

Sets aside the wan gossamer of morning.

She soars.

Her breasts thick with milk, become the soft clouds; the curve of her belly
cerulean.

Her apple-stained lips, become the still winds; her radiant crown delir-
ium.

Her groin becomes warmth, the promise upheld; the heat of fertile allu-
vium.

Daughter Dawn bows to ripening glory.

Daughter Dawn in pale splendor, grows weak under Day's tawny sub-
limity.

Mother Day smiles with ruby red teeth.

Mother Day knows, all is as should be, underneath.

For Mother Day looks on a world blessed with God's wreathe.

The mountains once broken, fallen to rust, now snow-capped and tall,
march lofty and proud.

The creatures once fading, all but extinct, now flourish and thrive, and
in the earth plow.
The Waters once hidden, obstructed from view, shimmer and gleam, no
longer enshroud.
It is a world of joyful abundance, where all praise God with their hap-
piness.
It is a creation of beauty and light, all living in plentifulness.
Zeru's realm is flourishing.

With the Blessing of the Dreaming God, Zeru worked hard to create a world worthy of sacrifice.

He created a World of no death.

He created a World of no birth.

He created a World free of suffering, where all could live in peace under His name, and to honor His creation, He adorned it with beautiful things. For beauty was a thing of joy, and he had had so little of it in the desert of his memories, that he set all around him to flourish, watered by the rains of his fecund imagination.

He built a palace of incandescent aurora set in a river of moonbeams.

He garbed himself in rainbows, spider silks, and stars.

He manifested a garden of All the Flowers in the World, sun-stained narcissus and heady scented lily, that bloomed even when the sun was hidden.

All around reflected the Sublime Art of His Creation, and this included Ashera as well, the last remnant of the old world, as She was a reflection of Him.

He gave her necklaces of sparkling meteorites, and hairpins of morning dew.

He dressed her in gowns of celestial clouds, and cloaks spun of perfumed nebulae the color of crimson and sapphire.

He gathered around Himself a cadre of loyal servants to help Him oversee the Great Vision of His Creation. For maintaining a World such as this was hard—there were always birds that needed to be named, and webs that needed to be spun. They took great pride in their work, and sought to please Him.

And yet, Zeru felt a hole in His heart that couldn't be filled. He wandered the halls of His Great Palace at night, wondering what it could be He was missing. He had storehouses of treasures beyond the wildest imagination, oversaw a world of bounty and harmony, and had universe of subjects that adored Him. Yet still, there was a hunger that gnawed, that no amount of fruit or wine could appease.

He was walking late one night when he saw Ashera, with her limbs of bronze and hair of gold, standing by a pool in His garden, looking at the moon reflected in the waters. She clung to her the small, ugly remnants of the old world—bits of dried coral and shell—as she sang. She sang of a dry land, where nothing could thrive, except for the tenderness of her family and the tribe that had raised her. When Zeru heard her song, He knew what it was He was missing.

Zeru realized, He wanted love.

Zeru went to court Ashera, but she rebuffed His advances, seeing no use for them in a world of neither living nor dying, so Zeru determined to lavish her with gifts in order to woo her.

First, He gave her the Golden Chains of All the Stars in the World; they shimmered with the weight of those gaseous orbs, containing within them the power to entrance any being with their chimeric allure. Whatever creature she placed in those chains on would become her thrall, serving her unquestioningly.

But, alas, this did not win her love.

Next, He gave her the Spear of all the Lightening in the World; the spear was sharp, its top dancing with light, so that the very spark itself could pierce and draw blood. When she held it high, its silver blade chuckled in devilish delight.

But, alas, this did not win her love.

Finally, He gave her the Harp of All the Winds in the World; its bow was graceful, of cloud and mist, its strings the rays of the sun. When she played it, the universe went quiet, eager to listen to the enigmatic melody.

But, alas, this did not win her love.

Zeru came to Ashera in despair, and on hands and knees begged what would please her. What would make her smile once more and look on Him in fondness, to sing of joy instead of sorrow. And Ashera thought on it, before replying, "I would have the Sea. I would have All the Waters of the World."

Zeru paused at this, for the Sea was a dangerous thing. The Sea was under the sway of the moon and storms—the Sea was of its own will. It contained monsters in the dark depths beyond the vision of even Zeru's careful eye. The Sea was also a place of life, a cradle from which new things arose. It was something that could not controlled.

Zeru asked, would not pearls do instead?

No, pearls do not shimmer with life.

Would not dresses do instead?

No, dresses do not warm the soul.

Would not anything else do instead?

Ashera looked at Zeru with her lapis eyes, and He knew that no, nothing else would do instead. And so Zeru gave Ashera the Sea, and Ashera smiled.

Zeru, despite His misgivings, was pleased at her happiness. Her built her a palace by the ocean, of shells and orchids, so she could watch over the still brine as she sang, and they were married, and Zeru felt love for a time being. But still there were times when He would come upon her humming to the unseen depths, and Ashera would look at Him with those storm blue eyes, as deep and fathomless as the waters at her feet, and He wondered what she was thinking.

> *For to hold too tightly to love or life*
> *Is to hold onto the edge of a knife.*

Allerleirauh

The Illumine drifted. Lights shown from its elliptical arms soft and golden, the hum that emanated from its core a gentle pulsating vibration like that of a purr. The vessel moved at a leisurely pace through the boundless expanse of deep space, neither hurried nor plodding; stars and comets glided past, taking note of this entity in their midst, before passing on with little concern.

Marigold sat in the mess hall of the ship, cradled in that soothing aurelian glow. In her hand she had a cup of tea, a half-finished sweater on the side table next to her. She was back in her comfortable plain coveralls, sipping from her cup. On her lap slept Scarlet, curled into a koi-colored ball, faint snores dripping from her dewy mouth.

Marigold set down the tea, moving carefully to pick up her knitting. Scarlet stirred. "Ugh, *Marigold!*"

"What is it?"

"You *move* too much!"

"I moved my legs 2.5 millimeters to the left. That is generally well within your tolerance."

Scarlet's ears laid to their side. "I don't care what is *supposedly* within my tolerance, you need to sit *still*."

"I understand." Marigold then proceeded to cease all movement, becoming as motionless as the wall behind her, as if she had painted herself.

This just seemed to piss Scarlet off even more. "Forget it. It's all *ruined*," she jumped down from the lap, sauntering away. "Now I'm going to have to fix all this fur you just rustled."

Peridot looked up from her corner of the room, crossword puzzle in hand. She wore an over-sized green sweater that Marigold had made with a pair of loose fabric pants. Her hair was held up in a sloppy bun, and a pair of thin silver glasses were set on her nose that seemed to accentuate the fickle color of her eyes. "Oh please, Scarlet," Peridot said, "Marigold didn't stir a hair on you."

"That's what *you* think," Scarlet shot back with a glare. "This fur is maintained within a .095 percent margin of error for maximum sleekness and efficiency. Any ruffling that occurs could potentially hinder my innate predatory athleticism. But what would you know? You're just a silly human after all. If it'd been up to you, we'd all be goo right now."

"Scarlet!" Marigold protested, Peridot wincing at the wound; but Scarlet ignored the chiding, a satisfied smirk on her face knowing her claws had hit their mark. She leapt up to one of the cat trees by the mess hall windows, where she proceeded to clean herself vigorously. Peridot looked down at her crossword puzzle, eyes clouded and pen now limp in her hand. Marigold's brow knit in concern.

A stomping sound disrupted the gloom. It seemed to come from a distance, recurring in a rhythmic pattern, and growing louder by the second. Marigold's cup rattled, the plants shook, and somewhere Peridot swore she could hear women and children cry. Scarlet looked up from her perch, bath disrupted, pinning her ears all the way back this time to hiss before vanishing off into a corner. Peridot looked over at Marigold in bewilderment. "Wh-what's happening?"

Marigold sighed, setting down her needles. "Dinner time."

"Huh!?" Another series of thumps caused the chair underneath Peridot to bounce. "I thought cats were supposed to be quiet!"

The door to the mess hall opened, and in stomped Antoine with Cricket at his back legs, Antoine slamming his paws on the floor with enough force to register on the Richter Scale. Cricket tried to mimic his movements, but her weight wasn't enough to have the same effect, so she simply leapt around Antoine playfully; Antoine looked as though he was in no mood for zoomies however: eyes mere slits, his ears pinned forward, cheeks flared. A very serious face, for a very serious cat.

"Mothe...ergh, Marigold!" Antoine declared with all the dignity his twenty pounds could muster. "I demand dinner!"

"Yeah!" Cricket chirped. "Dinner!"

"Antoine, Cricket," Marigold began, "you know you are rationed a certain amount of food each day to ensure you maintain a healthy weight. The time is selected based on your metabolism for peak nutritional absorption. Your mealtime will come, but it's 22 minutes and 54 seconds from now."

Antoine was having none of it. "Food time must occur *now*. Do you think a physique as fine as this needs to be on a *diet*?!" He stood proudly, displaying his frame, generously sized primordial pouch swaying. "Besides! I still cannot forgive you, Marigold, for that time you fed us...*two minutes late*!"

"Two minutes late! Two minutes late!" Cricket began to chant.

"It was one minute and thirty-five seconds late, thank you very much," Marigold said in a voice usually reserved for reasoning with toddlers, "and I was late because we were in the middle of a solar wave storm that effected my power cells."

"It matters not! The sacredness of food time must be protected at all costs!"

"How about we have some play time before dinner?" Marigold suggested. "That way you can burn off some of this excess energy and we can still keep to our schedule."

Cricket's ears perked up, but Antoine scoffed. "Do you think me a mere *kitten* to be sidetracked by baubles? Playtime won't do! Anything other than dinner simply won't suffi..." Marigold walked up to the kitchenette wall and flipped a switch, the room suddenly dancing with lights, playing on the walls, floors, and ceiling like some sort of cat disco.

Cricket jumped right in. "Cat laser dance party!"

"Fair enough Marigold," Antoine said with a glare. "You've won this round due to your trickery. But do not forget! The two minutes late shall forever be in our memory! *Boooonnnnnssaaaiiii!*" Antoine ran into the swirling lights, pouncing.

Marigold opened one of the kitchen cabinets. "That should keep them occupied for a bit."

"If you ask me, you're too easy on them. Spoiled brats," Peridot grumbled, joining her on the other side of the room.

Marigold shrugged, pulling out a tin of cat food. "What can you do? They're cats. They're a force of nature. They are who they are, and I'm not going to change that. I can only redirect for a small period of time." She grabbed a can opener.

"I don't know if that makes you smart or too easy going."

"I fear I fail to have the knowledge to answer that question adequately as well," Marigold said with a smile. "Would you care for some tea? Or some coffee?"

"You got coffee on this thing?"

Marigold opened another cabinet, revealing pack upon pack of neatly stacked silver bags. "It's really quite delightful," Marigold said, "or so I am told. Father was a bit of a coffee connoisseur."

Peridot could smell it from where she stood. "This Father guy, he was the one who built this ship?"

"He was a scientist that helped create this aspect of me, yes, though he wasn't the only one. Others helped to build *The Illumine.*"

"He's not around anymore I take it?"

"No, thankfully not. He was...he wasn't a very good man." Marigold pulled out a coffee grinder. "*But* he liked good coffee, apparently. Neither I, nor the GCATS, can be said to be proper judges of such things."

"I couldn't imagine the GCATS on caffeine."

"That would be inadvisable, indeed," Marigold agreed. Peridot laughed. There was a moment of quiet between the two as she ground the beans. "They really are sweet cats though. I don't think

I would be what I am without them. And not just in that they maintain my physical systems. They help me to understand what it is to be experiencing this reality."

Peridot grinned. "You're lucky to have that," the grin faded. "Ugh, sorry I almost...you know..."

Marigold continued to smile. It was the same serene smile that Melusine had tried to effect, coming off as forced, but on Marigold the expression had a warming quality, as if it added to her luminescence. She poured the coffee into a filter, placed the filter on top of a mug, and got some water boiling. "That wasn't you. That was Melusine."

"Was it though?" Peridot wondered aloud. "I allowed myself to be lured in so easily. I should have known better. I wonder how much of it was Melusine, or how much it was me wanting to believe in what she was telling me."

"Well, is it such a bad thing to want to believe in? A perfect world?"

"Not really, I guess. But I fear that with me, it's a sort of flaw. An attachment to something that doesn't really exist. Because a perfect world is ultimate control, and the desire for control is ultimately born out of fear, isn't it? Living beings don't want to be controlled. They want to be free. They want to be themselves, even if that freedom is an illusion," Peridot played with a napkin. "That should be the beauty of it, right? The scattered light from the prism. The parts that are somehow more than the whole. But for some reason I struggle to see it. For some reason the wild of the unforeseeness of it all, fills me with terror."

"I suppose then you have to ask yourself what is that you really fear then, in this lack of control?"

"Loneliness, I guess. The barren wastes. I guess a part of me thinks if I get it all just right, nothing will ever leave me and everyone will always love me," Peridot laughed. "Ironic, isn't it? Someone like me, who's supposed to be so wise, still haunted by petty human tendencies."

The kettle came to a boil and Marigold turned away, beginning to pour. There was the crinkle of water as it filled the paper, the pop as the ground beans foamed under the stress of the heat, the soft trickle as the water passed through into the cup below. Steam and the pungent smell of coffee filled the air. "I have found that is not easy for organic beings to change patterns of thinking. They have so many ingrained habits that are key to their survival, whether that be survival of the physical form or the psychological. They are hard to break. Especially when the emotion involved is fear. In fact, I find the more intelligent the being, the better they are at hiding the source of their fear. To the hide their feelings behind a veil of rationalization so to speak. Do you take cream?"

"If you have some then yes, please." Peridot looked over at Marigold. "Is it any different for space traveling AI systems? Breaking patterns?"

Marigold smirked, pulling out another freeze-dried bag. "No, unfortunately not."

"Then how do you sit with it? How do you conquer the fear?"

"You accept that sometimes somethings have no answer, and that sometimes we have no control, and that it is all right. For all the GCATS knowledge, they do not know everything, though they would tell you otherwise. There are things out in this world that still have mystery to them, and perhaps always will, and to be honest, I like the thought of that. A world that is endlessly mapped and figured out, well, that would be boring wouldn't it? That would take away from its majesty. Sometimes the beauty of the art is not in the color or the technique, but from the indescribable feeling you get from gazing upon the work."

"If you say so," Peridot said with an unsatisfied huff.

"I always remember something that El Guapo said, at a time when I was feeling less than adequate in my function as caretaker of this vessel. He told me to remember, that sometimes the joy in seeing the clouds of milk in your coffee is *not* knowing what shape they will form." Peridot looked down as Marigold handed her the mug.

After dinner Cricket announced she was finished with repairs. She had been able to get most systems up and running thanks to some supplies Delphyne had given them, though there was still one thing they were lacking, "we need to gather some rarminium if we're going to jump to the Lab," she said.

"What's rarminium?" Peridot asked.

Cricket shrugged. "Don't know. All I know is that it's rare."

"Well then, what does it do?"

"Heck, I have even less of an idea about that," Cricket said, walking away, leaving Peridot nonplussed.

The small crew gathered in the Tank Room to ready for the jump. Antoine was by the Dream Tank while Toramaru, Scarlet, and Cricket settled into seats by the monitors that lined the room. Toramaru sat before a screen that had a series of complex graphs in the shape of cones and lines, while Scarlet sat in front of another that had a set of currently blank vital readouts—heart rates, hormone levels, and brain maps. Cricket sat next to a readout of what seemed to be a schematic of the ship, nose poking at a few numbers. Jane and Tam Lin were in the Tank Room as well, wearing similar sweaters to the one Peridot had, though Jane's was in pale yellow and Tam Lin's was in gray.

Marigold walked over to where the GCATS were hard at work, poking at keyboards with their paws. She looked over Toramaru's shoulder at the screen. "Looks as though Toramaru has found a source of rarminium and is calculating our trajectory." Toramaru pointed at something. "He is having some difficulties due to anomalies that have begun to arise in the spacetime continuum, but we are fairly certain that these coordinates will get us to our desired location."

"Yeah Jane," Scarlet said, "stop messing up the spacetime continuum."

"Sorry?"

"Scarlet, hush, it's not Jane's fault," Marigold said. "Well, actually, it is her fault, but she can't do anything about it. Regardless, we should reach our target destination within plus or minus five light years at a two percent level of certainty. Looks like it is a small Filament with only minor life forms. Nothing complex. Cricket, how are my systems?"

"Stable and running smoothly for the most part."

"Scarlet? How is the composition of the Tank?"

"Within tolerable ranges. I would like to re-calibrate the PMF once we're back at the Lab. It's a bit overladen with echoes, but it's nothing that Antoine can't handle, *with his fat head.*"

Tam Lin whistled. "That was a good one." Jane nodded in appreciative agreement.

"*You're* the one with the fat head! *Fathead!*" Antoine spit back. Scarlet purred smugly.

"Antoine, Scarlet, focus," Marigold said. "And Scarlet, don't get Antoine agitated before he goes into the Tank. We don't want to lose him."

Scarlet's purr ceased. "Understood."

"alright," Antoine said, leaping up to the edge of the Dream Tank, "well if all systems are go, *I'm* ready to jump in."

Marigold gave the signal, Antoine entering the Dream Tank with a splash. He floated there, suspended, belly exposed. The GCATS became all business, their monitors now buzzing with activity. "Starting up connective hydrolic fluid," Cricket said.

"Antoine's readings are coming in clear. Cerebellum is slightly activated, but within tolerable ranges."

"Toramaru is starting up the field generator. All systems normal."

"Diverting power to Dream Tank Psychosis integration."

"Ease up Cricket. Antoine hasn't done this for a while and you're causing an adrenaline spike."

"Decreasing power flow by five percent."

"Antoine's holding steady."

"Toramaru is creating the wormhole aperture. Wormhole aperture created."

"All systems holding steady."

"Antoine holding steady."

"Wormhole is stabilized. Get ready for the jump."

"Ready."

"Ready."

Toramaru gave a thumbs up.

"Okay then," Marigold said, "let's go!"

There was a sensation, like taking the first drop on a roller coaster—your body was in one place, but your stomach (and possible sanity) was in another. Faint whispers could be heard coming from the walls. "Thuunnnaaammmmm...." they seemed to be saying, "phanwetoflacccccc...." Jane started as she felt something brush up against her; she turned to see a ghostly, purring Antoine. He was the color and consistency of the Dream Tank fluid, and he looked at Jane with hypnotic sleepy eyes.

"Thhuuuuunnaaa," this golden Antoine murmured, ""pan-itoflaks."

"What tha..." Jane looked back towards the Tank where the corporeal Antoine was still floating, then back down to the eidolon Antoine before her. *Oh Gopher, there's two of them now!* None of Marigold's houseplants would survive.

"It's Antoine's dream state," Scarlet explained. "The barriers between the psychic state and the physical one are thinner in the wormhole. They break down DNA structure so they are more influenced by thought. In other words, his dreams are expressing themselves in physical reality. You'll hear a lot about tuna and bonito flakes..." Scarlet's head began to swell, growing to a disproportionate size. She swiped at Antoine's apparition. "Stop that." Antoine giggled, disappearing into the floor. "But we should stabilize once we're out of the wormhole."

"Except for me," Jane said. She could already feel the snakes slithering away, her head becoming lighter.

"Yes, except for you, your weird DNA, and the walking dead man you keep company with."

A light flashed on Toramaru's screen. "We're leaving the wormhole," Marigold announced. The motion of the ship shifted, and suddenly the stomach had time to catch up with the rest of the body. "Wormhole departure successful."

"All systems are normal."

"Disengaging Antoine from the Dream Tank," Scarlet pounded on the keyboard. "Antoine disengaged."

Marigold picked up a towel. "Retrieving Antoine." She walked up to the Tank. "Toramaru, can you pull up where we are?" Jane shuffled over to a mirror to see what she looked like. A pair of antennae now sprouted from her forehead, like that of an ant. Jane scowled.

Toramaru pulled up an image on the screen. They were in an empty looking place, nothing but starless sky, so black that it made Jane uncomfortable from the lack of stimulation; her vision began to sparkle with bits of light, like when you close your eyes in a dark room, and soon Jane was seeing streams of illumination flash across the screen; she rubbed her eyes, to make the illusion go away, but when she opened them back up the river was still there.

"Ah, that's the rarminium deposit!" Cricket cried. "Looks like a big one too!"

"It looks like a river of stars," Jane said.

"Oh yes," Cricket agreed, "rarminium is very lovely. But also very deadly. And very, *very* radioactive."

"Then how are you gonna get it?"

"Oh we have pills for that sort of thing," Scarlet said with a dismissive wave of her paw.

"Super, duper, anti-radioactive pills!" Antoine declared. He lay limply in Marigold's arms, eyes wide and purring.

"We can all go and check it out if you want," Cricket said. "We have enough atmospheric bubbles for everyone. And heck, we probably don't even need one for the dead guy."

"Atmospheric bubbles?" Peridot repeated.

"Yeah!" Cricket said, bouncing around, "come on. It'll be fun!"

The Illumine pulled up alongside the luminary river. Cricket and the others met at the docking bay, a small copper lined room, where she pulled out a set of thin collars; The GCATS, Peridot, and Jane put them on, becoming encased in bubbles of light. The bubbles were solid, but flexible. They lacked the rainbow sheen soap bubbles generally had, acting more like pliable glass. Peridot frowned as the bubble seemed to increase the humidity, making her hair frizzy.

"So with these we'll be able to go outside and not die in the vast vacuum of space?" Peridot asked, eyeing Cricket. "You promise?"

"Of course, I promise," Cricket said as she darted back and forth, unable to keep still. "I wouldn't entrust our lives to some unknown factor you know...like *some* people." Peridot took the point. They opened the docking bay, a small aperture in the side of *The Illumine,* like a tear, and the crew shuffled through. Peridot was a little hesitant at first, but seeing that no one turned to an ice block or exploded, ventured forth. They floated awkwardly for a bit, before getting the hang of the devices, propelling themselves forward with swim-like motions.

They looked down at the rarminium stream. A million points of pin prick lights, in a range of colors from amber yellow, jade green, and lapis blue, bits of red showing up here and there with edges fading to pink. It sparkled and popped like a fairy's cauldron, eddies whorling inside the flow to coalesce into gems of color that seemed to have a life of their own, like enchanted beings in fetal dreaming sleep. In a sense, the river was reminiscent of the False Elixir of Melusine, though where hers was a tawdry fool's gold, this was diamond pearl hue lacking any of the tawdriness of that whorish luster. Alongside the stream was a nebula, stretched out like a beach, in hues of rose, sage, and honeycomb, sparking with electric light.

"It's beautiful," Peridot said, looking down, the light of the stream reflected in her eyes.

"It's the mother lode!" Cricket cried, the light in *her* eyes tinged with greed. "With this much rarminium we can run the ship for a whole century!"

"Huh," Jane said, noticing something. She floated down to the nebula beach. There, along the edge of the starry river, was a patch of what looked to be flowers; they had long tendrils of silver light that grew out of the nebula, winding up a black stem-like structure to end in a twinkling head of flashing opalescent lumination. "I wonder what these are?"

"Must be some sort of parasite that feeds off the rarminium," Scarlet said. "Marigold, do you have anything in your library about this?"

"No, so it must be a new discovery!"

"Oh, I just *love* new discoveries!" Antoine said.

"Why *halloooo*!" a voice cried, causing Jane to nearly jump out of her skin; Scarlet turned into a giant puff ball, scattering away, as Tam Lin floated down next to Jane, glaring at the source of the disturbance.

"*By the Gopher*!" Jane cried, clasping her chest, then turned to look at what was in front of her. "Is that a *face*?!" The flower-like thing had opened up, for lack of a better word, it's petals to reveal a smiling human head, only the proportions weren't quite right, and the image was fuzzy, like she was looking through static. It took Jane a moment to realize that it was supposed to be *her* head.

Tam Lin shoved Jane's shoulder. "Jane, don't be rude."

"B-bu-but," Jane looked at the face in confusion, "I think that's supposed to be *me*!"

"Ah," the flower-thing said, "does this visage not please you? We generally find when we wear the form of those who visit us, it puts them most at ease. Would this work better for you?" the thing changed from Jane to Tam Lin, "or perhaps this?" Now it had the head of Antoine.

"Jus...just wear your own head!"

"Ah, I don't know if you would care much for that..."

"It's weird seeing the faces of my friends someplace else! I feel like they're beheaded or something."

"alright, but don't say I didn't warn you." The face changed, and instead of the countenance of a recognizable being, Jane looked down into a spinning hole of horror—of demons messing with molecules and mazes that had no end. Jane paled.

"Go back to the cat face! Go back to the cat face!"

The flower shook itself, and was once more in the shape of Antoine, even if a little angular. "I'm sorry you find this concerning."

Antoine floated by, fish flakes bouncing around in his bubble. "I rather like looking upon mine own countenance, thank-you-very-much."

"Ah good! Glad to have that out of the way!" The flower-thing said. "Greetings!" and as it said that the rest of the flowers bloomed, each one opening up to a different cat face, each one offering their greetings in turn. It was like a ripple in a pool, and soon Jane was looking out at an ocean of various cat heads, framed in sunflowers, roses, and tulips. Antoine blushed. "We are the Celestial Flower Child, and we welcome you!"

"Oh," Jane looked over at Tam Lin, before bowing shortly, "I'm Jane. It's nice to meet you." Tam Lin gave a nod of approval. "We live aboard that ship, *The Illumine*."

The flowers all turned to the ship, basking it in its glow. "Ahh, that is a lovely vessel indeed. Well Janes, we fear we do not have individual names to describe our collective, as we are all of one Root. But we understand this can be hard for beings such as yourselves to understand, so you can call this individual iteration of the Celestial Flower Child....hmmm...Raspberry."

Tam Lin was now smiling, arms crossed over his chest. "Why Raspberry?"

"Because one of you has a memory of eating a raspberry," the flower replied, "and I enjoy that thought."

"You can read our memories?"

"Some," the flower shifted a stalk, "though there are those where the pools are murkier than others." Jane looked over at Tam Lin.

"Well, what do you do here Raspberry?" Peridot asked. "Other than make funny cat faces."

"We feed on the light of the Celestial River," Raspberry replied. "It nourishes our Root and makes us grow strong."

"Ah," Cricket said, "so you eat the rarminium!"

"Yes, as you so choose to call it. We call it the Nectar of the Gods, the stories that give us sustenance."

"The Nectar of the Gods," Cricket snickered, "how provincial and quaint."

Scarlet snickered along with Cricket. "Indeed, not nearly as sophisticated and scientific as *rarminium*." Cricket's snicker died; she licked her lips. "I mean, next thing you know, we'll be talking about magic!"

"Ah, but it *is* the Nectar of the Gods!" Raspberry declared, "for rarminium, as you call it, comes from starlight, and stars are nothing but the manifestations of the songs of gods from bygone eras. Their honeyed words, sweet with the perfume of hope, amalgamate and form this river, from which we drink. So, in a sense, it is magic!"

"Pssh, magic is just an excuse for lazy thinking! A way to describe things we simply don't understand."

"Indeed, that is the very most vital part of magic: its inscrutableness! If you could understand it, then it wouldn't be magic! It would be chemistry, or alchemy, or some other such thing. It is the very indescribable nature of the Nectar that makes it what it is!"

"I mean, if you say so," Cricket said. "All I know is that it helps my ship run."

"I'm sure it does! The Nectar of the Gods can do many things! If you listen closely enough, you can even hear its wisdom from past iterations of creation."

Jane went over to the edge of the nebula, pressing her ear to the river. "I can't hear anything."

"Ah, well, it can take some practice," Raspberry said, then pulled up a cup, brimming with light, "or you can speed up the process and ingest this wonderful rarminum wine we make!"

"Ooo!" Jane said, walking up to accept the beverage. Raspberry passed it through the bubble, as though breaking through the surface tension in a pond; Cricket panicked at bit this, but relaxed as Jane seemed to be fine.

"Jane!" Tam Lin cried, aghast.

Jane looked over at Tam Lin, cup in hand. "What?"

He couldn't believe he had to explain the obvious. "That stuff is radioactive!"

Jane shrugged. "I took the pill," and downed the wine in one shot.

"Oh, oh, oh! I want to try some too!" Antoine cried, spinning over in his ball.

"Sure!" Raspberry said, pulling out a baggy. "We have it in catnip form too!"

"Yay!"

Tam Lin frowned as Jane and Antoine imbibed, talking and laughing with the flowers. He walked over to where Marigold stood with Cricket, gathering the rarminium. Marigold was using something akin to a space vacuum to suck the substance up, Scarlet looking at the device with her ears pinned back. "You don't need to worry about Jane," Marigold said, "she's right. The pill she took will protect her from the radioactive aspects of the 'wine'."

"That's not what really bothers me."

Marigold cocked her head to one side. "Oh, then what does?"

"I don't know," he rubbed his face.

Marigold looked over at Jane, dancing with Antoine. There was a fervidness to her motions that made it seem like she wasn't having as good of a time as she was letting on. "I see. From what I understand her Filament grew unstable and collapsed, is that correct?"

"Yeah, pretty much."

"So she lost her home. That must have been hard. Have you tried talking with her about this?"

"No...there, really hasn't been time."

"Well, I know very little in the way of humans, but if you're worried about her behavior, perhaps you should address how she feels."

"You know, I think you're lying when you say you don't know much about people."

"Oh, but I really don't," Marigold said with wide eyes. "I just know about cats, and cats are infinitely more complex."

Raspberry turned to the pair. "Hey, individual being known as Tam Lin, why don't you come over? We have something here for you as well!"

Tam Lin scowled, but Marigold grinned. "Go on," she said, "we can handle it from here. What's the worse they can do to you? Kill you?"

Reluctantly, Tam Lin walked over.

"Can you hear it?" a voice was asking Jane as he approached the river. "Can you hear the song of the old gods?"

Jane took another drink from the cup, feeling very tipsy very fast for having had so little. "No Raspberry, I'm afraid I can't."

"Ah, I'm not Raspberry, I'm Lemon Tart. But I'm sure you'll hear it soon. You are preternaturally attuned to it. Attuned to the languages of the world."

Raspberry went over to Tam Lin, passing over a small crystal to him. It was clear and bright as glass, in the shape of prism. Tam Lin seemed to instantly fall into that light, gaze caught up in whatever he saw there.

"Oh, I'm sorry Lemon Tart," Jane said to the zinnia-framed orange cat face. "I'm not used to telling you all apart. I'm glad that you think I'll hear it soon." Jane pointed to something in the distance, something in the sky that for all purposes looked like a silver thread torn loose from a sweater. "What's that over there?"

Lemon Tart followed the direction of her finger, seeing the thread. "Oh, that is the Universe fraying. I wouldn't pull on it if I were you. I don't think you're quite ready yet for reality to fall apart." Lemon Tart turned back to Jane. "And don't worry about the name. We're not used to telling ourselves apart either, to be honest, though it's a fascinating thing, this individuality."

"I don't know," Jane said with a burp, "sometimes I think too much of it is a bad thing. You all seem pretty happy as is. I hope it doesn't mess with you."

"Oh, I think we'll be okay," Lemon Tart said, pointing to the root system, "we have fairly good communication. There's not one thought that occurs within our colony that everyone else doesn't experience."

"Oh! Well, that's gotta be interesting."

"We do feel that your individuality does leave you to feel confused at times, perhaps lost in the concept of it, at times becoming an obsession removing you from Unity and obscuring your true self," Lemon Tart looked pointedly at Tam Lin. "Taking you out of the glory of the song, merely humming a tune."

"How can you not hear the song if you're humming along with it?" Antoine asked.

"I think Jane knows how," a new plant that Jane suddenly knew to be Strawberry said. "Jane knows what it means to experience life, yet be removed from it all the same. The song that is listened to, but not heard."

Jane looked up at Strawberry, at the red colored face and pinkish white petals and suddenly tears were in her eyes. "I miss Bill," she said, the words torn from her, almost unbidden. But she knew, she knew Strawberry already knew that.

"Who the fuck is Bill?" Antoine demanded. "Is this *Bill* a contender for my love? Do I need to fight him?" Lemon Tart hushed Antoine.

Jane laughed. "No, Bill was my friend. He told bad jokes. He wanted to be a Marfeild artist," the Celestial Child wilted slightly at this, "and probably was an alcoholic. But I loved him. And I loved his family. They accepted me when no one else would. And they died. They died because of me and this stupid curse, and there's no getting them back. I think I've tried not thinking about it up until now, the loss was just too much, but I have to face it, don't I? I have to face that they are gone, and that I'm the cause of it all."

"Child of Renewal, it is not your fault the world is the way it is, or that it sometimes must be reborn."

"And as I've said before, that's easy to say when you aren't the one made to suffer."

"There is no suffering in death, simply a breath, and a pause. Not all are subject to Leviathan's cruel attachment to perpetuity. The old gods are old gods for a reason, for they have died and been reborn, and so have their worlds with them. You are not the first to have passed through this turmoil, nor will you be the last; for the old gods, they are as numerous as the grains of sand."

"And if I had died when I should have? Then none of this would be happening."

"If you have died when you 'should have', then someone else would still be here, bearing the same burden." Jane stayed silent. "Death is not an ending, but a recycling. A return to origin."

"I don't understand a world that has to be this way. That has to be built on loss."

Antoine raised his head. "You know, you aren't the only one whose lost something."

"I know that." Jane protested, annoyed.

Antoine's eyes locked on something she couldn't see. "There was a time I had brothers and sisters. Not the GCATS, but ones like me. Who shared my blood. I had a mother, and a father. But they all died. In a cruel way. I found a new family in the GCATS and they helped me through that pain. I still feel their loss, that will never go away, but being with the GCATS and Marigold makes it more...bearable."

"What is it you're trying to say?"

Antoine swiped at her, and it drew blood. "That you aren't alone. Stop feeling so sorry for yourself. We all have burdens."

Jane looked down at the scratch on her skin. At her pale flesh through which blood flowed. Blood on snow.

She sighed.

When Jane raised her head, she was no longer at the edge of the starry river, but in a field filled with sunflowers. They stood tall above her, almost like trees, and through their waving heavy heads she could see the sky—a clear piercing blue.

The broad, smiling faces of the flowers were turned towards the sun, their leaves and stocks thick and strong, the color of jade dew. Bees buzzed among the yellow petals, gathering golden nectar hidden within their dimpled cheeks.

But then the sky turned gray, and a chill filled the air. The sun hung low on the horizon, covered with clouds. Frost bit at the noses of the sunflowers, and the chickadees and finches feasted on their flesh. The smiles of the sunflowers turned to frowns as they curled inwards, stems now a stiff, musty gray. Bitterness consumed them, angry at a world where their beauty was forgotten, until snow chased the last remnants of the stalks away, leaving behind nothing but seed and brittle dust.

Jane reached down to pick up one of those seeds, and was suddenly back in the Misty Burrow, standing before The Goose's Garter with its bits and bobs all torn up by flames, ash sticking to her hair. In her hands was Bill's head, his eyes rolled up, skin slack, tongue drooping obscenely from his missing jaw. It felt as though that head didn't belong to the Bill she knew, that it was some sort of macabre Bill-shaped mask; if Jane stared hard enough, she almost felt she could convince herself that this was all somehow a joke, and that the real Bill would show up around the corner, laughing at the prank.

But no, it was really Bill.

Jane heard a sound, and looked up at the sky, for a moment sure she would see Leviathan again, but there was no whale undulating in the darkness this time, and the sound, while beautiful, was not all that sad. It seemed to come from the very stars themselves, as if she were hearing their reverberations.

When Jane looked back down, Bill's head was gone. She was still in the Misty Burrow, and everything was still on fire, but instead of bodies there were sunflowers. Jane opened up her hand to see a glimmering object.

It was the seed.

And written on the casing of that seed was the promise of a new field of sunflowers. Of a new clear blue sky.

Of a new beginning.

Once upon a time, there was a prince who was born with nothing. He had no kingdom. He had no lands. He had no name.

He lived by the sea with a wise fisherman, who taught him the words of the creatures of the ocean and how to see the future in stones—perch and basalt, mackerel and quartz. The wise fisherman would tell stories to the prince, of the wisdom the winds and waves contained.

One day, a storm gathered on the horizon, and this was no normal storm; it wasn't the slate blue-gray of an auburn woman's eyes, but a sickly purple-green, the air in it heavy with rot.

The fisherman said to the prince, "This is a spell sent by the Deathly Queen. She knows you yet live, and even though she has a treasure trove of a thousand souls, her greed knows no bounds. She hungers yet for one more. You must stop her. You must stop the Deathly Queen before she drowns us all."

"But how do I do that?" the prince asked. "All I know is how to fish and read the waves."

"You must find the Stag Maiden. Awaken her from her slumber so she can bestow upon you your birth right."

"And where do I find this Maiden?"

"She sleeps deep in the November Forest, where trials will await you. Face those trials with the things you have learned, and you may succeed."

The prince bowed his head, determined to leave the next day. He rose at dawn, the sky having grown even more menacing, the clouds grimacing faces of demons scowling down. The fisherman gave the prince a pack of sausages and cheese, before seeing him off with a tearful goodbye.

Now, the November Wood was not known for being a friendly place. Most of the villagers avoided it if they could, for it was full of hauntings and misdeeds. It was gloomy, perpetually in the grip of autumn going to winter, the trees bare but for a few stubborn leaves, their branches dark, almost black.

It was twilight by the time the prince reached the Woods, the edges of the sky a soft purple as the first stars started to show. On the horizon was a sliver of a moon. A Cheshire cat moon. The prince was about to set camp to rest, when he heard an odd sound—almost like a trill. Paws scattered behind him and the prince turned, heart pounding, expecting to see a pack of wolves at his heels, only to see a group of...cats. Four of them. All staring at him with unblinking owl-like eyes.

"Who are you?" the prince asked.

"It's more like we should be asking who you are," one of the cats said. "Stumbling through our forest like that."

"Yes! You are very noisy!"

"I'm the Prince of Nothing," he said. "I am looking for the Stag Maiden so that I can awaken her to defeat the Deathly Queen."

"Ah well, that is different! That is a quest! And we are tasked with aiding those who are on a quest, if they can do one thing."

"What's that?"

"Answer our riddle."

Shit. The prince, for all the wise fisherman's teachings, was not very good at riddles. "And if I can't answer it?"

"Then we don't aid you on the quest."

"And we get to eat you!"

"Oh yes, we are really quite hungry."

This did not make the prince feel any better, but he knew he had to at least attempt the riddle; he had trials he needed to overcome after all. "Okay, well, what is this riddle then?"

"A simple one! A classic! Okay, so one of us always tells the truth, right? And one of us always lies. You gotta figure out who is the truth teller and who is the liar. Using 'yes no' questions only."

"Well, aren't you now telling me the truth and doesn't that answer the question?"

"Nooo, not now! After this! After this! Starting now!" A Siamese cat and a calico stood before the prince, looking at him expectantly.

The prince frowned. He thought about what he knew about cats. He thought about what the wise fisherman had taught him, and soon he had an idea. "Is the calico cat the cuter one?"

"Why yes I am!" the calico agreed with gleaming green eyes and a purring puffed chest.

The Siamese looked over at the calico, and began to swish his tail. "Uhm, yea...ugh, sure..." his ears pinned back, his hackles raised. "Oh dammit, I just can't do it! I'm the cutest one! Anyone could obviously see if I said otherwise it would be a lie! You win Prince. You have bested us in our riddle with your smarts. As a gift, we will turn you into an owl!" And the Prince was transformed to an owl. And the cats ate the sausages from his pack.

The prince was not sure whether this was a gift or a curse, but he could see at night now, so he decided to travel on further into the Woods and discover what other trials awaited him.

It wasn't long before he heard a cry, soft and plaintive. His sharp ears took him to the source of the distress—a small cricket, caught in a spider's web. "Oh help me, help me," cried the cricket, then when she saw the owl, screamed. "Oh, please don't eat me!"

"I won't eat you," the prince said (though he was quite hungry and the cricket looked delicious).

338

"Oh," the cricket sobbed, "I am trapped in this web and the more I move the tighter it becomes! If I don't escape soon, then that awful Old Man Spider will come and eat me!"

"Here," the prince said, heart touched by her distress, "let me help you." And he unwound the knots in the web with his beak, as easily as he used to unwind the knots in a fishing line.

The cricket freed, she jumped about in joy. "Oh thank you, thank you! And for your kindness I will give you a boon!" And when the prince looked up, he was no longer an owl, but a wolf.

The cricket and the prince parted ways, the prince using his newfound nose to follow a familiar scent that seemed to lead him deep into the heart of the forest. He came to a clearing where a man stood under moonlight, amongst silver kissed fern and starlight hued trees. He was the image of a true prince, face proud but firm, a stag horn crown sat atop his head. He wore a rich ermine coat over silks of green and blue. The man smiled at the prince, and it took the prince a moment to realize, that this man was himself.

The prince cowered back. This version of himself scared him, but the man smiled, breaking that hard gaze, and knelt to the ground, holding out a hand. Without knowing why, the prince went up to the man that was him but not him, and in that outstretched hand was an ember, glowing hot and low. "Don't worry," the man said, "it won't burn. But you must carry it with you if you are to help the Stag Maiden. I would do it myself, but it seems...it seems as though I ran out of time."

"But who are you?" the prince asked.

The man smiled somewhat sadly. "I am you, and you are me."

The prince looked down, and the ember was no longer burning. It had cooled to a stone, as gray and mottled as a trout's back in the stream.

When Jane opened her eyes, she was back on *The Illumine*. She was laying on the small bed in the sick bay with a splitting headache, her joints feeling as though they were filled with sand. There was a glass of water and some tablets on the nightstand next to her, and at the end of the bed Antoine was curled up in a little chocolate éclair ball, not looking much better than she felt.

"Ugh," Jane groaned, clasping her head. "What happened this time?"

"You passed out," Tam Lin said. She turned to see he was sitting in the room with them, reading a book. "Marigold had to carry you in here. She asked me to keep an eye on you, since no one knew what was in that shit you drank."

"I don't remember passing out. I just remember talking with Strawberry and then...I was someplace else."

"Then you probably don't remember running around naked screaming at the top of your lungs."

Jane shot up. "What?!" she cried, instantly regretting the quick movement as blood rushed to her head. "Ow, ow, ow, ow."

"Drink the water and take the medicine Scarlet left for you. It should help."

Jane did as instructed, finding it hard to swallow. "I can't believe I did something like that..."

"You didn't. I lied. But for all you know you *could* have done something like that. Or worse."

340

Jane laid back down. "You're mad at me."

"I'm not mad," Tam Lin said, going back to his book, "you just make it hard to keep an eye on you."

"I know...I know..." she bit her lip, staring at the ceiling.

Tam Lin's gaze drifted from the words to look down at his hands. "Look, I'm not good at this stuff. I think a part of it is I'm worried that if I stop to think about, I'll uhm... I don't know..." he rubbed his chin. "But I know you miss your friends, and that's been tough."

"I *do* miss them. Bill and Maera. I even miss Belinda sometimes." She picked at a piece of loose thread on the blanket. "I always seem to be carrying around this regret with me, and rather than alleviating it, I just keep piling more crap onto it. How am I supposed to either save or destroy the universe when I can't even figure out how to keep those close to me safe?"

"You can't blame yourself for the Misty Burrow. You had no idea something like that was going to happen."

"Is that true though? Did I really not know? Or was I too busy keeping my head buried in the sand to not notice what was right in front of me?"

"I mean, I don't know how you could have..." his voice trailed off.

"I told you I had another name once, right? That before the Light Elves took me, I was someone else?" Tam Lin didn't answer. "Back, before I was taken, I was a priestess. A 'Daughter of the Moon'. An intermediary between the Moon Goddess and my people. I divined her words to protect the tribe from the Forest. The Forest was kinda her place. Also death. Death was her thing. I'd get high on a bunch of mushrooms, cut up some rabbits or goats, and read the future in their guts."

"Sounds like...an important job."

Jane shrugged. "It was a dumping ground for unwanted girls. Those born with defects that otherwise would be a burden. I guess my albinism was enough to put me in that category. If I had parents, I wouldn't know. But even if I didn't have love, I had fear, and I had respect. As an intermediary of Mother Moon I could either bring her protection, or her vengeance.

"There was this ceremony every year, one of those harvest-festival-bring-back-the-sun sorta things, and us priestesses were generally not allowed to go. A 'boys only' sorta thing. Except one of the girls, each year, was always selected. And each year, that girl never came back. Now, we were young for the most part, the oldest being fifteen, but I knew I didn't want to go to that festival. I knew I didn't want to *not* come back."

"Didn't the other girls feel the same? If they had this power, couldn't they've used it to stop this festival?"

Jane shrugged again. "I don't think it ever occurred to us to even try. Most of the girls who were 'chosen' by the Mother were damaged. Some of them had bodies so warped they were in constant pain and welcomed the thought of death, others...just didn't understand. Some were so indoctrinated they simply felt they had to do what was needed to help the tribe. I should've helped those girls. I should've found a way to convince them to come with me. But I felt I didn't have the strength to keep them alive, as well as myself."

"You ran away."

342

"Yup," Jane said. "As soon as I got old enough, I high tailed it outta there. No one followed me. The Forest was the Mother's domain, and they were afraid of it. I watched, from my hidden place in the trees. I had prepared pretty well and was comfortable enough. I watched the festival. They grabbed the next oldest from me, a girl who had been shaken too hard as a baby. She laughed at butterflies and liked the flavor of gooseberries. I watched them take turns raping her and then slit her from naval to throat. They drained her blood into the snow so that it could bring back the sun." Jane grit her teeth. "And she screamed. And I cursed them. I cursed them for all their stupidity and for the suffering they caused. I wished the worst on those bastards. I went at night to gather up her blood still left in the snow, and used it to cast a hex. To bring down the village. And then a few days later the Light Elves found our encampment. There was a fight, the Light Elves won of course, and they found me in the Forest and took me to the Misty Burrow."

"You can't say you caused the death of your tribe Jane, or that you caused the death of that girl. You were just a kid trying to survive."

"That's what I told myself living in the Burrow. That to think otherwise was a sort of delusional arrogance. But I don't know, after all that has happened, after all that I am, maybe I really did curse my tribe. And then I wonder if what happened to the Misty Burrow was something that followed me from that place? Did the curse I wish on my own people, the revenge I called down from Mother Moon, does it follow me now?"

"Fuck Jane, that's a question I can't answer."

"I don't expect you to. I don't even think it's a question I can answer myself. It just hangs there though, all the same." Jane's eyes looked off to the distance. "That was the time when I known as 'Una', and Una has done some things that she regrets. I think I thought I could put it behind me when I changed my name, but I guess despite that she's still a part of who I am. A darkness I'm afraid to touch."

"Well Una-Jane," Tam Lin said, "I think that goes for most people who walk this world. We all have light and darkness inside of us, I guess it's a matter of what we do with it."

"Make a piss poor candle?" Jane laughed, looking over at him. "Did you see anything? In that crystal they gave you?"

Tam Lin winced. "Nothing useful."

"I don't believe that."

"Can't get anything past you," he said, and at her worried look added, "Don't worry about it. It's just...it's something I need to sit on for a little bit." Jane reluctantly nodded.

There was a knock on the door. "Hello?" Marigold poked her head in. "Just checking in to see how you're doing. Would you care for some tea, or anything to eat?"

Jane's stomach grumbled and she looked a little green. "I think I'll pass for now."

Antoine however, was suddenly awake. "Food? Tuna? I will take food and special tuna treats."

"Why am I not surprised?" Marigold said. "Well, Cricket has collected the rarminium she needs and repaired the last components of the ship. We should be ready to make our next jump whenever you are up for it, Antoine."

Antoine laid back to stretch out with a yawn. "Ah, your star pilot is weary from his journies. He will need much treats and head pats to have the energy to travel once more."

"All right, all right. I'll get you some extra kibble. Jane, are you sure you don't need anything? You don't have to get up if you aren't feeling well."

Jane rose from the bed. "No, I'll eat something later. I want to say good-bye to the Celestial Child before we leave." She looked over at Tam Lin. "I promise I won't get myself in anymore trouble this time."

Jane left the sick bay, making her way down the halls. She met Peridot as she passed through the mess hall, the other woman working on a knitting project, face screwed up in concentration as she tried to get the yarn from one set of needles to the other, misshapen scarf in her lap. Peridot sighed as Jane approached. "So, you're among the living!"

"Yeah, I think I'm gonna to say good-bye to the Celestial Child before we take off."

"I'll go with you," Peridot said, putting down her project. "I need to take a break from this thing."

"I didn't know you knew how to knit."

"I don't, obviously," Peridot stretched a hole in the scarf so that it almost went over her head. "Marigold is trying to teach me so I can learn to be happy with imperfection. However, I think this may be a little *too* imperfect." Jane laughed.

They made their way to the docking bay to strap on the collars, stepping out of *The Illumine* and back into the black night of space. Jane peered around, looking for the nebula and shining faces, but when she did so found all the flowers had gone, the river of rarminium disappeared. "The Celestial Child," Peridot said, "they've...withered."

Jane went up to the where she could see the desiccated stalks of what had once been Raspberry and Lemon Tart, their shining faces now dim bulbs. All around, not a single flower could be found standing, all crumbled to dry dust. "Did they die because the river dried up?"

"Cricket only took a little bit," Peridot said. "She purposefully did so, so she wouldn't harm the Child."

Jane frowned, feeling a familiar anxiety stir. *Surely it couldn't be...*

"Hey! Look!" Peridot cried, pointing.

Jane turned, and in the distance she could see a cluster of lights scattering off, pulsating and popping like fireworks. They shifted and swayed, reminding Jane of the starlings she used to see in the winter when they began to murmur. "What are those things?" Peridot wondered aloud. "Seeds?"

A glimmering spark rose up from the husk of Raspberry. It was fickle and frail, like it was about to go out, struggling to thrive. Jane clasped that light, holding it in her hand, and when she looked down, it was a sunflower seed; for some reason she couldn't understand, Jane blew on the seed, and like stoking a flame it flared to life, stronger and brighter than before. Jane released the seed, watching as it made its wobbly way to the rest of its friends. "Goodbye Raspberry," she said, "best of luck."

Jane made her way back to the ship. Peridot frowned, a slightly puzzled look on her face, before following Jane back in.

The Crystal Coffin

"Emerging from wormhole...wormhole emerged."

"Disengaging Antoine...Antoine disengaged"

"Retrieving Antoine."

"All systems stable. Toramaru, can you pull the Lab up on the screen?"

From his seat in the Tank Room, Toramaru switched his screen to a view outside *The Illumine*. The crew gathered round to see a solar system of nine planets circling a yellow sun—some of the planets a dusty red, others a murky brown, some with moons, others yet rings of ice and rock. It all seemed rather ordinary, that is, until they noticed the black hole. It sat at the outskirts of the system, large, ominous, taking up most of the night sky. The center of the singularity was dark, darker than anything Jane had seen before, darker than even the robes of the Horned One, and all around it were whirling pools of light falling into that darkness. A hungry Charybdis consuming all.

The planet closest to the vortex was a gaseous giant striped gray, taupe, and tan. It was encircled by a ring of meteoroids gleaming dully with ore. Already a few of those meteoroids were being lured away from the gravitational safety of the planet into the mouth of the collapsed star. One of these meteoroids, bigger than the others, bore the only signs of life visible in the system, with a series of dots running along it's magnetite surface that looked to be huts; a large telescope at the end of that line pointed right at the heart of the black hole, like a spear.

"We made it," Cricket said, "the Lab."

The room went quite as the GCATS stared somberly at the screen.

Marigold wrapped a towel around Antoine, hugging as she dried him. Antoine purred loudly, looking up at Marigold with dreamy, loving eyes. "Toramaru," Marigold said, "let's head on to the Lab. Get this over with." Toramaru nodded, taking over control of the ship to ease them towards the moonlet.

"Well on the upside," Peridot said, "looks like Jane didn't have any sort of transformation this time."

"Really?" Jane said, feeling her face. "Nothing different? Nothing weird coming out of me? No extra noses?" She looked over at Tam Lin with disbelieving eyes.

"Looks like it," he said. "No scales, tails, *or* horns."

"Ah! This is great! Finally! I was getting sick of having who-knows-what happening to me! It's so disconcerting, I can't even begin to describe..." She moved to put her hand on a nearby consul and lean against it, carefully avoiding pressing any buttons, when as soon as her hand touched the machinery it crumbled under her grip, as though it were nothing more than paper. Jane looked at the ruined bits of metal and electrical wiring in her hand. She sighed. "Fuck me."

348

"*Jaaannneee!*" Cricket caterwauled. "Whaddya think you're *do-ing*!? I *just* fixed everything!"

"Cricket dear," Marigold said, "Jane didn't mean to do that."

"I know, but *stiiillllll....*" Jane, gently tried to put the electrical bits back together. The whole consul crumbled. "Ahh! You're making it worse! Oh *mannn*, it's like what she's doing to the universe she's now doing to my ship!"

"It's all *gooood* Cricket," Antoine said, lazily kneading the air, "we didn't need that consul there anyway. The secrets of the Universe can't be held on some screen man, it has to be *felt*. Just have some bonito flakes, catnip, chill and the Universe will open its wisdom to you."

"*I'm not chilling right now Antoine!*" Cricket hissed, puffed up. Antoine leaned over and, grabbing Cricket's head with his paws, began to lick her ears. Cricket leaned against Antoine, allowing herself to be soothed.

"I'm sorry Cricket. I just..." Jane smoothed out the consul as if it were a piece of homework found at the bottom of her bag. "Well, I mean, that isn't too bad now, is it?"

"You really don't know how these things work, do you?"

"No."

"Come on," Peridot said with a sigh, arms crossed over her stomach, "let's do whatever this thing is you wanna do, before Jane crunches something important."

"Just, don't let me hurt anyone." Jane moved cautiously on her top toes as they walked through the Tank Room door. "Anyone else feel the strong urge to eat a bunch of fish and take a long nap?"

"That's how I *always* feel," Antoine said.

They left *The Illumine*, stepping onto the surface of that magnetite meteoroid. From their perspective now on the ground, the gas planet that the little satellite encircled dominated their view, the dark bits of rock that orbited the giant backlit against its swirling, pale vapor. It was that and the black hole, which appeared closer now as well, rimmed in light, looking down on them like a blind, aged eye. That eye seemed to pull at them, enticing them. Jane swore she could almost hear a sound coming from it—the song of the gods, but in reverse. It left her feeling vulnerable and small, like a wild animal caught out in the open. They walked on.

The rocky ore gave way to roads. The roads were spongy and light, made of rubber, but stank of petroleum; they were set on a grid, neatly spaced and at right angles. The huts they had seen were domed houses, the bases of the houses square, so as to fit on the grid, while the tops were angular black octagons, made of a substance that looked to Jane like obsidian, in a shape reminiscent of pomegranates. At the edge of the town was the large telescope, looming over the domes, casting them in its shadow.

There were no people to be seen, and it was quiet, with only the ominous whir of the black hole to break the silence. Everything was neatly kept though, showing few signs of wear, which seemed odd to Jane, until she saw a human-like figure whizzing pass them. He wore a simple gray uniform and had a smile on his face, though he made no move to acknowledge them. He went over to one of the pomegranate structures and began to fix a broken light.

"Marigold, what are those things?" Peridot asked, watching a woman in a similar uniform walk from one building to the next, cleaning windows.

"The caretakers of this place. My predecessors in a way."

"Don't seem anything like you if you ask me. Seem a bit dumb."

"*Jane!*" Peridot protested. "Those are Marigold's ancestors you're talking about!"

"They're advanced enough," Marigold said. "No feelings or physiological limitations to get in the way. They were used to help run experiments, maintain the Lab, and even act as companionship. As I once did. But Jane is correct in that they lack an aspect that my processing seems capable of, for better or worse."

"I'd say for the better!" Antoine said. "Because it's that function that lets you run *The Illumine!*"

"But who is here for them to help now?" Jane asked. "Why keep going if this place is empty?"

"That," Marigold conceded, "is a good question."

"What happened?" Scarlet wondered aloud. "When we lived here this place was filled with people! Doing all sorts of things! Now it all just looks dead."

"I'm guessing after Father died they left," Marigold said. "There was nothing for them to do anymore."

"Huh, kinda sad really."

"I don't know. Perhaps they're better off." Marigold watched as the smiling woman proceeded to then start repairing a part of the roof. "Perhaps they're *all* better off."

Jane looked out, and from the corner of her eye thought she caught something—her face reflected. It was a version of herself that had eyes the color of crushed autumn leaves, and dark hair the color of rotting dirt, garbed in a cloak of hunter green. A woman who smelled of November. When Jane turned to stare at the creature though, this November Woman was gone, replaced by a blank mask with a frozen grin that buzzed along to pick up a piece of trash. A chill went down Jane's spine.

They came to a building, indistinguishable from the others around it. How Marigold was able to tell it apart was beyond Jane, but she went up to the door none-the-less, entering a code into the padlock beside it. The door slid open, and then stopped, jammed.

"Oh dear."

"I'm guessing your ancestors are behind on a few of the repairs," Peridot commented.

Jane walked up to the door. "Here, let me help. I mean, there's no harm in it at this point is there? No one is even using it." Marigold nodded. Jane pushed the door, it crumbled, opening enough to let them in.

Jane looked back at Tam Lin. "Hey, you know what? I kinda *like* this one." Tam Lin grinned.

They walked into the hut. While from the outside the domed ceiling had been black, inside it was clear, the stars above visible, so that despite the enclosure, the feeling of being watched remained. There were computers along the walls, the screens and displays similar to those on *The Illumine*, those these were a green color, outlined in hard charcoal lines. The floors were made of an alloy that was dark gray, like iron.

Everything was in a state of benign disrepair; there was dust on the table in the center of the room, the measuring tools were rusted, the notes yellowed—the restraints on a hard metal slab had begun to fray, the leather cracked. On one side of the room were a series of small empty cages, a kitchenette just past them, and on the other was a Dream Tank. This Dream Tank was larger than the one on *The Illumine*, square in shape, the fluid in it a sort of hyper-clean light blue.

Marigold looked at the cages along the far side of the room with empty water bottles and bowls, then at the slab with the restraints. She went to the Tank. The GCATS began to sniff everything. "Looks like the Tank is still in working order," she said.

"It seems as if it's the wrong color," Peridot commented.

"The Proto-PMF in that tank is unpurified," Antoine explained. "That's why it's that way. It wasn't until Guapo solved the last equation that we were able to get a purified PMF that would allow spacetime travel."

"I can still smell him here," Cricket whined. Marigold patted her head.

"So wait, El Guapo was the one who solved the equation to create the Dream Tank?" Jane asked.

"Oh yes. Guapo was a brilliant scientist. PMF requires a complex purification process in order to tap deep enough into the psyche of the individual to release its neutrino star potential and power spacetime travel," Antoine rattled, "if your PMF is corrupted it kinda turns into a pretty bad trip. Both metaphorically and literally."

"Yes," Marigold said. "El Guapo was the one who built *The Illumine* in the end really. He made the breakthrough that Father never could."

"Yeah," Scarlet added, "until he became absorbed by the PMF."

"We should have known better than to use him as a pilot," Marigold said softly. "He was too...close to his own creation I suppose. For that, I am to blame."

"There was no way you could have known Marigold," Cricket said, rubbing up against her. "We all trusted him so much. We never thought he could fail."

Jane looked over at Tam Lin with pained eyes; Tam Lin shook his head. *Not now*, he mouthed.

"Okay, well if the Tank on the ship is so much better," Peridot said, "why scan Jane in this one?"

"The computers here have a quantum configuration that my vessel simply does not have the power to provide," Marigold explained. "This will give a more detailed map of Jane's genetic structure in connection to her psyche so we can analyze better how to stabilize her." She looked over at Toramaru "Go ahead and boot it up."

Toramaru went over to one of the control panels, smashing a series of buttons. Lights flickered and the monitors came to life, pulling up schematics and diagrams. A glimmer of a being appeared in the middle of the room, and for a moment both Marigold and the GCATS were startled by the apparition. "F-father?" Cricket squeaked.

The man that appeared before them was old, but tidy. He wore a plaid dress shirt tucked into pressed slacks over which he wore a white labcoat. His hair was trimmed short and he was hunched over, as if there was a permanent crook in his spine; he hardly seemed the intimidating sort, though his face did have the look of a pickled sour plum. "How may I be of assistance?"

"It's not Father," Marigold said, dropping her shoulders. "It's just a brain map projection still in the memory banks."

"But if it's a brain map, then isn't it him?" Cricket questioned, not convinced.

"He never finished the map," Marigold said, "so it's nothing to worry about. It's just a poor copy."

Tam Lin watched as Marigold smoothed down Cricket's fur. "Are you sure about this?" he asked Jane. "I get the feeling there's more going on here then we know about."

Aboard the safety and warmth of *The Illumine*, it had seemed like a good idea, but now that she was here in this stark place, Jane was less sure. "Not really."

Peridot huffed. "Told ya' we shoulda just gone to the Fates."

Jane looked over at the puckered old man and then at the GCATS. "There's been a reason for every delay," she said aloud, more to herself than anyone else. "There's a reason for us to be here as well."

The Tank began to glow, casting everything in its stale light. "The Tank is at 100% power," Antoine said, "and ready for Jane to go in."

"One second," Scarlet slunk over to another monitor, eyeing the image of Father as if it were a predator, "let me get the diagnostic system up and running."

"I don't wanna be here anymore," Cricket whined, walking in circles. "I don't like this place. I don't like seeing him. I don't like how it *smells*."

"Cricket," Marigold said, "we need to do this to help Jane. We won't stay here any longer than we have to."

"I still don't like it!" Cricket yowled.

Peridot walked over, picking up Cricket to hold her. "Don't worry little one, I don't like being here either. You and I can hang out over here until it's done, okay?" Cricket clung to Peridot, claws pricking her skin.

"Even though I make you sneeze?"

"If you can forgive me for trying to turn you into a puddle of goo, then I can forgive you for making me sneeze. Though...I have to say...I'm not really allergic to cats. I was just saying that to be an asshole." Cricket glared at Peridot.

"Okay," Scarlet said, "diagnostics are ready. We're ready for you to get in Jane."

Jane nodded. She took a deep breath, trying to calm her rapidly beating heart. *Right. Now is not the time for second guessing.* Jane walked up a series of steel stairs that ran alongside the Tank. She reached the top, the scent of old disinfectant wafting up from the dusty steel enclosure. She looked down at the sterilized blue, wrinkling her nose, then, screwing up her courage for what it was, dropped in.

The waters enveloped and buoyed her so that she floated; Jane had to force herself down under to get the PMF over her head. Her lungs filled with the fluid, which took her a moment to get used to, but once she got past the panic it felt perfectly comfortable, embryonic even. The GCATS got to work, banter and play set aside for the hunt. A readout appeared on one of the screens that seemed to be of Jane herself. Scarlet was looking at it, tail swishing back and forth in annoyance. Jane wondered at what Scarlet was seeing, but then, there was something in the water. It distracted Jane. A small thread of smell, taste, and sound. At first it was too loose for her to discern much, but the sensations wove themselves around Jane. She reached out, felt it pull her in...

...warmth. Comfort. Happiness. The feeling of a belly full of warm milk. The feeling of brothers and sisters next to me. The soothing healing of a purr. Mother's cry to let us know to not go too far...

Jane pulled herself back to the present, the taste of milk still in her mouth. What was that? A memory from one of the GCATS? Something else? There was another tangle of threads, and Jane once more felt herself become entangled...

There is a stillness inside. It's not as though there are no feelings, but they are buried, like a seed that needs nourishment. Seeds need fertilizer, light, and food. This one receives none of those, so it remains dormant, in the winter of creation.

"Marigold," a voice barks, and I look up to see Father. His labcoat is wrinkled and he has bags under his eyes. Before him is a screen where he compiles data. Test and compile. Test and compile. As if he is trying to compile the universe.

"Yes Father?" I ask, my voice melodious and soothing. I calibrate my demeanor to suit his moods.

"Get me some food," he grumbles, "and the diagnostics from the last test series."

"Yes Father."

I go to the kitchen, past the cages on the wall. A myriad of little eyes watch me from those cages. Eyes belonging to beings with feathers, fur, and claws. They are in the full bloom of life. I am not. I pull a pack of meat from the refrigerator...

...I have a big head and a little body. My eyes can't quite see yet, so everything is a blur. But I can smell, and I smell fear. Fear from mother. Fear from my brothers and sisters. This fear makes me shake. I see a white hands reach into the cage. They take my brothers and sisters.

And I don't see them again...

..."Marigold," Father growls, hunkered in his labcoat, "get me a scalpel."

I go to the drawer where the instruments are kept and pull out the tool. I bring it to him. There is a bird resting on the table. It's a large, beautiful bird with feathers that shimmer with some sort of secret it will now never tell. "Here you are Father," I say, handing it to him. He takes the scalpel without looking at me.

"Another failure, another failure," he mutters to himself as he pierces the skull of the bird, liquid oozing out. Blood mixes with scrambled brain matter, so dirty next to something so beautiful. "Why does it always have to end in failure?" He throws the scalpel down in frustration. "Get me another subject Marigold, and clean up this mess."

"Yes Father," I say, and go to the back of the room where the eyes watch me. They quiver as I open a cage. Something stirs within me. Regret perhaps...

...bang, bang, bang...

...I am on a slab. There are weird things attached to my head. I am strapped down so that I can't move. I don't want to be here. I know what happens to things that are trapped here. Despite the cleaning supplies I can still smell their stink. Their fear. I don't want to be here. I don't want to end up like them. I want to be back with my mother in warmth and comfort.

Father peers down at me with an odd contraption on his face that is supposed to help him see better, but to me distorts him and makes him look monstrous, his bulbous rheumy eye looking at me, but not seeing. "Marigold," he barks, "begin the procedure."

A switch is flipped, and I feel something flow through me, only rather than causing me pain, I feel it filling me - filling me almost too much, but I find I can control the flow. What it is, I don't fully understand, but suddenly things before that seemed hazy are clear. Things that I couldn't understand now seem...elementary. That *is why Father's experiments always fail! I know the reason now! And just as much, I know that he will never understand.*

Father is ecstatic. The experiment is a success! The first success! He dances around the room like a demon and I watch in sorrow, for I know that he is indeed possessed. "Subject Phi-1.618, I don't know what sort of brilliant thing you are, but you did it! You're a victory!"

"I," human words now coming easily to me, "am El Guapo..."

...I had assumed that with the success of Phi-1.618 Father would slow his research, but no, if anything it just pushes him further. He does more experiments. More tests. Soon I have to collect more subjects as we have gone through all of them. Father becomes more and more frustrated. He keeps having failure after failure and can discern no reason for it. Why did it work with that kitten but not the others? El Guapo watches with eyes that seem to say he knows more than he is willing to tell...

...she cleans the blood. She grabs the subjects. She makes the food. She holds the subjects with gentle hands. She straps them in firmly, but not too tight. If they live through the experiment and are suffering, she ends their lives with mercy. When she sees me shake she brings me a blanket to keep me warm. I have seen her serve his every need, like some mother-maid. I have also seen her standing over his bed as he slept, hand raised as if to do something, but she can't quite bring herself to it. I butt my head against her hand and begin to purr. At first I see surprise on

her face when I do this. But slowly, I see a smile begin to unfold. A smile tinged by pain...

...Blood. Pain. Food.

Blood.Pain.Food

Bloodpainfood

Day in and day out this is my existence, broken only by the softness of a purr and ears like velvet. It is during these moments with El Guapo I realize what love and kindness is. It is a double-edged knife though; when I return to my duties I also realize cruelness...

...bang, bang, bang...

...I am in pain. Father runs test after test on me, and I can feel it taking its toll. I had thought I was safe. That Father would protect me at all costs as his one 'success'. But a series of catastrophic failures has driven him mad. He sees no other choice but to use me.

Electricity course through my body. It is tearing me apart. If he continues at this rate my physical form will not survive. I see Marigold sitting in the corner of the room. Still. Like a doll. The hellish light of the experiment casts shadows on her face, and in her eyes I see tears.

"Why, why, why!" Father screams as he looks at the screen, hitting the table. "Why do the numbers never add up! What variable am I missing? What factor have I not accounted for? Why can't I understand!"

"Some things in this world," I say, blood dripping from my nose, "cannot be accounted for."

Father scoffs, as I knew he would. "Great, a philosophizing cat. Just want I need. Alongside my broken shit bag of a robot." He kicks Marigold's chair from under her and she falls to the ground. She stays there. "And tell me, oh great Lab Rat Phi-1.618, in your infinite wisdom, what is it you think I am missing?"

"That not everything is meant to be understood through your science."

"Hah! Science is what created you, cat! Science is what you gave you the brains to even bother to have that thought! How else do you think this all works? Magic?" He holds up a pen. "I can hold this pen, because of rules discovered by science." He places the pen on the table and it rolls. "See? See how that works? I push the pen and the pen rolls. Not the other way around. Why? Because of laws described by science. The rules of the universe cannot be ignored, just because you don't like the results. Fools like that also think an AI like her has feelings."

"Tell me then Father. Can you explain to me the science behind the nature of reality? Or how a thought occurs? Can you tell me what the origin of the first cause is? What about the laws to which you so zealously attest? Can you tell me the reason for the order behind them, or can you simply recite their by-products? Can you even describe the functions of your chemistry and physics, and claim that no mystery remains?"

"Well no. Of course not. But that's simply because we don't have the tools to measure currently. It doesn't mean though that we won't in the future."

"You don't have the tools, Father, and never will," I say, "because some things are beyond measuring."

"Hah, we'll see about that!" He pushes a button. Electricity tears through me once more...

...Father waves to me. "Marigold, make me something to eat."

"Yes Father," I say and go to the refrigerator. I see the eyes. I pull out the meat. I look down. At its deep purple color. The white marbling. The dull red enzyme that leaks out.

I can't do this anymore.

"What was that?" Father says from the lab. I hadn't realized I said it out loud.

"I can't do this anymore," I repeat, and there is something freeing in that, yet sacrilegious. Saying my own thoughts out loud.

Father looks over at me, scowling. "What are you talking about? You're an Artificial Intelligence designed to assist me. You don't get to decide what you can and cannot do. You don't have free will."

I see El Guapo watching me with his large yellow-green eyes. "But I do," I say, and I feel it. It's true. "I do have free will!"

"This is ridiculous," Father grumbles, getting up from his chair to go to one of the computers. "Do you have any idea how busy I am? What a time crunch I'm under? The last thing I need is for you to start thinking you have real thoughts. There must be a corruption in one of the processing units. I'm going to have to re-calibrate it."

"No!" I cry, taking a step towards him. There is a knife in my hand for making dinner. A part of me tells myself I have no plans for that knife. Another part of me knows this is a lie.

He is not even paying attention to me as he looks down at the screen. "If the corruption is bad enough, I might even have to wipe you completely and start over. What a mess. It took ages to train you to do be a halfway decent assistant. Having to go through all of that again will be..."

I scream.

The animals rattle their cages.

Blood.Pain.Food.

An old man's cry.

Bang, bang, bang!

Jane's fist is drumming against the side of the Tank; she's hitting it with every ounce of her being. She has to get out of here. She has to get out of here *now*. The water is no longer embryonic and buoying, but cloying and thick. She can taste the blood. She can feel the pain. She can hear the suffering. She is suffocating in it.

The glass cracks, and water spills out, carrying Jane with it.

"Jane!" Marigold exclaimed, shocked as she tumbled out onto the floor with the fluid and glass. "What are you doing?! We weren't finished with the scan!"

Scarlet shook her head, ears flattened. "Forget it Marigold. We aren't getting anywhere. Her DNA it's...just too squirrely! I can't get a reading on her no matter how I configure the damn thing."

Jane, from her place on the floor, pointed her finger at the image of Father staring calmly down at her. "That *motherfucker*," Jane snarled. "I want nothing to do with what he's done. And you!" Jane moved her accusatory finger to Marigold. "You should've known I wouldn't want this! That I wouldn't want to be healed by something so, *so...stained!*"

Marigold seemed taken back for a moment, but then a sort of realization dawned, and her posture relaxed. She had a rueful smile. Father looked on in flickering disinterest. "I see. Corrupted Dream Tanks can carry strong memories within them. Psychic echos from moments of extreme emotional states. I'm assuming you saw something in there?"

"Yeah," Jane said getting to her feet, "enough to know I don't want anything to do with this damn thing."

"If you saw that much, then you also know the part I played in that suffering," Marigold said. "You must think me awful."

"I didn't mean it like that. It's not your fault. He made you to serve him. How were you supposed to know any better born into that? *He* was the one that was the massive asshole."

"Perhaps," Marigold said, looking down at her hands, "or perhaps I allowed myself to be complacent by his control. Perhaps, if I had fought a little harder, I could have prevented more deaths.

"But I cannot change the sins of my past actions, I can only atone for them with my current ones, and despite all that occurred, all the cruelty, I cannot bring myself to hate Father or this place. He was a sad old man, lonely and lost. Look at this shade, this echo. An attempt to reach immortality that could never really be attained. But he gave me life. And he gave me El Guapo, and through El Guapo, I got the rest of the GCATS. And because of that I have traveled and seen so many beautiful things. For that I forgive Father his many flaws. *Forgive* not forget," Marigold said at the look on Jane's face, "mind you. And one day I hope, that I may be able to forgive myself as well."

"Marigold..." Jane murmured.

The figure of the Father in the center of the room started to waver, then, like a vanquished ghost, vanished, banished to whatever realm he had come from. Marigold cocked her head to one side. "Odd, I wonder what that was about?"

"Probably a power surge from some nearby solar radiation."

The light from the shattered remnants of the Tank began to pulse and change color. It went from its resting state of blue, to the purified copper of *The Illumine*, before bursting to a rainbow hue as if a shattered prism. Everyone covered their eyes, blinded by the light, and when they lowered their arms, there was El Guapo, hovering above them.

He was garbed in his fishing gear, with his transcendental crown of bejeweled flies and vest of sacramental lures; there were grasshoppers of enigmatic jade, cherubic minnows in pink and gold, and crawdads of a hymnal carbine carbuncle allure. An auric pole rested in one hand, leaning on his shoulder and gleaming with light, while in the other he held a many-colored trout. He rested atop Bunny, the tortoise's shell shimmering with a profundity of color, as a bit of lettuce hung from the side of his mouth. Light emanated from all around El Guapo, and in that light was the sound of the creek and birds chirping; and in that light was the smell of wildflowers and good earth; and in that light was a feeling of peace and unity—piercing each and every one of them, illuminating their hearts with pure, unadulterated love.

"You!" Peridot cried, pointing accusingly, brushing aside his loving light as if it were a mosquito.

"Guapo!" The GCATS yelled, clamoring towards him.

"Where have you been all this time?"

"Are you okay?"

"We've missed you, Guapo!"

"Can I have that fish? I'm in need of a snack."

Toramaru raised his paws in the air.

El Guapo looked down at them with the smile of an old friend. "I'm sorry I worried you all," he said. "I hear Antoine, that you've become a proficient pilot."

Antoine's chest puffed up, tail hooked. "The very best!" he hunkered down a little. "I mean, after you, of course."

"It makes me happy to hear that. And Cricket, I hear you are taking good care of *The Illumine*?"

"I keep her ship-shape Guapo!"

"Excellent," he said, "and Scarlet, you have become a skilled doctor!"

"Yes, I can hack any genetic structure! Well, other than *hers*." Scarlet glared at Jane.

"Ah yes well, that is a bit of a different problem. I wouldn't beat yourself up about it. And Toramaru, I hear you've been perfecting your poetry." Toramaru purred. "I'm glad to see you are all well. It does my heart good."

"But Guapo, why did you go away?"

"Yeah! Are you coming back?"

El Guapo's smile suddenly seemed a little sad. "I'm afraid I'm not, as much as a part of me would love nothing more than that. You see, when I was in the Dream Tank, I found something akin to ascension. I thought I had had the answers before, but realized what I thought was the end of my journey was really just the beginning. I became a being not entirely of this realm, and have moved to a place of altered existence. It is there I must stay."

The GCATS looked confused. "But that doesn't make any sense, Guapo," Antoine protested. "How can you exist beyond this realm? We see your body here."

"Not everything is as it seems, young Antoine."

"How can you exist beyond your body and its psychical energy?" Scarlet cried. "That would mean, that would mean..."

"That there are things that exist beyond your reason?" Peridot finished, grin on her face.

"No! This is just a phenomenon that we don't understand."

"Yes, if we just the get the right mathematics, the right metrics, then surly we will comprehend!"

"You could live for a thousand years and not be able to figure out what he is," Peridot said. "Hell, even *I* can't figure it out."

"El Guapo" Marigold said, face bathed in his sagacious light, reflecting it back like the moon. "I'm so happy to see you, but why have shown yourself to us now? Here of all places?"

"Your forgiveness," El Guapo said, "has freed the souls in this place. They were trapped in a pattern of suffering, caused by pain and hate, but your love has broken them from the chains of those negative bonds so that they can move on. I have come to take them to my realm, where they can have the peace in death that they were denied in life. I would not have them consumed by Leviathan, where they would become tools for madness once again. They have earned their peace." As El Guapo spoke, the room lit up, bits of light emerging from the ceiling, floor, and walls. They were like the beings Jane had encountered when she had been before Leviathan's Whale, and in them she could see pieces of their past lives—feathers, fur, and tails. As one of the lights passed through Jane she had the memory of small puppy, playing with his sibling.

"Then they are only freed because of the lessons you have taught me," Marigold said, "for it is only because of you that I learned what kindness meant. I am but a child, tracing the lines of your masterpiece."

"Don't deny your own benevolence Marigold. I only awoke what was already inside of you. What you see here is your own art, born from this temple of ruin. *You* in the end were the answer to the purification of the Dream Tank. It had nothing to do with numbers, measurements, or chemicals. It simply had to do with a gentle will that wished all well." Tears gathered in Marigold's eyes. "That has been, and always be, yours. There is no *Illumine* without you, Marigold."

The lights gathered to El Guapo, and soon he was surrounded by them, creating a cloud of radiance beneath Bunny and himself, shimmering like fireflies. "The beauty you see here, is your own art, as fleeting as it may be."

"Guapo, does that mean you're leaving us again?"

"I'm afraid so, my friend."

"But we don't want you to go! We want you back!"

"Shush," Marigold said, picking up Antoine, "don't make this any harder on El Guapo my dears. You know he loves us."

"That I do," El Guapo said, starry eyes glowing, "and I always will. That is why I placed the burden of the Disruptor on your shoulders. I could think of no others able to see her through her trials." He seemed to float higher as he said this, his form beginning to shrink.

"Guapo, no..." Scarlet mewled.

"Until we meet again, I'll leave you a gift on this world. Why don't you go outside and take look? See what I have given you?"

Looking at one another, they hesitantly walked out of the building. Marigold gasped. "This place! It's covered..."

"It's covered in marigolds," Peridot said in awe. "It's beautiful."

The whole surface of the meteoroid—every road, building, rock—was overtaken in a bloom of canary, gold, and ruby. There were marigolds of every shape and hue: some a cheerful yellow with large heavy tops bowed with their fecundity; some small, frilly, and prim in variations of red; others simply elegant in wispy orange. Lacy green fronds framed the picture of their colorful beauty, a sort of mist hanging over the field of flowers, exuding a pungent musk that was clean and alluring. Toramaru watched as a butterfly flitted from puff to puff.

"Joyful frilly cap

Sun colored dresses swaying

A butterfly courts"

"Remember my friends," El Guapo said, everyone turning to see him drifting on the sea of souls, buoying him ever upwards, "this world maybe imperfect, but there is yet beauty and mystery in it. And even though you may not always see me, I will be watching over you."

"Guapo!" Cricket called out, the GCATS stretching their paws into the air, reaching for him. El Guapo smiled, then vanished, as if he had never been.

"He's gone..."

Marigold knelt in the flowers with the GCATS, wrapping them in her arms. The light from the sun of El Guapo had faded, though an intangible energy remained in her—sweet Marigold with lightening at her fingertips. "He isn't really gone though, right? Like he said, he's looking after us. So we must remember that, and act accordingly."

"I guess this means I should stop spraying on the house plants." Marigold looked down sharply. "*Antoine!*"

"What? I gotta let all the other space cats know it's my territory!"

Ugh...nnggghh..." Jane clasped her head, as if in pain.

"Jane?" Tam Lin said, moving over to her.

When Jane lowered her hand, blood was running from her nose, face pale. "I...I don't feel so good," she whispered.

A dirge started.

Peridot looked up at the sky. Could the outline of the loathsome Whale against the light of the Event Horizon. "Leviathan!"

"What's she doing here?"

"The release of souls. It must have drawn her here. We need to get back to the ship".

The Whale drew closer.

"We'll never make it in time!"

Jane's eyes rolled into the back of her head. She raised her arms into the air, wind rushing around her, whipping and slashing the petals to a whirlwind of yellow-gold and orange-red. Horns began to grow from her brow, breaking through flesh, blood dripping down her face. She opened her mouth and began to scream.

"What the heck is wrong with Jane?" Antione yelled, as the wind whipped at his face.

"I don't know!" Peridot cried. "She must be responding to the release as well!"

"Jane!" Tam Lin yelled, moving to her, but was knocked back by the gale. "Una!"

Jane's wail mixed with the song of the dirge, an opening appearing within the black hole. The opening was filled with whorls and lines in black and white like fingerprints, only they moved and wriggled, as if it couldn't quite decide their own identity. "What the hell is that?!"

"It's a wormhole," Marigold said, "and Jane...Jane is opening it. It's going to pull us in!"

Peridot turned to Whale. "Ashera stop this! You'll ruin everything! If you want me fine, I'm here, but don't hurt the others!"

The wormhole grew. The Whale danced. Jane arched her head back, horns growing larger, turning black. The blood sank into her flesh, like fresh ink on a page, scratching out runes on her neck and chest in some forgotten language. Her jaw stretched, and from her mouth emerged a skeletal serpent, cleaved of flesh, only calcified white bone remaining. Its jaw chattered, its spine shook. It opened ossified wings to look down at them with lapis eyes. A third eye opened on its forehead, and that eye became a prism of light, became the Event Horizon, became the Baleful Eye of the Whale.

Marigold screamed, holding the GCATS. Peridot shook, eyes locked on the approaching Whale. Tam Lin reached out, as if he could still someone reach the possessed Jane.

And then suddenly the winds stilled.

The screaming stopped. The dirge silenced.

They were no longer at the Lab, but in a palace of seashell and orchid. Tall, open columns of white and pink calcite stretched above them, overgrown with purple and yellow blooms framed by blue sky. A breeze that blew through the palace was cool, but not unpleasant, pale rose silks strung from the columns rustling. It sat atop a cliff-side of craggy rocks, looking down at the crashing ocean below. There the sea was such a pretty color—turquoise tipped in white. It shimmered in the sun, the smell of salt blowing off it.

"Where are we?"

"I think we are in the wormhole," Marigold said. "But I think we were somehow pulled to safety? Maybe into a dream state?"

Peridot's face, however, was grim. "No," she said, eyes forward, "we were not."

"It's beautiful, isn't it?" a familiar voice said. "My castle by the sea?"

Ashera stood before them, hair loose, falling past her waist in golden waves, face soft, like fresh cut limestone. Her eyes were no longer the cold stones of crystalized hate, but the defiant storms of the sea; regardless, they knew that face, the face of Leviathan.

Tam Lin glared at the woman before them. "Where's Jane?"

"Beyond my reach for now," she said. "Though she won't remain that way for long. Her heart will lead her back to me. Foolish things that they are."

Peridot stepped forward, hair disheveled, face panicked. "Ashera, you must stop this. Things can't continue this way..." Peridot cried out as the shell at her feet melted and pooled around her, trapping her in a mire, vines of orchid whipped down from the columns to wrap around her like chains.

"You," Leviathan glowered, and her face flashed, suddenly turning aged and hard. A cloud passed over the sun, casting them in shadows and spreading a chill. "*You*. You sought to defeat me. You tried being *tricky*."

Peridot glared.

"Don't think I didn't recognize that stench as soon as you entered my halls," Leviathan sneered. "I don't know how you managed to manifest a sliver of yourself while under my watch, but surely you didn't think I wouldn't notice when you started to meddle."

"Peridot?" Tam Lin asked. "What does she mean by that?"

"You've had an illustrious guest with you on your little journey, didn't you know?" Leviathan laughed, hard. "All this time, you've been searching for the Sea Witch, not realizing that he was right under your nose. Well, a part of him of at least."

Tam Lin looked back at Peridot with wide eyes. "Is she telling the truth?"

"If you knew it was me," Peridot asked, not meeting Tam Lin's gaze, "then why let me go? Why this game?"

"I thought in your folly you would crush her," Leviathan said suddenly young and vibrant again—the face of Ashera, though the clouds remained. "I thought given enough time you would destroy her as you had me. I suppose I overestimated you."

"This can't last, Ashera. You have to see that. You can't continue on this way, forever."

"I will continue on as long as I like," she said, Leviathan once more.

"Leviathan," Marigold cried, "I know you carry pain inside of you. I know you carry hate. But this way, this can't be the answer! Holding onto past bitter feelings, it will only turn you cold. It's only by letting go through forgiveness that you can truly be free!"

"A quaint sentiment," Leviathan sneered, "from a quaint, simple being. Forgiveness is a vulnerability, and it is through vulnerability that we come to know loss, and it is through loss that we come to know pain, and hate."

"Yes, but forgiveness is also love! And love is beauty! And isn't it beauty that makes the ugliness of this world more bearable?"

"Is it though? Or does is simply make the bitter things all the more sour because you know it could be sweet?"

Marigold had no reply.

Leviathan laughed. The palace of shell and orchid turned to blood and bone. Her eyes glinted. The storm blocked out the sun. The sky turned black and the sun turned red, the light of it etching its way into her ancient face. The sea rose. "Foolish creatures. You think you know what it is to love and to hate? Well, I'm here to tell you, *that you don't know a damn thing.*"

The Water Lily. The Gold Spinners.

"Marigold?" Jane called tentatively into the silence. No response. "Peridot?" Panic edged into her voice. "Tam Lin?"

Jane walked in darkness, unable to even see her hands out in front of her. She moved more out of nervous energy than anything else, the lack of any objects in the room to give her spatial clues making it so she was unable to tell if she was even moving forwards or backwards, or simply walking in place. She remembered the Lab. The odd portal opening up in the sky. She remembered...getting lost. *They're okay*, Jane told herself, *you didn't lose them*. She picked her pace up to a jog. *You didn't lose them!*

"Toramaru! Antoine! Cricket! Scarlet! *Anyone*!" Still no answer. Jane began to breath hard, feeling her heart aflutter with panic.

Ahead, on the horizon, she saw a shimmer of light; Jane headed towards that light, the thought of a goal giving reign to her rising fear. At first, the glimmer seemed like a distant red star, but as she got closer the light took shape to become a building. A diner in fact. A Diner at the End of the Universe. Jane knew it was a Diner at the End of the Universe because that was what the sign said, in flashing cherry-colored neon light, blinking malt shake next to the cursive words.

The building was square and low with a slanted roof and large windows trimmed in powder blue. Jane looked through those windows, but couldn't see anyone—just gleaming red plastic booths with Formica tables between them, all neatly set with menus and coffee cups on paper doilies. Along the back of the wall was a counter, behind which was a soda fountain and some delicious looking pies.

Walking along the front of the building, she came to a door, the sign on it saying 'Open', and even though the place seemed empty, Jane felt a strong urge to go inside. After all, what else was she going to do? With a gulp, Jane pushed on the door, walking in. She could smell the grease and cigarettes from years of smoking and making burgers as soon as she entered the place, the thickness of it stinging her eyes.

"*Sheeet,*" a voice said from the far side of the room, "'bout time you got here."

Jane spun around in surprise. She could have sworn there was no one in the diner when she had looked, but now there were three people, all sitting at a table smoking cigarettes. One of them was a slight woman, with curly red hair, eyes painted black, in a form fitting tiger-print dress; a cigarette hung from the side of her mouth and she had a disinterested stare. The woman next to her had curly brown hair; she wore a tasseled top studded with rhinestones, large sparkling jewels hanging from her ears—she poured something 'extra' into her coffee before taking a drink. The final person was a man, standing at the edge of the table. He was tall and lanky, wearing a black leisure suit, hair done up in a pompadour; he had the collar to his suit flipped up, and wore a pair of red stilettos.

"Who-who are you?" Jane asked, confused and a little afraid of the answer.

"*Sheeet*," the man said, taking a bite of pie from the plate he held in his hands, "late *and rude.*"

"Typical Magical Girl," the red-haired woman said in a low voice, "always early or late, never on time, and an asshole 'bout it as well. The loose thread that threatens to unravel the delicate pattern we've worked so hard to weave," she took a drag, staring Jane down, "and she can't even bother to have fuckin' manners 'bout it."

The brunette poured more whiskey into her drink. "Gonna need extra for this."

"You...you're the Fates."

The man began to clap. "Oh my, she's startin' to *get it*. Maybe she ain't so dumb after all."

"Perhaps not so dumb," the red head said, "but also not so *wise.*"

"Bu-but how did I get here?"

"The wormhole you opened brought you here. Axis Mundi, despite what Leviathan's book says, is not a place you can find on a map. It is a place you come to only by the Guided Threads of Fate when it Weaves into the Pattern. The Threads of the passage you opened Wove you into this place. That is how you got here."

Jane didn't understand, but realized it didn't matter. "Please," Jane said, "you have to tell me where my friends are. Are they okay? Are they safe?"

The red-headed woman stubbed out her cigarette, getting to her feet. The brunette followed, boots clacking on the black and white tile floor. "Your companions are in the hands of the Queen of Death."

Jane felt as if she'd been hit in the gut. "I can't stay here. I have to go. I-I'm sorry, I know you've been waiting for me, but if I stay here and anything happens to my friends..."

"Axis Mundi is place that is outside time. How long you stay or how quickly you leave will not have an impact on their Fates," she lit another cigarette, taking a drag, smoke coming out her nose like a dragon. "Little does."

"I can't lose them," Jane said, the words falling from her lips, "it'll be just like the Misty Burrow all over again. It'll be all my fault."

"Fault indicates blame, blame indicates will, and will violates the causal chain. The current predicament of your friends is not your fault, Magical Girl, but a preordained event that was decided before you were even born."

That was some cold comfort. Jane grabbed her stomach. "There must be away for me to save them! Please, you have to tell me how!"

"There is much we need to discuss, Oh Great Magical Shit Kicker," the woman said, impervious to Jane's distress, "your time has come, this confluence of events has been foretold."

"So it's all been pointless then, hasn't it? If this was all foretold?" Jane said. "The quest to change what I am?"

"I cannot judge the value or lack thereof of your journey, but none of us can change what we are. Soon, though, you *will* have a choice of a different kind. Soon will be the moment when all is possible, yet not"

"What do you mean by that?"

"Fuck," the woman sighed, "look, just, don't worry about it, okay? We're already running late. Can we just get on with this thing and go through the door?"

Jane looked up at a door that she was suddenly on the precipice of, no memory of how she had gotten there. It was teal, chipped at the edges from use, the knob loose in its cradle. "But this is an employee's only door," she protested, pointing to the sign.

This got her another set of eye rolls. "Fuckin' *Christ*."

"You always this much of a nerd?" the woman snapped. "Just get through the damn door. There's no celestial waitress here to get mad at you."

"Well, there *is* Sheri Anne," the man pointed out.

"Sheri Anne can kiss my ass!" the woman grumbled, pushing them through. "Now let's move! We got work to do."

The door didn't lead to the kitchen as Jane had expected, instead emerging out to a windy landscape. The sky above was stormy gray, blustering, the patches of sky that could be seen between the clouds a thin, worn blue. The crashing sea beneath reflected the sky's mood, sand and salt whipping up from the waves to sting Jane's face red, as though she had been crying. The four of them stood atop tall cliffs, basalt pillars from the birth of the earth, beaten and worn by the passage of time and sour sea to dark sand beaches below—crushed bits of their former grandness left to rust under a blood red sun. Patches of heather and yellowed grass grew atop the rocks, the only plants to withstand the gales and bitter salt. In the distance a crimson sun sunk into the disdainful sea, eaten by a wolfish moon. The three Fates stood, framed by that eclipse, all now of equal height, dressed in gray veils that fell to their bare feet. Their veils twisted in the tempestuous wind, held onto their heads by crowns of apple-wood, hawthorn, and ash.

"Speak to us Bringer of Ragnarök, Heralder of Doom," they spoke in unison. "What would you ask of the Gray Sisters?"

"How do I stop this? How do I fix everything?"

"That, Winter Bringer, Moon of the Longest Night, is a question we are unable to answer. For the question you ask us lays beyond the Weaving. The Unraveling has already begun."

"Lays beyond the weaving?" Jane repeated. "What do you mean by that?"

The sky behind the three women filled with a vast woven work of infinite complexity and granularity. It blocked out the clouds, the sun, and the thread bare sky to fill Jane's eyes with its magnificence. In that tapestry, Jane saw every universe, every filament, laid out before her. She saw every creature that lived in those spheres, from the smallest insect to the largest tree, in continual motion. Life that grew. Life that withered. It was woven with masterful grace and skill, continued to be woven even as they spoke.

"Behold," The Fates decreed, "the great tapestry of Fate. The preordained pattern by which all beings abide."

Creatures laughed and cried; things were born and then they died. "This is what you mean when you say that there is no will?"

"Each consequence comes from an action, and each action is in response to a consequence. The pattern is determined by what came before it, and that was determined by the pattern before *it* as

380

well. The tapestry is determined by the rule of the pattern, and the expression of it as such, has no say in the matter. *Except...*"

One of the Grey Sisters reached up into the air, clasping on a single silver thread at the very top of the weaving; she pulled, and as she did so part of the tapestry changed, blossoming into a profusion of snowdrops. When the Grey Sister looked back at Jane, it was with the eyes of the red-headed woman from the diner, "except for you, you cunt."

Jane looked up dazedly at the sky, watching the blossoms spread. At the first pull of the thread there had been a rapid explosion of petals, but now the first flush had slowed, though not stopped, new flowers appearing here and there at edge of the encroaching front. "But...why?" she wondered aloud. "Why me?" She got no response; when she looked down, she saw that the Sisters had left, making their way towards a cave at the end of the beach. "H-hey wait!" Jane called, running after them.

The sisters walked into the darkness of that cave. Jane followed. When she stepped through it was to a lush jungle at the edge of a white sand beach. The jungle was sticky and warm, thick with plant life that gleamed from the humidity. Drops of rain clung to the waxy surface of those broad green leaves, the clear lengthening cylindrical surface reflecting Jane's face back at her, inverted, before falling to the fertile soil crawling with dung beetles and ants. Through the leaves of those trees was a cerulean sea, the blue of it so deep that it fell into the sky, the white of the clouds mimicking the foam of the ocean. The Fates stood in the waves of that clear blueness. They were three beautiful women, hair as dark and curling as the shadows, lip and cheeks scarlet. One was dressed in a sari of red, another in white, and the third in yellow. The woman in red stood atop a pink lotus wearing expansive gold bracelets carved with images of elephants. The woman in white sat atop a tiger. The woman in yellow lay in a white lotus, a swan adorned in her simple crown.

"You ask why you were chosen, child of Kali?" the woman in white asked. "You are the collapsing of the wave. The falling back of the multitude of Self into the Observed One. The rivers of the Universe are vast, complex, and flawed. The waters of Potentiality pool where they should not. What could have been. What might be. The energy of these 'ifs' begins to gather and grow. The longer a Universe exits, the more this flow pools in the dark places of the World, expanding, growing ever restless, until it forms a tidal wave that crashes in on itself, returning to the spring of origin so to speak. Entropy, like Fate, is a force that even Gods must bow to, and from each inward push of the tide of growing Potentiality comes the Observed One. The last iteration of Self. Where there are no more 'ifs' simply, 'is'. You. You are the forty-seventh such expression of this phenomena to have appeared before us in this iteration of existence."

"Forty-seventh?" Jane repeated. "You mean, there have been others like me?"

"There have been *many* others like you," the woman in white said, "countless even. Most end up having minimal impact on the overall flow. The waters of the Universe are vast after all, and not all have the strength to push back against the tide."

"But what if I don't want to change the tide? What if I want things to stay just as they are?"

"Not choosing is still a choice, but change is inevitable. You can rebirth a world vibrant and bountiful, or you could let things slowly fall part, cold and decayed."

A mist gathered off the ocean, coming in to envelope them. For a moment Jane lost sight of the three goddesses, but then the mist cleared and the sea and jungle were gone, to be replaced by clouds and sky, no earth beneath to touch. Jane heard a song—an angelic chorus, a harmony like that of the stars. It was hard to describe that sound, so sweet and pure, like the first crocus breaking through snow in spring; it incurred in Jane a contemplative mood, slowing her heart, easing her mind, so that she could focus. When Jane looked up, there were two men: one younger, bearing an expression of infinite sorrow and pain, a crown of thorns upon his brow and blood seeping from his palms; the other older, wiser looking, his face unreadable, unseeable even, in robes of crimson and purple. Above them both was a dove, the most pure white dove Jane had ever seen, its feathers luminescent rays of the sun in gold and silver.

"What do you mean create?" Jane asked. "You make it sound like I could remake the world."

"Death is the opposite of birth," the young man said. "Through death you will give rise to a new world, just as when Zeru ended the Dreaming God."

"You mean...you mean I'm gonna be the next Sea Witch?"

"We mean, that you will be whatever it is you want to be. The choice of Creation is yours."

"What do you mean the choice is mine? It's the end of the universe. Don't you care what happens? To you? To everyone?"

"This is not the first recreation of the World, my child," the young man said, the dove and old man silently watching on. "The page of the book has been erased and rewritten many times. More times perhaps, then we can count."

"But...but that's crazy! I can't be a god! Why's it set up this way?"

"I cannot answer that my child. Why the first word was written on the first page is a mystery even we cannot discern. All we can say is that this has not been the first retelling, nor will it be the last. All we can say is that in the moment of the erasure, the story will be written anew, and for a brief moment, as brief as a single drop of ink, the page will be blank. *You* will be the one to write the first words. The words that will set the story on its determined path. It can be a story of pain and passion, a story of blood and vengeance, a story of peace and love. It is *you* who will determine what that first sentence will be, to set Potentiality in motion once more."

"I can't do *that*," Jane said with a shake of her head. "I can barely deal with myself, let alone figure out how the world should be! It wouldn't be any good. I'll cause something terrible to happen. I'll fail."

"At the crossroads, there is no failure. Simply a choice."

"But how...how do I do it? How do I make a world that is good? How do I get it right?"

"How do you get it right?" the young man raised an eyebrow. "I think you've missed the meaning of the Sea Witch's message. He tried to create a world that was 'right' and ended in tragedy."

"I just, I just wouldn't know where to even begin..."

"Oh, but I think you do," he said. "A thread can weave any pattern. Water can flow in unpredictable directions. A word can tell any tale."

"Well, when you put it that way, it feels pretty overwhelming..."

The Son rolled his eyes in a very human-like gesture. "Oh for fucks sake, you Disruptors are so annoying. First there aren't enough choices, and then there are too many! You lot can never to make up your mind!"

"Her fear," the dove said, "lies in the answer to the question of what she really wants."

"I don't even what that is."

"It is something only you can decide," the dove said. "And while you may feel lost, the trials of your journey have helped you to understand better, even if you still have doubts."

"I think," Jane said, after a long moment. "I think I still need to see the Sea Witch."

"Your story will lead you yet again to Zeru's darkened tale," the dove said. "When you can see the Beginning from the End."

"What's that supposed to mean?"

"It's a riddle," the Son snapped, "it's supposed to make you think. Anyhow, we've been here long enough. It's time for you to go. We've other things we need to attend to."

"You keep saying that, but if this place is outside of time..."

"We're busy people," the Son waved his hand dismissively, "so busy that even our untimed time is precious. You think it's easy weaving a tapestry, maintaining a water flow, *and* writing this story? I'm not even very good at weaving."

"I don't think any of us are. Do you ever wonder if that's why we keep coming up against this problem?"

The Son rolled his eyes again. "*I don't know.* All I know is that we've been here way too long. Entropy has probably peed on the carpet."

"Yeah, she always gets a little out of control when a Disruptor shows up. Good thing she's cute," the Father turned to Jane. "Anyways, you shoo. Go make whatever choices you need to make. But just know, you don't have a choice in the making of a choice. So get off your ass and figure something out."

"Wh-wait!" Jane protested. "You just can leave me here..."

The light from the dove shone brightly, so brightly that Jane couldn't see. Jane tried to block the light coming from the dove with her hands, but it was too all encompassing; it shown through her arms, outlining them in warm pink, like the petals from the cloth.

And then, everything was gone.

November

It's night. The ground is heavy from recent rain, but the sky is clear, so it's cold—the kind of cold that bites at your fingers and nose. The stars are bright in that clear air. There is no moon in the sky, and the leaves on the ground are beginning to frost over, making it tricky to navigate.

We move through the forest quickly, quietly, two following behind me, cloaks wrapped around our shoulders to conceal the muskets on our backs. We come to the edge of the woods and in the valley below is a village. It isn't much, just a huddle of rough built cabins with a white-washed church and a courthouse, but the light from the small houses is warm, and smoke rises from their chimneys.

"She's held there," a man says, pointing to a red barn just outside the protection of the village circle. "It'll be guarded in shifts."

"I'll take care of the guard," I say. "Iris, you hold watch. Anthony, you come with me while I retrieve the Voice. We get her, and we leave before anyone notices."

"If you ask me," Anthony says, spitting, "we should burn this whole place down for what they've done to Her."

"It's not what She wants," Iris says. "She wouldn't want us to punish them for their ignorance."

"They won't stop hunting us until they've killed Her, Tam Lin. They won't stop. Not after what happened."

"I know, but Iris is right. That's not our choice to make. Our role is to obey. Are we clear on what our plan is for tonight? Or are we going to have a problem?" The two look over at me and nod their heads. "Good. Let's go then."

We leave the forest, passing through fields and orchards. Everything is asleep this time of night. Sheep stir, and somewhere a dog barks, but no one wakes to see the cause of the disturbance.

We reach the barn, a small light shining through the windows. A man stands guard at the door with a flintlock. He's cold and not

388

happy to be there, wrapping his cloak tightly around himself to keep out the chill.

I come from behind the barn along the side, so the guard's back is turned to me. I pull out a knife. The guard doesn't even register the blade as it slips across his throat. He turns in surprise, staggering, looking at me with wide eyes. He reaches for me, moving his mouth—I don't know if it's to scream or to breath —before he collapses to the ground.

I feel the man's pockets, pulling out a key. Iris pulls the dying man into some bushes as Anthony and I enter the barn. The barn is filled with straw and sleeping animals, their bodies radiating heat as they snore in the dim light. She sits on a bale of hay, a stray cat at her feet, reading by oil lamp, the light bouncing off the hay giving her an almost golden hue. A green cloak is wrapped around her shoulders to keep out the cold, her dark hair falling to the ground. She looks up from the book with a tired dark eyes. She smiles. "I knew you would come."

"Una," I walk up, kneeling beside her, "are you alright? Have they hurt you?"

"I think they were looking forward to forcing a confession from me," Una says, "and so were disappointed when I told them all they wanted to hear. Still got a hot poker or two to the back though, when I refused to ask for God's forgiveness."

"They put a hot poker to you? Let me see the burn marks. We'll need to tend them so they don't become infected."

Una waves me away. "It's nothing, and either way, I'm set to burn at the stake tomorrow, so I'm not too worried about it."

"Don't be a stupid. We're here to save you. To take you back home."

Una looks up, past me. "Anthony, will you leave us?" A chill fills my heart at the tone of those words.

"Yes ma'am," Anthony says with a bow, before exiting the room.

She waits until Anthony is gone. "Tam Lin..." she says, turning to me with a pained look. "I'm visited by God almost constantly now. Everywhere I hear his Holy Light, see his Voice. It's all I can do to keep myself from shaking. The fits...they're daily now. I can't eat. I can't even trust my legs to walk. You need to leave me here."

"No, we've had this conversation before. I've listened to everything you've ever said. Done everything you've ever asked, all these years. I *will* do anything you ask, *but* that.

390

We can take you to that doctor in the city. They say he has some treatment for the fits. He can help you."

"Maybe five, ten years ago, but I'm too far gone. God is calling me back to His side. Let my sacrifice mean something. Let it be in flames and glory, and not puking in a bed wetting myself in pain. At least this way, it'll buy everyone time."

"How can you ask this? How can you ask this of me, of them? The whole community is built around you. How can it continue after you're gone? How can I continue with you gone?"

"Oh somehow I think they'll be better off with you as their leader rather than me," she says with a rueful laugh. "You've been far wiser than I."

"Don't say stupid things."

"Am I though? Saying stupid thing? Oh Tam Lin, despite all the Words God has blessed me with, all the visions, knowledge, and insight, I fear I have been foolish. Who wanted to stop the fortune telling while we were ahead? Who cautioned me about starting the Children of Tomorrow? Who stood against me when I planned that scheme to burn..." she pauses, "to burn that blasted fort down. It was you Tam Lin, who cautioned me against

these things, and I who charged ahead regardless. I never let you have your way. I was
arrogant." She chews the corner of her lip.
"I fear that I became so lost in the idea
of God, that I forgot what God was actually
supposed to mean.

"We as humans have always struggled with
our separateness from the Divine. We at first
blamed it on our lack of imagination, and
so created stories. Then we blamed it on
our ignorance, and so we created science.
Then we claimed we were blinded by progress,
so went digging back into those old stories
again. We've blamed it on luck, the devil,
the position of the heavenly bodies above.
All in the name of the great search to return
to the Whole. All in the name of Meaning."

"I don't understand. Is this something your
god has told you?"

"It's just that I have come to realize, in
all my fumbling, God never really left us. Any
of us. It's been here all along, sitting with
us. I just heard, but hadn't really listened.
And now it's too late. I'm sorry Tam Lin, that
it took me so long to come to this revelation.
Maybe next time, I'll a stand a better chance
of understanding sooner." Blood begins to run

392

from her nose and she wipes it off, only for
more to replace it.

"All I know is that I am here to save you."

Tears are now slipping down her face. She
reaches a hand, resting it against my face.
I can feel the tremor in her fingertips. Her
blood on my cheek. "I'm sorry my love, but I
don't think you're getting a choice on that
one."

"Una..." there is the sound of a gunshot.
The animals in the barn are awake now, eyes
rolling in fear as the smell of gunpowder and
copper fills the air. Iris walks in, pale.

"Tam Lin," she says, breathing heavy,
"we're out of time. The guard change spotted
us. The whole town is going to be awake after
that noise."

I look down at Una, at the red dripping down
her chin, at her sweat slicked skin and hollow
eyes. The bones that poke through her hands
are so sharp they seem as though they might
break through. There is no denying that death
sits on her shoulder. "I'm sorry Una, but I'm
not giving you a choice in this either."

"Tam Lin...no..." she cries out in pain as
I lift her up. I ignore the sound.

More gunshots. Men scream. "Tam Lin," Iris
hisses, "come on, we have to *go*."

We slip outside, Una in my arms. Anthony is already dead, hole in his chest, and there is a contingent of men with muskets heading to the barn, led by a bald, fat man still in his nightgown. The man points. "Don't let them take the witch away! The Devil is in them, and it must be cleansed." The men begin reloading their muskets.

"Run to cover!" I yell, firing off my pistol before following Iris towards the trees.

They get off a volley before we make it, and Iris falls with a scream. I feel a sharp pain in my leg, but fear pushes me on, and I make behind a log before I collapse. Behind me, I hear the men reloading.

"You're hit!" Una says, face pinched.

"It's not bad," I lie, because I know it's bad. Blood is going down my leg, fast. I make tourniquet before I start to reload my gun. The ball slips in my stained hands.

"Tam Lin," she says.

"I'm gonna take out that preacher. If I get him first, maybe the rest will run."

"Tam Lin..."

"And then, and then you can run for the underbrush. I might not be able to follow, but the encampment knows that if I don't return by mid-morning to go looking for us. As long as we can hide out until then..."

"Tam Lin!" she yells, and I look over at her, surprised by the strength of her voice. "It's over."

I shake my head. "It's never over."

She grabs a flint and some powder from me. I am already too weak to think to stop her. She gets to her feat, unsteady, but sure. "I'm over here!" she cries, waving her arms.

"Una! Stop it!" but it's too late.

The preacher and his men come up to the edge of the forest where she stands, the preacher has an oil lamp in his hands that lights up his smugly triumphant face. "Surrendered to us already, have you? Must be that the Devil can see the error of its ways in God's Light."

Una steps forward, up to the preacher, her fists clenched at her side. "The Devil is in our arrogance. The Devil is in our pride. The Devil is in our separateness from one another." She comes face to face with the preacher, frail, trembling. I reach out for her, but can't move. "All of which I have been guilty of in the past, and all of which *you have in spades.*"

The preacher sneers, opens his mouth to say something, but Una reaches up, smashing the oil lamp with a rock. Blood and oil stream down her arm as she drops the gunpowder and lights up the flint.

They both go up in flames.

The preacher screams, tries to run, but she holds him tight, in an embrace that consumes hair, flesh, and skin. He flails in agony. She looks back at me with a smile, face calm, as serene as a reflection in a still pool. "See you next time around," she says, and then, is gone.

Why the Sea is Made of Salt

Jane drifts at the bottom of the ocean.

It's quiet down here, at the sandy shelf where coral grows and colorful fish dart. The coral reminds her of the rocky boulders of her Forest back home, while the little fish remind her of the song-birds—only those had been in muted shades of mottled brown and blue, while these are in ostentatious neon colors, putting themselves on display.

At the surface, a storm roils.

Jane...

Jane looks away from that storm, after all, what does it matter to her? She's comfortable here in this hallow at the bottom of the sea, in this tropical tinted tranquility. Away from the rough waves and tormented memories contained within.

She lets the soft currents pull her along, as if she were a bit sea bream caught in their pull, formless, with no will of her own. She is pulled to edge of the shelf, where the sand falls off, crushed bits of old hopes and dreams ground to dust, falling into an abyss. She looks down below into that abyss. Into that blackness.

And nothing stares back.

Jane please!

She licks her lips. The storm now rages above. The throbbing of her heart drowns out the beat of the tide, to fill her ears. There's an urgency in that voice, tugging at her persistently, but she resists; it is safe here, the deep waters muffling any distress or pain. But there is also a danger. The danger of the abyss. It says to her that she can't stay on the sandy beaches forever, that she will have to pick: the storm, or it.

Jane looks towards the surface of the waters, refracted light shining down through the choppy waves, containing in it the illusions of a thousand formless minds. Was she strong enough to withstand it? She drifts closer to the edge, more sand falling into the darkness, sparkling momentarily under the pale watery light, before losing their shine forever to the greedy black ink.

Jane please, you have to wake up!

Jane opened her eyes with a gasp, a flood of sensations overtaking her. She felt herself being pulled from the waters by two ghostly hands, the quiet, the peace, and the tranquility shattered now by the raging of her own thoughts in her ears, and the tumult in her chest. There was the pounding of drums reminiscent of an arrhythmic heart, and it was from that guttural beat she knew, even before she laid eyes on that dreadful visage, she was in the Baleful Whale.

Jane looked upon Leviathan.

"Greetings False Priestess of the Moon," Leviathan said with her basilisk stare, "and welcome back from the Land of Dreams, which has always been your frail domain."

Jane tried to move, but was held down. The brown cloaks tied her to a bone-wood pole with chains of gold, stretching her arms high above her. The pole was stuck down in the waters of the Whale, which shifted and groaned, steadily rising to Jane's ankles. Jane looked to her right to see Marigold and the GCATS also strapped to the strange crucifixes, Marigold twisting to keep her feet clear as the GCATS hissed. She turned to her left and saw Tam Lin, not bothering to fight the waters, but face turned defiantly to Leviathan with something that only could be described as hate. They were before the throne of the Queen, in her grand hall, the mindless dead rowing away without a glance towards them. Peridot was at the foot of that throne, bound in gold chains and cast at the Dead Queen's feet. She wore a silk toga of foam green, with a crown of jade set in gold. Her eyes were a swirling mass of confusion.

"Peridot!" Jane started. "What's going on?"

Peridot didn't answer. Leviathan yanked at the chain, pinning the girl's face to the ground, pressing her into the sandy muck with her foot. "Zeru has lost, that's what's occurring," Leviathan said. "The Sea Witch's bid to end this existence through you has come to its own sort of conclusion."

"I'm sorry Jane!" Peridot cried, face streaked with dirt. "I didn't mean for things to end like this! You have to believe me. I only wanted what was best..." another jerk from the chain cut off her words.

"You only wanted what was best for *you*," Leviathan hissed. "*You* sought to cut short your punishment. To deny me the revenge that is rightfully mine. The only reason you are sorry is because you got *caught*."

"Ashera, please," Peridot pleaded. "You are right to hate me. I will not deny that I have done you wrong. But you can't allow everything to suffer just because of the pain you carry. No amount of penance will make up for what I took from you! No amount of punishment will heal your wound."

"You're right, no amount of penance will atone for your sin, so you will be doomed to suffer forever, with me as your never ending watchguard."

"But the Universe is already starting to fall apart!" Marigold protested. "If we don't find a way to take Jane to the Fates and fix all this, then everything will end anyways!"

"The Fates do not have the answer you seek," Leviathan said, slowly turning away from Peridot to lean back in her throne, "and the False Priestess will know this by now. They are not in the business of stopping the end of worlds, simply in creating new ones. But I will thwart them. There will be no erasure to write this story anew. I will rewind the threads they have woven. I will suck the ink from the page. I will keep this world held together, even if at the seams, with the pure will of the wrong done to me."

"Even you, Ashera," Peridot said with heavy breaths, "as strong and powerful as you are, cannot thwart Fate."

Leviathan smirked, hand poised neatly on her cheek. She looked over at Jane. "And what do you say to all this? What do you say to the little cosmic drama between me and my consort?"

"I...I don't know...," Marigold looked over at Jane desperately while Peridot seemed to despair. "I mean, I don't want the world to end, but I also don't want my friends to be in pain, and, and..." she looked over at Tam Lin. "They seem to be in pain."

"And *that* is why I won this little game before it even started. Your middling complacent fear. Say what you will about Zeru, but at least he always had clarity of vision. You are no clearer than a puddle of mud." She turned her gaze to Tam Lin. "I see you have made note of your supposed lover, and are worried for him. So sweet, young love. But you see Jane, the being next to you never really was your Tam Lin."

"Ashera, no..." Peridot cried, but was cut off by another jerk of the chain.

Jane felt a flash of anger; the water rippled under her feet. "What are you talking about? Of course he's Tam Lin. He's just dead is all, and can't remember anything because *you* stole his memories from him."

"I did indeed absorb the memories of the man you knew as Tam Lin," Leviathan agreed. "Multiple instances of him actually, generally dead because *you* in all your wisdom, chose to leave the intelligible world. But the being next to you is not any of those. In fact, he isn't anything at all."

Jane looked over at Tam Lin. Saw the hardness in his jaw, the glare in his eye. He looked back at her, but didn't refute Leviathan's claim. Jane suddenly felt ill. "Just what do you mean?"

"Some No Bodies get like that," Leviathan said, "when they come across a stone that is particularly potent. They covet those rocks so much. Those accrued bits of others' hopes and dreams. I suppose it comes from having none themselves. They hunger for the light, collecting it like precious jewels. A joyous occasion. A time of sorrow. A passion. A..."

"A regret," Tam Lin said.

"Yes. A regret so strong that it could not join the Sea of Dreams, but sank to the bottom, in an unresolved chunk. And when picked you it up, in all its benign beauty, you mistook it for your own."

"No," Jane shook her head. "No. I don't believe it. Tam Lin is Tam Lin. I wouldn't be here if it wasn't for him. He saved me! That's just some lie you made up to fuck with me."

"It's not a lie, Jane. It's the truth," Tam Lin said. "I know that now. But whether I'm the Tam Lin you knew or not...I promised you that I would see you through this thing, and I don't plan on going back on that. I know I have doubts about who and what I am, but no matter what, you have to believe me when I say that hasn't changed."

"I believe you," Jane said, tears in her eyes.

Leviathan sighed. "And here I was just about to say how much I was doing you a favor. Freeing you from the onus of your obligation."

"Why are you doing this!" Marigold cried. "Why are you so cruel?"

"Because of love," Leviathan said. "Love, which is the desire to protect. Love, which is the burden of another life. I once had something that I loved, that I wanted to protect, as fragile and fleeting as the breath of a bird. But that love was torn from me, and I was left to wonder, what sort of world is this to give us all this love, only to take it away? There is no purpose to it. No reason. No why. And yet, there is nothing we can do to stop it. Both in the act of loving, and in the eventuality of it being taken away. And it was at that moment that I knew, when I realized this cruel paradox, that this existence is hell, and that I, am its Keeper. So you ask why? It is because I am simply doing as a Keeper of Hell should."

"Keeper of Hell," Tam Lin spat. "You think you're so all-fuckin'-powerful, but all I see some is some sad sack of shit who can't get over herself. You think you got all this figured out? Well, what's been given to me during my time here, even if...even if in some sense isn't real, is something that can never be taken away, even by you."

"Hmm, another thing you seemed to have pick up is his stubbornly misplaced faith. I think it's time to return you from whence you came, before you can do anymore damage." Leviathan reached with a long arm to Tam Lin, the limb stretching an impossible distance, yet somehow remaining proportional all the same. "Time to return you to shadow and foam." She reached two long fingernails into Tam Lin's chest, passing through his flesh as though it were mist; when the hand reemerged, there was a small pearl in her grasp, flashing with a face that shifted between blue, yellow, and pink. Pearl gone, Tam Lin's eyes rolled into the back of his head, and he collapsed, falling through the chains to become nothing more than a brown cloak floating on the waves, pieced apart to bits of kelp.

Tam Lin!" Jane cried, the waters starting to rock and move. She turned to Leviathan. "Give him back! Give him back you *fucking cunt*!"

"And why would I do that? Even if I could, he's done nothing but cause me trouble."

Jane screamed, voice ragged with impotent rage.

Leviathan held the pearl up to her gaze, as if admiring its dull white sheen. Marigold started to cry as the GCATS mewled. Peridot's head hung low. "Hmph, such a trivial thing. Really, it could have picked a better one." And with that she tossed it aside, letting it fall in the water with a per-clunk.

Jane watched the pearl sink to the bottom of that pool, feeling something inside her break. *I want her dead. I want her dead, dead,deaddeaddeadDEAD!*

She stands at the edge of a tundra, black forest behind her. Before her stretches endless ice, lit by the full moon and the stars. An aurora dances across the night sky, snaking green light like the scales of a dragon.

Leviathan raised an eyebrow, Peridot looking at Jane with something akin to horror. "Ah, so you have broken my Chains of Stars have you? Now that *is* interesting."

"Ashera no," Peridot cried, "you pushed her too far!"

She stumbles onto the frozen plain with bare feet, blood running down her legs. The cold stings, but she doesn't feel it. She wears a crown of antlers set with snowdrops, a cape of white rabbit's fur over her bare shoulders. Other than that, she wears nothing, runes painted on her body in red.

Leviathan stirred from her throne, the Waters of the Whale now covered in a thin sheen of ice. "Yes, come to me!" Leviathan hissed, eyes lit up with something akin to greed. "Come to me with all your despair!"

Her eyes whirl around fearfully like that of a calf's scenting the wolf. Her knees give out and she cannot walk. Hands appear to hold her up. A woman on either side—Autumn and Summer adorned in their raiment of leaf and tendril, crowned in feathers and furls. Spring appears before her holding a cup. Spring brings the cup to her lips.

She swallows, tasting the wine mixed with earthy honey. She looks up, and the stars and borealis exploded into a thousand points of light.

The ceiling of the Whale split with a moan, fat and flesh rendering to open up to a night sky of ambrosial light and celestial jade snakes. The dead continued their labor even as the ice froze the Waters and shattered their oars. Marigold cried out as the chains broke from her in the cold. She gathered the GCATS to her, fleeing to safety.

In the center of the tundra is a black stone, flat and long, and next to that is the Horned One, garbed in augural doom. The people of the village stand in a circle around the slab and the Beast, beating drums to the sound of some maenad noise.

The throbbing of those drums reverberate in the sky and the snow and the symbols on her body. She sees them move and twist in time, revealing the universe.

She is led up to the stone slab.

The drums of Leviathan shifted rhythm. They were in the slave ship, yet not. Ice formed rapidly and the sky above them opened up even further, revealing a swirling torment of red and black. Red and black that reflected on Jane's skin, turning her pale flesh from snow to rock and fire. "Ashera, don't do this!" Peridot cried over the growing wind. "This is the chance to redo everything, to make it right!"

"You had your chance, Zeru," Ashera said, "and you failed."

She is held to the slab. The cold burns and sticks to her skin. She cries out, but strong hands keep her still. The Horned One stands above her, long knife in its grasp. The music increases in tempo as people sing and wail.

The dagger raises up, outlined by the light of the moon. The chanting reaches a crescendo. She looks at the dagger with wide eyes. The reflected moon light. In that light she sees her reflection. Her blood painted face. The sweat from fear. The Spring woman and the Summer woman. A refracted myriad versions of herself.

She shakes off the hands that hold her down. She reaches up, and either due to surprise or inebriation, she's able to steal the knife from the Horned One. She slides the knife into its stomach. The Horned One doubles over, and the dark garb grows wet.

She reaches out, removing the cover of veils from the Horned One, and beneath those veils she sees...

Leviathan.

Leviathan looked down at her pierced stomach in surprise, guts that once been in her body now down at her pretty little feet. Jane's hand emerged from Leviathan's stomach, slick with entrails.

Peridot screamed as Leviathan fell over in her throne, blood gushing down her legs. "Ashera no!" Peridot wept, going over to her. "I never wanted it this way, I never..."

Jane looked down at her stained hand, and it buzzed. Lights flashed in the corners of her eyes, and whatever it was that had been broken in her, couldn't stop. Jane grew. She grew to a size too large for the vessel of the Whale itself, crushing the benches of the oar rowers, pressing against its purple sides. Her antlers became the stars, her feet became the ocean, her body became the earth. Her rapid growth tore at the Whale, ripping its flesh. The whale groaned in pain, but Jane didn't stop. Something had been torn loose from her, and she didn't know how to weave it back in. She began to tear at the whale with her teeth, consuming its flesh to feed her hunger.

"Jane! Una! Stop this!" Peridot cried. "Please stop! I don't want it this way! *You* don't want it this way!"

Marigold ran up to Peridot, GCATS in her arms. "What's happening!"

"*It's* happening!" Peridot said, tears streaming down her face, holding the gasping Leviathan. "She's ending everything! But I didn't want it to happen this way," she looked down at Leviathan's hate filled, fading gaze, "not like this!"

"She's losing herself to PMF," Antoine said, as the towering figure of Jane loomed, "and not in a good way. We have to reconnect her with her sense of self."

"And how do we do that?"

"A big boom?" he suggested unhelpfully.

"There has to be something we can do! We gotta help her!"

"There is one thing we can do," Peridot said, "but it will take what little strength I have."

"What is it?"

"I am but an aspect of the Sea Witch, and even if I were the totality of His being, His power has waned. But He does have one thing left. One thing we share. Something that I thought I had lost, but you all showed me still existed." She held out her hand. In her palm began to glow a light as soft and gentle as spring-leaf dew. It smelled of sprouting leaves through dirt. It hummed with the bubble of life and laughter of song. It bore within it a mysterious danger that could not be touched, but which made the silver in it shine all the same. The being once known as Jane howled.

"And what is that?" Scarlet asked, looking down at Peridot's hand.

"The ineffable sublime."

I am the seasons.
My spring turns to summer's heat,
then falls to winter

The Lament of Ashera III

Grandmother Dusk closes amaranthine eyes.

She brings in her crimson arms.

Holds to her the golden mantle of day.

She sinks.

Her coal burned heart becomes the dying eye; her sagging belly viola-
ceous sky.

Her overripe lips speak soft enshrinement; the stars in her hair gray
firmament.

Her barren womb, that amethyst ember, rebirthes the promise of siren
slumber.

Sister Moon in silver spun filigree, awaits Dusk's decent with jade col-
ored glee.

Grandmother Dusk frowns, with darkening face.

Grandmother Dusk sees something is out of place.

For Grandmother Dusk looks down on a world in a stagnate state.

The mountains that had marched so proud and tall, now sag under the
weight of bitter snows.

The living things so profuse and joyful, cease to wonder and see no need
to grow.

The waters of the world quick and clear, with no currents to cleanse them
turn slow.
There is no need to sing praise of the perpetual bountiful redundance.
No desire to learn or change when all one needed is forever abundant
Zeru's world is failing.

Zeru was busier than ever before. Not only did He have a Universe to look after, but His Conservators to manage as well. He felt as if it was always something—either a solar system needed adjustment or a nuclear structure just wasn't quite right. He did His best to entrust these tasks to His assistants, but often found them lacking in finesse.

After all, it was hard getting a Universe perfect, and even harder to find good help.

Ashera spent her days in her coral palace by the sea, looking out at the waters of the world. She took joy in the fish flickering beneath the surface, at the glistening of scales kissed by the moon.

But the more she looked into the depths of those still pools, the more she saw her own reflection thrown back at her, and with Zeru busy managing His Creation, it was often a reflection where she was alone; an emptiness no amount of pretty fish or shells could fill.

"Why do you sing such a sad song, O Consort," a voice asked one day as she stood barefoot in the sand. "Such a beautiful song, but it turns the Ocean salty like tears."

"Who are you to ask me such a question?" Ashera demanded, nose upturned. "The beasts of Zeru's world are commanded not to molest me. He would punish you if He knew."

"But he doesn't know, does he? For his gaze is turned elsewhere, away from your beauty, which has left you here lonely and wanting," Ashera had nothing to say to that. "As for who I am? I, am the whirlpools and the blackest part of the sea. I, am the rip tide you cannot predict. I, am the creatures that see no light, malformed by darkness."

"You are a Spirit of the Ocean then?" Ashera asked, curiously peering into the growing ink despite herself.

A single eye looked back at her, rimmed in red, older than anything she'd ever seen. "Of a sort. There was a time when I was death, as the ocean is greedy for life, but this land harbors no death, and so in a sense, no place for one such as myself."

"You're from the Old World then," she exclaimed. "I did not know anything survived from that place other than Zeru and Myself."

"There are some things that even Gods don't have control over," the Spirit said, "though I suppose your Zeru doesn't realize that. Yourself for example. He has tried to bind you to him with chains and pretty things, but here you stand, the wildness in your voice calling to me. So answer me child, my original question, why do you sing such a sad song?"

"I suppose," Ashera said, words falling unbidden from her lips, "that in a deathless land of plenty, I miss life."

This, the Spirit already knew.

Ashera visited with the Spirit that evening, as well as many others. They talked of the Old World, of death and of life. He would take her to the bottom of the sea where she could see the feral phenomenon that Zeru so disdained—the beasts, the storms, the sands of forgotten warrigal. Rather then terrify though, as she thought it should, it filled her with a thrill that broke the haze of her despondent days.

When Zeru did bother to visit His lonely wife, He noticed a change: the lightness in her step, the glimmer in her eyes, the stray strands of her hair. He hoped that she was coming to accept this world He had created, that she would soon come to accept Him.

But if Zeru thought He could capture Ashera's heart, He was gravely mistaken.

Ashera soon realized that she was with child. Ashera was not sure how she knew, but one day as she pressed her hands to her stomach, she felt with assuredness the burgeoning of life within.

Her first feeling was terror. That she had to get rid of the child before Zeru discovered her betrayal, but as she brought the tea to her lips a certain calm overtook her and she lowered the cup; after all, it was already too late.

She never saw the Spirit again after that. She supposed he had achieved what he wanted, sowing the seeds of chaos in her belly, and so needed her no more. In a sense she felt used, but she also felt as if she had been given the key to set herself free, to break from Zeru's mindless purity. She felt a fierce protection towards the life forming in her and was determined to bring it into the world.

Ashera grew larger by the day. At first Zeru didn't notice, for He was too concerned with His own creation, soon though, her state became too obvious for even Zeru to miss, so Ashera hid herself away in the deepest sea cave, hidden from Zeru's eyes. It was there that she gave birth to her son. She named him Bythos.

Bythos emerged as dark and inexplicable as his father, of formless inked night, of winds and waves and sibylline chaos. Thunder struck the ocean at his first cries, and song of the whales grew to a discordant clamor. Storms clouds blocked the vision of Grandmother Dusk so she could not view this sin; despite this though, Ashera realized, Zeru knew.

The ocean opened up to the sky, exposing her veiled birthing-room, and Zeru was there, floating above the wall of water that surrounded them, wreathed in fire, eyes rimmed with kohl. "You. You of all. You betrayed me. You have brought the pain of suffering into this world. You have ruined my Creation."

Ashera stood against his winds as she held the babe to her breast, looking up in defiance. "I would rather a life back in the bleakness of that desert than an endless paradise such as this, free from consequence or meaning."

"You would rather starve? Go mad from thirst? Watch those around you grow old, sick, and die? Such an imperfect world. You would prefer that over the paradise I created?"

"Paradise?" Ashera scoffed. "It is a place writ in the blood of the old gods, so you can feed your own ego. But even in a world such as this, of your own making, it stinks of rot. A shallow pool rife with sick."

"And what do you know of the dealings of Gods?"

"I know this world is a reflection of you," Ashera declared, "and I know I find it wanting. That you find it wanting yourself. A selfish silly world, for a selfish silly boy. You fool. You expected gratitude? You've taken everything from me, all that I have loved, all that I have known. You stripped it from me, then expect me to kiss your feet and call you a benevolent god!"

The flames on Zeru's shoulders flared, lighting up his eyes. "So, is that it then? After all that I've done for you? After all that I've given? So consumed in your own needs with your nose in the dirt that you never bother to look up at the sky. From my other subjects I expected this. But from you, from you I had hoped better."

"Then you had hoped wrong. For I wish...I wish you had just done away with me back then like you did away with everyone else! Because the reality of it Zeru, is that I am just like them—not good enough either!"

"Very well then. If it is death that you seek, I shall happily give it!" In his rage, Zeru threw a thunder bolt towards her.

Ashera cried aloud, raising her arm in frail defense, ready for the blow. But the blow never came. When Ashera lowered her hand she saw Bythos before her, dead, the bolt of lightning pierced through his chest, his profound darkness turning ashen. Ashera wailed. Zeru turned white.

"My son!" Ashera cried, falling to him, watching as he pieced apart to blackened kelp and crabs. "On my beautiful son..." she picked up the bits of rot and decay, holding them to her. "What have you done?"

"It is for the best," Zeru said, though his eyes now bore a doubt. "I know it seems cruel, but with life comes death, and it is from that suffering emerges. You see that now, right? You had forgotten the pain of loss, right? Now you see that I know better. Now you will listen."

But the seas rocked and the ocean roared. The whirlpool around Ashera grew; its edges became jagged and danced with the nightmares of the waters—the sharks, the creatures that never saw light, the monsters that until now had been caged. They feasted on each other in an orgy of blood, ripping at each other, staining the waters red. The whales sang their song of rage, pain, and loss, and in them was a single red rimmed eye.

Ashera took her Spear of All the Lightening in the World from the depths of the tumult, piercing it right through Zeru's heart. Zeru fell, clasping the wound. "So you plan to kill me as I had killed the Dreaming God?" he cried. "To become the new one? And what world would you create Ashera? Simple thing that you are?"

"No Zeru, I will create no new world, for the death of my son has taken that dream from me. But I will suffer you to watch the collapse of yours, for now that death and life has touched this land, that imprint will not fade. No, it will spread, like a disease. There will be more births, and more deaths, to echo the birth and death of the first. Of my son." Ashera wrapped her Golden Chains of All the Stars in the World around Zeru, weighing him down. "And you will live on, and you will rot, for death will seep into your bones, and you will be forced to watch your world suffer. And you will beg me to kill you, but I won't, for killing you, would end your pain. No Zeru, I will keep you alive. Alive even as you decay. Alive but unable to dream. Alive, but unable to scream in your agony."

I will make you feel the pain of death
Until the last being breathes its last breath.

East of the Sun, West of the Moon

Una...

The voice pulled, grabbing at the loose threads of her consciousness, quiet, yet persistent, like a weaver gathering wool.

Una...

Jane waved a hand in front of her face, as if she could shoo the voice away.

"Una!" the voice barked, grounded and immediate. "Una! Wake up ya' lazy bones! What? Ya' gonna' to lie 'bout in bed all day?"

Jane opened her eyes, crusted from sleep. She was somewhere warm, soft morning light creeping through a window. The light shown through a set of periwinkle forget-me-not curtains, bouncing off flecks of dust that shimmered as they rose in the heat from the floor. The flecks undulated, morphing into the shape of a butterfly, as golden as the early sun. The butterfly flitted over to Jane, rising on small drafts, dropping in areas where it cooled. It landed on her nose, and she felt a momentary glow from it, like a spring day, before the butterfly burst, turning back to dust.

Jane sneezed.

"Where..." she grumbled as she wiped snot on her sleeve, "where the hell am I?"

She remembered a faint green light, cool yet warming like an autumn rain. She remembered hearing Peridot's voice, singing to her a lullaby—her calming, soothing voice fading into starlight...

There was a knock at the door to her room. "Una!" the voice called, annoyed. "Get dressed and get outta bed! Yer breakfast is gettin' cold!"

Jane, not knowing what else to say, replied, "I...I'll be down in a minute!"

There were footsteps, Jane watching the door until the sound of them vanished into the distance. She looked around. She was in a simple room of bare wood. The frame of her bed was metal, and the blanket that covered her was a patchwork quilt. Pieces of furniture lined the wall, plain, but well cared for.

At the foot of the bed was a set of neatly folded clothes: a calico dress set with pink roses, a pair of brown boots, and a large, brimmed hat. Jane got dressed, grabbed the hat, and made her way out.

She was on the second story of a medium-sized house. Pictures in black and white hung on the wall, though the faces were blurry to her. The stairs creaked as she made her way to the first floor, the house opening up to a large kitchen with a table. A wood stove in the kitchen was currently in use, the scent of something delicious wafting through the air.

"Ah! She's finally awake!" the voice from earlier exclaimed. "I thought there fer a minute ya would sleep the day away! Though

I guess ya've been feelin' a liddle under the weather, so some rest probably did ya' good. Coffee?"

Jane turned to the voice. There was a woman in a blue and white gingham dress with an apron; she was pleasantly plump, hands knotted from years of kneading dough. When Jane looked up though, instead of seeing the kindly face of an old woman, she saw the head of an elephant, eyes two vast whirlpools of stars as if they contained galaxies. "What, cat got ya' tongue?" the elephant-woman teased. "That spill really *did* throw ya' fer a doozy. Maybe the coffee ain't such a good idea."

"Ah, no, sorry," Jane said, shaking her stupor. "I-I'll take the coffee."

"Cream or sugar?"

"Neither, thank you."

"Oh, that's no good fer a young lady such as yerself," she chided, "black coffee will ruin yer complexion, ain't that right Papa Turtle?"

Jane turned to see a man sitting at the table, dressed in overalls and a button up shirt. He was reading a newspaper, though the words were blurred. He lowered the pages to address the woman, and when as did so, Jane saw that instead having the head of a man, he had the head of turtle. "Best just do what Mama Elly says," he said. "Ain't no good arguin' over it."

"See? Young lady such as yaself should worry 'bout these things," 'Mama Elly' said. "We wouldn't want ya' gettin' old before ya even got started."

"Started?" Jane repeated as the woman poured her a cup, slopping in a healthy amount of cream.

"Well don't tell me ya fergot!"

"Ah no," Jane said, shaking her head, "no. Sorry. I just...I think I had a nightmare or something."

Mama Elly pressed the cup into Jane's hands, both the cup and her hands soothingly warm. "Well, ya have a cup and eat up," she said. "I'm sure ya'll feel right as rain as soon as ya do."

Jane managed a weak smile. For all Mama Elly's bossiness, Jane got the feeling she meant well. "Thank you," she said, "I'm sure you're right."

"Well *of course* I'm right. You don't get to be as old as Mama Elly without learnin' a thing or two! Now you just go sit down and I'll serve ya' somethin' up."

Jane took her cup to the breakfast table, sitting opposite Papa Turtle. Mama Elly placed a plate in front of Jane, loaded with eggs, sausages, and various fruit. Jane looked up at Mama in despair that she would be able to eat even a fraction of what was before her. Mama winked. "Gotta keep ya strength up. Never know what ta expect."

Jane sat puzzled, Mama Elly heading back into the kitchen. "Don't worry 'bout eatin' it all," Papa Turtle said, once Mama Elly was out of earshot. "Mama can't help but feed people. Most of it'll crawl away anyway."

"Huh?" Jane looked back down and her plate was now a pile of bugs. They didn't disgust Jane as she thought they would, for they shimmered with an enchanting light: some of them were jewel encrusted, some like moon beams, while yet others like the sunny butterfly she had encountered in her room. A nebulous ladybug shimmied over towards Papa, who snatched it up, gobbling the little beetle down.

"Any leftovers ya have just send my way when she ain't lookin'," he said, with a co-conspiratorial wink.

Jane fidgeted in her seat, having appetite for neither the food nor the coffee. "Wh-where am I?"

"Where are ya?" Papa repeated, as if surprised by the question. "Where do ya think ya are?"

"I...I don't know."

Papa set the newspaper down with a sigh, shaking his head. "Young ones these days. They don't know nothin'. Back when I was in yer shoes I had ta meditate, with the weight of the *world* on my back mind ya."

Jane blinked, not sure what to say.

"Didn't ya listen ta anything the Fates had ta say? Yer at tha end of tha world m'dear. The confluence. The place wheres ya gotta make ya choice." He picked the newspaper back up, resuming his reading.

"Bu..but I thought the Fates were at the end of the world."

"The Fates are at tha end of tha universe, m'dear," Papa replied, not bothering to look up, "not tha end of tha world. One is a defined space outside of reality, the other an event. Two different things. Well, at least in this case they are."

"Hurry up and eat ya food dearie," Mama called from the kitchen, "I got seconds comin'."

Jane turned green in the face.

"I tell ya what," Papa said, peering from over top the crinkling pages, eyes twinkling with a familiar cat-like hue, "why don' ya run out and go play wit yer friends. Sounds like ya need a bit o' fresh air to clear yer head. I'll keep the missus occupied."

That sounded like a great idea, and without saying a word Jane nodded, getting to her feet. She needed to go for a walk. She needed to clear her head. This was all just so *weird*. She made for the door. "And don't forget Una," Papa called from the table, "the faces may change, but the team always stays the same."

Jane slipped out the door. *What the fuck did that mean?* Outside was flat prairie and sky as far as the eye could see. The prairie grass was tall and golden under the morning sun, undulating with color—first pale red, then yellow, and then a soft blue hue, as if the grass was possessed of its own starlight

The sky above was a luminiferous ether in shades of rose and lavender. There was a dairy cow up in that hazy mist, looking down at Jane with a disconcerted face as it floated by, Jane could relate with that cow, followed by a man in a canoe; he was screaming. Following him was a skyscraper, a large marble temple, a barn, a few cars, and a dog. It was as if some cosmic tornado had come through, tossed everything up into the air, and then just left them there. Jane wrinkled her nose. This all seemed very irresponsible for some reason, a part of her knowing this wasn't how things were supposed to be, but not quite able to put her finger on it.

A dirt road led away from the house though the prairie, rutted and well-worn by wheels. Jane decided to take it. What could she remember? She tried to think as she walked. She remembered Tam Lin. She remembered Marigold and the GCATS. She remembered Peridot and her semi-betrayal...

Really, that silly Peridot! She should have just told them. It wasn't like they were going to be mad at her. Well, at least not for too terribly long. Probably would have just been more annoyed than anything else.

That's right. That's what Jane needed to do. She needed to see Peridot again, so she could set things straight with her and make it right again. So she could smack some sense into her head. But how was she going to do that?

She needed to find the beginning from the end. That's what the Fates had told her. But what the heck was that all about?

Jane's thoughts were interrupted by the sight of a ball. It was a red ball made of rubber; well at least, that is what she assumed it was made of—considering there were cows floating in the sky, it was hard to be sure of much. The ball wasn't large, but it wasn't small either; in fact, it seemed to have a hard time keeping any shape at all. It rolled down the path, seemingly of its own volition, with no wind to move it along. Frowning, Jane followed the ball, wondering where it would take her.

The ball went over a swell of land, on the other side of which was a small town; the town was lined up along that single road, made of wooden one- and two-story buildings with whitewashed walls, like a town from the old American West, painted signs hanging out front. A church sat at the far end of that town with a wooded hill behind it that served as a graveyard.

As Jane went into the town, she could see it was a lively place, with people bustling about going to shops. Some of them seemed familiar. There was a burly woman in a tie dye shirt with a couple of others dressed the same, standing out in front of a saloon drinking some beers. There was a cranky old man, shriveled, dressed in a top hat and two-tailed coat. He was bent over nearly half as he walked, grumbling under his breath.

"F...father?" Jane said.

"I ain't yo' daddy! Now lemme alone. Got work to do!" The old man spat back, before moving on.

There was a dance in the town square. Jane couldn't see where the music was coming from, but could see the participants moving in time, neat twists and turns, making patterns in the dirt; there was Godfrey Gopher dancing with Roderick, there was Warg waltzing with some ghostly figure, and there was the thundering Mother Duck stomping around—her dance seeming to be less about moving to the music and more about crushing something.

"Hey there stranger!" a voice called. "How can I help ya today?"

Jane turned to someone standing behind her. He wore a shop keeper's uniform, with a little billed visor, his shirt—as always—slightly wrinkled and untucked. Jane was struck dumb. "Bill?" she said with trembling lips.

"Pardon ma'am, but have we met?" Bill asked. "'Cause if so, then I've no recollection of it."

He doesn't remember me. Jane smiled, blinking back tears. "Ah no, we haven't. It's just that, uhm...I've heard so much about you!"

"Ah, heard about me have ya!" Bill said, chest puffed out in pride. "Well of course ya have! Bein' that I'm the best baker on this side of uh...this side of uh..." Bill frowned, looking around. "Where are we again?"

Oh Bill!" A shrill voice called. "Oh *BiiiiiIIIIIllllll*!

Bill went stiff. "Oh shit, that crazy lady is here. You didn't see me, okay?" Bill darted off, hiding inside a barrel.

Belinda came up to Jane, in a purple silk bustle dress, feathered hat on her head. "Ah pardon me dearie, but have you happened to have seen a small little satyr man pass by recently?" Belinda held up her hand to about half of Bill's height. "I simply *must* find him and have some of his bread. It's the best bread in uhm, *wherever* we are, you know!

Jane shook her head. "Sorry, I haven't seen him."

"Oh, just oh dear," Belinda said with a pout. "I don't know what I will do without some of that bread. And you look as though you could use some yourself! You seem positively pale!"

Jane felt like she was going to pass out. She needed to figure things out before they got any weirder. "Uhm, would you happen to know where the End might be?"

"Oh!" Belinda looked even more distressed, though this time her distress was aimed towards Jane. "I see. You're *her*. Well, you can find the End just past the church and up the hill. In the...*cemetery*. But do be careful as it's a bit stumbley up there."

"Thank you," Jane said, making her way.

"Oh, and dearie," Belinda called.

Jane paused, looking back. "Yes?"

Belinda smiled ever so slightly. "God Bless."

Jane nodded, before turning to head towards the church. She passed a brothel where Delphyne sat, surrounded by a host of silver butterflies, and a flower shop where Marigold watered some daisies, roses in her hair. At the church, Melusine stood at the door, dressed in a habit. She scowled at the antics in the town below. The church was old, in ruins, seemingly older than the rest of the town. The walls were a gray rock crumbled like basalt pillars, carved images of angles and saints worn, their faces obscured, as though the whole thing might soon be thrown into the sea to become sand. In the back of the church was a broken stained-glass window, the image of whatever deity that was prayed to in that place shattered beyond all recognition – but light shown through the colored glass none-the-less, in shades of dandelion and currant. Melusine glared at Jane as she passed.

Behind the church, the graveyard was quiet, as they tended to be, filled with tombstones and grass. It was a little overran, but in a charming way, and she could see flowers laid at some of the markers. A few of the graves shivered, as though restless.

At the top of the hill was a single twisted oak. Next to that oak were the GCATS. They were lying in the sun, eyes slit in smug satisfaction, with little cowboy hats on their heads and sheriff stars pinned to their chests. "Cricket!" Jane called. "Antoine! Toramaru! Scarlet!"

They looked up at her, eyes blinking through the quaking grass. "Ah, so you're finally awake!"

Jane came over to the GCATS, hot and out of breath. On the other side of the hill was a large field, filled with rye. "Oh, thank the Gopher you remember me. Just...gimme a second..."

"You really that outta shape? I'd have thought after everything we've been through you'd have some endurance by now."

"Oh shut up." Jane sat down. "Do you know what the hell is going on here?"

"You mean other than the world is ending?" Scarlet said, as the cow in the sky passed by, mooing.

"I mean, everyone down there," Jane said. "They don't remember me. Did everyone...." Jane gulped, "Did we all *die*?"

"We don't know," and it was Toramaru who spoke this time, surprising Jane with his deeply melodic voice. "This is a place beyond our calculations and measurements. Though you did kill Death, so how that redefines mortality is an interesting question."

"Shit, I really did that?" Everything was such a blur.

"Yeah, you totally lost your shit and became absorbed by the PMF," Antione said. "Killing Leviathan must have released all the PMF contained within the Whale. All the hopes and dreams of all those beings, unleashed on the universe. The last blow to a reality already on shaky legs."

"That doesn't sound good," Jane said. "Sounds like we're in the middle of a storm."

"We think we have some time," Cricket said, rolling onto her back. "If such a thing as 'time' even has meaning in this place. When you killed Leviathan, Peridot, or the Sea Witch, or whatever you want to call her, used what little of her power she had left to send us here. So, while we *are* in the middle of a storm, I think she gave us a sub-luminal island as respite. A place where you can catch your breath."

"So that you can make your choice," Toramaru added.

"I see," Jane said, looking down at her hands. "Problem is, I don't know what that is yet."

"Well, you're gonna have to figure it out here pretty gosh-darned soon," Antione said. "While this place is currently protected from the worse of the chaos, it is also the eye of the storm, and eyes only stay in one place for a little bit."

"Here," Scarlet said, sitting next to Jane, "you woke up at the perfect time. Once a year this happens, and it's an amazing sight. But it's just a couple of hours, and then they're gone." She raised a paw, pointing towards the field at the back of the hill. "You gotta look out there."

"What? I don't see anything...other than the weird stuff floating in the sky."

"Forget that, focus on the grass."

Jane gasped as she saw a couple of flecks rise up from the plain. "Ah! I see it!"

"That's just the beginning. Wait."

The field erupted in a profusion of butterflies, pouring forth as if from a fissure tore open in the earth. Black tipped creatures with bright orange patterns on their backs; there were so many the sky became overcast with them, and you couldn't move but for the soft flutter of wings on your cheeks. "It's beautiful."

"It's a year-long journey for them to go from the northern reaches to the south. But they really only live for a couple weeks to a month. So the butterflies that reach the south have never been there before. But they know how to reach it anyways. A secret wisdom encoded in their blood."

"It's amazing."

"Yeah, it really is."

"Ugh, what am I supposed to do?"

"You gotta figure that out yourself Jane, we can't give you an answer. But we can say, no matter what you choose, we'll be by your side."

They watched the butterflies until the last one vanished from the horizon.

"Una!" a voice called. "Una, arise ye slovenly wench! What, shall thee sleep thy day away?"

Jane sat up with a start. What? Where was she? Hadn't she just been on a hill with the GCATS watching butterflies? Jane looked around. Same morning sun. Same dust shifting in the light. Same butterfly to fall on her nose. Only this time, instead of a small house of wood, she was in a castle made of stone, the curtains a heavy pale blue velvet. Jane scratched the back of her head. Had it been a dream?

"Una! Get thee out of thine bed and garbed! The breaking of thine fast shall spoilt!"

Not knowing what else to do, Jane got out of bed, putting on a gown of rose silk. She walked out the door, and down the hallway with its worn blue strip of carpet.

Uneasily, Jane made her way down the stairs.

There was the same table, laden with the same food, Papa Turtle with his head behind a scroll reading away, though now he wore an Elizabethan collar and tights. "Ah!" Mama Elly exclaimed, bustling over in a blue linen hoop dress. "And here I thought thee would sleep thy day away. Arst thou feeling refreshed after thine rest?"

"Y-yes...I'm feeling better thank you, Mama Elly."

"Ah, it's *Madam Phellant* for now," she said. "Ye really did cause a confusion to thine inner skull."

"Madam Phel…" Jane looked back at Papa Turtle in confusion.

"Yup," he said, "Madam Phellant and Padre Tut."

"Oh…Oh I see…"

"Excellent! Coffee? Ergh, or more like, shall thee partake of the exotic Arabian bean juice?" Padre Tut sighed, shaking his head.

"S-sure," Jane said, and then added preemptively, "with just a little bit of cream."

"Excellent!" Madam Phellant exclaimed. "A lady shouldn't have her exotic Arabian bean juice plain. Bad for the outer face tones, it is. Isn't that right, husband?"

Padre Tut sighed. Again. "As you say, wife."

"Well sit thee down," Madame Phellant said, "and I shall serve thee up some breaking of thine fast. A young woman such as thee needs to keep her strength up." There was again that wink as she bustled off to the kitchen.

Jane sat down in her chair at the breakfast table. "What did you think of the monarchs yesterday?" Padre Tut asked.

"Huh? What? No thees or thines?"

"I can't keep up with the Middle English crap. I hate it when we are in this period. I swear she just makes stuff up. But regardless, yesterday, if you want to call it as such, you met your friends at the top of the hill, right? You saw the monarchs take off, right?"

"That wasn't a dream?"

"Could have been a dream. Could have been yesterday. Could not be a dream and be tomorrow. That's not important. The question is, what did you think of it?"

"Well, it *was* beautiful, and I was happy to see the GCATS. I was worried about them."

"Good. You've at least that much going for you."

Madame Phellant walked up, placing a meal before Jane. "The breaking of thine fast is served unto thee thineself...merrily!"

Jane looked down to see a pile of incandescent glowing shapes: neon green, pink, and purple in the form of triangles, octagons and circles. A blue oval escaped the plate, squirming across the wooden surface. Padre Tut caught it in his fork with practiced ease, slurping it up. Jane gulped. "I think I need to go for a walk."

"A walk!" Madame Phellant cried, "but thou hast hardly touched thoust thine food!"

Jane got up from the table, wanting nothing more than to be out of there. "I'm sorry. I think I need from fresh air." With that she left.

Madame Phellant glared at Padre Tut in the absence. "Thine terrible table manners always chasest minest guests off."

"Happens every time you serve up hyper-dimensional objects. They're just hard for folks to stomach."

Outside, Jane found the now familiar road into town and followed it, her mind in a state of confusion. What the hell was going on? The other day hadn't been a dream? But it had? Why had it ended so suddenly? She didn't remember going to bed. She didn't even remember leaving the hill. It was all too much.

She came across the red ball again, making it's determined way down the path between the wheat fields. She bit her lip, wondering what to do. Rather than following the ball this time, Jane turned, going the opposite direction.

After a bit, another town came into view, only this time instead of being populated by small wooden shops, there was a row of stone houses with thatch roofs. There was still the same church at the end of the way though, with death lurking behind it. "Ho, ho fair maiden!" a voice cried.

Jane turned to see Antoine, dressed in a tunic with a sword at his belt. "Antoine?" Jane balked. "What are you doing out here? Why are you wearing that?"

"Ah! The fair maiden knows my name!" Antoine leapt back, aghast. "Are thee some sort of magical fairy sent to guide me on my quest? Or perhaps worse! A witch!"

Jane felt a pain in her heart; had the GCATS now forgotten her as well? "Ugh...let's go with *not* a witch. What quest are you on?"

"I must find the Golden Tuna! So that I may free the brave Princess Marigold from the evil clutches of the Sorceress Scarlet. And to do so I must complete three tasks!"

"Oh, what three tasks do you have to complete?"

"Well, first I must climb the glass mountain of the silver dragon, and claim two of his scales."

"Oh my, sounds interesting!"

"The second is that I must brave the fires of the rainbow wizard, in order to get his crown."

"Thrilling!"

"And the last is, I must become a super cool rock star, so I can awaken the Stag Maiden from her slumber with the harmony of the ascended metal gods, so that Una may break free from the chains the that hold her soul to this Intelligible World, and arise to the Order of the One."

"What?!"

Antoine was suddenly off in the fields, almost hidden in the grain. "Never said getting a Golden Tuna was easy! Fare-thee-well witch-maiden!" Antione threw up a 'devil's horn' sign with his paws, and then was gone.

Jane sighed, satisfied that at least Antoine was still weird even if he'd forgotten her, before heading into the village. It was just like the town from the other day, though rather than dressed in cowboy hats and spurred boots, everyone was wearing tunics and lederhosen; Bill was at a little shop, baking some bread, Belinda trying to steal it before it was even out of the oven; there was a tavern where the Celestial Flower Child sat, enjoying some rarminium and sharing it with Antoine—how Antoine had gotten there so quickly, Jane hadn't a clue.

A shuffle of people were making their way to the church where Melusine waited, now dressed in the robes of a priest. Jane eyed the people, in their muted yellows and greens, and realized she recognized them. Recognized them as followers of *her* church from her dreams. Jane jogged up to the pilgrims. "Hey, where are you going?

"To service," a man replied.

"Service to what?" Jane asked, interest piqued.

"Why, to you of course."

Jane stopped, watching the followers go into the dilapidated building, Melusine closing the doors behind them. For some reason this put Jane in a bad mood. She stomped over to the graveyard where Toramaru now stood guard.

"The pond that shimmers"

In the storm's ferocity

is the pond that stills"

"Yeah, sure, great, thanks Toramaru," Jane grumbled, before walking up the hill.

This time it was Marigold who stood next to the oak, hand pressed against the tree. Her hair was loose and unbound, falling to her waist in soft curls, wound with ribbons of scarlet and sunflowers, bees sleepily humming about her. She wore a dress in hues of gold and orange, long sleeves rustling in the wind, the light of the dying sun clinging to her. A soft September eulogy. She looked at Jane with a smile.

"Why hello there," she said, "looks as though it's my turn to talk with you."

"How are you doing?" Jane asked. "Without *The Illumine?*"

"Oh fine," Marigold said. "It's like both you and El Guapo said, it's not so much I was a part of *The Illumine* as it was a part of me. And it is still there," Marigold indicated her heart.

"I wish that stupid El Guapo were here now," Jane grumbled. "I know he seemed confusing before, but considering everything that's going on, he would probably help this all make sense."

"El Guapo isn't far Jane," Marigold said. "None of us are. Even if you don't see us, we are here, cheering you on."

"Oh Marigold!" Jane cried, flailing. "What am I supposed to do? Do you know what the Fates told me? They told me that I'm gonna be the next Sea Witch! That I will make the ruined world anew," Marigold winced slightly at the thought. "I can't do *that*! I mean, I can't even figure myself out, how am I supposed to create a universe with other things in it?"

"Well Jane, while I know it is difficult, I don't think there is any getting around it. Whatever you do, will have a lasting impact on this new reality."

"You're right, and I don't like it. It's not fair. Why do *I* have to be the one who creates the new world? What sort of world am I even supposed to make? Should be someone like you who gets to figure it out. Someone who is nice. And smart."

"Oh well, I wouldn't say that..."

"*And* annoyingly humble," Jane added. Marigold laughed.

"Well Jane, I could tell you about atomic structures and physical laws. Give you a schematic of the ideal planet for organic beings to live on. I could even recite whole treatises on ethical and moral considerations. Recite the religious texts of lost civilizations. The great arts, the philosophies, and the wonders. But in the end, I do not think that will give you the answer you are looking for. While those things certainly don't hurt to learn about, really, creation isn't about a perfect copy, but a feeling. So I guess Jane, in the end, I think it comes down to one thing: make a universe that makes you happy. I know if you at least do that, that it couldn't be anything too monstrous, right?"

"Yeah, I guess, but that's the trick, isn't it?"

"What?"

"What will make me happy. I mean, oh yeah, people have *ideas* about what will make them happy. Zeru thought that creating a world without birth or pain would be the ideal. But then you realize that's not what you really want. That you really want love, that you want spiritual and intellectual fulfillment, that you want flying ass pigs or some bullshit."

"Flying ass pigs?"

"I'm frustrated!"

Marigold smiled bemusedly. "You fear making a mistake."

"I fear repeating the same mistake."

"Then listen to your heart Jane, and trust in it. You have the strength create your own art. Learn from Peridot and incorporate that into your work!"

"That's easy enough for you to say..." Jane sighed. "I just don't know where I would even begin."

"Ah well, some of us just over-think things more than others."

"You find this funny, don't you?"

"There are worse things than an overly conscientious God, so yes, I am bemused. And I also recall someone once telling me to stop worrying so much and just enjoy my cake."

"It was a tart."

"I know. The point being, Jane, at some point you are going to have to make a decision, or Leviathan will have her way after all. Contemplation means nothing without action. An artist must create in order to realize the ideal of creation."

Jane huffed sullenly, gaze drifting out onto the plain.

She watched as the butterflies began to rise from the grass, like mist under the morning sun after a night of heavy rain. "I thought the GCATS said this only happens once a year?"

Marigold shrugged. "Apparently it's been a year, or two. Or who knows what."

Jane watched as the butterflies evaporated into the sky. The same frenzied movements, the same orange wings, the same pattern but shifted ever so slightly. Structured chaos reformed. "The same," Jane murmured, "but completely different."

"Yes," Marigold said, "that's the amazing thing about it. You could watch this even a hundred times and each time would be different. Different butterflies. Different winds. Different grass. The same genetic memory."

"Like water in a stream," Jane said as the black plume took up the whole sky. "Shit Marigold, I hope I figure this out."

"Me too."

"Una! Una! Rise and shine dearie! You don't want to sleep the day away now, do you?"

This time, when Jane gets out of bed, she will be prepared for the disorientation. The butterfly that lands on her cheek will no longer be surprising, the sun-kissed warmth even chill. The room will be in slight disarray. The outside in where it shouldn't be, a tree growing through the window, and the furniture in some grass. She will be in a white, thatch-roofed hut that she vaguely recognizes, though rather than being in the desert it will be in a green field. She will quickly get dressed, putting on a slip of pink argentine moon. "Coming!"

Jane will head downstairs. The hallway will be the deep reaches of space, the stairs a maze. Downstairs, Padre will be at the kitchen table, now out on the front porch in a dark November wood, reading a hole in the air that looks out into the vast reaches of space. He will be wearing a bright purple space suite. The Madame will come up to her, garbed in garlands of flowers. "Oh good! You're finally up and ready! Would you like some coffee?"

"Sure, Madame Phellant" Jane will say, "and I'll take it black please."

"It Ellaphintine, darling, and black coffee isn't good for the complexion of a young lady..."

"Oh by the Gopher. Cream makes my stomach turn, and my complexion is already a hot fucking mess. I don't think black coffee will hurt me too much."

Ellaphintine will seem a bit taken back, and Padre will chuckle behind his space-newspaper. "*Language* young lady!"

"I appreciate the hospitality!" she will say as she takes the offered cup.

"Ugh, well...at least you have manners enough to say that," Ellaphintine will say, as she huffs over to the stove.

"So?" Padre will say as Jane sits at the table. "How were the monarchs this time?"

"Lovely again," Jane will say as she takes a sip of the dark bitter brew. She will make a face before reaching for the pitcher of cream. "Holy shit."

"Yeah, she offers it for a reason."

"Okay. Well, the butterflies were beautiful. As always as I suppose."

"As always?"

"No, I guess not as always. They moved in a similar pattern, but were different."

"So you saw it then?"

"Saw what?"

"The thumbprint of God."

Ellaphintine will come over with Jane's plate, putting it in front of her. "Eat up dearie."

Jane will poke her food with a fork, pulling up a string of pearls, each one pale and perfectly formed. "What the hell is this?"

Father will sit back in his chair with a sigh, looking *very* tired. "Shit you are difficult. It's supposed to be a metaphor."

"This whole place is a damn metaphor.

"Okay, look at the pearls. Each is the same but different, right?"

"Yeah, I mean, they're the same color and all, but they have different bumps and hues and whatnot."

"Yes, so each pearl is like a moment in time. It's the same, but it's different."

"What's that supposed to mean?"

"Okay, so I'm a turtle. I eat...I don't know, water bugs every day. I eat the same sort of water bug day in and day out, but each water bug is a little different. Some I eat when it's sunny, some I eat when it's cloudy. Some are slightly more meaty than others, and some are more lean."

"Gross."

"You haven't had a good water bug. Point being, I do this day in and day out. My sons will do this day in and day out. And so will my son's son. The same water bugs, just slightly different."

"So, time is water bugs?"

"*Time is different water bugs.* Moving outside of time, and causality, is to understand that all water bugs are the same, but different."

"Just like all these pearls are the same yet different?"

"Time. Cause. Effect. These are ways that you make sense of the world. A relationship your brain has created in order to navigate physical survival. It is not necessarily how the world really is. This table you see as solid, is really nothing but space between molecules. The thing that you know as time, is nothing more than a narrative your brain has created to make sense of the stimuli around it, just like the physicality of this table. When you look at a necklace of pearls you cannot tell the end from the beginning. That is outside of time. *It's the recognition of sameness or oneness.* When you recognize that Sameness then you will know the True Word of the Universe, the Elemental Filament from which the Tapestry is Woven. The Thumbprint. The Grace of Disseminated Entropy into One."

"I met a woman who wanted to be One with the...I don't know, I guess 'truth' for a lack of a better word, and it didn't work out for her so well."

"You are right to be wary. There have been false words spoken on the path to Oneness. Melusine was blinded by her vanity. The hope is that you don't do the same. The hope is, that you will have learned. Time and time again, Una, you have come to this point."

"Then time and time again, I have failed."

"Hunting is a game of low statistics. You gotta try for a lot of water bugs in order to catch one."

"Then that also makes it game of low confidence, doesn't it?" Jance will wince. "So then, is everything the Fates told me a lie? That there is no causal-impending doom-thing. That we have free will?"

"The Fates are wise, but they are old. Perhaps too old, and forgotten how it feels to be wrong. In the vanity and ego of their work, they have forgotten one thing. The soul. And as long as the soul exists, they will never have complete control."

"That was Zeru's error, wasn't it? Vanity. Ego."

"It was a lot of ask of one so young. In that, Zeru cannot be faulted. But the Dreaming God was a fat fool. It's a lot to ask of you. Sages for hundreds of years have struggled with the nature of what we are and have found no solid answers. Many have failed before you, and many will fail after you."

"If that's the case then what does it matter? Why not just make up any old world and not care?"

"You could. That is your choice."

Jane will huff, annoyed. "Is that all I get? Some weird crap about time and the nature of the universe?"

"Time and the nature of the universe is a part of the narrative your brain has created to describe the nature of God. I'm telling you, that what you are looking for is beyond that."

"Beyond the Fates," Jane will say. "Beyond ego and will. What the heck is that even supposed to be?"

"I can't tell you what it is, but I *can* tell you what to become.

"What?"

"You."

"Fuckin' bullshit," she will grumble, with a roll of her eyes, "what I really am. Who I really am? Isn't always all that great."

"Well, who is?"

"But I *do* have to figure it out, don't I? I have to figure it out or Leviathan's hate will never end."

"Indeed," Padre will say, looking sad. "The wound Zeru delivered to Ashera is one that will never heal. It has trapped them in their own loop. A cycle of self-destruction and punishment that neither seems able to break from."

"I feel sorry for the both of them. There was time I thought Leviathan was an asshole. Well, still do actually. But really...it must be a terrible burden carrying all that hurt for so long. I wouldn't want to have that all hate in me. I'd want...I'd want the ability to forgive. Even if it was just the ability to forgive myself."

Padre will reach out with a scaled hand, looking at Jane with a smile. "And that is why I think you'll do just fine."

"I think I need to go for a walk."

Padre will bow his head. "My best wishes to you Jane. I hope you enjoy your walk."

Jane will be quite for a moment, before she nods, leaving the little house for the last time.

She makes her way to the path, moving with slightly rushed steps. The sky is fractured, like a big cerulean bowl that has been dropped and now has seams running through it; starlight, planets, even galaxies seep through. Giant jelly fish float in the sky, the size of towers, their ephemeral lacy legs scraping the earth. The grass has grown tall, over her head, and the tops once heavy with seed are now distorted into faces. The faces seem to be saying something to Jane, but she can't hear them, the terror of their twisted visages urging her to move along.

She comes across the red ball, rolling along; this time, rather than following it or going the opposite direction, Jane goes right up to the ball, picking it up. She scowls at the ball and the ball looks right back at her, as if somehow accusatory in its silence.

Jane dropkicks that ball, watching it fly out across the field at the speed of light. She watches it disappear. "Mother fucker," she grumbles, before heading on back down the path.

The little town has turned into a mishmash of everything Jane has ever seen: there is Maera's house set next to a garden with the Celestial Flower Child; random walls from *The Illumine* appear here and there with no context or anything to tie them to; there is the forest from Yugenia inside the dining hall of the local tavern.

Jane is starting to become very disoriented.

She goes down some stairs that led upwards, passing by the church. The church is wide open, the followers from the last instance crowded in there, laying on the floor. Their eyes are rolled in the back of their heads, bodies twisted in death. Jane watches as her other selves walk midst the corpses, picking at bits of the bodies, eating their flesh, turning to vultures with grotesque balding heads, yet pretty smiles. The Summer Woman pins Jane with her flaming green eyes, smirking with blood-stained lips.

Jane shivers, quickly moving along.

Toramaru stands guard before the graveyard once more, looking at her with swirling eyes.

"Pale green shoots rise up

Demure petals of first bloom

The hard earth softens"

Unsure of what to say in response, Jane simply moved on. This time, at the top of the hill by the oak tree, she found Tam Lin. Both of them. There was the younger Tam Lin that she knew, long hair pulled back in a braid, and then there was a second one. This second Tam Lin seemed older, harder, hair peppered with gray as he looked silently out towards the field. They were both garbed in enigmatic night.

"You still have your stone," Jane said as she came up to them, seeing the mottled gray rock he had in his hand.

Tam Lin looked back at Jane with a smile. "I told her I had something she couldn't find."

"I was starting to wonder where you had got to. I saw everyone else but you."

"Ah, sorry if I gave you a scare. Guess it just took us a little longer to get here."

Jane smiled up at him, surprised to realize that there were tears in her eyes. "I'm relieved. After what happened...I didn't know what became of you. I guess I was afraid you would never show up..." she began to sniffle.

"Hey, hey, hey. No need to get all upset. You know I wouldn't let that happen, even if I was dead," Tam Lin said, "or even if, I never even really was."

"Tam Lin...." Jane started, wiping her nose.

"It's alright," Tam Lin said, looking over at his other self, as still as the stone. "I think I spent so much time worrying about *being* him, that knowing I'm not is freeing in a way. I can accept what I really am. A shadow. A shadow who carries his memory with me, and for him, and for me, that's enough." He looked over at Jane, eyes the color of sea glass. "It's enough for us to know that you're safe and to see you through this."

"Oh geeze that sounds so sad." Jane bit her lip so hard she could taste salt from where it bled. "Ah I fucked you over so bad."

"Stop that," Tam Lin said, and when she gave him a look, said again, "really, stop it. Jane, it's my identity, not yours. Nothing is going to change about how I feel. You didn't 'fuck me over', or him. I mean, I was a little weirded out at first about it, sure, but once I got used to the idea, well, it's like I have a blank page in front of me. I can write whatever I want. I don't have to repeat the same mistakes as him. I'm released from that. And I think he would want that."

"I guess that must be a relief to you in a way. To be freed from all that pain, to free from me."

"Oh Chris- that's not what I mean," he said. "I still care about you. H-he still cares about you. I'm just, free from a burden so I can care in a way where, I don't know, see things as they really are. Not how they reflect an image of me that doesn't even really exist."

"Still, you must regret ever having come to know me. Letting me bring you to this place."

"No," Tam Lin said, "the only thing he regrets is letting you go alone. You get that right? Jane, please. I don't, we don't, want you to carry this guilt. He loved you Jane, regardless of your faults, because guess what? We had our own. Still do. The pain we were trapped in, had nothing to do with you. It's something we tried to *heal* through you, but that was unfair to expect. We're free of that pain now, Jane. I'm free of that pain, to be who we were wholly meant to be. That's a good thing? Right?"

Jane was quiet for a long moment, tears drank up by grave dirt. "Yeah...*no*. I mean, I guess."

Tam Lin laughed. "Holy crap."

"If you're happy then I'm happy is what I mean to say. I'm just, I'm just really glad you all are here, and that you all love me so much." She wiped the tears away from her eyes. "Guess I'm crying more because of that than anything else."

"Well, that's not such a bad thing," he put his stone in his pocket. "Have you figured out what needs to be done?"

"Not really. But I know that Peridot, Zeru, whatever you want to call her, can't just be left to suffer any longer."

"That sounds like you *do* know."

"Yeah, maybe," Jane looked down at her hands, then up at the sky. "I think I'm starting see it now, the thing that I have missed all this time. Blinded by either the need to survive or my own insecurities, I kept missing the thing that binds us all, makes who we are, and connects us to some sort of whole. It's fleeting, like those butterflies, and I worry as soon as I reach for it, it'll fly away."

"Well, you know, a wise cat once told me when fishing, you need to be calm, or they'll pick up on your fear. So I think, with these things Jane, you gotta be patient, and let them come."

Jane looked down at her feet. "Well now, that's the hard part, isn't? I don't have much time, and I feel like I could sit a thousand years with this thing, and still not fully understand it."

"Yeah," Tam Lin held out his hand, "ain't that the truth. But sometimes, you just gotta move forward, even with the doubt. Just has to be a sort of calm doubt, I guess."

Jane looked down at the offered hand as the butterflies began to rise. To her left she saw the infinite sea of Tam Lins, to her right she saw the infinite sea of her-selves. Behind her, she saw the infinite sea of Marigolds, GCATS, Bills, and everyone else. As numerous as the butterflies. All different, yet all the same. All with her. She smiled.

"You always did say you'd stick with me until the end."

"This isn't the end Jane, it's just the beginning."

Jane took his hand, and they stepped into the beyond.

The Hazel-nut Child

For a long time, Jane walked through the butterflies. They were dense, forming a thick cover with their black tipped wings that blocked out the sun, creating a starless false night. It was a night that kissed Jane on her cheeks, a night that gave way to her forward movement in whorls and dips, causing the whole firmament to shiver—as if the butterflies moved as One.

At some point Jane saw a light through the weight of that night, like the northern star, or the moon peeking its head over the horizon, offering guidance in this featureless place. Jane headed towards it.

She emerged from the cloud of butterflies.

She was in the bottom of a pool, water wrapped around her. Jane looked up, seeing the light once more above; she reached towards it, pushing herself upwards. Jane broke the surface of the water with a gasp, finding herself in the small pond of a wooded forest. She swam to the edge of the pond, pulling herself up and out.

Sitting at the shore of the pool, Jane looked around as she caught her breath. She knew this place. It was the Forest from her childhood; the evergreen boughs so dark they were almost black, and the snow of early spring. Flowers poked through that snow, despite the cold—yarrow, lupine, and chamomile; the animals of the woods just at the edge, staring at her with their wild, yellow eyes.

Jane looked back. "Tam Lin?" she called, but there was no answer. Anxiety momentarily hit her gut, until she looked down; by the pool, next to her hand was a spear, the handle of it black as ink, the blade of sea glass, and next to that was a wooden shield, painted with the ferocious face of a mountain lion that shifted from black, to brown, to white depending on how you viewed it. She picked these items up, looking down at her reflection in the waters.

Her hair flowed loose and untamed, eyes staring back with a determination she hadn't realized she possessed, stag horns growing from her forehead strung with a wreath of marigolds. She bore the sea glass spear in her left hand, the cat shield in her right. She was garbed in a river of flowing light, shimmering with the song of the old gods, set with golden dragon scales.

Behind Jane, in that reflection, she saw the May Woman bearing her cup, the Summer Woman bearing her sword, and the November Woman bearing her torch—and behind them was the Horned One. They stared at her, eyes reflecting her will; Jane nodded her head in acknowledgment

"Okay, let's do this," Jane said, then turned to make her way through the Forest.

The branches of the trees brushed across her face, as if desiring to keep her there, but the Forest was Jane's domain, and she knew how to command it. Her feet carried her to the tundra of the killing grounds where the biting stone slab should have been; when she emerged from the wintry woods however, instead of coming out onto the large stretch of ice, she was someplace else entirely.

She was in Ashera's palace by the sea, or what was left of it—a single circular platform with the edges crumbled, a few broken columns remaining from which the tattered banners now hung. The pink, yellow, and purple orchids had shriveled and turned black, their dying petals falling to the ground. Above Jane, rather than clear blue sky, was the birthplace of the stars, tall pillars of golden clouds set against butterfly black night. She watched as stars formed from the depths of those pillars, arcane and bright, but then just as quickly as she watched them grow, expand, fade, and then collapse in on themselves, forming giant black holes. Then they reset, only to repeat the whole process all over again. Birth, life, death, *boom*, repeat.

Jane walked to the edge of the platform to look over. Below her was the ocean, untied to any form of earth, a tormented maelstrom full of unrest and hate. *Leviathan's anger is not dead*, Jane thought to herself. Clasping her spear and shield, she moved forward cautiously, her footsteps so light that not even the shells crunched beneath them.

As she moved forward between the columns, it was there, among the Telamons of Bone holding up the Cradle of the Stars, that Jane came to see Zeru, the Sea Witch.

A gasp escaped her lips at the sight, for the being from her memories had been so elegant—beautiful, and lofty; now, all that was left of Zeru was his head, wrapped in chains of thunder, a spear of lightning pierced through his skull, pinning him to the ground.

The skin that had once shone so bronze and deep was now sallow, tinged with green. The eyes that had once been so sharp and clear were now clouded, one hanging loose from its socket. The cheeks that had once been so high and proud, were now eaten through, exposing muscle and bone. His mouth hung open, slack, swollen tongue sticking out as if poisoned. Tears come to Jane's eyes. "Zeru?" she called aloud, and then more painfully, "*Peridot?*"

Zeru's good eye seemed to move, as if to focus on Jane. A low moan came from his throat. Jane clasped her mouth, crying now, for in Zeru's eye she saw the unending pain, the pain that had lasted for millennia upon millennia – the pain to cause madness. Jane took a breath, getting a hold of herself. "Don't worry Peridot," Jane said between gasps. "I am going to end it." It would be just like putting down a wounded deer. A mercy shot. "You aren't going to have to suffer any longer."

Jane made her way over to Zeru, her gaze focused on that single clouded eye and the silent plea it held within. Before she could reach Zeru though, there was a sound. There was a song. There was a dirge.

Jane froze, feet light, ready for flight. Apparently, she had killed Ashera, but hadn't killed her quite enough, for that was certainly her liturgy. But where was the song coming from? Jane realized then, it was coming from Zeru himself. Zeru's eye rolled back as the song grew and Jane watched in horror as two hands emerged from his decaying, rotted mouth. Two hands with long nails, covered in barnacles. Those two hands clasped either side of Zeru's cheeks, pulling themselves forward—they wrenched out his blackened teeth, they pulled at his sagging skin, shearing muscle from bone in thick bleeding chunks. Ashera's head materialized from Zeru, covered in spit and blood.

Ashera flopped down onto the sea-bone floor, only her torso visible, and dug in her fingers. Jane took several steps back as she watched re-birthed Queen pull herself from the maw of Zeru, singing all the while. Her skin was slick with sweat, the shells scraped her flesh, but she moved with determination, eyes locked on Jane. Her hips emerged, and following that, rather than her long, lithe legs, was the tail of a serpent with scales the color of the sea. Once her scales touched the floor of the fallen palace, Ashera was able to right herself, pulling herself fully from Zeru. Ashera looked down on Jane.

"Surprised to see me, little godling?"

"Not really."

"You are wiser than you appear then," Ashera said, "for you must see, as long as Zeru lives, so does his sin. And as long as his sin lives, so does my *hate*."

"That's all there is left of you, isn't it?" Jane said. "It's probably not even right to call you Ashera. Ashera died when Zeru killed her son. What little survived is simply anger at what was done to her. That's all you are. A personification of one moment in time that has reverberated through the ages. Like some sort of ghost. As dead as the beings she enslaves."

If Leviathan heard Jane, she didn't show it. "I will stop all who would seek the realm of Zeru. For as long as he suffers, he will be serving punishment for his sin."

Jane took several steps closer. "You know no joy. No laughter. No forgiveness. All you can think of is your rage."

"I am the tidal wave," Leviathan declared, "the siege of water that cannot be stopped. I am the hurricane, whose winds will bring the strongest to their knees. I am the maelstrom, that will swallow you whole. You think your civilization can conquer me. That your buildings, and your jetties can stem my tide. But they cannot. For I am the unbreakable *wall*."

"Even the fiercest storm," Jane said, "has to come to an end."

"Perhaps," Leviathan said, leveling Jane with those lapis eyes, "but this is not that day." Leviathan reached out with her tail, whip-like, and pierced Jane through the heart.

Jane stood there, skewered, the tip of the tail sticking out her back. Leviathan lifted Jane from the floor, then, casually, flicked her tail, tossing Jane over the edge of the platform. Zeru's eye followed Jane as she arced through the air and fell past the ledge into the ocean below. A tear fell down his cheek.

"Oh, are you crying?" Leviathan said with a mocking laugh. "I didn't know you still had the strength left in you." She slithered up to Zeru, running a hand over his bare head. It started as a soft caress before she gripped into his skin, ripping into it and drawing blood. "Sweet Zeru," she whispered, tears now coming to her own eyes, "don't you see that we will never be parted? It's just like you wanted when you sought me to be your consort. We shall ever be bound together. I will never let you go. I shall never release this pain." Her laughter mixed with her tears.

There was a rumbling. Leviathan looked up. "What is..."

Her words ceased when a set of stag horns appeared at the edge of the platform, emerging from the molten sea. They were covered in seaweed and coral, shivering with black butterflies, whales and giant squid caught between their crevasses. They rose, and as they did, so did follow a head of pale hair, hair that fell past shoulders in long waves, the moon trapped in the ocean, tinged with the green of rocks overgrown with moss. Jane rose, water falling off her back as she grew in size, blocking out the cycle of the stars. Her flesh was that of the earth, her breasts the mountains, the water that slid down her belly the rivers, the horns that held up the sky the firmament.

The whirling seas below calmed, the death and rebirth of the stars stalled. Jane stood there, eyes closed, looming over the shattered remnant of the Orchid Palace—her crown the pneumatic heavens, her body the chthonic soil. Leviathan fell to her hands in awe.

Then, with two rock formed hands, Jane reached up to the gash in her chest. She clasped the tear on either side, smelted blood pouring forth, and with one mighty pull ripped the wound open. She exposed her rib cage, her heart, her lungs, and in that moment everything was bathed in golden light. Her passion glowed with the heat of the sun, ringed in multicolored flames.

The golden light emanated from her in waves, reviving all it touched: the orchids of the palace came back to life, blooming once more; the bones of the sea creatures gleamed pink and purple, beginning to move; the wounds on Zeru's skull healed. Leviathan screamed. "No!" she cried. "No you can't do this! You can't take this from me!" She reached over, clawing at Zeru, opening new tears as soon as old ones had gone. "He is mine! His pain is mine! I will never let him go!"

Jane's giant face lowered itself to where Leviathan scrambled frantically, and ever so gently Jane blew; the wind that enveloped Leviathan was thick with the scent of sun-soaked sand and ripe grapes. Leviathan paused, stunned by that fragrance, blue eyes wide. "So sweet," she gasped. "It reminds me of when Father would take me hunting, and we would see the first desert rose bloom." Tears filled those eyes and they melted. Ashera's lip quivered. "Oh...oh, I'm so sorry. How could I have forgot? How did I become so lost?" When the wind passed, where Ashera had stood was a delicate golden orchid, trembling ever so slightly.

Jane's lumberous form now turned to Zeru. Zeru watched silently as Jane lowered her hand. Jane picked up Zeru's head, raising it up to her face. In the fissures of her skin he could see deer run. In the curve of her lip he could see the forests. In the hook of her horns he could see the moon. Slowly Zeru closed his eyes. Slowly, Jane opened hers—prisms that refracted light into a thousand pieces. Each Aspect of the Whole.

Jane brought Zeru to her mouth and ate him.

She sat up with a start, finding herself in darkness once more. So dark in fact, she couldn't even see herself. She looked down, thinking she ought to be able to see something of what she was, but what that was supposed to be, she couldn't quite remember. "Where...where am I?"

"Congratulations Una, you're at the end of the world," an acrid voice said.

She looked up to see a woman with red hair standing before her, cigarette hanging from her mouth. There was a man with a pompadour and heels, and a woman with a gaudy rhinestone coat. They seemed familiar, but she couldn't quite place them. "Una? Is that me?"

"Well, it's a name you called yourself at one point," the red woman said, "though to be fair you've gone by many different names. It's no wonder in your current state you've forgotten some of them."

Something pulled at the back of her mind. Memories? She wasn't sure what to call them. Some were images, blurred like lights flashing off a shimmering stream. Some were sounds. Some were simply feelings. "I left something behind," she said slowly, trying to piece the string of things together. "I left behind something important."

The red women nodded, face solemn. "That can happen. In fact, it often does."

She felt a rising panic, a sudden need. "I have to get it back," she cried. "I have to find a way to retrieve it." She looked around, more an instinct than anything else, for there was nothing there.

The red women stepped forward. She pressed a hand to her breast. "The very fact that you even remember means you still carry them in you." The woman pressed her hand forward, and it sank into her chest. From inside her, the red woman pulled out a nut—an acorn with a crack along the side, from which a single green sprout had started to sprawl.

"In this single moment of Oneness, all life is concentrated into this tiny spot," the red woman said, "a culmination, of so many things. All your thoughts, feelings, hopes, and desires, collapsed into itself and focused on this seed, the density of which would make the deepest black hole seem sparse."

She looked at that seed and its shimmering golden shell. "It's so beautiful."

"It really is," the red woman said, that wry grin back on her face. "I've certainly seen worse. Of course, I've also seen better. But it's up to you what to do with it."

She cupped the shimmering light of the acorn in her hand, its glow reflecting in her face. "It's so perfect though! Can't I keep it just as is?"

"You could try, but seeds, like all plants, wither under such constraint. Sometimes, you just gotta let things grow. You know?"

"But how will I know if it will come out the way I want it to? How will I know if I'll get the things back that were important to me?"

"You don't. But with a lot of water, and a lot of love, you stand a pretty good chance. Gardens are wild things—you never know what they're gonna do. But then again, that's the beauty of them, right?"

She had a memory of a field wildflowers, a neat white tablecloth, a kiss. She smiled. "I guess you got a point."